WRITE MURDER

Eric Shaw Quinn

A Write Murder Mystery

To Anne and Christopher Rice
for always, always, always being there.

WRITE MURDER

1

Paige had promised himself he wouldn't cry over her again.

At that moment, he was uncertain he would be able to keep his promise.

He hadn't seen her or spoken to her in over a year. But as the events of that day coalesced into fresh defeat and new humiliation, everything reminded Paige of her. He glanced at the cardboard box on the passenger's seat beside him. Its Amazon smile mocked him.

The contents of the leering, stained brown cube along with the thirty-four dollars in his checking account were all he had to show for the past eight months. A frowsy-looking begonia clung to life as its crispy-edged leaves sagged over the ragged flaps of the box. The bedraggled plant had managed to survive the same neglect and fluorescent light they had both endured since Paige's indignity at receiving it for Secretary's Day. The sickly plant, a few meager possessions, show swag and assorted purloined studio office supplies were all Paige had to show for the better part of a year of his life. *Perhaps next time I should ask for some magic beans*, he thought. He laughed bitterly and came perilously close to breaking his no-crying promise.

It was just a show. It was just a job. It wasn't even a good show or, for that matter, a good job.

But with *Show Talk* cancelled, Paige had no show and no job—not a good job, not a bad job, just no job. Again. The show had offered a lifeline, however slim, to Paige's fading dream of a career in the entertainment industry. It allowed him to believe that he was still a writer. With the network's abrupt cancellation that day, even that had slipped through Paige's fingers. He felt stuck in a cycle.

He took a breath and looked out at the beautiful late-spring day.

It was Southern California, so late spring was the only season on offer. Turning off Santa Monica Boulevard, he began the steady incline into the Hollywood Hills—more accurately the West Hollywood Hills—that led him home. Leafy silhouettes danced across the broad hood of his ancient Mercedes convertible. Tree branches knit together into a canopy overhead. Prematurely tall and thickened, their trunks and limbs were gnarled by the continuous growing season that turned the flora of Los Angeles into freakish botanical hyperbole. The youthful monsters, combined with the absent-mindedly assembled façades of the residences along the avenue, heightened the backlot quality of the not-very-old buildings designed and dressed to look anything but. The neighborhood, like so much of this place, strove to be what it was not.

In just the last half-block, a French chateau beside a turreted Tudor castle nestled up to a Spanish Hacienda that gave way to a California Mission Village. Paige had been told two things about the eclectic apartment buildings that lined his street and so many others in the small town of West Hollywood. One: most were built as temporary housing for the actors who had come to the constant sun of the sleepy hamlet of Los Angeles to work in the movies between "real" acting jobs on the New York stage. And two: Paige had been assured that Marilyn Monroe had lived in each at one time or another. Though the rumor was that the screen siren had died of a drug overdose, Paige's theory was that she succumbed to exhaustion if she had, in fact, had to move into and out of all those buildings.

Or perhaps it was all bullshit.

There was a fair amount of that in the greater Hollywood area as well.

Paige found out the hard way there was less to Los Angeles than meets the eye. Hollywood's *trompe l'oeil* isn't the tired Tinseltown trope. Rather, like the granite chateau on the corner, L.A.'s secret identity is that it's lamb got up as mutton. The illusion was a desperate effort to attain enough gravitas to be taken seriously. People in L.A. are as real as anywhere else—more so, perhaps. They are more likely to be not only camera-ready but also naked in pursuit of their dreams. Elsewhere, in what passed for the real world, discretion, and even a bit of subterfuge, is prized and often rewarded. Folks running for president spend years pretending that they aren't. But in Hollywood, subtlety is the most certain path to failure. Through bitter disappointment, rejection and hard luck, Paige had come to understand that in his adopted home the choice is between dreams merely dreamt and denied or ambitions pursued with all the unscrupled tenacity of the starving.

Beyond the required bleached hair and fake body parts, no one in Hollywood can afford the luxury of phoniness. Not even the richest and most successful. Not even—in fact, particularly— those who have nothing to do with the entertainment industry.

Nowhere else on Earth is being taken seriously as important as it is in Hollywood. Paige knew it only too well. Here there is no reality, only perception.

He aimed the dusty old convertible into the concealed lot beneath what a real estate ad would describe as his "Hollywood Regency" apartment complex—code for no air conditioning and paper-thin walls. He expertly conducted the '80s behemoth down the Model-T-thin driveway, picking up just enough speed in the turn to fishtail into his improbably narrow parking space. The smell of dust and dry rot filled his nostrils.

Paige turned the key.

The car began its St. Vitus' dance, wheezing itself into an automotive coma. Most days he'd simply abandon the car, leaving it to perform its nightly death ritual solo. That day, though, he sat with both hands on the steering wheel, ten and two as he'd been taught. His knuckles went white as he gripped.

It wasn't until he caught his own glance in the rearview mirror that the tears came.

2

As Paige struggled to negotiate his keys, the ill-tempered old door lock and the box of stolen pens and Post-Its, the Secretary's Day begonia fell, its novelty terra cotta pot smashing at his feet just as the oversized front door relented and swung inwards.

"I wonder if this means I'm really not the world's greatest secretary," he said to himself, stepping over the ruined planter that had formerly proclaimed as much. "Time to snap the head off my Oscar."

Paige left the mess where it lay. He didn't have the energy. Leaning against the door, he closed it from the inside. The sound echoed, a greeting from the empty house and a reminder of the bleakness he felt.

Through the archway to his right, and down the single, fashionable, polished mahogany step, with its coveted hardwood floors and wood-burning fireplace, Paige's empty living room amplified the clunk of the ill-fitted door and rusty hinges. He paused. The forsaken room's sole furnishings were the unopened cartons of the last book he'd written with her. The books awaited her signature and the promotional tour that would never come. Paige sat on one of the stacks. He had arranged the boxes into a sort of chair.

He had actually planned to buy real furniture for the room with the proceeds from the stillborn book launch. The unopened and unread tomes were a bitter memento of a failure he had not caused—and for which he alone had suffered the consequences. Though he often thought of burning the books to spare himself the pain and the reminder, he knew he would lose only a place to sit. His sense of failure would still fill the room.

The tears came again as he remembered her betrayal.

Shaking it off, he got up. The echo of his hollow footsteps pursued him up another fashionable, dusty step and beneath the fluted Regency archway. Paige made his way across the daunting and completely unfurnished, book-carton-free formal dining room, through the architecturally obligatory swinging door into the kitchen.

He abandoned the box of what remained of his most recent former job/life on the cozy room's ceramic tile counter. As he filled the kettle, a huge bubble belched inside the large upended Arrowhead water bottle poised precariously on its stand in the corner. The gas flames licked up the pot's sooty, enameled sides with a whoosh.

Paige stared into the refrigerator in search of life's meaning or perhaps something for dinner. His quest yielded only a few aging and highly questionable condiments and a bottle of bubble bath that, for some reason, required refrigeration. Surrendering, he closed the door.

The kitchen, a largish room, served as an informal dining nook and did triple-duty as his office, research center, and library. The multi-tasking wasn't entirely due to the apartment's lack of furniture. Paige liked the crowded little portmanteau. Paige did most of his writing perched amidst the kitchen's cluttered comforts. The pages of a manuscript littered the table and filled several of the chairs. It was a memoir of sorts that he been working on, as he tried to capture the highs and lows of what he'd been through with her.

He flicked on the small television. It was wedged amidst a strange mix of books, periodicals, an engraved crystal angel and his Gilded Garland award—a ring of golden acanthus leaves standing erect on a mahogany base with a testamentary gold plaque.

The TV blurted to life mid-sentence.

A bay window wrapped around the small, squeaky, white table. The room's only glimpse of the outside world was over the top of a preternaturally large boxwood hedge that seemed on the verge of strangling his apartment. Along with the glass in the upper half of the apartment's back door that offered an unobstructed view of the brick wall on the other side of the alley behind his building, the room managed to capture a bit of sunlight, if not much in the way of scenery. There, in the kitchen's shadowy confines, Paige could indulge his insatiable tea habit, grab a snack and watch a *Perry Mason* rerun or a half-hour cycle of cable news, interspersed with bouts and fits of writing.

The television awakened, still tuned to the channel that featured the talk show Paige used each morning to deaden his feelings enough to allow him to return to the front desk at the former *Show Talk* HQ. He recognized the familiar tortured strains of "Hooray for Hollywood" repurposed into a theme song for the syndicated entertainment news program *Star Reporter* so long ago that no one still remembered its true origin or Johnny Mercer as the author of its lyrics. Paige ignored *Star Reporter*'s host/newsreader's babbling as he fiddled with the teapot. She prattled cheerfully about the weekend box office and celebrity sightings and what everyone wore. Paige counted out bags of cheap black tea into the stained old pot with the chipped spout. He kept meaning to replace the homely little vessel once he got his head above water in the career he'd been drowning in going on—how long was it since she'd come into his life?

The whistle on the kettle interrupted his count. He moved to pour the water.

"One of Hollywood's oldest and most venerable hotels tonight plays host to one of entertainment's hottest couples," the bleached blonde talking head teased in that smarmy *couldn't-give-a-shit-entertainment-reporter* kind of way that had replaced carbs as Paige's dinner-hour staple. "Here, with live coverage, is *Star Reporter*'s star reporter, Busby Barclay."

Video champagne bubbles wiped the screen from the studio to Busby's stand-up in front of the venerable old hotel.

"Hollywood power couple Angela Panderson and Seth St. James will be celebrating their engagement at an intimate, star-studded gathering here tonight with fifteen hundred of their closest friends at the legendary Argyle Hotel on the world-famous Sunset Boulevard," Busby chirped.

Moth-to-flame, Paige was drawn into the report. He sank, teapot in hand, into one of the molting white chairs that matched the table and each other only in their squeaky, chipped distress.

"We're here live under the Argyle's art deco porte-cochère to await the arrival of the happy couple and their many glittering guests," Busby went on.

As the show broke away to a taped review of the parade of stars who'd already made their way into the live event that Busby was covering, Paige craned his neck to look up and out the bay window and over the hedge.

The Argyle was literally across the street. If he looked out of his kitchen window and up at just the right angle, he could see the hotel's ornate art deco tower as it crested above the trees in the park across from his building. It was only a short walk to where Busby, a moblet of paparazzi and a smallish crowd of gawkers had gathered to await the arrival of Angela Panderson.

"Angela Panderson, known as Angel to her many fans, is arguably the most famous woman in the world," Busby's voice went on, narrating the little taped filler segment. "Her tumultuous marriage to legendary rock guitarist Bill E Blaze—from their high-profile courtship to their scandal-filled divorce—is still the talk of Hollywood. Her life has become a model for many young starlets looking for their big break today."

Paige smiled at the cynical ease with which Busby teased the phrases "arguably the most famous" and "legendary rock guitarist" to mean "has-beens."

Distracted, Paige raised the teapot to his lips to drink. Still laughing at his mistake, he rose to get a teacup.

He could not remember making the conscious decision.

With his steaming cup of Earl Grey in hand, he found himself leaving his apartment and crossing the street to Barrymore Park. He wondered for a moment if he'd even closed the kitchen door. Not that it mattered. Paige couldn't have turned back to put out a fire. He was drawn across the lawn of what had once been home to one of Hollywood's famous first families, long ago donated to the city and more recently turned into a public park. Paige walked easily beneath the low hanging branches of the ancient olive trees lining the walkway.

He was a small man. Just short enough to be overlooked but not so short as to attract attention. His size, along with his unprepossessing looks, was a kind of curse he'd come to accept. The world in general and Hollywood in particular had become so noisy that all but the most hyper-pneumatic went unnoticed. It was, Paige thought, the age of exaggeration. An epoch of billionaires and larger-than-life personalities, where movies and art were judged by their box office take and people's true worth was determined entirely by the size of their bank accounts and body parts. In such a world, physical merit had become so exaggerated as to be cartoonish. More was more and less was just that. The world had told Paige that he was—quite literally—not enough for so long that he was in grudging acceptance of the fact. Though he'd grown accustomed to being ignored, he'd never been entirely comfortable with the idea.

A couple of tourists brushed past him as he made his way up the steep staircase that rose from the park's plaza to Sunset Boulevard and the Argyle Hotel beyond.

Still balancing his steaming teacup, he turned and headed the few steps west past the real palm trees and the stylized art deco palm sculptures that lined the path to his destination. Paige took up his place on the sidewalk in front of the Argyle Hotel to await his first sighting in more than a year of the woman who had ruined his life.

He took a sip of his tea and waited.

3

Angela Panderson was best known to those who could still remember her simply as Angel. She became the Angel of the centerfold in her days as a nude model in men's magazines. The name stuck. She had yet to retire from the field, though age, grace, or even a shred of dignity might have indicated otherwise to someone less intoxicated than she. Angel had been the perennial party girl ever since she'd first hit town and, like a bad guest, she steadfastly refused to leave, even though with the obvious exception of that evening's self-congratulatory festivities, the celebration was long over.

Somehow, Angel found her way to Hollywood from a small and unremarkable town in Manitoba. Raised among the sort of pickup-truck-driving, shotgun-toting, alcoholic, strip club habitués of what she liked to call the "nothing-better-to-do-than-fuck" region of north central Canada, Angel had come to the big city with dreams of pole dancing at a "nice" place. But, in keeping with the old adage "God looks after drunks, fools, and little children," Angel managed to turn a one night stand into an invitation to a party at the infamous home of a famous magazine publisher. The magazine mogul had made his name and peopled his bed with the bodies of young women whose intelligence was often greatly exceeded by their ambition and their bustlines.

Like so many before and after her, Angel was soon spread across—among other things—the glossy pages of his magazine. Unlike most of her predecessors, however, her intelligence greatly exceeded even her surgically enhanced breasts. Overnight and, in what appeared to the untrained eye to be a complete accident, she attained a kind of respectability not available to so many other women who made their living with their naked bodies. She engineered her way into a series of relationships with very high profile men who helped her career more than they compromised it. The medium of exchange remained the same, except that she traded her company for opportunities instead of direct payment. In short, she got a few auditions in lieu of money left on the bedside table.

A bit part on a hit sitcom that required Angel to wear something tight and jump up and down a lot made her a star. Her seismic jiggles caught the attention of the networks and legendary super-manager Lefty Flynn. Audience and access led to a series lead where the role demanded that she had to wear something tight and run toward the camera in slow motion a lot. Dazzled by her own star quality, Angel ditched Lefty to pursue her career on the big screen. Following her movie debut's flop, and a nasty lawsuit, Lefty kept all of Angel's profits from the hit show, and although she lost the access and the money, she kept the tight wardrobe. Later, she starred briefly on her own short-lived sitcom where she participated in helping the producers to make fun of her for doing the first two shows.

Hers was not much of a career. No one would probably have remembered her at all but for the footage recorded by VIP room security cameras at a private party she attended with her then-husband, rock star Bill E Blaze. Unbeknownst to Angel and company, the room's concealed cameras captured the evening's festivities. Highlights included her enthusiastic sex with Bill E and his awe-inspiring unit. Though Bill E passed out after their romp, the video and Angel kept going as she took on the rest of the members of Bill E's band, his touring crew, and an impressive number of his fan base. Excerpts of the scorching security tapes somehow wound up posted on the internet and later circulated in their entirety in wide release on video and DVD under the title *The Devil in Angel*.

The salacious scenes eventually paled beside the live spectacle generated daily during her ensuing earth-shattering divorce from the aging bass player. Highly publicized incident followed glaring episode. Heinous allegation was heaped upon egregious assertion. New shocking video after blistering video was revealed. Damning testimony filled page after degrading page of court records and sensational newspaper headlines. And a huge number of photos and digicam shots, which were just plain lurid, flooded the media and the email of millions.

Angel and Bill E might have become the long-forgotten, mediocre has-beens to which their lack of effort and talent entitled them. Instead, they rose to become pop-culture jokes. They entered the language not as household names but as perennial punchlines. They became immortal.

Angel was one of those absurd public figures who spent her time demanding privacy on national television, bewailing her fate at the hands of the very paparazzi and tabloid press whose efforts and attention had created her career and generated her fame and her infamy. Had she simply moved back to Manitoba and ceased her regular appearances, half-naked, at drunken brawls in and around nightclubs packed with people half her age, the press would have left her alone entirely. In fact, with each passing year she had to work harder and harder to get the attention she needed to fuel her ridiculous complaints about that same attention paid her next television or court appearance.

Her upcoming marriage to the newly minted media titan Seth St. James promised not only the ratings boost her sagging career and bustline needed so desperately, but it also offered the chance of that rarest of Hollywood commodities: a second act. What made Angel's prospects for a second act rarer still was the fact that she'd really never had a first act. A second act for Angel and those like her was more akin to singing the finale after making a scene in the lobby at intermission.

Seth St. James' Hollywood black card had "bought" about the impossible: the promise of another run for Angel at being a movie star. It was an ambition she'd destroyed with her bare hands and legendary antics on the set of the only movie she'd ever made. Her on-shoot orgies of sex, drugs, and rock-and-rollers gave the shocks on her trailer an Olympic workout. Her movie's delays and budget overruns made *Heaven's Gate* look like an art house film. Lawsuits had been threatened just to get her to show up for work. All this, combined with the fact that her performance stank up theatres around the world, had long since rendered any question of her viability as a movie star moot.

In fact, the camp value of her single film was second only to that of the offscreen performance to which she'd treated fans and critics alike. Her only appearances on the big screen since her catastrophic debut had been tiny walk-on parts—parodies designed to underscore the joke she'd become. The kind of parts that late-night comedy show cast members typically played, performing a demeaning imitation of the celebrity in question. But pride was not enough to come between Angel and a camera. She was too vain to be humiliated.

Yet through the grace of holy matrimony and her improbable new alliance, Angela's foundering fortunes seemed on the verge of change. Billionaire venture capitalist Seth St. James, with his newly acquired studio and media empire, could afford her the kind of credibility that came only from the implicit nepotism of sleeping with a really rich and powerful man. So bad was her reputation that the only way that she would ever star in another film was to marry the guy who owned the studio.

And so, she was.

Television is more forgiving than movies for someone like Angel. Even in her drunken debauchery she could easily spare the one day a week she'd actually have to show up for work to do a sitcom, though in truth she'd managed to screw that up, too. The real jewel in the Hollywood crown is the movies. Though she downplayed her interest in the big screen, she was a woman made out of ambition and a good deal of silicone. Seth was a man who could make those ambitions a reality without need of pesky things that she couldn't have surgically implanted, like hard work or talent or showing up. Seth was perfect for her.

Standing beyond the scrum of the media and fans crowding the fringes of the Argyle's red carpet to await her arrival with fiancé Seth, Paige reflected on one of the first warning signs he'd had about Angel's true nature. At the beginning of the end of her literary ambitions, his career, and their partnership, Angel had insisted that Paige edit out the truth behind Seth's fictional doppelganger in their second book. The two novels Paige and Angel had created were "loosely based" on Angel's life. The big selling point was the implied smearing of the fictionalized but recognizable Hollywood players who peopled Angel's bed and the novel's pages.

Paige's writing skill had managed to make their first novel fun and even earned a somewhat-less-than-terrible critical reception. "Not crap" was Paige's personal favorite note from their editor on the project. But it was the promised glimpses of Angel's soiled linens that sold copies. So when she decided at the eleventh hour to launder their second book of all its dirt and turn it into an inane, sizzle-free flop, it was the first assault in her campaign to kill the project and with it Paige's career, prospects and livelihood.

Thirteen months after the debacle, Paige stood on the napless side of the Argyle's red carpet, sipping tea from a chipped cup as Angel made her second-act entrance as consort to a mogul and born-again movie star.

The Argyle is the jewel of what is known the world over as the Sunset Strip. The famed few blocks adjacent to the hotel are pocked with the rock clubs, tourist traps, theme restaurants and trendy hotels that give the place its name and make the little town of West Hollywood rich. In return, the little city endures a nightly incursion of drunken invaders. Their cars clog the streets in the same way their garbage, vomit and blood clog the sewer drains.

But the Strip's big draw isn't the clubs, the hotels or the restaurants; it is their partiers, patrons, diners and overnight guests. Tabloids and assault-video shows would vanish were it not for the steady supply of embarrassing footage and paparazzi shots captured along the Sunset Strip. Angel's security tape fiasco had been filmed there. Attracting the attention of the freelance photographers who are the denizens of the storied street is in fact the PR plan of a sizable portion of those in Hollywood and beyond who are famous more for being famous than for any particular talent they might possess.

Paige thought it was the perfect place for Angel's engagement party.

4

For nearly an hour Paige held his tiny piece of real estate in front of the Argyle.

Attracted by the potential proximity to a genuine, newly-minted movie mogul, the guest list far exceeded the bona fides of the marital alliance being fêted.

"What's going on?" one breathless young woman asked another within Paige's hearing.

"Some kind of party," the girl answered with a shrug. "But I hear Luke is going to be here!"

"Luke!" shrieked the new arrival.

She was joined in chorus by a sizeable number of crowd members—not all or even most of them teenaged girls—screaming the name "Luke" in a frighten-the-livestock, nerve-shattering register. Paige hardly flinched, though he did wonder who the hell Luke might be.

"Will the others be here?" a middle-aged woman wearing a business suit asked in a bordering-on-hysteria-tone unrecognizably different from the first two young women. "I'm all about Ashton!"

They all screamed Ashton's name for a while despite the fact that neither he nor Luke had apparently arrived. During the Luke-and-Ashton-non-arrival-pandemonium, an Academy Award-winning actress disembarked without attracting attention even from the media. She waved gamely and went inside.

"So why are Luke and Ashton having a party?" asked another of Paige's curbmates—a man in his mid-to-late twenties and a tie, visibly shaking with excitement.

"It's actually an engagement party for Angel Panderson and Seth St. James," an irritable middle-aged man said in a dismissive manner that Paige himself might have adopted for people speaking during the feature.

"Who?" one of the girls asked in a tone of genuine bewilderment.

"Only the most famous—"

"But Luke will still be here, right?" the first girl asked, clearly worried.

Paige joined in the renewed Luke chorus just for something to do, shrieking the name as though he knew or cared to whom it referred.

Versions of the same conversation were repeated around him for the remaining forty-five-or-so minutes he waited for Angel and Seth. His tea went cold and he stopped drinking it. He regretted bringing the cup and considered throwing it away, but thought better of it. He could hardly afford the tea, let alone a new matching cup for the china he'd foolishly bought when his first novel came out—back before Angel was even a cloud on his horizon—and he thought his career was actually getting underway.

The crowd declined, repopulated and ebbed again. People got the chance to shout incoherently at their favorites. The paparazzi and entertainment reporters devoured the glittering guests like wolves enjoying slow-moving and surprisingly willing antelopes.

Not only did Luke and Ashton come to the party, but they brought Callum and Michael, and there was a moment when Paige feared for his safety and the mental health of those around him. He wondered if Luke and company were really as young as they appeared or was he really as old as they made him feel. He figured the four of them must be part of a band, but they might have been the stars of a Saturday morning kids' program—they seemed the right age. *How old had the Monkees been when they were a Saturday-morning phenom?* he wondered.

Jostled and trampled by the crowd as the fans and paparazzi around him jockeyed for access to more temporally relevant guests, Paige had surprisingly little competition for the alleged main event: Angel and Seth's arrival. By the time the happy couple's limo rolled into the drive, none but the most dedicated members of the press and fan base were still on hand.

Busby was still there. His live shot had long since timed out and he chatted on his mobile as he waited to capture some footage with the guests of honor. Despite the fact that it was their wedding, Seth and Angel were, after all, a venture capitalist and an aging centerfold who hadn't been on television for more than a decade. "Most famous woman in the world" was a nickname she'd earned when she had still arguably deserved it. Paige thought the title was only ever still used ironically. It was certainly how *he* used it.

At last, the lights came on. The scene was transformed from mere hotel driveway into a magical Hollywood tableau. The maître d'hôtel himself stepped to the curb to open the door.

Seth was first to emerge from the car.

He greeted the photographers with a smile and a genial wave that gave him up as a neophyte and made it clear to the fans that he was no celebrity. Seth was the sort of studio mogul one might expect from central casting. Tall, fit and styled to within a frame of sartorial perfection, he bore no resemblance whatever to the doughy post-middle-aged, middle-management types of men and women who actually ran the studio on his behalf. In truth, Seth had more than his dashing good looks in common with his actors. He was really just playing the part of media mogul. It was a role that he was already becoming bored with, just as he had previously tired of tech mogul, electric car mogul, hotel mogul and the many other parts and titles he'd purchased with the proceeds generated by his true skill, the manipulation of his family fortune. Still, Paige had to admit Seth looked great, even if no one was looking.

All eyes were on the woman who took Seth's hand as he guided her effortlessly out of the back of the limo.

Angel was the opposite of Paige in so many ways, but none more so than in how she looked. It wasn't just that she was a woman, though that was a really, really big part of it. And thanks to surgical assistance, her feminine traits were bigger still. But everything about her was bigger than life. She was the portrait of the age of exaggeration that had rendered Paige largely invisible. With her enormous, mercilessly bleached hair, her Oompa Loompa-orange skin, her stucco-and-Magic-Marker makeup and her pneumatic chassis, Angel could have stepped into a cell-animation and made Betty Boop look underplayed. In short, she was—or at least had been—everything regarded as beautiful and desirable in a crass world that had crowned her queen for a day so many, many days before.

It was in fact her extreme *passé célébrité* that made her of any interest at all. God, and anyone who'd ever seen her work, knew it wasn't her talent.

Nonetheless, she looked great on Seth's arm. Big boobs and a billionaire made for perfect TV. The morbid non-Luke-and-Ashton-fans who'd stayed to confirm the rumors that Angel, in fact, was not dead, as well as the dedicated paparazzi who were willing to waste the disk space on confirmation-of-life documentation shots, were distracted by their prurient fascination with Angel's continued but clearly flagging defiance of gravity. Even what remained of security seemed to be looking past their charges as if they might catch a glimpse of Luke and the boys or other more noteworthy *célébrités* at the horizon.

Seth and Angel managed a couple of back-and-forths for the photographers. Two lefts and one right was all they got before the photographers started to power down to preserve battery life for shots they could actually sell.

Paige felt the lull.

Busby was setting up for his three-shot with the happy couple. Seth was distracted talking business with the one reporter on the scene who was aware that entertainment was the country's number one export and Seth one of its principal exporters. Angel signed books, magazines and photos for a few stray fans.

Paige simply stepped past the barricade and walked up to her.

No one paid any attention, of course.

"I've always thought that looked more like vandalism than an autograph," Paige said of her limp-wristed signature.

She looked up at him, eyes wide, her head blindingly blond. The effect was undeniable, even to Paige who knew the monster behind the mask only too well. The harsh video lights behind her and the crude theatrical makeup created their well-known alchemy. It was as if he was seeing her under carefully hung studio lights, through a well chosen lens filter and burned into high quality film. It took him a moment to remember that he beheld not an angel but a goddess of destruction.

"Paige!" she shouted, startled. And the spell was broken.

Her little cry caused the otherwise oblivious security guards to look her way.

"Angel," he said, with a curt nod.

"Paige Blanche," said the dismissive middle-aged fan who had been standing next to Paige for nearly an hour as he belatedly recognized his curbmate. "Can you sign my book, too?"

"Why not?" Paige said, snatching the book out of Angel's hands.

I'm with stupid! Love, Paige, he signed. "There you are." He beamed as he handed the book back.

Given that Paige and Angel were signing autographs together, security personnel who weren't even old enough to know who she was took little further notice of the two.

"So, Angel," he said, extending his hand. "Congratulations."

"What are you doing here, Paige?" she snarled, grabbing his hand and stepping forward as much to head him off as to offer her stiff embrace.

Paige smiled when he saw the terror in her eyes.

"It certainly isn't because I was invited," he said.

"Well, there were only a limited number of places," she assured him, trapped. She tried to back away and tug her hand from his grasp.

With his cup of cold tea clutched in one hand, Paige held fast, matching her step-for-step in their uncomfortable little dance up the red carpet.

Seth, distracted by the idea of his own famousness, busied himself playing for the cameras and speaking to the reporters who were largely ignoring every word. Clever about making billions but clueless about the mercurial whims of the entertainment press, Seth was oblivious to the fact that even as he spoke, most lenses stayed focused on Angel. Her conversation with Paige or whoever was the story. Though no one could get close enough to hear what the two were saying, Angel was the money shot. Seth was just the money.

"Yes, only a scant fifteen hundred guests, I hear," Paige said. More than a year's unrequited anger crept into his voice, though his smile never wavered.

"You'd be surprised," she answered. Her tone rose to meet his as she relaxed into their red carpet duel. Only her eyes betrayed her, darting past him as she looked for an escape. Her icy paparazzi smile turned to bared fangs.

"Nothing you do would surprise me," Paige said, gripping her hand with both of his. His teacup still tangled awkwardly in his fingers. "In fact, the only thing that seems out of character is that you'd be stupid enough to tell me where all the bodies are buried and then screw me over so completely. I thought you were smarter. I guess I was wrong about that, too."

They were the first harsh words he'd ever said to her and, though her press-packet smile remained fixed, the shock in her eyes was perhaps the only genuine emotion he'd ever seen them register.

"So, what are you doing here?" she asked, her tone sharper than before.

"I live right next door, remember?" he said. He gestured in the general direction with his head.

"Then I suggest you go home," she said, snatching her hands up and away from his.

There was no plan. The teacup was in his hand. Her abrupt motion as she yanked free jerked his hands violently upward. In the whiplash, the last of his Earl Grey flew out of the cup across the bodice of her rather expensive looking white gown and into her face.

Both regarded one another in shock and surprise at first as they realized what had happened.

Paige began to laugh.

Security didn't know what to do.

The press did.

Photographers and reporters overran the line. Paige and Angel were surrounded. Security's task was not to get to Paige but to get Angel out of the media riot and into the hotel. Seth was unclear on what was going on. Ignored and indignant about it, he shoved his way through the Argyle doors.

Paige was equally ignored.

True to bad form, the media pursued the biggest name and not the story. They only focused on Angel; none thought to get Paige on camera or even to ask him who he was or what had happened. He stepped backward through the rush. Their eyes locked for an instant. Paige half-expected the stunned and spitting Angel to melt like the Wicked Witch. A brown stain spread across her white bodice as her face puddled and began to drip off her chin. On the verge of being so publicly unmasked, she turned to shield her face and pushed through the crowd with the ferocity of woman in fear for her life or maybe just afraid of the truth.

Paige simply stepped away and went for a walk in the park.

All in all, other than the becoming destitute and getting fired parts, it was the best day he'd had in a long time.

5

The incident made national news. Their moribund book sales even got a small bump. It was just a happy accident for Paige that photographers and television cameras had surrounded the two of them when the dregs of his cup of tea splashed into Angel's face. As an added bonus, the news of it eclipsed Angel's engagement party and became the story. Although there wasn't much tea left in the cup by the time she finally arrived on the scene and, sadly, it had gone cold, the moment was captured from dozens of angles and as a result looked like a lot more than Paige had either intended or achieved.

He hadn't thought what he might do when he walked across the park to the nearby hotel. In fact, he was so preoccupied with his hurt and confusion he'd hardly noticed the park, let alone contemplated acts of revenge. All he really wanted was some kind of answer or apology from Angel. Her expansive silence over the previous year had been the hardest to bear after their regular and garrulous acquaintance.

Afterward, back in his apartment, Paige smiled all through his dinner of ramen noodles and expired canned tuna. He laughed out loud at his fleeting moment of infamy, already picked up on the local news. And he glowed with triumph as he managed to record the footage of himself throwing his tea in Angel's face from one of the many TV news reports, along with angles of the incident that followed as the cable channels picked up the salacious clip. He played it over and over again, laughing harder each time. Somehow, it didn't matter nearly as much that *Show Talk* and his livelihood had been cancelled.

Paige was still savoring his private laugh as he drifted off to sleep. The sounds of Angel's party across the street wafted in through his open bedroom window but somehow, having eclipsed the announcement of her engagement and its lavish celebration, Paige felt a little less resentful.

At three forty-three, he awoke.

It took him a moment to realize he was hearing the sound of breaking glass. He fumbled on the bedside table for the phone, growling when he realized the cordless handset was elsewhere. He struck the charger base in frustration, which set off the cordless phone's pager. The handset began to ring. From the echo, he guessed it was in the living room or the front hall but he couldn't be sure. He was certain that his cell phone was in the charger in the kitchen.

He heard a small scream. Terrifying quiet followed the involuntary bleat, as whoever it was located the handset and silenced it.

Paige's panic set in.

The intruder knew he was awake. Paige could hear the floorboards creaking as the sound of footsteps drew nearer his bedroom door. In the darkness, he tried to find something to use as a weapon.

His slipper? Too angry mom.

The lamp? Too bulky and too awkward.

The clock? Really only good as a projectile.

Paige staggered toward the closet door. His toe connected with the corner of an old metal footlocker he had bought at a garage sale and kept meaning to throw out. He fought to suppress his yelp. Hopping on one foot, he slipped on a small fake oriental rug he'd acquired to hide a stain on the hardwood. As he fell, he overturned a small table by his reading chair. His hand came to rest on one of a pair of Lucite platform heels Angel had sent him when they first began working together. A memento of better times, he kept the pair on the little table he'd upended in his fall.

The impossible footwear arrived at his door after an early meeting with a handwritten note:

Paige –

If you want to walk a mile in my shoes, here they are!

Angela

Paige had been charmed and impressed by her powers of observation, or at least her ability to guess his shoe size. Later she swore him to secrecy when he realized that they wore the same size—and not because his feet were so small.

A Lucite heel was the perfect weapon, but he had second thoughts about possibly damaging a souvenir of their lost friendship. Then he remembered the many miles he'd walked since the heels' arrival and Angel's fancy footwork breaking her every promise. A little blood would make them a truer memento.

His faceted glass bedroom doorknob began to turn. The breath stuck in his throat. His heart pounded. The door creaked as it eased inward. He drew back the deadly seven-inch stiletto, poised to strike.

"*Paige,*" the intruder whispered hoarsely through the gap. "*Are you awake?*"

The dark figure stepped into the room. Light from the window glinted off something large, grasped firmly in one of the killer's hands.

Paige lunged. He skidded again on the cheap rug, lost his footing and fell on his assailant. The two crashed into the bedside table. The lamp and phone base rained down on both of them. The pager went off again.

Paige grasped for the attacker's weapon. They struggled. The object fell heavily from the assailant's hand, tumbling across the hardwood before settling with a solid thunk just shy of under the bed. He strained against his attacker's powerful grasp as he attempted to gain the upper hand and angle the shoe into striking position.

"Get off me, you big girl," the invader demanded. "What are you going to do with that thing? Put it on and kick my ass?"

"What the hell are *you* doing here?" Paige exclaimed. Freed of the need for his continued and incompetent self-defense, he located what was left of the bedside lamp and switched it on.

There underneath him, their legs wound together, her makeup and hair in dire need of a touch-up, was Angela Panderson, the most famous woman in the world.

"I have to talk to you," Angel said, struggling to sit up.

"Now?'

"Get off of me for fuck's sake." Righting herself in a sudden deft move, she easily took the fall and pinned him to the ground.

"You broke into my house in the middle of the night to talk?" Paige sputtered. He struggled but she held him fast.

"You wrestle like a girl."

"Takes one to know one," he said, giving up. "What is so important that you need to talk to me about it now?"

"If I let you go, will you stop this?" Angel asked.

"I was happy with our little tea party," he said, giggling. "Have you seen the news? It's really priceless. You should see the look on your face."

"Yeah, yeah, really funny, Paige." Angel let go of his hands and sat back on his chest. "But I'm afraid there's going to be a whole new angle on the story in a few hours."

Paige looked at her in horror.

"What is that all over your dress?"

"Blood."

"Are you okay?"

"It's not *my* blood," she said irritably.

"Oh my God," Paige shrieked. "I'm bleeding. What have you done to me?"

"It's not your blood either." She sighed.

"It's not? And you got it all over me. Look at this. These are white silk pajamas. Do you have any idea how much these things cost?"

"I gave them to you."

"I bet you still don't know."

"Paige, really, can we talk about this a little later?"

"Sure. You want to break in again? Say around six? I could be sound asleep again by then."

"I came here for a reason."

"Well, you're the one sitting on me."

"Seth is dead."

"What?" Paige tried and failed to sit up.

"I woke up in our suite at the Argyle, next door, covered with blood. Seth was dead on top of me," she said flatly. She stared beyond Paige, lost in the shock of the memory.

"Cheese and rice!" Paige still wished Angel ill and he was not sorry about throwing his tea in her face—he'd do it again—but he felt a numbing horror.

"Tell me about it," Angel said. She shivered.

"I'm so sorry," Paige said. "Are you okay? What happened?"

"No idea," she sighed.

"Did you call the police?"

"So you can visit me in jail?"

"As if," Paige snorted, then started. "Did you kill him?"

"God, no!" she said with conviction. "Well, I'm pretty sure. I mean, I don't remember coming back up to the room, but I'd had a lot to drink."

"You? Got drunk and blacked out? *Quelle surprise*."

"And when I woke up he was dead."

"Oh my God, you did kill him. You killed him in a black-out," Paige said, trying to crabwalk away but unable to escape her. "It was really only a matter of time."

"No, I didn't kill him," she said, rolling her eyes and grasping him with surprisingly powerful thighs. "Why would I kill him?

I was just about to marry a three-picture deal. In six months, maybe I'd kill him, but now?" She made a dismissive, farty noise.

"True," he said, again giving up the struggle. "So, what do you think happened?"

"I don't know."

"Then why come here?"

"Because that's what the murderer used to bash his head in," she said, pointing at the shiny, bloody weapon he'd knocked from her hand in their earlier struggle.

"What is it?" he asked, turning his head in the direction she was pointing. Then, even at his odd angle, he recognized it. It was a crystal angel. One of a pair their publisher had presented them upon the launch of their first book, custom-made, one personally engraved to Angel and one to Paige, to commemorate their publication day. "Your angel?"

"No," she said, shaking her head and sliding off him to sit on the floor. "*Your* angel."

"Mine? How the hell?"

"Either I'm not the first person to break in tonight…" Angel trailed off with a shrug and a smirk.

"Or?" he demanded, sitting up.

"*You* did it."

6

Paige could only stare at Angel.

They sat on the floor of his bedroom, still breathing hard from their exertion and the horror that they were smeared with Seth St. James' blood. The murder weapon, engraved with Paige's name and dripping gore, was partially concealed under his bed. He had to fight off his inner drama queen to keep from going into the well-deserved state of shock he could ill-afford. Next door, a man lay dead. Both of them were clearly implicated in his death, if not outright suspects in his murder.

"God," he sighed. "And I thought yesterday sucked."

It had been more than a year since they'd spent any time together unless you counted the tea incident. He smiled as he remembered it. After so much enmity and betrayal, what was there to be said?

"So, why did you really come over here?" he asked.

Folding his arms, he fixed her with an unflinching glare. He knew her well enough to know that if he stared at her silently long enough she'd begin to talk, even if, as was most often the case, it was to lie.

She made an indignant noise and held his eye.

They glared for a long tense moment.

"Because you live next door," she said, blinking at last.

"And?"

They stared at one another for another long while.

He could almost see the lie forming.

"To protect you because the murder weapon…"

"*Ennnhhh*." He made a noise like a game show buzzer. "Liar."

"Because I realized I had been wrong about you—"

"*Ennnhhh*."

"Because I needed to get cleaned up and I thought I could talk you into—"

"*Ennnhhh*."

"—*threaten* you into helping me."

"Well, you see there, I was wrong. You actually can tell the truth if your life depends on it," Paige said. He laughed grimly. "You really do look like crap. I think you've got brains in your hair."

"Ewww," she said, gagging. "Can I borrow some jeans or something?"

"You're lucky I'm short and you're tall," he snorted. She helped him to his feet. He accepted her assistance and then shook his hands free of hers.

"Try not to get blood all over everything." He stalked toward the back of the house. "And you are paying for that window."

"Won't your landlord—"

"*Ennnhhh*."

"Fine."

"You seem really broken up about old Seth biting the big one," Paige said, flipping on the bathroom lights as the two began to get out of their bloody clothing. They had dispensed with the need for separate dressing rooms during their book tour. Neither was affected by or had the slightest interest in the other's nudity. Paige was just too clean-cut for Angel. And Angel was just so very indisputably a girl and as such, aside from her potential BFF factor and dish potential, she held no interest for Paige.

"God, you're right," she said as she tried to unhook her bra with one hand and turn on the shower with the other.

"Careful of the hot water," Paige said. "The boiler's right below so it's unlimited but it's scalding."

"Perfect," she said, adjusting the head of the flexible neck on the shower massage. "I guess I'm sorry about Seth, but I've felt like his prisoner for these past months."

"I don't want to hear the sordid details of your little sex games," Paige complained, tossing his bloody pajamas in the sink. "Is it cold or hot water for blood stains?"

"I think it's salt and Perrier." Angel kicked off her panties and stepped into the shower. "Anyway, it wasn't a sex game. It started with the book. And since when don't you want sordid details?"

"*Our* book?" Slipping on a robe, he made his way into his glass-strewn kitchen for salt and fizzy water.

"No, the Encyclopedia Britannica, volume WTF!" Her shout echoed in the tiny stall. "Yes, our book."

"What about it?" he asked, returning with salt and seltzer.

"There was something in it, something that we made up about the fictional version of him that turned out to be true." Angel began draping bloody, wet hair extensions over the top of the rippled glass shower door.

Paige shuddered.

The expired club soda hissed sullenly as he twisted off the cheap aluminum cap. He took a sip to test it. Flat. He poured it over the ruined pajamas anyway.

"Remember that time you made something up from my childhood that I didn't even remember and my mom freaked out about it being in there when she read the book because it turned out to be accidentally true?"

"That was so weird," he answered. He rubbed salt into the stains with a fingernail brush. "And what do you mean *we*? You can only type with your thumbs."

"We, you, potato, whatever, it was the same with Seth," she said, rinsing soap out of her hair. "I gave him a copy of the manuscript and he totally lost it. Came over demanding to know how I found out. Said that if it got out it could ruin him, or worse."

"What was it, I wonder?" Paige asked. "Clearly, Seth has arrived at the 'or worse' part of that prophecy."

"I have no idea, but he tried to get the publication canceled. And when he couldn't, he started marking out whole sections of the book. You remember? Where's the conditioner?"

"Yes," Paige growled. He most definitely remembered the humiliating and demeaning process of getting story notes for his book from Seth along with Bill E and even ultimately random friends of Angel's. He tossed the conditioner over the top of the glass shower door as hard as he could.

"Ow!" she wailed. "That hurt."

"Sorry," he said, clearly not. He went back to scrubbing, though the task was hopeless. The conditioner made fart sounds when she squeezed the bottle. She giggled. "Excuse *you*," he said.

Paige laughed. The juvenile silliness of it reminded him how much fun they'd had together before she ruined everything. He held up the pajamas, disgusted. So like her to spoil something nice for someone else without ever pausing to consider. He dropped them back into the cold, flat club soda for a vain soak. "So no idea what was in the book that freaked him out?"

"No," she said.

"But he thought we did?"

"Well, really, he thought *you* did," she admitted.

He hiked himself up onto the counter. One leg tucked under him, he considered her answer until he understood what she meant. "Because you'd never actually read the book?"

"Well, not all at once, I mean... Well, I didn't exactly not read the book..."

"So much as you just never got around to it?"

"Don't get mad at me," she pleaded, popping her dripping, tangled head from behind the door.

"Too late."

"Well, I read some of it. At first. In the first book, anyways."

"Oh honey, I never thought you'd read the book," he said, tucking both his cold feet underneath him on the purple-and-yellow ceramic tile counter top. "And that is *so* not why I'm mad at you."

"Why *are* you mad?"

"One murder at a time. Let's just get cleaned up and figure out what we're going to do." It took a conscious effort not to give himself over to his anger and answer her question. But he knew it would consume him. First, like it or not, he had to save their lives. His only alternative was to trust her to effect their rescue, and he didn't trust her at all. He took a breath. He remembered the cup of tea and the look on her face. He smiled.

"So, Seth thought *I* knew whatever it was and put it in the book for some reason?" "Yeah," Angel said, closing the shower door and stepping back under the spray.

"Do you think whatever was in there was bad enough to get him killed? Like, did it seem like it was that kind of bad?"

"He basically held me prisoner since he read it, cancelled the book tour and made me change the whole book." Through the stall door Paige could see her scrub herself more furiously.

"So, naturally, you decided to marry him?" Paige literally threw up his hands. "Your taste in men."

"For a three-picture deal. Millions against the gross," she added when he didn't respond.

"Oh, you meant that literally."

"Duh."

"Well, now, that's a real Hollywood prenup."

"Yeah," she said, turning under the stream. "We were actually supposed to sign the prenup papers when I got back to the room." She went silent.

The handles of the old shower squeaked as she closed the taps. He tossed her a towel as she stepped dripping from the stall.

Her strangely orange, salon-tanned skin glistened like freshly minted pennies.

"So, he changed the book. Then why kill him?"

"And make it look like we did it," Angel added. Wrapping herself in the first towel, she took a second one to her hair.

He sat up. He was suddenly alarmed and awake in a way he had not been since Angel's unwelcome arrival.

"To get rid of us," he said.

Bent over, she bundled her hair in a towel. "What?" Angel asked, looking up at him through her legs. She stood, tossing her head back and completing her terrycloth turban. She too had gone serious.

His nerves tingled like sunburn on a cold night.

"Lookit," he said. "Whoever it is has already gotten rid of Seth because of whatever it is they think we know. If they can make us look like the murderers, then who'd believe us if we told whatever it is they think we might try to tell?"

"What?"

"They're trying to shut us up, without killing us." He slid down off the counter. "If we don't get blamed for the murder, then I think we're next."

"You think someone's trying to frame us both?"

"How else do you explain the crystal angel? I mean, why else go to all the trouble of stealing that from me and then bashing his head in with it? Was there anything else odd about the room?"

"You mean besides the dead guy?"

"Un-hunh."

"I woke up covered with, well, Seth," she said. Her eyes went glassy. "I realized he was dead. I pretty much freaked out. I didn't scream. I didn't know if I was alone. I was too terrified to make a sound. I got out from under him. I got to my feet and I ran."

"What about the angel?"

"I tripped over it. Thought it was mine at first. Then I saw it had your name engraved on it. That's when I remembered that you were next door. Now, if I could just forget everything else."

They sat in silence for a bit. Paige pondered.

"We have to go back," he said finally.

"Where?"

"To your room."

"Gross, no way," she said vehemently, almost shaking the towel off her head.

"The angel isn't enough to make their case," he said. "If they wanted to frame us, there's bound to be a lot more evidence implicating us. We've got to retrieve it before the police get there."

"Who are you all of a sudden, you big Ellery Queen?"

"Come along, my dear Watson," he said, heading for his dressing room. "What should we wear?" He opened the door and pulled the cord on the dowdy overhead light.

"Ew, I love this," Angel said as she followed him into the little windowless room. The walls on one side were lined with mirrored French doors. Behind the two sets of double doors was not only hanging clothes racks but the kind of built-in shoe racks, hat shelves and tricked-out closetry typical of old Hollywood apartments. Opposite the elaborate closets were enough shelves and built-in chests of drawers to accommodate a wardrobe far more considerable than Paige's. He assumed it had been built to appeal to some potential temporary actor resident traveling with the sort of jewels and furs to justify not only the opulent accoutrements but also the room itself. The door even locked, as did all the old fashioned interior doors in the apartment, with a shared antique skeleton key. Paige had always figured it as a sort of safe room should the need arise. He kept the skeleton key in the lock in case of an emergency—although it had not occurred to him during that night's break-in.

After playing dress-up for a bit, they settled on black jeans, black T-shirts and black shoes. "It's slenderizing and it'll hide blood stains," he explained. "And of course, we'll need gloves."

She chose a pair of heavily fretted driving gloves made of leather and stretchy material so they were only a little too big for her. He reluctantly wore a pair of leather gloves he worried about ruining.

"Oh, I love these," he sighed. "They're the only other solid black pair but they're like kidskin and so comfortable and warm. I hate the thought of messing them up with God knows what goo from the murder scene."

"Touching," Angel said. "Your life actually depends on this, Paige."

"Right," he said, pulling them on like a surgeon in the scrub room.

"You might want to wait until we get there," she said, patting him on the shoulder. "It will still be Los Angeles when we go outside."

"Conspicuous, hunh?"

"At least." She nodded.

Desperation was once again their bond.

Three Years Earlier…

In the Beginning

From the start, Paige and Angel's ill-advised and ill-considered partnership had been based on expediency and self-interest. With no sense of direction between them, the path they forged together led them inexorably to the grisly scene and their tenuous fate. On balance, other than being in a room with a dead body, a scavenger hunt at a murder scene would not really be an outlier for the as-yet-unindicted co-conspirators.

Their improbable introduction began shortly after the critical success of Paige's first novel. Praised as "fresh-voiced" and "a remarkable debut," the book had earned him the Gilded Garland award for gay literature and something in the neighborhood of 250 dollars in royalties. The earning power of fiction, despite its long and storied reputation, is not what it once was. In short, Paige had been feeling the pinch.

He had learned the hard way that no one in publishing will talk to—let alone pay—writers unless they were willing to offer up a tragic "true life" story and sell it as a "memoir" or—if anyone knows or cares who you are—a "tell-all/biography" and then only if something salacious or hideous has happened to you or someone famous you're related to—with a bonus if you have the same last name. If your traumatic childhood leads to a worthy enough redemption, you might get to go on the *Today Show* or the Oprah Winfrey Network to promote your tragedy, and then retire on the proceeds.

As Paige began to pitch ideas for a second novel to his publishers, he found that not only was there little or no market for fiction but that what market existed was glutted with bad fiction foisted off as memoir—known in less literary circles as lying. Writers possessed of enough integrity to call their alleged memoir the fiction it truly was got compensated with the cold comfort of principle and—if they could actually write—a few good clippings for their scrapbooks.

Paige chose integrity and found himself fully stocked on principles and cupboard-bare on the rent. His publisher had not only declined the manuscript of his second novel but taken his beloved first novel out of print in favor of publishing an internet-spawned blogger who had written a book on the same topic but without wit or imagination—i.e., a nonfiction memoir.

Writing is already a very solitary profession, but when you are spurned and broke, it can quickly become a credible motive for suicide. On rent day, in an effort to combat the urge to move to swifter means of self-annihilation than authoring fiction, Paige elected to take himself out to lunch at the neighborhood diner for a dollar-cup of tortilla soup.

Eating out, even at The Monkey Bar, was an extravagance, given Paige's complete lack of funds. He had some money put aside, but he was saving up for bankruptcy. He would have declared chapter-whatever months earlier but the legal fees required for filing were a bit too dear. Paige could not even afford to go bankrupt. He had been squirreling away every penny since his free legal consultation. Despite such lofty goals, Paige could not face another day swallowed by the semi-darkness of his kitchen/library and the absolute necessity of either finding a roommate or writing something he could sell. Instead, he elected to spend a dollar, plus taxes and tip, of his legal fund on a lifesaving cup of soup.

Despite Paige's resolve, he almost didn't make it out the door.

In the little enclave of West Hollywood, every day is swim-suit competition. The tiny city, surrounded by Los Angeles on three sides and Beverly Hills on the fourth, is home to pretty much all of the underwear models, commercial actors and gay porn stars in the whole world. The majority of the city's other residents are people who just *look* like they belong in one of the aforementioned categories. It makes for great scenery, but a trip to the gym or the grocery store or the neighborhood diner often felt to Paige like a plank-walk down the runway, if his ego or his outfit wasn't *haute* enough.

In Hollywood, successful people are expected to go out dressed like slobs. It's a sign of success. In fact, if you are really successful, you can even stop bathing. But it's a fine line, because if other people don't know you're famous, they just think you're homeless—not worthy-homeless but crazy-homeless. Since Paige's self-worth had gone the way of his first novel and his fortunes, he was forced to wear something flattering and spend extra time on his hair.

In the end, hunger more than a satisfying reflection propelled Paige out the door.

A former Italian grocery store turned coffee shop turned sidewalk café, the low-budget Monkey Bar bistro was only a block and a half away. Paige was enjoying the scenery and the unrelenting spring weather as he made his way to a late lunch. His mood was actually lightening a bit.

He froze as he came within sight of the outdoor diners.

Bobby, who had three commercials running and who had stopped returning Paige's phone calls after their second date because he was "out of minutes on his cell plan," was there—worst-case scenario—with the ex-Marine/actor/masseur/hooker Paige hadn't heard from since they'd spent New Year's Eve together.

Well, that wasn't entirely true. Their paths had crossed one recent afternoon when Paige was dining on free samples at the local market. Marine/actor/masseur/hooker had managed to let Paige know about every single showcase, one-man-show and brush with fame he'd managed to scrape together since their last night out together, without ever once asking about Paige. It was a very impressive display of self-obsession in a city noted for its epic narcissism.

As Paige drew nearer the two, it became clear that things were worse than he had supposed at first glance. Both Bobby and the Marine were not only seated at the same table but were talking on their respective cell phones. This proved conclusively that they were sleeping together regularly and were possibly an item. People who are just dating don't take more than a quickie phone call during a date for fear that other people will think that they are married to the person they are with and, hence, off the market.

Ignoring one another and talking on the phone at the table in a restaurant was a brazen show of intimacy if not outright commitment. The only possible exception was at a business lunch where the more important of the two can and will take calls as a show of power and dominance over the lesser diner. But Bobby's three-commercials-in-rotation equaled the Marine's one-man-show-that-got-a-good-mention-in-*Backstage* magazine, so whatever was going on between them was obviously serious.

Paige remained motionless. He was afraid to proceed and equally terrified that running away would only attract their attention. He tried to remain perfectly still in the hope that, as happened with other, less harmful predators, they would think he was part of the scenery. But it wasn't a busy street and there was no one else around. Still, Paige might have managed to capitalize on their natural self-absorption had he not been standing in The Monkey Bar's driveway. An irritable woman in workout togs and a Prius began honking. Startled, Paige screamed slightly.

"Paige!" Bobby called, spotting Paige before he could flee the scene. "Just the man I need to see. I'll call you back," Bobby said into his mobile. He tossed the phone dramatically aside. Rising, Bobby began to cross toward Paige with the sort of unmotivated gravitas one might expect from the reigning bite-and-smile-queen of national-fast-food-thirty-second-network-commercial-work.

Paige briefly considering throwing himself in front of the entitled honker's Prius. Realizing that mortal injury would deter Bobby only if *Bobby* was mortally injured, Paige resumed walking in Bobby's general direction. He attempted to smile, though the results were unclear.

"Paige," Bobby repeated. He kissed the air by Paige's left cheek and embraced him coldly. "Perfect timing."

Paige's smile broadened painfully.

The Marine looked up without discontinuing his phone conversation and nodded, almost irritably, to make it clear to Paige that his arrival had interrupted a very important call. Paige resisted the urge to scream and run down the street, though he did look longingly at traffic. It was bad enough running into a date-gone-bad. To run into *two* at once was a catastrophe. And to run into two ex-dates out with each other was one of the biblical signs of the end of days.

Why was Bobby talking to him? He had hardly spoken to Paige while they were dating.

He endured the embrace and pointedly resisted Bobby's offer of a chair. Bobby sat down again, across from the Marine, who turned away, shielding his phone from the injurious effects of live conversation.

"You are just the person I needed to see," Bobby repeated. Clearly, he was caught up in the miracle of the coincidence.

"So you said." Paige began hoping that Armageddon would begin or that his heart would stop before he found out why he was just-the-person.

"What does guileless mean?" Bobby asked earnestly.

"What?" Paige asked. Though he knew the answer he was a bit unclear about the asking and still hoping for even a minor cataclysm or possibly rain, which counted as epic disaster in L.A.

"Well, I was reading the review of the play I'm in," Bobby began. He picked up the strategically folded copy of *Backstage* from his table. "I'm in *Love! Valour! Compassion!* Did you hear?"

"No," Paige sighed, as it became crashingly clear just why Bobby was talking to him. "Which one do you play? *Valour*, I bet. You've always looked like a *Valour* to me."

Bobby broke into the laugh that Paige had not missed once during their recent estrangement. It was insincere yet completely artificial.

The Marine put a finger in his free ear and rolled his eyes lovingly as he exchanged a look with Paige. Paige felt lightheaded and fought the desire to sit down.

"So, the reviewer says that my performance is guileless," Bobby said, searching the text for the exact quote. "Is that a good thing?"

"I guess it depends on what part you're playing." Paige shrugged, unwilling to be sucked into Bobby's exceedingly guileful line of inquiry. "It would make for a dreadful Iago." Paige smiled at him, knowing full well that Bobby didn't have any idea who Iago might be. He waited to see if Bobby would ask or pretend he knew. Paige's ploy foundered, because talking about Iago didn't steer the conversation back towards Bobby or his recent *Backstage*-vaunted triumph.

"Well, I play Ramon," Bobby said, by way of explanation.

"Really?" Paige puzzled. He gave Bobby's surgically enhanced but still oh-so-Waspy looks a quizzical sneer.

"Well, we're actually calling him Raymond, in this production."

"The one who takes his clothes off all the time?" Paige clarified.

"Yeah, that's the one," Bobby said with a reprise of the affected laugh.

The Marine scuffed the legs of his metal chair across the pavement as he rose and moved away to continue his phone conversation in quieter, mirth-free surroundings.

"Hmmm," Paige mused, knitting his brow over the question. The character was a guileful little whore, but Paige knew the reviewer to be a dreadful old pederast so it was anyone's guess as to whether or not guileless was meant as a compliment. Paige was not about to say any of that. "I guess it depends on what you were trying for in your portrayal—how you see the character," he said, turning his palms skyward.

Bobby's smile faded. At least he didn't laugh. "So, then it means what exactly?" He turned to look at the article again, considering for the first time the possibility that he'd actually gotten a bad review despite the extra hours he'd put in at the gym preparing for the role.

In that moment of petty triumph, Paige's luck began to change.

His cell phone rang.

It would be some time before he realized his fortunes had actually taken a turn for the worse, but it was a moment of jubilation all its own.

"Oh, it's my editor," Paige said, examining the caller ID. He played it off as though he and Honoria were in constant contact. The truth was he'd not heard a word from his New York editor since her complete mismanagement of his debut novel.

"I'd better take this," Paige said, trying not to run.

"Hello?" He made an effort to mask the shock he was sure must be in his voice by affecting a puzzled tone, which offered the added fidelity of being true. Bewildered might have been truer still. Stupefied would have been right on the money.

"Paige!" Honoria bellowed. Her pretentiously exaggerated tone suggested that Paige was an old and dear friend, but he knew from experience that it really meant there was someone else with her. She had cut him dead almost two years earlier, following her move to a larger and more prestigious publishing house and, presumably, larger, more prestigious authors. They had not spoken since.

"It is," Paige said, bemused. He threw himself into a vacant booth.

"It's Honoria," she gushed.

"So it says on the caller ID," he said. He was wary of the trap he sensed near at hand.

"I didn't know if this was even still your number," she said. "I haven't heard from you in ages. I'm so glad I still have it in my cell. How are you?"

"I'm okay," he admitted. "You?"

"I'm desperate!" she exclaimed.

"Really," Paige said. He made teapot and cup hand signals to the Israeli waiter who looked great in a T-shirt but clearly had very different cultural imperatives regarding the role of waiters in modern society. Paige had often wondered if the place was a terrorist cell of some sort. Since all waiters in L.A. are going to be famous someday, they are consistently surly and indifferent because the waiting job they've had for fifteen years is only temporary. The staff at The Monkey Bar was even more rude and indolent than most of the typically negligent and disinterested L.A. waitstaffs, so their cover would be above suspicion. Once, at the Beverly Hills Cheesecake Factory, Paige's waitress had actually turned to him and demanded, in reply to his request for silverware, "Can't you see I'm busy?"

So Paige was abandoned to fiend for tea while Honoria went on a bit about herself and the work she'd done since their parting. She named a few high-profile books she'd edited and hinted at a couple more to come.

"That's great, Honoria. Could you hang on just one sec?" Paige sighed as the waiter dropped off a pitcher of pancake syrup. "Thanks, and could I get a pot of green tea when you get a minute?" he called vainly to the V-shaped back receding down the aisle.

"You and your tea," Honoria said, as if reminiscing about a closeness they had never shared.

"Sorry, yeah," Paige said. "I'm just sitting down to order breakfast."

"Is this a bad time?"

"Not really," Paige said. "I'm on my own, so you can have breakfast with me. What would you like?"

Her laugh was rich and vicious, like that of a '50s movie star.

"The salmon wrap is particularly good."

"No thanks, I just got back from lunch. It's late for breakfast there, isn't it?" she asked.

"I got to the gym early today," he lied, vamping as he waited to discover her angle.

"You must be ravenous, so I won't keep you long." The charm drained from her voice. "The thing is, I've got this project I need your help with."

"Oh, really?" he asked, trying to sound more interested in her scheme than food. He poured syrup into a spoon and licked it off. "A writing job?"

"Yes," she said. "This is going to sound strange, but I'm working with someone who needs help with a book. I can't tell you who it is, but I'm wondering if you're available?"

"What kind of book?" Paige asked. He hated the generic use of the term *book*, as though novels and instruction manuals were interchangeable.

"Do you know the old term *roman a clef*?" she asked, pronouncing the *f* and making him wonder if she, in fact, knew the term.

"So it's fiction," he said.

"Based on the life of a certain celebrity."

"Whom I would be working with."

"And I can't tell you who it is."

"Do I have to do anything?" he asked. "Send samples, take a meeting, find my agent?"

"Not yet," she said, a bit awkwardly.

"Will I know if I've gotten the job? Or will I just read about it in the trades?"

"Oh, Paige," she said, with her Ida Lupino laugh. "You're going to be perfect for this."

"Great," Paige said with a shrug. What did he have to lose? Perhaps he'd even earn enough money to go bankrupt. "So, I'll wait to hear from you?"

"Probably," she said.

"Okay then," he said, oddly comfortable with her lack of clarity. "Will I hear if I don't get it?"

"I doubt it."

"That makes sense," he agreed, making hand signals to the waiter for a menu. "I mean, how can I be turned down for a job when I don't know what it is?"

"Exactly," she said as though that really explained everything. "Well, I've got to fly, Wonder Boy. Kisses."

She hung up without waiting for Paige to say goodbye.

He stared at the phone a moment before setting it aside.

The waiter/terrorist delivered Paige's check with a knowing smile.

7

The primary entrance to the Argyle is on Sunset. The famed boulevard snakes along a ridge carved deeply into the bedrock at the foot of the Hollywood Hills. The elevation offers spectacular views of the nearly flat seaside city that stretches on for hundreds of square miles beyond. Just below the venerable hotel's lofty perch was the park Paige had traversed to crash Angel's engagement-party red carpet.

Built into the side of the hill above Paige's apartment with several stories of the hotel below street level, the hotel's service and garage entrances were conveniently located just a few steps from Paige's front door. It seemed a relatively simple task for the two of them to make their way across the dark street, into the garage entrance and up the back stairs to Seth and Angel's suite.

Scaling the eleven flights of hotel stairs, plus the three flights in the parking garage, was not quite as simple as Paige had theorized. Both he and Angel were exhausted by the time they reached her floor. Finding the hallway accommodatingly abandoned, they made their way to the doors of the suite with the gasping subtlety of a pair of out-of-shape marathon runners crossing the finish line.

Their first discovery upon arrival was that Angel's key card was back at Paige's, if she'd ever even had it, a fact about which she was far from certain.

"Well, excuse me but there was this dead body and I got all distracted—"

"Shhh," he hissed, dragging her from the hall back into the stairwell.

By the time they'd traipsed back down to the parking garage, gone back to Paige's, had a fight, eventually found the cocktail purse she'd used to break in his kitchen window, discovered that it contained pink lip gloss, a tampon, an American Express black card *and* her room key card, sneaked back into the parking garage and climbed the fourteen floors' worth of stairs, Angel was limping, Paige had a hot stitch in his side and both were gasping for breath.

"I could kill you," Paige wheezed as he summoned the strength to swipe the card.

"Get in line," she said, pushing past. They tumbled into the room.

Momentarily distracted, they were unprepared for what awaited them.

Paige screamed when he saw.

"*Shhh*!" Angel urged, slapping her hand over his mouth.

They fell awkwardly onto a leggy little sofa so fashionable that it threatened to collapse.

"Sorry," Paige said, gagging as Angel removed her hand. "I just wasn't ready."

"So." Angel sat up, all business. "What exactly are we looking for?" She scanned the room as she tried to avoid focusing on her fiancé. They sat for a moment to recover their breath and keep dinner down.

"Well, things that will connect us with the crime." Paige shrugged. He hadn't thought through exactly what evidence they needed to find. "Look for anything strange. Anything that makes it appear as if we were here or gives us a motive."

"This is my room," Angel said. "It would be strange if it didn't look like I was here."

"Great," Paige snapped. "We can go get the murder weapon out from under my bed. I'm sure it already has your fingerprints on it. You can call *WeHo 5-O* and confess. I'll just go home and get back to sleep."

"Or I can just tell them that when I woke up I found your bookend thing here and since you attacked me earlier on national television…"

"The footage really is funny," Paige agreed. "I recorded it. You have to see it. You'll just die."

"So, what do you suggest, queen?"

"That's Mr. Queen."

"Not Miss?"

"That would make it princess. I'm thinking we should make it look like you didn't stay here, so that you can say that you went home or something." He really wasn't paying attention to her. It was a practice he'd perfected during story meetings for their books. His answer just happened to be in reply to what she'd asked.

"Why did I go home without my fiancé?"

"Yeah, that's no good." Paige grimaced. Looking around, he spotted and stared wistfully at the honor bar a moment before thinking better of it. "They have such good food here. It's a shame we can't call room service."

"We can see what's left in the mini-fridge," Angel said. Rising, she stepped gingerly around Seth.

"Yeah, don't touch it," he sighed. "I thought about that, too."

Heedless, she opened the faux deco cabinet, which contained the Toblerones and a dorm room fridge.

Dozens of typed pages cascaded onto the floor around her feet.

Angel leaned down to pick them up with her sportily gloved fingers.

"What is that?"

"I don't know, but it says it's by us." She began to shuffle the pages.

"A manuscript?"

"*Fallen Angel*," she read, from the cover page. "We didn't write a book called that, right?"

"You could at least *try*," Paige said, disgusted. He snatched the pages out of her hand and scanned the first few. "Wow, this is really bad. Lucky we found it."

"What? What is it?"

"Oh, I don't know where to begin," he sighed, leafing through. "Bad structure, juvenile word choices, the dialogue is wooden at best—"

"Oh, for God's sake," she cut him off irritably. "I thought there was something incriminating."

"And there's that," he added with a nod, still reading. "Find all the pages. It looks to be mostly about Seth."

"What about?"

"Just a lot about him, or rather some guy called James Saint," he said with distaste. "So, not only is it poorly written, but it might possibly be nonfiction."

"I don't see what that has to do with anything," Angel huffed, gathering up the last of the loose pages.

"Me either, but there's a book we didn't write with our names on it left at the scene of a murder," Paige said, handing her back the rest of the pages. "I think it may have something to do with anything."

"I see what you mean. So this is the kind of thing we should be looking for? Things that shouldn't be here."

"Or anywhere, as in the case of a manuscript we didn't write."

"Got it," she said, going to the closet to get a bag to put things into as they found them.

"Like this bloody letter opener, lying here by the body," Paige suggested. "The one shaped like a penis?"

"I have one just like that," Angel said. She emerged from the closet, stuffing the manuscript into a smart little leather valise.

"Exactly," he answered. He began looking through the drawers in the faux deco bureau.

"Don't you think we should take it with us?" she asked, leaning down to pick it up.

"Yeah, hold on a second," he said. Rummaging through the drawers a moment longer, he found the plastic laundry and shoe-shine bags he was looking for. "Put it in one of these so that we can use it as evidence later if we need to."

"Do you think that's a good idea?"

"What do you mean?"

"Well, isn't it evidence that we did it?"

"Yeah, it is, but it's also a crime or something to destroy it," he said, holding out the bag for her to drop the bloody knife into.

She regarded him a moment before thoroughly wiping the blade and much of the handle on Seth's jacket before dropping it into the bag.

"Fair enough," Paige conceded, queasily. He folded the bag and added it to the valise with the manuscript. "What else?"

"I don't know about you, but I'm having a drink," she said. "My stomach." Before he could stop her, she stalked back over to the mini fridge.

"Isn't that how all this started?"

"Oh, my God," she all but shrieked, slamming the fridge door.

"Sorry, I don't mean to nag but—"

"It's not that," she said, rushing to him. She clutched his arm so tightly that it hurt. "Well, it's not only that. There is a head in the refrigerator."

"A head?" Paige asked incredulously. "What kind of head?"

"*This* kind," she said, grabbing Paige by the chin.

"There is a human head in the mini-fridge?"

"Yeah, and if the M&Ms are nine dollars, you can only imagine what they must charge for *heads*."

They laughed and held each other until tears were running down their faces. It was all just too much.

"Any idea whose... head?" he asked at last.

She only grimaced as she wiped her tears, crying more earnestly.

He comforted her stiffly as he considered their circumstances.

After a moment's thought he held her firmly at arm's length.

"Okay, so I think we should discover the body," he said.

8

It would be an epic understatement to say that the staff at the Argyle was not easily surprised. It is equally true of all Sunset Boulevard hotels. The Strip's location and reputation make its goings-on both legendary and notorious. A favorite playground to the world, the super-rich neighbors from Beverly Hills, points west and north, and the luminaries of the music and entertainment industry, the Strip's well-burnished reputation serves to further jade playground personnel.

Busby Barclay's *Star Report*—filed most often from those few golden blocks—had drawn Paige to Angel's engagement party that very evening. Busby's and a number of other television shows captured almost all of their most salacious footage outside the Strip's clubs and hotels after midnight as the celebrated, drunk and debauched stumbled out to their cars.

Angel and Bill E had done their part to help launch the trend, with their frequent after-hours skirmishes with the paparazzi.

The Sunset Strip is party central, but, like the rest of Los Angeles County, it closes at two A.M. New York might be the city that never sleeps, but L.A. is the city that's late for a nap. There is actually a second rush hour at two in the morning, particularly on Fridays and Saturdays. But by three, the sidewalks roll up and everyone goes home or up to their hotel rooms for more private entertainments.

Diligent paparazzi take up their vigils outside the last-known whereabouts of the noteworthy in hopes of a revelatory shot made more meaningful by the hour of its capture. Typically, there's nothing to see. But since everyone else is home and in bed, it's much easier to spot when there is something going on. Despite the occasional imbroglio and hubbub, the boulevard usually settles into the kind of small-town three A.M. quiet you'd find in any hamlet the size of West Hollywood.

It was the habit of the night manager at the Argyle to use the quiet of these anticipatory hours to complete the tedious paperwork that most required his concentration.

That night's *t*'s were not destined to be crossed.

Dressed with all the subtlety of a couple of Vegas showgirls, Angel and Paige stumbled into the Argyle lobby near sunrise. They were singing the *Laverne & Shirley* theme song and wrestling over a bottle of champagne, which somehow got smashed on the lobby's marble floor. No eyebrows were raised. The doorman and valet captain did battle with a couple of determined paparazzi who had clearly been following the two.

"Oops," Angel said, putting her fingers girlishly to her lips. "Looks like we're out of Cristal."

Angel and Paige then collapsed onto the lobby floor in a fit of drunken laughter.

"Good evening, Miss Panderson," the night manger greeted them. Emerging from behind the desk, he joined the doorman, two security guards and the bellman in their efforts to get Paige and Angel to their feet. "We'll get some more champagne sent up to the room, right away."

"Not champagne, my good man," Paige corrected, hanging from the manager's lapels. "Miss Panderson only drinks Cristal. Don't you read *People* magazine?"

Paige and Angel exploded into hysterics and fell into each other's arms. Paige lost his footing and he and Angel collapsed into the growing number of hotel staff involved in helping her up. The entire group tumbled to the lobby floor like uniformed dominos.

A flash went off. Then another flared. Security ran to the hotel doors to fend off the second wave invasion of the paparazzi, but it was a little too late. This only made Angel and Paige laugh harder. To make matters worse for all concerned—except the photographers—the two refused to get up until more champagne was served, fending off all offers of assistance.

Eventually, the night manager gave in to their relentless demands. Room service arrived with a rolling cart groaning with enough chilled Cristal and champagne stems for a small reception. Appeased, the two consented to climb aboard the rolling cart with their spoils. Waving to the press like pageant winners on a holiday float, they were wheeled into the elevator. With much fanfare and the two security guards appointed to help make sure they "got to their room safely," Angel and Paige vanished from view.

9

"Somebody call an ambulance!" Angel kept repeating, between grand opera sobs. "He can't be gone! Get an ambulance!"

The night manager looked up from his receipts. The quiet that had settled over the Argyle lobby following Angel and Paige's comic departure was shattered minutes later as they returned, hysterical, blood-covered and screaming the place down.

"Get the police! Seal off the hotel!" Paige commanded. He leapt over the desk and attempted to use the very complicated phone but in fact only managed to wake the occupants of room 911.

"What's happening?" the night manager asked one of the security guards as he wrestled the receiver from Paige's hands.

"There's been a murder," Paige announced dramatically. "A man's been killed!"

"*Noooooooooooooo!*" Angel screamed, going off into another crying binge that quite impressed Paige. Despite her years on television, he'd never suspected she could act. She can *overact* at least, he thought to himself, smiling at the absurdity of the moment.

Her wails and his repeated shouts of murder attracted the attention of the still-lurking paparazzi. Surging past the distracted doormen and security, the press fray was on. No more hotel paperwork got done that night.

10

The West Hollywood Sheriff's station had excellent Wi-Fi, Paige discovered. As soon as the police finished their initial questioning and he and Angel were left alone, Paige's quick search on his phone revealed the world was discovering what he knew all too well:

Hollywood_Executive_Murdered—The_Times.com

Brutal_Murder_Rocks_Hollywood—LA_Confidential.com

INSIDE: Angel's_Blood_Soaked_Love_Nest—Exclusive_Nude_ Photos—Examiner.net

Hollywood's_Dirty_Little_Secret!_Angel's_Fiancé_Killed_in_Satanic_ Engagement_Ritual—WorldNews.org

Ten_Surgically_Enhanced_Murderers—Bottom-Feed.com

Psychic_Reveals:_Elvis_Fathers_Angel's_Love_Child—Inside_ Reporter.com

How_Will_Hollywood's_Murder_Spree_Affect_Presidential_Race?— Internet-Post.org

Paige clicked on a link from Busby:
BusbyBarclay.com/Lurid_Pix_of_Panderson_at_the_Scene_ of_the_Murder

**Pictures from the tony Sunset Strip Argyle Hotel,
scene of joy and tragedy for Angel Panderson.**

The Argyle Hotel was the scene of Angela Panderson's lavish engagement party to newly minted media titan Seth St. James (<u>photos of the couple just before the party opposite</u>). In the early morning hours, Panderson returned to the hotel with frenemy and writing partner Paige Blanche after what appears to have been a drunken spree—<u>seen here together</u> entering the hotel and disrupting the lobby with their pre-tragedy antics.

The two were bribed with a cartload of Cristal to return to Panderson's suite. Their good-natured departure was <u>captured here</u> as they made their gracious and raucous exit. The Argyle lobby returned to its pre-dawn quiet but it was the calm before the storm. A moment or two later, chaos. (<u>See photos, after the jump</u>)

Paige groaned, though he was pleased with their reviews.

Coverage was more than comprehensive. And why not? The story had everything: celebrity suspects, a rich and powerful victim, posh setting and an unidentified head in the mini-fridge. Those elements the story lacked, the tabloids and the blogosphere simply made up.

Busby Barclay had apparently been webcasting from outside the West Hollywood Sheriff's station almost since before Paige and Angel's arrival. The story wasn't just interesting or noteworthy: it was the sort of fuel that kept the 24-hour news cycle alive. Minute-by-minute developments, or the lack thereof, were reported with equal gravity.

Busby had scooped them all by establishing a special coverage blog Avenging-Angel.org which had the advantage of being both pro-Angel—as in "avenge Angel, the victim"—and con—as in, maybe, she was "the murderous avenging Angel." Busby had been the first to post the lobby photos from the Argyle and each subsequent guess, supposition and unfounded rumor since. He was already being quoted on network and cable news. It was gold. Busby had successfully staked out this murder as his vehicle and he was going to ride it as far as it would take him.

Judging from his online posts, Busby could almost touch the perfectly manicured shrubbery that trimmed the low-profile, red-brick sheriff's station. Nestled unobtrusively next to the party district, the station offers the security of easy access to West Hollywood's two world famous party streets—Boys' Town and the Strip. Concealed in plain sight underneath the gleaming, primary-colored geometry of the Pacific Design Center, the station is so low-key it avoids harshing the party going on all around it.

Inside, the sheriff's offices achieved a cheerful institutional drab that eschewed the shopworn jade more typical of police stations. It resembled a national bank chain branch more than a police or sheriff's station—real or cop-show variety. The much-persecuted minority who had built the little city created a policing environment that was based more on customer service than shock-and-awe.

Weary and on edge, Angel and Paige sat in an unused office at the station. Though he was morbidly curious about the head in the fridge, Paige had other worries, not the least of which was Angel. From the moment they first met, she'd screwed up his life. Now, someone was trying to frame him for murdering a man he'd only ever met once—twice, if you counted the tea-throwing incident, which Paige did not.

It was almost enough to make him regret the tea. *Almost.* There was too much justice about Angel tossing Paige's tea in her own face on national television to make him lament being a murder suspect. Even if he was found guilty, it would almost be worth it.

Almost.

2 Years, 11 Months and a Few Days Earlier...

The Beguine Begins

Paige often joked that he expected to die of colorectal cancer from all the smoke he'd had blown up his ass over the years by agents, producers and editors. Honoria's ludicrous promises and the absence of even the appearance of follow-through were less surprising to him than an actual offer would have been. His concerns at the time were focused nearer to home. The prospect of finding a roommate to help meet his ever-more-challenged expenses was uppermost.

He placed a roommate-wanted ad in the West Hollywood rag *Vanguard*. It had garnered a sizeable response, but not for roommates. One unproductive tour was pretty much like the next.

"And through here would be your room," Paige said.

Turning back, he found that the candidate had removed all of his clothes. He stood facing Paige in the strong afternoon sun coming into the hall from the kitchen. Paige could not help noticing that the latest applicant's erection cast a shadow like a sundial across the black and white tile floor.

Paige sighed. "Not again."

"I thought maybe we could negotiate something on the rent," Naked Guy said.

"Get out," Paige said without much conviction.

"Or maybe we could just have some fun."

"I'm actually looking for a roommate," Paige replied.

"You're not serious?" Naked Guy asked, genuinely surprised.

"Doesn't anybody place ads for roommates in West Hollywood who's really just looking for a roommate?"

"No."

"Get dressed."

"Couldn't we—"

"Get out."

"Wouldn't you like to—"

"Yes."

It was the third time this had happened. Paige was starting to feel guilty. He would have placed the ad in *Vanguard* long before if he'd known this would be the result. He'd just never needed a roommate before. It wasn't so much that he felt guilty for taking advantage of the unexpected windfall. He felt guilty because he really did need a roommate. The rent was three weeks past due, there was no word from Honoria and no sign of income from any other source. Paige's own agent had shown no interest in his latest book ideas and stopped returning calls.

"So, I'll call you?" formerly Naked Guy said as Paige shepherded him out the door into the courtyard.

"That's great, yeah," Paige said, rushing to get back inside before Armie, the building manager, spotted him.

"Oh, Paige! A word?" Armie called. Paige slammed and locked the door. After a covert look out the window, he ran for cover.

He ignored the pounding.

"I know you're in there," Armie shouted.

Paige put water on for tea. He began searching the refrigerator for something he could make into a meal. Clean dishes were the only things still in the cabinets. The refrigerator contained a jar of pickle juice and a few random grease-marked packets of grated Parmesan cheese, cracked red pepper, soy sauce and honey packets from various takeout orders. There weren't even ice cubes in the freezer.

In an effort to kill the hunger pangs, Paige extravagantly squeezed the last of the honey into a cup of tea. When the phone started ringing, it was a defeated and hungry Paige who answered.

"*Paige*," his building manager said. "I know you're in there. I'm having pot roast tonight if you'd like to come to dinner."

"That's low, Armie," Paige accused as he slid down the wall of the kitchen, weak from lack of food, funds and self-esteem. "Luring me out into the open with the promise of food. That's how they trap animals."

"And not the smart ones," Armie pointed out. "Look, just because I'm going to have to start eviction proceedings doesn't mean you have to go hungry. Or that we can't be friends."

"No, I often throw people I care about out into the snow," Paige said, looking up at the kitchen ceiling as he lay on the floor.

"I don't own the building. The woman who does is a crazy French control queen. It's August and it hasn't snowed in Los Angeles since that freak occurrence in nineteen forty-nine."

"You're still throwing me out," Paige insisted.

"You haven't paid the rent."

"I don't have the money."

"Duh."

"Oh, that's nice. I'm trying to get a roommate in here and come up with the money. I just need more time."

"Yes, I saw you conducting that in-depth interview on your kitchen table a few minutes ago."

"You saw me?"

"Paige, your kitchen door has a window in it."

"You were spying on me from my kitchen door? Which opens onto the alley, by the way."

"I came around back when no one answered my knocking."

"Oh," Paige said. "I did hear something. I just thought it was the table. It's old. I wasn't even sure it was going to survive."

"So, is he moving in?"

"Moving in?"

"The roommate you were interviewing?"

"Yeah, right. You've got no idea what roommate ads in *Vanguard* are really for."

"Oh Paige, *everyone* knows what roommate ads in *Vanguard* are really for, except apparently you. What about getting a job? Or at least charging the roommates by the hour?"

"I sent off a manuscript of the new novel to an agent in New York who's agreed to read it. Maybe I can get the deal going again—"

"A *real* job, Paige."

"Writing is a real job. Everyone was so keen on me moving into this bigger apartment when the book was first out and there was talk of a movie deal. Including the French control queen who said my work was '*splendide.*' Where's my fan club now?"

"Paige, don't act like you just got to town. We live in L.A., remember? Everyone's nice to you when they think the movie's going to get made."

"Crawl up my ass and eat a ham sandwich."

"There is no need to take that tone with me. I've tried to work with you on this and you've been dodging me for days now. I've been there for you right along. I'm a better goddamned landlord than you deserve, given that—"

Paige hung up the phone.

It started ringing again.

"Ham sandwich," he said into the receiver and then hung up again.

It rang again.

"Are you coming to dinner or not?"

"Seven?"

"Eight's better."

"Go to hell."

"See you then."

"Eight it is."

Paige hung up and immediately began dialing.

"Ham sandwich," he said when Armie answered, and then hung up again.

The phone immediately began to ring again.

Paige answered and then hung up, clicking the answer and end buttons in rapid succession. It rang again. Again he cut off the call. He kept that up until he got bored and then just let the phone ring.

Paige decided that a bubble bath was really the only thing to do at such a moment. He needed a treat and there was blessed little available to him on that front, at least until the next room-mate interview. He collected all the fanciest samples from the bowl where he kept the booty from the hotels where he'd stayed on the promotional tour for his novel. He poured the souvenir bottles one after the next into the steaming water in the vast old tub. The room filled with the heady scent of a half-dozen signature corporate fragrances. Gathering the phone and the latest *Vanity Fair*, he submerged himself into the cloying bubbles. He leafed through the glossy pages. The phone continued to ring intermittently. Periodically, Paige answered and hung up.

Once he got the bath drawn and got himself situated with sponges, candles, his favorite mix disc on the CD player and the obligatory George Clooney article, he answered the phone. "Ham sandwich!" Paige screamed into the receiver.

"'El-oo?"

"Oh, that's very convincing, Armie!"

"Oo iz Ar-ME?" demanded the preposterous and possibly female voice.

"Oh, come on," Paige said, rolling his eyes so far back in his head it could be heard in his voice. "That is the worst, most fake accent ever, Armie. Keep your day job."

"Vhy do you keep callink me Ar-ME?" she asked indignantly. "Iz zis Paige Blanche?"

"Oui," Paige said, playing along.

"My name iz Grizelda."

"As if," Paige groaned. "You're totally overplaying it. No one is really named Grizelda."

"You are a very strange man, Mr. Blanche," she intoned with a very stagy clucking of her tongue. "But you come most *eye-ly* recommended."

"Oh, here it comes," Paige said. "By whom? The guy who just did me on the kitchen table, I suppose?"

"Truly, Mr. Blanche," Grizelda said gleefully. "Your temperament matches my client's exactly. You are zee parfait writer for zee *roman a clef.*"

"How did you know about that, Armie?"

"Please, Mr. Blanche, my employer iz *très privé*, so I am acting in zair be-alf."

"Did I tell you this? Armie? Dear God, tell me this is not really—"

"Grizelda Lamar, personal manager to someone who iz considering you as ghostwriter for a *roman a clef*, a novel vis a key, zat key being my client."

"Well, I have to say, Grizelda, that's pretty convincing," Paige said, sinking up to his chin in the bubbles. "I'm sorry to be rude. I thought a friend was having a little joke at my expense and I'm still not totally convinced. You've got to admit that this whole thing is a little strange."

"Cautious yes, but zis iz no joke, Mr. Blanche," Grizelda said very dramatically. "I am callink to arrange a rendezvous for you viz my client."

"Okay, well, as it happens I have a lot of free time coming up," Paige said, coyly. "When's good?"

"Tomorrow you vil take a taxi at nine A.M. from your 'ouse to zee Chateau Marmont."

"I can just walk. The Chateau is really only a couple of blocks from here."

"Never zee less, zee taxi vil call for you at nine sharp. Ven you arrive at zee Chateau, speak vis zee concierge. Tell 'im zat you 'ave a message from Minnie Mouse. 'E vil give you furzer instructions."

"You're kidding." It was all Paige could think to say.

"I am very serious, Mr. Blanche. Security iz most très importante to my client."

"Okay, I like a scavenger hunt as much as the next fellow. I'll be out front at nine, but so help me, Armie, if this is you, 'am zandvitch."

11

"Why did you hire me?" Paige asked Angel.

The police had already questioned them several times, together and separately. Their well-reviewed performances in the Argyle lobby had established their mutual alibis. "Discovering the body" together and in front of multiple and credible witnesses, as well as the press, had distanced them from the murder but not enough to eliminate all doubt of their innocence. Their blood-smeared clothes had been taken from them. Though they were not under arrest, it was well into the day after the murder and still they remained at the West Hollywood Sheriff's station. The only difference between under arrest and whatever they were was a matter of the few yards that separated the office from the cells.

"What do you mean?" Angel somehow managed to look smarter than she sounded in the scrubs the medical examiner had issued her in trade for her evidentiary clothing.

"Why me?" Paige raised the sickly blue green shoulders of his scrubs, a match for Angel's, though she clearly wore it better. "Why not hire some other writer? Someone who writes celebrity books? Or who *is* a celebrity? Or some TV writer you'd worked with?"

She gave him a dazed smirk. "I don't know, but I'm glad I did now. You've been great through all this."

"Thanks," he said without thinking or meaning it. He looked around nervously for signs that they were being watched or overheard. His nerves were on edge as much from lying as from getting up at quarter of four. "Let's talk about that later."

Why me? The question ran like a rat on an exercise wheel in his head. No one was in a better position to have set him up for the murder than Angel, yet there was no figuring why. But, facing a capital crime, the question still came down to it: why had she hired him in the first place? Did the plan go back that far? And why come to his house instead of calling the police if she did in fact discover Seth's body? Had she been coming to plant the evidence of the bloody crystal angel or bash in his head? Was she the murderer or just framing him? Or—what seemed the least likely—did she really want his help?

He gave her a sweaty smile. Conversation was out. He was afraid to engage her lest she blurt out something to give them away. And he couldn't warn her that their current accommodations offered them no expectation of privacy for fear a sheriff might in fact be listening. All he could think about was getting out of the station and into a hot shower and then maybe going to a foreign country and hiding under a bed.

"Miss Panderson, Mr. Blanche. May I come in?"

Angel started and made a high-pitched little noise like a sneeze or a bad porn film. The tall, well-dressed man at the office door looked strangely out of place in the worn and institutional surroundings. Lost in thought or just half asleep, neither of them had heard him approach.

Paige jumped up and dropped the ancient copy of *Los Angeles Magazine* like he'd been caught reading it. He locked eyes with this Armani model of a man who'd wandered into the sheriff's station in the expensive well-fitted suit and who somehow already knew his name. "Who are you?" Paige asked.

"I'm Roy Slade." Their visitor extended his hand. They hadn't yet invited Roy in, so he leaned in from the door, like a vampire technicality. "I'm a lieutenant with LAPD homicide."

"Really?" Paige answered. This is a pleasant surprise, he thought, as he rose to take the man's well-manicured hand.

12

"Lieutenant!" Angel leaped to her feet and cut Paige off. Stepping forward, tits first, she managed to slip her hand into the policeman's large and powerful, but well-polished, paw. "Nice to meet you," she said, tossing her hair in Paige's face. "Won't you come in?" Without releasing Slade's hand, she led him in and guided him into a seat next to her own, pushing Paige aside as she passed.

"Nice," Paige muttered, giving her the stink-eye behind Lieutenant Slade's back.

Angel responded by taking the chair where Paige had been sitting so she could face the lieutenant as she maintained her hold on his hand. Paige took up a perch on the edge of the desk, managing to get his feet between them.

"What can you tell us, officer?" Angel asked.

"Well, I have some background," he said, making no effort to extricate his hand. "Really, though, it's more what you can tell me."

"So, what exactly is it you think we can do for you, Lieutenant Slade?" Paige asked, trying for enough sincerity to mask the suspicion he feared his voice might give away.

"Well, first, I just wanted to say hello, find out if you were okay, and see if there's anything we can do." His glance swept easily to include them both. Slade's manner was a pleasant change from the parade of men and women who'd been and gone and never raised their gaze above Angel's legendary augmentations. "And may I just say how sorry I am about all this to both of you, though especially to you, Miss Panderson. When were you to be have been married?"

"Married?" Angel repeated.

"To Seth," Paige said irritably, folding his arms. "Your fiancé? The *dead* guy?"

"Oh, yes, Seth," Angel said, almost taking her hand out of the lieutenant's. "Well, we hadn't actually set a date."

"They weren't very close," Paige put in. He played it off as though he was making a little joke of it, but shot Angel a warning look.

Angel laughed nervously at Paige's little jest, though her eyes threw daggers his way. "Paige, don't be cruel," she said, wiping away invisible tears. "It's too soon to joke about it. Though I know your sense of humor will get me through this."

Taking Paige's hand with her free one, she squeezed it painfully, secretly skewering his palm with the pink-blush-lacquered, porcelain hawk talons she maintained like a fetish. Paige managed to keep his composure as she tried to draw blood. He struggled to free his hand from her death grip, eventually placing his other hand over hers to try and tear the two apart.

"How fortunate that you were with Miss Panderson at such an awful moment," the lieutenant said, putting his hand over Paige's. The reassuring gesture, combined with the intense pain Angel was inflicting, played havoc with Paige's body temperature.

"Yes," Paige sighed. He looked into Slade's cool blue eyes, his agony momentarily forgotten.

"How was it that you happened to be with each other last night?" Slade asked with a practiced ease. "The clip of the two of you with the teacup just a few hours earlier looked more like the stuff Hollywood feuds are made of than the start of an evening together."

He's good, Paige thought. He stared, stunned, at their charming interrogator, his mind racing for some kind of answer.

Paige and Angel exchanged a look and to his relief, she retracted her claws from his injured palm, though to his consternation she took the lieutenant's other hand in hers as she wrapped their hands together affectionately.

"Well, that's just how I am," Angel said shyly. "I just can't stay mad, especially at the people I love and care about. Paige means the world to me and I just couldn't go to bed without setting it right. He lives right next door to the hotel, so it made the perfect escape from the crowd."

"And your fiancé," Paige added.

"Oh, Paige, *you*," she said. Unable to recapture his hand, she wagged a scolding finger.

"It meant so much to me," Paige gushed. "That you'd humble yourself, coming by like that to admit that you did lie to me, cheat me, and leave me financially destitute on a whim. And it touched me when you insisted that it really was all your fault to begin with." He flicked the end of her nose playfully with the tip of his right index finger. "It really is just the kind of person she is, to take responsibility when she's been such a complete, almost criminal fraud, to cop to it and put things right between us."

"Now, Paige," Angel said with a nervous laugh. Her smile slipped and her grip tightened on the lieutenant's hands.

"Don't be modest," Paige said, taking another swipe at her nose, this time with a clenched fist and a pulled punch. "Where would you be right now if you hadn't come to me? Hmmm? So just admit it."

Angel treated Paige to a blistering smile. She took a deep but unsteady breath as she fought for composure. "What can I say?" She shrugged. "It's just the kind of person I am. Friendship first."

"And when you're wrong, you're wrong," Paige coached.

"And I was," Angel said, nodding and not breaking the look the two shared. "I was soooo wrong. You just have no idea, lieutenant."

They smiled malice at one another.

"And second?" Paige addressed the lieutenant without looking at him.

"What?" Angel asked, confused.

"Lieutenant?" Paige clarified, again looking into his dangerously blue eyes. "You said that *first*, you wanted to see if we were comfortable or needed anything. *Second*?"

"Oh, right," Slade nodded as though he'd forgotten his true purpose for being there. Paige found the officer's performance very convincing. He could see how easily others might be taken in by his practiced casualness. Angel seemed to be buying it.

"Yes?" Paige prompted.

"Well, I'll be taking a public role in the investigation," Roy explained. "I'll be speaking to the media about the case. For the department. So I just want to be clear about the facts. Be sure I get it right."

"Like a spokesmodel?" Angel asked, nodding.

"Well..."

Paige tried not to laugh but failed.

"I guess you could call it that," the lieutenant admitted, smiling.

Is he blushing? Paige wondered.

"So, Lieutenant Spokesmodel, what are you worried about getting right?" Paige asked.

"Well, for instance, Angel," the Lieutenant began, and it didn't escape Paige's notice that Slade started on the weaker link. "I'm unclear on the legal nature of your relationship with Mr. St. James."

"The legal nature?" Angel asked. "He was of age. I am."

"God knows," Paige snorted. "The lieutenant wants to know who gets Seth's money. 'Fiancée' is a largely ceremonial title."

"Oh, legally," Angel said, considering. "We were working out the prenup—in fact we were supposed to sign it last night after the party. I think there was a draft of a will as part of that. But I think his last wife is probably still his beneficiary. Or his son maybe. Not me anyway. At least, I don't think so."

"So close," Paige said, in a conciliatory tone.

Both the lieutenant and Angel gave him an uncertain glance.

"Well, there you are," Roy said. "There's an heir."

Angel shrugged.

"So, opportunity, but not motive," Paige said.

"*Paige*," Angel scolded, putting her hands on her hips. She shot him a quick, dangerous grin.

Slade rose to his feet to get away from her when she finally let go of his hands.

"So, lieutenant…" Paige began.

"Please, Mr. Blanche, call me Roy."

"Thanks, Roy," Paige said, with an inadvertently flirtatious smile. "Feel free to call me Paige."

"Paige," Roy repeated.

"Um, yes," Paige stammered, forgetting his question briefly. "Um, well, um, do you need us or me any longer, or would it be okay if we…" He trailed off with a little gesture, which might have meant "take the dessert cart away" if they were at the Four Seasons, or "hurry up and kiss my ring" if they were in a rush at the Vatican.

"Oh, certainly," Roy said, patting and then grasping Paige's shoulder. "You have been through more than a day's worth already today and it's not even lunchtime. Here's my card—home and cell are on the back. Let me know if you think of anything. Or if I can help in any way."

He gave Paige the card and a sincere look that Paige found quite piercing.

Angel grinned again, but for a different reason.

"And you, Miss Pan—"

"Now, you call me Angel—everybody does," Angel said. She rose with perfectly rehearsed choreography, dragging her breasts against the lieutenant's arm.

"Well, not the people who really know her," Paige said with a little bleat of laughter. The temperature of the room seemed to lower a couple of degrees.

Roy and Angel both laughed, though not for the same reasons.

"I'll probably want to talk to the two of you again, if that's all right?" Roy asked as he escorted them to the door. "It would really help me with my spokesmodel work."

"Of course."

"Anytime, Roy," Paige said, beaming. He managed to get in one last handshake as he shoved Angel out the door with his free elbow. "Maybe over lunch?"

"I'd like that. I'll call you," Roy said to Paige, following them out into the hallway and escorting them through the unfamiliar building like a subtle dance partner, leading from behind.

13

"Angel! Angel!" Busby shouted at her. He had earned his place at the front of the mob of reporters and photographers who surrounded Angel and Paige in front of the West Hollywood Sheriff's station. "It's Busby. Busby Barclay, with *Star Reporter*. Angel, are you okay? What do the police think happened?"

In response to his familiar voice, Angel turned to Busby and offered a brave smile before she and Paige were shoved past him and toward the SUV, left over from the engagement party, that had brought them over the night before.

"Lieutenant," Busby called to Slade who stood just outside the door. "Any new developments to report?"

"No statement at this time," Roy said, giving Paige and Angel cover as they made their way past the swarm of paparazzi. They were almost home free.

"Murderer!"

A man stepped into their path and began shouting the word over and over again.

Angel turned to Paige and gave him a pleading look.

"What fresh hell?" Paige said under his breath.

"It's Seth's son, Jay," she gasped into Paige's ear.

"Murderer! Murderer!" the young man continued to shout. He towered over Paige and Angel, but to be fair that wasn't much of an achievement. Paige could see that Jay was his father's son, though clearly his mother's beauty had also contributed to the striking final product who stood blocking their way. Jay had his father's coloring and imposing stature, but there was a fine-boned delicacy to the young man's face. Contrasted with his six-foot plus frame, the strikingly pretty face gave the kind of patrician mien usually reserved for state portrait galleries in aristocratic countries.

The lieutenant forgotten, the press was closing in on the three of them like kids at a playground fight.

"Jay St. James!" Paige shouted. "So sorry about your father. Are you here to identify the body?"

The paparazzi and press, suddenly aware of the accuser's identity, turned from Paige and Angel, briefly distracted, ready to surround the surviving son. Surprised, Jay stopped shouting his repetitive accusation.

"We don't believe for a minute that you or your mother killed your father for his money," Paige said, thinking on his feet, stunning even the paparazzi into momentary silence. "We want you to know you have our full support, no matter what the police think."

That was all it took. The press was on Jay like dogs on red meat.

"I have the prenup!" Jay shouted after them. "It proves you're a murderer."

Paige and Angel were forgotten just long enough to dart past their surprised-but-consistent accuser and into the waiting SUV. Even in the crush, Paige could not miss Jay's familiarity with the prenup. He found it more than a little unsettling. Angel claimed she hadn't seen it, but her word was far from the gold standard. Realizing they had been given the slip, the press quickly surrounded the vehicle, but the darkened windows rendered their attentions moot. Jay's face was pressed against the glass as the paparazzi crushed him against the side of their car.

"That son of a bitch," Angel growled the instant the driver closed the door behind them. The blackout windows separated the two of them from the phalanx of photographers and army of reporters shouting themselves hoarse trying to make themselves heard over one other, as they all asked the same few questions. "Paige, you are brilliant!"

"I really am, right? You should pay me," Paige said. "How well do you know our driver?" He watched the man through the window as he pushed and shoved through the crowd, making his way around to the front door.

"Not sure," Angel muttered. "He might work for the caterer, or the hotel. It was all such a blur on the way over here."

"Then put your head on my shoulder, act like you're crying, and shut the hell up until we get to... Where should we go?"

"We can go to my place at the beach," she suggested, her anger fading as they switched back into unindicted-coconspirator mode.

"Yeah, the press will never look for us there," Paige said.

"The press will follow us wherever we go," Angel replied, the voice of experience in such matters.

"True enough." Paige's mind raced. "And even you were able to break into my house, but we still have to go back there."

"We'll send somebody for your things," Angel said.

"Like my crystal bookend?" Paige asked just as the driver climbed into the front seat. "We'll get a suite at the Argyle. No one will have thought of that."

"Gross," Angel made gagging sounds. "Wonder why?"

"Where to?" the driver asked, looking at them in the rearview mirror.

"What's your address, Paige?" Angel asked by way of answering.

14

"Is there Wi-Fi?" Paige asked the driver as soon as they were underway. "Access code?"

"Honestly," Angel said irritably." I know I'm bad about texting, but now is hardly the time to go web-surfing. Oh, no. You're not looking for that clip with the tea?"

Paige gave her a rakish smile for the driver's benefit and a good kick when the driver looked away. He wanted to find out what he could, during a moment when no one was watching him. Paige was already worried that the lieutenant would be able to trace his search on his phone at the station somehow.

He quickly found Busby's Avenging-Angel site and a cache of just the dirt he was digging for. Aside from exhaustive reporting of the most trivial aspects of the case, there was a rogues' gallery lineup of the field of players and suspects. His and Angel's bios led the list, but there were other more useful assessments that were just what Paige was searching for—including the 411 on their handsome and suspicious Spokes-Lieutenant Roy Slade, and Seth's handsome and scary son, Jay St. James.

Hollywood_Murder_The_Unusual_Suspects/Lieutenant_Roy_ Slade.Avenging-Angel.org

Busby Barclay, Star Reporter, Outside WeHo Sheriff Station

Star Reporter has learned… Lieutenant Roy Slade is coordinating the investigation for the LAPD and the county sheriff. Because the murder took place within the city of West Hollywood, the crime technically falls within the sheriff's jurisdiction. The issues surrounding such a high profile case and victim go well beyond the boundaries of the approximately nine square miles that comprise the tiny city that lies near the geographic heart of Los Angeles and L.A. County.

Slade, who works as part of a new specialty unit of the Los Angeles Police Department, has been brought on to the St. James investigation with the blessings of the county sheriff and West Hollywood authorities. Aside from looking like a Milan runway model, Lieutenant Roy Slade (photos after the jump) is tasked with managing the sort of high-profile cases that are the occupational hazard of law enforcement officers in all company towns everywhere.

Here in the entertainment industry's company town, dating news and weight gain can make national headlines. So a murder like this with all the celebrity trimmings ranks right up there with natural disaster on the Star Reporter's news radar.

By any standard, Lieutenant Slade's education, exemplary academy performance and spotless record actually over-qualify him for his position. And his looks may actually have been as much of a deciding factor, though neither he nor his bosses would confirm the obvious. With his on-camera poise, well-spoken good manners and above-average appearance, he clearly fits more easily into the milieu of this case. Even his charming denial of the *Times'* assertion served to confirm our supposition.

"I'm an L.A. police officer. I passed the lieutenant's exam. I applied for the job," Slade told the *Times* article LAPD'sCentralCasting-Cops. "I'm lucky I got it. Like anyone in the department, I'm sure I'll be judged on my performance."

In such a high-profile case, the West Hollywood branch of the L.A. County Sheriff's department, more accustomed to the bright lights of celebrity celebration, has been besieged by national and international media attention. Whatever rivalries and turf issues exist between LAPD and L.A. Sheriffs seem to have been set aside to bring in a detective who actually took camera technique classes, along with his weapons and self-defense training, to prepare him for his job.

Next Page: Jay St. James Goes On the Record.

Of course Paige clicked, unable to resist finding out a bit more about their most vocal accuser so far.

Hollywood_Murder_the_Unusual_Suspects/Jay_St.James. Avenging-Angel.org

Busby Barclay, Star Reporter

"Murderer, murderer, murderer!" Jay St. James chanted outside the West Hollywood Sheriff's station as Angel Panderson struggled to escape. (Video after the jump)

Jay St. James, only child of billionaire media executive Seth St. James, made his suspicions known regarding the death of his father moments ago. The younger St. James pointed an unequivocal finger at his father's fiancée, famed actress Angela Panderson, who discovered the senior St. James's body in their suite at the Argyle Hotel early this morning following the official announcement of their engagement. Panderson, seen fleeing the younger St. James' accusations in the video, was detained for questioning for hours along with frenemy Paige Blanche, coauthor of her novels, who was with her when she discovered the body. Only a few hours before that, Angel and Mr. Blanche were engaged in a red-carpet altercation outside the hotel, as can be seen in the video Tea4Two, which has already gone viral and is now outpacing the top-trending music videos.

I was able to ask Angel about her well-being and the progress of the investigation, but we were interrupted by Jay St. James before Angel had a chance to answer.

Angel did smile for our camera, but then put her head down and moved on as Jay St. James kept chanting the word "murderer" again and again.

Jay is the son of Seth St. James and his first wife Anne, who was killed in a plane crash seventeen years ago. Following Anne's death, the senior St. James remarried socialite Lucrezia DeSole. Their recent and acrimonious divorce that cleared the way for St. James to wed Angel Panderson has obviously left some hard feelings that questions surrounding St. James murder can do little to soften.

Angel left the Sheriff's Station in her black SUV without comment, but not before her companion and former business partner Paige Blanche offered these words of conciliation to the young St. James.

"We don't believe for a minute that you or your mother killed your father for his money," Blanche reassured young St. James as Angel looked on with a gentle smile. "We want you to know you have our full support, no matter what the police think."

An emotional Angel lowered her gaze and fled the scene and her no-longer-prospective stepson's accusations. Other than claiming to have an allegedly incriminating copy of the St. James/Panderson pre-nup, Jay offered no further comment before going into the Sheriff's Station.

Next Page: Movie previews to die for.

"Busby is going to own *Star Reporter* after this," Paige sighed. He pocketed his phone as they pulled up in front of his building. "Go around to the side," he said to the driver. "We'll be back in a few."

"Do I have to come?" Angel whined.

"If you want me to come back," Paige said, slamming his door and heading for his apartment without a backward glance.

"I'd have a mantel full of Oscars if I could make an exit like that," she called to his back as she followed.

"When will you learn?" Paige said, struggling with his key. "It's all about the writer. Come on."

15

"Cheese and rice," Angel said, slamming the door behind the Argyle's hotel manager. The well-meaning celebriphile had dogged them up to the suite and even followed them inside in an effort to "help." "I thought we'd have to kill that man to get rid of him."

"What, again? That trick never works," Paige sighed. He heaved his bag onto the dresser in the largest of the penthouse suite's three bedrooms and began to unpack. "Well, Manager Bob is a fan at least," he said, doing a comic imitation of the way Bob said his name. "He'll be on our side, if the chips are down."

Angel stood in the doorway, folding her arms indignantly under her ridiculous breasts.

"What are you doing?" she demanded.

"I'm going to put the murder weapons in the hotel safe and go to bed," Paige said. "A sentence I never thought I'd utter in real life. In case you've forgotten—and since it doesn't directly involve you, that's likely—I was asleep when you woke me up at four in the morning to come to your bloody rescue after you murdered your fiancé. I've done that, and I'm going to bed now."

"But this is the master," Angel said without irony.

"Yeah and I'm locking the door when I go to bed," Paige said. Carefully, he wrapped the plastic bag that contained the bloody crystal angel in a towel and looked around for something more respectable to stash it in. "I don't trust you any further than I can throw an anvil in a swamp."

"Me?"

"Yes, you," Paige said, going an octave above her. "In case you've forgotten, you ruined my life and then you dragged me into this mess."

"Your life was already ruined when I met you," she said, sitting on the bed.

"I was a struggling artist when you met me," he corrected. "But I would hardly have spent the next two years working on your crappy novels, living below the poverty line, if you hadn't committed to doing everything you could to make our project a success. Do you have a jewel case or a little overnight bag?"

Her luggage was still in the hotel from the night before. What pieces hadn't been impounded by the police had been moved into their new room upon their unexpected return.

"I think so," she sighed, falling back onto the bed. "Why do you need it?"

"I'm going to put my bookend and your letter opener inside and send them downstairs to be put in the hotel safe."

"Are you crazy?" she demanded, sitting up. "What are we doing here anyway?"

"Well, whoever did the murder, and I'm not saying it wasn't you—" he said, rooting around in his luggage for the garbage bags containing their bloody clothes, the knife and the forged manuscript he retrieved from their hiding place in his apartment. "—But whoever it was has been in both of our houses. So there may be bugs or maybe they're watching or at the very least they know how to come back and finish the job. *We* didn't even know we were going to be staying in this suite until the hotel offered it to us a few minutes ago. And the hotel can hardly afford for things to get worse, so they have an interest in protecting us. Now get off my bed."

"That's actually pretty smart," Angel said, not getting off his bed. "But putting all the incriminating evidence in the hotel safe?"

"We're both suspects and it's only a matter of time before they search our houses and this room." Paige stared at her a moment. Then, grabbing her hands, he dragged her off the bed forcibly and pushed her toward the door. "I'm not going to tell them it's in the hotel safe—are you?"

Angel only shook her head with a sigh as he shoved her out the door into the parlor.

"So, get me a bag that locks to put all this in," he said firmly, blocking the doorway and her return. "Then call your new boy-friend Manager Bob to come and get it and lock it in the hotel safe. Meanwhile, I'm locking this door, taking a full-on shower and going to bed for a few hours. I suggest you pick a room and do the same. We've got work to do."

"What kind of work?" Angel asked as she dumped the makeup out of a largish white quilted leather Dior bag.

"That looks like a diaper bag," Paige said. "It can't be soft sided. That little Vuitton piece on the top of that pile over there—do you have the key?"

"I guess so," she said, annoyed at having dumped all the stuff out of the one bag.

"This one is already empty."

"We can't use that one," Paige sighed. He was too tired to argue and rapidly losing patience with the discussion. "Just a thought—find the key to the Vuitton before you dump the crap out of it. It's got to lock."

It turned out the key was in the pile of stuff she'd dumped out of the first bag.

"This is perfect," he said, taking the tray out of the top of the jewel case to reveal a large compartment beneath. He easily stashed their swag and then refitted the tray of Angel's highly questionable jewelry over the top to conceal it.

"So, what work do we have to do?"

"We have to find out who killed Seth before they kill us, too," he said.

"Really?"

"Yeah. Speaking of which, what was junior St. James doing with your prenup?"

"I dunno. *I* haven't even seen the final version."

"Were he and Seth close?" Paige asked, tracing the piping on the bag with his finger.

"Not really, I don't think."

"Is he close with the ex?"

"No, the ex is his stepmom," she said, shaking her head. "Jay's mom was killed years ago. Lucrezia, the ex, was Seth's second wife. She doesn't like me much, to put it mildly."

"And she's the heir?" he asked.

"I think," Angel said. "My financial benefit had more to do with Seth being alive."

"Until the new will?"

"I don't know," Angel said.

"So it looks like the ex is our most likely suspect," he said. "We have to find out who benefits from his death and why Jay is so convinced you're the murderer."

"We *have* to?"

"It's that or turn over the evidence to the police and let them do it," Paige said, holding up the bag.

"But the evidence will convict us!"

"Exactly." He put his arm around her shoulder and guided her gently to the room's double doors. "In return for wasting two years of my life writing your lousy books for practically nothing, and then having you screw me out of any profits, and wrecking my life, while refusing to return my calls as if *I'd* done something to *you*, I'm now running from a killer I've never even met while I try to prove my innocence of a crime I didn't commit, all without contacting the authorities because they'd just arrest me if I told them the truth."

"Is this why you're so mad?" she asked as he pushed her back into the parlor and handed her the bag.

"Oh, darling, that is just the beginning of why I'm so mad," he said, dropping the key to the little case into his own pocket. "Now, call your minion and have him put that in the hotel safe confidentially—that means it's a secret. And don't bother me again until I've had some sleep."

He slammed the doors in her face and turned the lock.

"*Touchy*," she shouted.

2 Years, 11 Months and a Few Days Minus One Day Earlier…

The End of the Beginning

Paige and Angel almost never met in the first place.

Once he'd heard the details of Paige's story, Armie spent their entire pot roast dinner trying to talk Paige out of going to his first meeting with Angel—though neither of them knew the appointment was with Angel at the time. Armie had been especially protective after a stalker, obsessed with Paige's photos in a gay magazine spread entitled "The Hot Writers of Summer," got into Paige's apartment.

"Paige, it could be anyone. You have no idea who this is or what it's about."

"How much trouble could I get into at the Chateau Marmont?"

After they finished laughing, Paige did agree to get in touch with Honoria before departing on the cloak-and-dagger interview. Of course, Honoria had not called back by the appointed time. Paige, though not heedless of Armie's cautions, was spurred on by his declining fortunes. He climbed into the cab for the two-minute ride around the corner.

Deposited in front of the impossible entrance to the Chateau Marmont, Paige made his way up to the lobby, where he managed after more than a little difficulty to round up the concierge. Surly and possibly drunk, the man had little interest in wasting time on someone who was neither a guest of the hotel nor anyone he'd seen profiled on MTV, *Behind the Music* or read about in a tabloid.

"I'm sorry to bother you, but I'm expecting a message from Minnie Mouse," Paige finally managed to inquire.

"Minnie Mouse?" the concierge intoned. "Why didn't you say so? Right this way."

The concierge led Paige back down the stairs to the valet parking area. Paige followed him to a windowless van waiting there. The concierge slid the side door open to reveal a single bench seat in the four-wheeled, gray metal cell. He stood expectantly holding the door for Paige.

"What is this?" Paige asked, suspicious of the rather sinister conveyance.

"This is your ride," the concierge explained as he held the sliding door open.

"Where am I going? Human trafficking distribution center?"

"No idea, sir," the concierge said.

"Well then how—?"

"The driver knows."

Paige caught the driver's eye in the mirror. They exchanged a small smile and a nod. The intimidating countenance of a formidable black man with a shaved head and a diamond stud in his nose gave Paige a small chill.

"Do you know where we're going?"

"Not sure yet," the driver said. "I'm supposed to call once my passenger gets here. Are you Minnie Mouse?"

"No, I'm here for tea with the Mad Hatter," Paige shot back.

"This is Minnie Mouse," the concierge put in, to try and move things along so he could get back upstairs to drink with the guests.

"Well, there you are," the driver said, dialing. The concierge took Paige's elbow in a civil effort to force him into the van.

"Miss Mouse is here," the driver said into his cell.

Paige reluctantly took his seat. The concierge slid the solid metal door shut with an ominous, metallic scrape, obscuring the world from view.

"Got it. What time?" the driver said into the phone.

There were no handles on the inside of the door. Paige felt more than a little insecure about the high-security arrangements.

The driver nodded and clicked off his phone.

"So, where are we—?"

The panel that separated him from the driver slid shut.

Left in the dusk of the van's light, Paige was not only cut off from sunlight but any idea where they might be headed. The vehicle lurched away from the curb. Paige scrambled to put on the seatbelt as he took in the spare gray interior around him.

"Oh, the things I do for art," Paige sighed, making himself as comfortable as possible. The shocks on the van were as spare as the air conditioning. No amount of shouted abuses and pounding on the partition could convince the driver to turn on the air or take it easy on the potholes.

It was more than an hour later when they reached their clandestine journey's end. Paige was hot and battered. He squinted as the driver pulled the door open. The late morning light ended his sensory deprivation by blinding him a bit.

"Are we in Mexico yet?' Paige muttered under his breath as he alighted. Once clear of his odious transport, he looked around to discover his surroundings. He recognized the place immediately from his brief but intensely unsuccessful stint as an actor. It was a private casting studio where he'd been to test for a focus group on a pilot he was ultimately cut from. "We're in Burbank?" Paige asked with some disgust. "I could have walked here in less time."

"This way." The driver motioned to him, oblivious.

He held the door to the studio entrance open for Paige. They exchanged the contentious looks of a parting neither man was sorry to see arrive.

"Minnie Mouse, I presume," said the odorless, tasteless and colorless little man in the lab coat waiting inside the entryway.

"Hello, Pluto," Paige said effusively in his best Mickey Mouse voice. It was as much humor as he could muster after the beating he'd taken in the back of the van. He was there for an interview so he felt some obligation to be friendly, even as he had no idea who the man was.

"This way, Ms. Mouse," the man with the clipboard giggled. He was either enjoying Paige's joke or one of his own.

"Is Grizelda here?" Paige asked genially. His hope was to get near enough to the author of his torment to hurt her.

"I'm only a technician," Pluto said.

"Technician? This is a casting studio," Paige said. He was incredulous at the level and absurdity of the charade. "What do you do? Repair broken egos?"

Pluto laughed again, but offered no further information as they headed down a long, grim hall.

"Here you go," Pluto said, opening a door marked "Focus Room A."

Paige peered inside. The room contained a single black leather swivel desk chair. The solitary seat faced a massive mirror mortised into the wall it dominated. An unhealthy amount of gray industrial broadloom carpeting ran a few feet up the gray walls like fuzzy wainscoting.

"There's no one here," Paige pointed out.

"If you'll just wait here." The little man reached up and nervously slid the *In Session* sign into place in the aluminum frame mounted on the door before closing it from the outside.

Paige was left alone in the strange chamber.

"I always liked Goofy better," he sighed. Paige moved into the empty room. The sound of the bolt being thrown caught his attention. He tried the handle. Locked in. He began pounding on the door.

"Hey, let me out of here!" Paige shouted. When he got no response, he tried in earnest to tear the door off its hinges. "Hey, you come back here right now!"

The voice that answered him came so suddenly and unexpectedly that he would probably have screamed anyway. "Thanks for coming, Mr. Blanche." The electronically altered and amplified voice sounded like the phone caller from *Scream* and inspired Paige's best Drew Barrymore ululation.

"Sorry," the strange, electronically augmented voice said.

Paige pressed his back to the pale gray wall opposite the mirror so that he could watch himself have a breakdown. "Jesus, what the fuck are you trying to do to me here?"

"Can we do anything to make you more comfortable?" the weird voice asked—at once polite and ominous.

"A week in the south of France would be nice," Paige said. Grasping for his dignity, he righted himself and moved away from the gray-carpeted wall. "Some water or, if you could manage it, a cup of tea would be great."

"What kind of tea?" the warped voice echoed.

"What kind?" Paige echoed. "My favorite is Jasmine pearls. But a nice green or even just good old English Breakfast would be welcome."

"I'll see what we can do," the voice said almost sadly. It was like talking to Hal the computer in *2001*—helpful but homicidal.

"Thank you," Paige said, regaining a bit of his composure but still on edge. He took a seat and faced the mirror. "Curiouser and curiouser," he said to the mirror. He'd done focus groups before and knew that the two-way mirror allowed the occupants of the room on the other side of the glass to observe unseen the occupants of the room on his side. The speakers were built into the walls flanking the mirror. Given the fractured tone of the voice, it was as if the mirror itself was speaking.

"Are you the person I'm going to be working with?"

"Yes," the voice said.

"So, here I am." He shrugged.

"Do you want to wait for your tea?"

It was just unnerving to be asked common questions by the altered voice. It seemed to Paige to be the sort of voice that should be demanding the secret plans or threatening excruciating torture and death, not asking if he'd like one lump or two. "No, we can go ahead, thanks," Paige answered. He managed to suppress his giggle.

There was a knock on the door, which gave him the chance to laugh. "Look at that, chivalry isn't dead. Come in," Paige called sweetly.

The door opened. Pluto entered with a bottle of Crystal Geyser and a steaming World's Greatest Lover mug. The cup bore a picture of Pluto—the "technician," not the cartoon dog—and trailed a sachet fob for Trader Joe's Organic Green. The string from the bag was wrapped loosely around the cup's handle to keep the sachet from sliding in.

"So, Pluto, you're the world's greatest lover, eh?" Paige asked, taking the cup. "I'm free on Friday."

Pluto gave a braying laugh, blushed and withdrew. Paige heard the door lock again. He decided against saying anything further about it. Everyone present had presumably witnessed the screaming and pounding from earlier so he felt his objection was already on the record.

He took a long pull on the bottle of water and then screwed the lid back on. He wiped his mouth daintily on his sleeve. "Thank you," Paige said, toasting the mirror with the mug. "What do you want to know about me?"

"Um, well, I guess I just wanted to get an idea of the kind of person you are," the eerie voice said, sounding as unsure how to proceed as Paige was himself.

"Like this? What have you found out so far?"

"Well, I haven't asked you anything yet."

"You could have called me on the phone if you just wanted to talk to me without being seen."

"Hey, that's right. Grizelda? Why didn't we just—"

The speakers went dead in mid-sentence. Paige sipped his tea for a bit.

"Who is your favorite writer?" the voice asked. It was sudden and Paige choked slightly, startled. He spilled some of his tea before answering.

"I am. Who's yours?" he choked out, brushing spilled tea off his shirtfront.

"I have a number of favorite authors," the voice answered.

"Really? Have you had them ride over here in the back of a windowless, unair-conditioned van and then locked them into a room to observe them like laboratory animals? Or am I a special favorite?"

"Um, hang on."

The microphone went dead again. Paige was less surprised when the voice returned.

"I've considered a number of writers but you're the first I've interviewed."

"So, which book of mine did you like best?" Paige asked to trip up his inquisitor. He'd only published one book.

"Um..."

The microphone clicked off once again. Paige grinned. He found that, having assumed the role of interrogator, he was enjoying himself a bit.

"'El-oo, yes, tzo I zuppoze I vould like to know how you vould feel about writing a book visout receiving credit?" the voice asked with an abruptly acquired and strangely familiar, heavy, Pan-European accent. Paige laughed out loud. It was like yelling into a fan, still the same voice even with the electronic alterations.

"Grizelda," Paige said cheerfully. "So glad you could make it. Did you come by smuggler's van as well?"

"Er, zis iz not Grizelda..."

"Okay then, 'Not Grizelda,' just to let you know. I've done a lot of uncredited writing over the years, so that's not a problem for me as long as I get paid."

"Why do we have to keep it a secret?' the original voice asked.

"I'm not really…" Paige began.

"Vee have been over zis, ant over zis," said Not Grizelda.

As the dispute progressed, it became clear to Paige that the question was not for him. He sipped his tea and pretended not to hear so he could listen for clues.

"It iz part of your mystique. People vant to read your verds."

"But they're not my verds—words—and no one will think so," the original voice pointed out to Not Grizelda. "If we make it a secret, it's just one more thing for people to find out."

"Look, darlink, vee can talk about zis anozer time. Zee point now iz zat no one vants to read zis guy's stuff."

Paige bristled a bit but tried to keep his composure and his cover.

"Then why do we want him?"

"Because 'e iz good and very funny."

"So, you liked his book?"

"Well, I 'aven't actually…"

"Oh God, is that microphone still on?" the original voice wailed. "What did he hear?"

There were a few muffled cries, some clattering noises and the sound of someone wrestling with the microphone a moment before it went dead.

Paige finished his tea and then the water. He began pacing the room.

"Are we done yet?" he asked, after a longish pause. He walked close enough to the mirror to press his face against it. "Not that I'm not having a swell time, but you haven't asked anything for quite a while and I could really use a break."

There was no response.

"Hello?"

He tapped on the glass.

"Please talk to me," Paige pleaded. "Can you get Pluto to come by and let me out for a minute? I need to go to the little ghostwriter's room."

Still there was no reply.

He pounded on the glass. No response. Frustrated, he went to pound on the door again. It was unlocked. He poked his head tentatively out into the hallway and looked around.

"Hello?"

He made his way down the hall to a door marked "Focus Observation A." He tried the handle. It was open. Gently, Paige eased the door inward. He peered into the darkened room. Aside from a few disarranged chairs and lipstick-stained Starbucks cups, there were no signs of life. Through the mirror he could see the room that now contained only his empty chair and Pluto's teacup. The microphone was turned at an odd angle in a stand in front of one of the chairs by the glass.

"Well," Paige said aloud as he made his way through the abandoned building back toward the front doors. "I guess the interview's over. I thought it went great."

16

There was one piece of evidence that Paige did not put in the hotel safe that afternoon. He hung onto that strange manuscript, *Fallen Angel*—the book attributed to Angel and him that they'd found at the crime scene. Not only had he not written it, but he'd never heard of it before. The fact that they'd found it in the room where Seth was murdered made it the only real clue that he had to the killer's motive and identity. And it was a pretty thin clue.

The night before, after their clandestine *CSI: West Hollywood* moment in Seth and Angel's suite, he and Angel had returned to Paige's apartment to prepare for their big scene in the Argyle lobby. They took the manuscript and all the evidence they had found during their search of the murder room. Anxious to get back to the hotel before someone else could discover the body and draw their own conclusions, Angel got cross with Paige when he took the time to locate a box of clear page protectors. He'd brought the tabbed plastic sheaths home a couple of weeks earlier to use in a project for the cancelled *Show Talk*.

"What are those for?" Angel demanded, when he offered her no explanations.

Ignoring her and her questions, Paige slipped the skeleton key out of the old-fashioned mortise lock in his dressing room door and locked himself inside. As she beat on the door, he slipped on the yellow rubber gloves he kept under the kitchen sink but had never actually worn. Carefully, he slid each page of the strange novel into the fingerprint-preserving sleeves. He hid the manuscript, along with the crystal angel, the penis letter opener and their bloody clothes in plastic garbage bags behind an old shoe rack built into the wall. Only then did he let Angel back into the dressing room. In this way, he reasoned, she couldn't reveal the location of the incriminating evidence, no matter how stupid she was.

"What were you doing in there?" she huffed, throwing herself onto his bed.

"Masturbating while I wore your bloody party dress and watched the video of me throwing that tea in your face." He began looking through the clothes rack for something festive they could wear to their upcoming alibi-creating lobby engagement. "You really should see that video. I laugh harder every time..."

"Fine, don't tell me," she snarled, leaving him to search for a drink.

Following their extended engagement at the police station, they returned to his place where Paige retrieved the manuscript along with the rest of the evidence on the pretext of packing a few things. The mere existence of the manuscript worried him so much that Paige debated locking it up with the rest in the hotel safe. Back at the Argyle, he took pains to hide it before he got in the shower, taping it to the bottom of a dresser drawer.

After nearly an hour under the hot water, he bundled up in his second-favorite pajamas—blue flannel with white fluffy clouds. His most-favorite pair was in the hotel safe along with the rest of the incriminating evidence. Retrieving the manuscript from where he had concealed it, he pulled the windows' velvet blackout curtains and crawled beneath the countless threads of the yummy Egyptian cotton sheets.

He switched on the bedside lamp and snuggled in. In the warm yellow light, he began to leaf through the plastic covered pages he'd clipped into a loose-leaf binder labeled *The Price is Right*, snorting Diet Coke from the room's honor bar to keep awake. Thanks to the edge of NutraSweet-laced caffeine, fear and adrenaline, he only just managed to remain conscious long enough to read the book in the slim hope that he might discover some vital fact that would lead them to the murderer and prove their innocence.

Fallen Angel was the badly written story of a Svengali character styled after Seth St. James himself. A studio mogul named James Saint, he was more the sort of movie executive that people imagine than one who might actually exist. In the novel, the rather obvious and obviously named Mr. Saint falls in love with a beautiful but hopelessly untalented party girl. The hapless heroine misses out on being a hooker only because she is not smart enough to charge for it.

James takes Ela, the no-talent drunk, under his dark wing. After a complete makeover that includes extensive plastic surgery, he transforms her into a physical ideal, changes her name to Gabrielle and makes her into a gigantic movie star. But, like Pygmalion and his Galatea, once Gabrielle becomes the ideal, she tries to leave James for another, more ideal man. James retaliates by holding her a virtual prisoner, controlling her life and her career as long as he can. But Gabrielle eschews fame and money for true love and escapes James' hold over her.

Heartbroken and blinded by his loss, James falls into the arms of an obvious, cheap tramp named Devila Pimpton—guess who. Aided by her confederate Leif White—AKA Paige Blanche—they contrive to swindle James out of his money. James discovers their scheme and confronts them with his suspicions. But, no fool like an old one, the tramp turns on her confederate Leif White convincingly enough that James believes her and marries her. Devila and Leif then drug James and drown him in a hot tub while he and Devila are on their honeymoon, leaving Devila in control of the fortune and, ironically, Gabrielle.

It was a cloying and insipid story, but it was filled with elaborate descriptions of James' shady partying, womanizing, drug use, questionable business dealings, money laundering, dubious associates and ill-gotten gains. It was too detailed, intricately conceived and, hence, dull to be entirely fiction. It was also incomplete. In the end it only raised more questions than it answered. Was Lucrezia his movie star protégé Ela? It didn't really sound like her, so had there been someone before Angel she had neglected to mention or didn't know about? It also made Paige question his relationship with Angel all the more. Had she simply sold him out to serve her own ends? He laughed, but bitterly. The answer seemed as obvious as the names of the book's "fictional" characters. But the novel, however crappy, did offer Paige a starting point.

Frustrated but unable to elude sleep any longer, he set the binder on the bed beside him and switched off the lamp. Lying there amid the four-figure thread count, he chuckled darkly as he considered their prospects. He hadn't the least idea how to conduct a murder investigation. Working with Angel on anything more serious than a bottle of Dom or a dime bag would end up being nothing more than a punchline. He was still smiling as he drifted off into fitful sleep.

He dreamed that there was someone in his room at the hotel and woke up screaming.

"What is it? What's happened?" Angel rushed into the room, light spilling in through the open doorway. "Are you okay?"

Paige pushed her away as she grasped his shoulders, trying to steady him.

"How did you get in here?" He knocked the phone off the bedside table as he fumbled for the lamp.

Night was falling in that abrupt L.A. way when, at the end of the day, the sun plummets into the ocean. The amber light of the largely decorative table lamp beside the bed dimly illuminated the curtained room around them. Even so, it was enough to make the two of them gasp.

The bedroom was shredded. The contents of Paige's suitcase and toilet kit were strewn everywhere. The cushions on the chairs were disemboweled, their down floating in the twilight. Instinctively, Paige's hand shot out to find the warm leatherette cover of the manuscript he'd been sleeping on.

"Jesus," Angel intoned, looking around at the tumbled up room. "I gotta stop coming to this hotel."

"I gotta stop coming here with you." Paige shuddered. Tossing the duvet aside, he grappled with the phone.

"What are you doing?"

"Yeah, I need the manager and hotel security up here now," Paige said authoritatively to the front desk. "Someone's broken into my room."

"While you were out of your room, Mr. Blanche?" the clerk asked.

"No, while I was in it."

"You don't think they're still here?" Angel asked.

"Well, I do now," Paige said, suddenly chilled and dizzy at the idea.

Angel grabbed him and tried to shield herself with his body until Paige succeeded in pushing her off the bed and on to the floor. His escape was brief. As he got to his feet, she was on him again. Dragging her with him, he managed to open the curtains, turning on as many lights as he could along the way.

"Hello?" a voice called from the other room.

They began screaming, grabbing onto one another. Two thuggish men in suits rushed into the bedroom. One of them entered with a gun drawn, the sight of which only made Angel and Paige scream more intensely. They began throwing bits of Paige's shattered room at their attackers.

"Hotel security!" the unarmed half of the rescue effort kept shouting. He waved his ID in through the door at them in a fruitless effort to stop them screaming and throwing things.

Eventually, the beleaguered security detail was joined by Manager Bob. Paige and Angel, calmed by his somewhat more familiar if irritating presence, stopped screaming, though neither would move much more than a few feet away from the other.

"You might have knocked," Paige gasped. He clutched his chest, which ached from the rush of the latest shock.

"It was open," one of the security men offered.

"Did you lock the door?" Paige demanded, shoving Angel away.

"Did *you*?" she countered, rubbing the spot on her arm where he'd shoved her.

"I locked the door to my room," he said.

"Well, it was unlocked when you started screaming and I came in," she pointed out, still rubbing her arm dramatically.

"True." He nodded. "And no one believes you're hurt. You're not that good an actress."

She stopped rubbing her arm and punched him in the shoulder.

"Ow," he said, making it two syllables.

"That does not hurt," she scoffed.

"No?" he said, hitting her back.

"Ow," she bellowed, shocked.

"Does it?"

"I guess it does."

"Then cut it out!"

"We're actually still in the room," Manager Bob pointed out.

"And I hope you're here to change these locks," Angel huffed, flouncing out of the bedroom and heading for the bar.

"Is there a copy machine I can use?" Paige asked, grasping the manuscript. "I need to make a copy of this and then put it in the hotel safe. Who has access to that?"

"I was just explaining to Miss Panderson earlier that it's more like a vault of safe deposit boxes with individual keys," Bob began, gleeful at having helpful information to share. "In fact, we'd already reserved a box for the gift Mr. St. James had intended for Miss Panderson, so we just added her jewel case to the existing—"

Angel's scream cut him off. Paige followed Manager Bob and the security detail as they rushed into the sitting room.

"Do all the rooms come with one of these?" Angel demanded, pointing to the woman's head, sitting on a shelf in the mini-fridge.

17

"What is this exactly?" Lieutenant Roy Slade asked. He leafed through the binder Paige had been clutching since his arrival at their hotel suite. The rest of the homicide detail, the coroner and the crime scene pathologist were about their business around them.

"Just an unpublished manuscript," Paige said with extreme disinterest as he watched the goings on.

"I thought you two weren't working together anymore?" the Lieutenant said.

"I said it was unpublished." Paige shrugged. He looked into Roy's oh-so-blue eyes and tried to seem casual about both the manuscript and the eyes.

"And you put sleeve protectors on each page?" Roy asked with a quizzical smile.

"I'm a little anal," Paige admitted with a nervous laugh.

"A *little* anal?" Angel piped up from the bed behind them in the unused third bedroom. Police and security had corralled them there since the fresh head had turned up in the refrigerator. "You should hear the story of the year his parents planted zucchini."

"Or the one about Angel and the periodic and unexpected return of the missing bunch of grapes," Paige shot back.

"Or not," Angel said tersely, teeth clenched in warning.

"Maybe some other time," Lt. Slade suggested, handing Paige back the manuscript. "Doesn't seem up to your standards."

"What doesn't?" Paige asked.

"The manuscript."

"Have you read my books?" Paige asked, at least partially feigning flattery and hoping to change the subject.

"All of them," Roy admitted, a little sheepishly.

Paige blushed sincerely.

"He's a Judy Garland gay book award winner," Angel put in proudly.

"Get off my side," Paige warned.

"Golden Garland," the lieutenant corrected.

Angel gave Paige a get-her head toss.

"Well, aren't you the homicide detective I'd have asked for if I'd been given a choice," Paige said, and smiled. Even as he enjoyed Roy's flattery, he couldn't help wondering if the lieutenant was feigning the shy tone to tease Paige into giving more away. "Although the second book with her was also hardly up to my standards."

"No," Roy laughed, a bit too heartily. "I figured that was why you weren't working together anymore."

"Yeah," Paige confided. "After the first one was a success, everyone else involved thought they were the bestselling writer."

"The sequel kind of has a committee feel to it," Roy agreed.

"And what do you know?" Paige shrugged and chuckled bitterly. "Bad reviews and worse sales."

"Does anyone want anything?" Angel asked. Without waiting for an answer, she stalked off in the direction of the bar.

"Sore subject?" the lieutenant asked quietly.

"Not sure," Paige said before he thought about it. He was definitely getting too comfortable around this guy.

"What do you mean?" Slade asked without seeming too interested.

Paige regarded him a moment, trying to determine if he was being played or if they were just making small talk. "I don't know if she sabotaged the second book intentionally," he said at last. "Or if she's really that stupid."

Whatever his motives, the lieutenant's laughter seemed sincere enough.

"What's so funny?" Angel asked, returning empty-handed to the room with a police officer firmly affixed to her arm. She was clearly being steered back into their art deco exile.

The officer deposited her inside the open doors before taking up a post just outside. "There's some Cristal on the way up, but don't go out there," she said. "That guy with the doctor coat on is really touchy about looking in the refrigerator or anything, even though that head is long gone."

"You see what I mean?" Paige said.

Roy broke up again.

"Come on, guys, what's the joke?"

"Any ideas on the identity of the first head?" Paige asked, ignoring her.

"It was Seth's business manager," Roy answered. "But don't say anything to the press yet. The assistant is also missing and we think that you might have found her, you know, in the minibar."

"Wow," Angel murmured. "I've spoken to her on the phone so many times. Such a bitch. I never met her, though. I thought she'd be more attractive."

"Maybe before the decapitation," Paige suggested.

"Maybe," Angel agreed, nodding absently.

Suddenly, like a hound on the scent, she sat up. Her eyes focused and her head turned in the direction of the door. The intensity of Angel's actions caused those around her to go quiet. It was almost imperceptible at first. A steady tinkling sound, too inconsistent to be a bell, but still too regular to be purely random. It grew in intensity.

"Cristal's here," she sighed, just before the cart rolled into view. The tulip glasses rang against one another in impotent little toasts with each bump in the carpet.

"Pavlov's lush," Paige remarked.

Roy tried not to laugh, but Angel wouldn't have noticed guffaws.

The waiter poured a glass. Angel snatched the stem from his hand before he could offer.

"Champagne?" the waiter asked, passing Paige a glass.

"No, thank you," Paige said, waving it away. "I would love a glass of iced tea if you could find one in the kitchen somewhere."

"After the day you've had?" Roy scoffed at Paige's choice. "I wish I was off-duty."

"What?" Paige asked, not understanding for a moment. "Oh," he said, realizing too late to stop himself speaking. "I don't drink."

"At all?"

"No, I'm allergic," Paige said. "I turn red, my voice goes funny and then I swell up like a peach in rainy season."

"More for me," Angel said, taking the second glass.

"And how conveniently you forgot me when you were ordering room service," Paige pointed out with a vicious little smile.

"I asked if you wanted anything," she huffed. She tossed down another glass and held out the empty for the waiter to refill.

"So, why did you want more champagne last night, when you two came back from your house?" the lieutenant asked.

"Cause we were out?" Paige suggested, without hesitation, while just managing not to faint. He had stepped right into that one.

"I just had the impression that the two of you were sort of drunk and disorderly when you returned from your house," Slade said seriously enough that Angel stopped drinking.

"Roy," Paige said, patting him on the arm. "I assure you, I am more than capable of being disorderly without the aid of champagne."

18

"Well, that was a close one," Angel said when they were finally alone together inside her massive, white, Malibu Barbie SUV, heading down Sunset toward the beach.

"That pedestrian you almost hit back there?"

"No," Angel said, with mild exasperation. "The lieutenant asking about our little Ashley and Rhett drunk scene in the lobby."

Though he had managed to gloss over the moment with Slade, Paige did not miss the warning shot. For that matter and maybe more alarmingly, clearly neither had Angel. If she got it, surely the lieutenant hadn't been fooled.

To her credit, Angel had followed the tense moment with an explosion of inane conversation that would have numbed the keenest of minds, taking over the room in a way attainable only by the truly self-absorbed. But even in her sea of non-sequiturs, the point had not been lost. It was official: they were suspects. *And* flirty Lieutenant Slade with the pretty blue eyes suspected.

"Do you think he suspects us?" she asked, glancing disinterestedly at the road.

"You can really only find so many disembodied heads in your room before it starts to attract negative attention," Paige said, clutching the armrest.

Angel weaved around a car that was stopped for the changing light, darted in front of another, and then ran through the intersection on the last flicker of yellow in a cloud of blaring horns.

"Do you think you should be driving?"

"If you're the only other choice, yes," she said, emphatically.

"You've been drinking."

"And you had a wreck in the drive-through at Burger King, stone cold sober."

"Oh, it's going to be *that* kind of ride."

"I'm just saying."

"Well, slow down then," Paige snapped, genuinely and as always unable to come up with a good reason why he should be driving. "We're in no rush and, even with you driving under the influence, this is the safest we've been in the last two days."

"I just can't wait to get home," she said, stretching against the steering wheel.

"I wish," he said, longing for the same.

"Your place just isn't safe," Angel told him. "And the hotel thing was so not working out."

"We're not going to be safe until we're either dead or in jail for this murder."

"Which murder?"

"Who knows? Why would someone kill Seth's business manager's assistant?" Paige asked.

"She was pretty horrible," Angel replied. "But there must have been some kind of funny business with the money and they knew about it." Without ever breaking eye contact with Paige, she roared through a whole series of nearly red lights at the impossible multi-acre intersection of Benedict, Canon, Hartford, Rodeo and Sunset, just in front of the Beverly Hills Hotel.

"But that only hangs a lantern on it," Paige said, trying to distract himself from the shattering sounds of squealing tires and horns from which not even the impenetrable Range Rover interior could insulate them.

"What do you mean?" Angel asked, making a sudden and terrifying left onto Bedford.

"Well, if they killed Seth over money problems, killing the money people only attracts attention to, you know, the money," Paige said. Though he was hanging on to the armrest, he was tossed about inside the car like a cork in the ocean. "I think it's about trying to keep people from finding out something."

"Something they think you know," Angel agreed. Careening onto little Santa Monica Boulevard, she homed in on Starbucks with the skill of a bat in a dark cave.

"Or they think we *both* know."

"You want a latte or something?"

"Some tea would be nice," he said. He put his hands out to try to avoid hitting his head on the dashboard as they went from sixty to zero into their parking space. "Maybe the whole fake manuscript is just a red herring."

"Sushi would be nice tonight," she said. "C. Shore?"

"I'm not sure that's a good idea," Paige told her.

"Come on," Angel urged. "We deserve a break after the last twenty-four hours. I need to forget, and we need to eat something."

"I guess."

As Angel disembarked, she pulled out her phablet and began scrolling through for the number of C. Shore Sushi. The trendy sushi bar had been their favorite hangout back when they were still speaking to one another. "What are we going to do? Go to the grocery store? Come on, who should we ask?"

"I really don't think it's a good idea," he said, shaking his head. "It looks bad and if someone is trying to kill us, maybe we should keep a low profile."

"I'll get a booth," she suggested.

"That should do it," Paige said with an edge she ignored.

Amidst the stares and countless surreptitious cell photos of every other Starbucks patron while they waited in line for her low-fat mocha grande and his iced green venti, Angel negotiated the intricacies of dinner reservations at one of the hottest sushi places in the city. It was harder than usual to for Paige to ignore the attention Angel aroused, as he tried to imagine what elements cut from his first draft of their last novel could have triggered the avalanche of bodies in the past few days.

If Angel was to be believed, whatever the book had said had caused his recent career demise, destroyed their second book and killed the project that had promised to be his livelihood. But the books were little more than the novelizations of the amateur porn movie that Angel's fame was based on. What could he possibly have made up in the inane, one-handed-reader piece of chick lit that could have gotten three people killed and now threatened to put their own heads on pikes?

For that matter, not that he was complaining, but why hadn't the murderer killed the two of them at the hotel instead of just ransacking their room? Paige took a thoughtful pull on the thick green straw protruding from the top of his iced tea container and wondered if it was safe to call Lieutenant Slade and ask him that question.

By the time they both had their drinks the paparazzi had found them. They silently negotiated the bad-photo-op-obstacle course back to the car.

"I think you should sleep with him," Angel said once they were inside the Rover. Without saying goodbye, she hung up the phablet she'd been chattering and typing into through their entire coffee run.

Paige realized she was staring. "Are you talking to me?" he asked.

"Un-hunh," she said, nodding. She put the key in the ignition and fired the lethally large engine to life. "It'll throw him off the scent."

"Throw *who* off of *what* scent?" Paige asked. He put his tea into the cup holder and strapped in as he braced for the remainder of their ride to the beach.

"The lieutenant," she said, in a well-*obviously* tone of voice. "If he's sleeping with you, he'll be less likely to arrest you. Just like in *Basic Instinct*."

"Yeah, that turns out great for everyone, as I recall," Paige said with a little snort. "Let's stop at Fred Segal for an ice pick on the way home. And why do you think it's me and not you that he wants?"

"Honey, he's a man," she said with a knowing laugh as she backed the car fearlessly into oncoming traffic. "If he wanted me, I'd know it."

The gathering paparazzi scattered for their lives.

"Maybe he's just keeping a professional distance," Paige said primly.

"Nope, that's not it," she said, shaking her head. She looked around for her mocha as she proceeded heedlessly west down Little Santa Monica without so much as a cautious glance in the direction of the front windshield. "A straight man would have made a play for me by now."

"I don't know how you can—"

"I touched him with my breasts," she said. "When we were competing for his attention back at the station."

"I was not competing—"

"You totally were," she crowed, her mouth full of laughter and low-fat mocha. "'Any time, Roy. Maybe over lunch?'" she said, trying to impersonate him, but really only sounding British.

"I was not—"

"Oh, give it a rest, Paige. I was there."

"Well, he is awfully nice looking," Paige conceded.

"And he was totally into you." Angel smacked him playfully on the arm.

"I'm not as sure about that," he said. "Especially now. I think he's just trying to catch us out by flirting with us and lulling us into a false sense of security."

"'I'd like that, Paige. I'll call you,'" she said in a silly baritone voice that sounded like Dudley Do-Right. "'Here's my card. Home and cell are on the back.'"

"You got a card," Paige argued.

"Check it out," she said, heaving her bag at him. "There's no numbers on the back of mine. Just the official one on the front."

"Really!" Paige said, his eyes lighting up. "That's pretty conclusive."

"No, *homo*-sabe," Angel said, shaking her head. "That's just a clue. Conclusive is if I meet a guy and he actually looks me in the eye and doesn't hit on me. He's gay."

"No one can not look at them," Paige said. "It's like the Grand Canyon. You just have to stare."

"True," she agreed. "But straight men can't look at anything else."

"A police lieutenant," Paige mused, grinning stupidly.

"So, I made a reservation at C. Shore tonight at eight," she said while Paige was distracted.

"Yeah, sure," he agreed. The lieutenant? It was a flattering thought, but he couldn't help but wonder about Roy's true motives.

Two Years, 11 Months and a Few Days Earlier

French for Beginners

Paige had been distracted when he agreed to his first lunch with Angel. He was busy avoiding packing his things in anticipation of his impending eviction. He had only managed to assemble a few boxes he'd bought flattened at the WeHo Postal Center & More. Instead of packing, he sat on an unsealed box of books reading the personal ads and bad articles in an old issue of *Vanguard* he was supposed to be using as packing material.

Armie had alerted Paige that the eviction notice was imminent. Even though the actual eviction would not happen until after a court hearing that had not been scheduled, and even then only when and if the judge set a date, Paige didn't want to wait around until the last minute. Or maybe he was just being dramatic.

Honoria had not called, nor had anyone else after the initial interview-slash-kidnapping attempt. He still didn't even know the identity of his abductor. He only knew it had ended badly. By the time Paige found his way out to the parking lot from the interrogation room at the casting studio, the van and driver and everyone else were long gone. He had had to get a cab home and borrow money from Armie to pay the driver. Paige was pretty furious about it, but on the whole relieved that he hadn't wound up in a snuff film or, worse, on reality television.

Still, things looked bleak.

Paige was less interested in the hopelessly outdated article he'd been reading on the clandestine network of gay bed and breakfasts in the "New Russia" entitled *Lenin and Lace* than he was in escaping from the reality of being evicted from his home. He had actually had an interview about a script supervisor's position on a series about game shows that was then still in development and would eventually be called *Show Talk*. It was not the job of Paige's dreams, but as he had no job at all, it was dreamy enough. As he reread the same paragraph for the third time, the phone began ringing. He scrambled through the piles of paper and boxes to find it, hoping it would be the show's producers phoning him back with an offer.

"Hello?" he answered breathlessly.

"'El-oO? Iz zis Paige Blanche?" the familiar voice enquired.

"No, he's still locked in a fucking observation booth in Burbank, starving slowly to death," Paige said hotly. "Can I take a message?"

"Oh, ho, you are zo very funny, Mr. Blanche," Grizelda chortled. "No vonder my client took zuch a liking to you."

"Oh yeah?" Paige said, playing with the tape gun as he talked. "Are you serious?"

"Very," she assured him. "Unfortunately, ve vere unexpectedly called away before ve could get deeply into zee interview. Perhaps ve could reschedule ..."

"Oh no," Paige said. "I'm not falling for that again."

"I am zo very zorry for zee inconvenience, but zee security measures ..."

"*No* means the same in French as in English, *n'est ce pas?*" Paige asked acerbically.

"*Oui*, Mr. Blanche, but the..."

"Then *no* it is, in English and in French. No, no, no. I will not do that again. Do you know you left me stranded in Burbank? It was a fifty-dollar cab ride home and not so much as thank you or have a nice day for all my trouble. I'm still black and blue from being transported over Laurel Canyon like cheap produce. And I'm no closer to an actual job offer. Tell your client to call me back when you're ready to meet for lunch at a nice restaurant—your treat."

He hung up.

There wasn't much profit in it. It was the only thing like a job offer he'd had. Still, there was such a thing as self-respect, which was, fortunately for Paige, still free.

He put the kettle on and took down the yellow Good Earth box. One teabag left. The phone rang before the steam blew the whistle.

"Lunch at Éclair on Zunset? Tomorrow at one?"

"Be on time," Paige said with a satisfied grin. He despaired of anything coming from another ludicrous interview, but there was free food involved. "And you owe me fifty dollars cab fare. Bring cash."

Éclair was one of a number of Eurotrash magnets lined cheek-by-jowl along Sunset Boulevard at Sunset Plaza. It was hard to tell where one bistro ended and the next café began. The tables were packed with overdressed people, encrusted with heavy gold jewelry so vulgar that it all looked fake but probably wasn't. Their totally insignificant identities were hidden behind their oversized Chanel and Gucci blackout sunglasses, gold and diamond designer logos at the temples as big as the lenses.

Paige passed through the clouds of expensive cigarette and cheap cigar smoke of a gaggle of smoker-exiles clustered the required and useless few feet from flocks of heedless outdoor diners feasting on the fumes of heavy boulevard traffic. He followed the hostess to the "Wilma Flintstone" table, his single concession to the afternoon's espionage. In the back, near the kitchen and behind a row of plants that had obviously been brought in just for this purpose, he found an immense horsey-looking woman dressed more for a hunt than a West Hollywood lunch. She took his hand and pumped it as though she expected water to come out of his mouth.

"El-oo," she said. "Ve are zo 'appy you could come. I am Grizelda Lamar."

"*Bonjour*," Paige said, dipping his head in a slight bow as he struggled to free his hand from hers. "I'm most happy to be here and not at some wild goose ranch in Pasadena."

"*Mais oui*," Grizelda said, stepping aside. "And zis iz my client."

Paige's gasp was naked and involuntary.

Seated at the table was, for all intents and purposes, a wide-brimmed hat and about twenty yards of nearly opaque black veils. The heap of fabric gave a nod in Paige's direction, the only real evidence that there was actually a person underneath. A woman's hand emerged awkwardly from beneath the veil, scrawled something on a small pad lying on the table, tore off the page and handed it to Grizelda. Paige fought back laughter.

"'Good afternoon, Mr. Blanche,'" Grizelda read. She then touched the note to the flame of the candle in the centerpiece, tossing the blazing bit of paper into an empty champagne bucket in a stand by the table.

Paige's eyebrows reached almost to his hairline. He bit his lip to keep from laughing in his host's veils.

"This way you cannot recognize either the voice or the hand-writing," Grizelda said. "Clever, no?"

"No," Paige nodded. He took up the heavy three-foot tall menu with purpose. He ordered pâté, caviar, a Caesar salad, the lobster/filet combo and had the chef put one of the house specialty chocolate soufflés in the works for dessert.

"I've already eaten," Grizelda read the note before burning it. "This vay zair iz no clue from vat is ordered who is my client."

"Well, with those delicate, beautiful hands we can tell it's either a woman or Zac Efron," Paige remarked, sipping his tea.

"I suppose ve can concede zat one," Grizelda said, with a genial and entirely artificial laugh.

"Let's get started shall we, Zac?" Paige suggested. He set his cup noisily back into its saucer. "I believe we left off where you two were discussing why anyone would want to read my work and whether or not to keep my participation a secret? Though I've got to tell you I'm not sure even I could make up stuff like these interviews."

The figure wrote while Paige poured a little more tea into his cup.

"'Ve 'ave not decided on zee billing,'" Grizelda read, exchanging a meaningful look with the shroud. "Might I add," Grizelda went on, departing from the text, "zat zo long as you are villing eizer vay, zee matter iz settled."

The veiled one was writing again.

"'Don't call us, ve'll call you,'" Grizelda read and then torched the next note.

He smiled despite his determination to sneer at the whole absurd, masked luncheon.

"'Tell me about vhy you are a writer?'" Grizelda read.

"By accident, really," Paige said. "I trained to be an actor and worked a lot when I was younger. I guess I read so many bad lines and bad scripts and so few good ones that I learned the difference without knowing it. Can you tell me a bit about what kind of book you have in mind?" he asked.

Zac paused for a moment, considering, and then wrote furiously for a bit.

Paige sampled the pâté.

"'Zmall town girl comes to zee big city and sleeps her vay to zee top,'" Grizelda read. "'But funny, not a victim or a vamp. I vant to make it zexy and fun—make fun of myself a little.'"

"Why not a biography?" he asked, intrigued by the answer if not the delivery.

"'Because I vant to tell the truth,'" Grizelda read.

Paige's laugh was genuine.

Most of the bizarre lunch was simple lunchtime banter conveyed in that most inane fashion. Paige refused to speak after the starter course. He insisted on calling his lunch companion "Zac" and began communicating only in written notes. He made Grizelda read them to the veiled specter with whom he was dining.

"'Pass zee salt, please.'"

"'Ow iz your lunch?'"

"'Could I get some more hot vater for my tea?'"

Grizelda read the entire luncheon to the two guests.

"'Vould you like to try a toast point vis a little caviar, Zac?'"

Most of Grizelda's reading was hardly worth burning.

Despite the clouds of smoke, things went well. Though he didn't get to hear his mystery date's voice, he did get to hear her laugh.

Had it been possible to overlook the bad theatre of the lunch itself, it was actually rather a pleasant meeting. Everything went perfectly until the dessert course. True to her word, his lunch companion declined all but a share of the tea. Éclair's chocolate soufflé was another matter.

"'Zac, surely you vill have some of my zhoufflé,'" a rather fatigued Grizelda read.

"'Vell, per'aps just a little,'" Grizelda then read the reply.

"*Très bon,*" Paige said aloud, breaking their silence. He spooned some of the warm, perfect little soufflé onto a bread plate and passed it to her. As luck would have it, Grizelda was just lighting off the note of acceptance when the lady in black leaned forward to take the proffered soufflé. The voluminous black veil sagged just far enough to touch the flame. No one noticed at first. But as she leaned back into her seat with her dessert, it quickly became clear that the mystery guest was wearing a flaming hat.

Paige was unsure how to proceed. Would it be ungentlemanly if he didn't snatch the flaming hat off her head to save her from being immolated, or was it unmanly not to respect her privacy and leave the hat in place? He did the only possible thing he could do. He screamed like a girl, leapt to his feet and overturned his chair. "Fire!" he shouted.

Naturally, his ill-considered cry began a stampede for the exits. The Flintstone party was seated near the kitchen. Everyone assumed the smoke and cries were coming from there.

Fortunately, Grizelda kept a cool head. She snatched the hat, tossed it to the floor and stomped out the flames with her riding boots, which at last seemed sensible.

In the process, Paige got his first up-close look at Angela Panderson, the most famous woman in the world.

"You must never speak of zis," Grizelda said, clutching his arm dramatically. She then took Angel's hand as they beat a hasty exit through the kitchen.

"Yeah, right."

19

Paige loved the tea and the sushi at C. Shore, in that order. The fare met Angel's basic dining requirements: a bottomless kir royale and eating with her hands. The restaurant became "their place." Initially, it was their celebration destination. They came after big book signings or to toast another click up the bestseller list. Eventually, as Paige grew more and more fatigued of the drunken wastrels in Angel's more typical hangouts, the trendy sushi bar was just something they could both agree on. C. Shore was loud enough that Paige didn't actually have to listen to Angel or her loopy confederates, without being so out-of-control that he was partially deaf the next morning.

Picking a restaurant in Los Angeles is actually more a fashion choice than a food preference.

L.A.'s restaurant-goers are a fickle lot, far more attracted to who's on the banquettes than what's on the menu. In other cities, consistency, reputation or the quality of things like the food or the service count. In L.A. whether or not the celebri-slut of the moment got drunk there with the cast of her reality show is as close as a restaurant gets to a four-star review. Hot L.A. restaurants are likely to have unlisted phone numbers, a private entrance and a waiting list for reservations that may exceed the establishment's life expectancy. Hot today and bankrupt tomorrow, a location closes, renovates and reopens under "new management." It seems like a new place: a trendy new name, fresh décor, recast celebrity investor and revised food group, though often it's just the same old food whores in fresh frocks.

C. Shore Sushi had hung on to its status as an "in" restaurant, though its A-List status was long gone and the end was near.

The awkward building on Beverly had previously been Quatorze, a French fusion place done up in distressed ormolu and rusty chandeliers with a patois-spouting waitstaff from the shores of exotic Burbank and sunny Reseda. Drunk with power, the management tried to silence the voice of the people and limit the fourth estate by banning the paparazzi. Alas, ravenous media addicts began to get their ego fixes elsewhere. The crowds followed the attention-starved celebri-whores, and for the restaurateurs it was soon off with their heads and their lease.

Before Quatorze it was Mecca, with fire pits, white stucco, geometric tile mosaics and signature hummus and flat breads with everything. The scourge of the low-carb jihad \wiped out Mecca's receipts when the faithful bowed in a different direction.

Prior to Mecca, the place was a celebrity theme restaurant Cydhartha. Owned by the Asian girlfriend of an action-adventure star, it was done up like a diminutive Angkor Wat lousy with Buddhas, elephants, pad thai and glass noodle salad. But when the action star's box office cooled off, so did the relationship. With him went the backing and the blessings of Ganesh, Shiva and the *Times*.

In its latest incarnation, C. Shore Sushi was just beyond its zenith. With no new ascendant on the horizon, their reign of tempura would continue until they were officially sunk by an as-yet-undiscovered new trend. For the moment, the fashion remained loud-sushi-place-with-drunken-screaming-Asian-chefs-and-round-eyed-matinee-idol-handsome-waitstaff.

"I invited Andy to join us," Angel said as the waiter pulled out the table to let her slide onto one of the black leather benches built into the blood-red walls. Rice paper screens, gouached with violent erotic manga images, made the black-lacquered tables with chairs opposite the benches into booths or little private dining rooms.

Theirs was always the first booth in the dining room in full view of most of the patio, the waiting area cocktail lounge and the entire sushi bar. In fact, as you walked in the front door, their booth was not only framed but magnified by the giant saltwater aquarium that formed the wall behind the hostess stand. It was a perk and a tribute that seemed less advantageous that particular evening. Paige scooched around the table and onto the comfy banquette beside her. They sat facing the stares of everyone except the people in the booth next to them.

"Andy, hunh?" he grunted, knowing he was in for a long night. "I'm glad we hired a limo." Paige knew from experience that after a few trips to the bathroom, Angel and Andy would be speaking a language that only they understood.

Angel had worn him down with an endless and relentless barrage of reasons they deserved a night out, countering Paige's expressed concern for their safety, if not the propriety of their being out in public the night after her fiancé's murder. They were murder suspects and possibly even targets. In the end, he just wanted out of her beach house.

Andy Lavautour, Angel's drinking buddy and go-to photographer, had become known as a high-camp, high-concept art house habitué who fancied himself a boy genius, though he had not been a boy for a very long time. Andy's studio was better known as the scene of wild parties and questionable activity than genius.

But Andy could still remind Angel of the time before Photoshop had become more important than hair and makeup to her modeling career and so his place at her table was assured. Paige found Andy polite but a little sketchy and a lot obvious.

"He's bringing Wiggie," Angel said hopefully, detecting Paige's less-than-enthusiastic response. "I tried to get the lieutenant to come along, but he was on duty or something."

Paige's eyebrows went up involuntarily as he pretended to look at the menu. "Big Wig?" he asked, ignoring her mention of Lieutenant Slade. "Wig" was their nickname for Ludwig Burgh, famous Eastern European supermodel and as much of an ex as Angel would ever let such a fine specimen become. "You're such a guy," he sighed.

"And you are such a lady."

Paige had grown accustomed to Angel's very masculine approach to sex. She would do or say anything to get a man she wanted into—or back into—bed with her. Because that often included saying "I love you," or "the part is yours," or "let's get back together" or frankly whatever her ever-hopeful suitors longed to hear, her bed and her personal life were peopled by a cadre of the walking wounded. It kept things interesting but also in a state of constant PTSD rotation as she returned again and again to her greatest hits.

Angel was a woman who wanted what she wanted when she wanted it. And just because Seth was dead and there was no new romantic prospect on her horizon didn't mean she was willing to go without the benefits.

She maintained sexually pragmatic, on-again-off-again relationships with many of her exes. Though they were long divorced, her ex-husband was still included in the mix. Angel confided to Paige that her relationship had always really been with Bill E's noteworthy penis. For his part, Bill E always got a little media boost from their on-again periods and, no small thing, he got to sleep with Angel. In many ways, not being together made them the perfect couple.

And Bill E was the rule, not the exception. Angel would meet some cute actor or model or reporter or circus performer or hustler and bring him home and play with him like a cat with a stunned chipmunk. Puffed up with his own importance, each successive trick would bask in the warmth of her spotlight as she indulged him and the public in the fantasy of their affair. Privately, she ridiculed the trick's intelligence, sexual skills and genitalia.

Then, when it suited her, she tossed each guy aside like a used tampon. She saved their anguished phone messages and pleading emails to share with friends as she added their pain to her repertoire of mockery.

In between feasting on the flesh and egos of her preferred prey, she often turned to "recycled cock"—Angel's colorful name for her former lovers, like Bill E and Wig.

At a holiday or a celebratory point in her life when Angel found herself between chipmunks, she'd call Bill E to accompany her to an event or to spend Easter or a birthday with her. If Bill E was in between groupies, he'd come oozing back, thick with his own dubious motives, aside from the obvious. A flurry of paparazzi sightings would follow, along with rumors of their impending reconciliation and secret plan to remarry. Bill E would confirm it. She would deny it. Then, like all the men in her life, she'd tire of Bill E and toss him back on the recycling heap. But from Bill E alone, she never asked for the key back. In fact, he was the only one who'd ever had one.

Perhaps most amazing to Paige was that Bill E and so many others were willing to return for second and third rounds of her stinging and humiliating rejection.

Seth had been the ultimate outlier in a very predictable pattern of behavior. The revelation that a three-picture deal was part of Angel's marital pact with Seth was at least a partial explanation for their much more formal engagement, but Paige was far from convinced. For him, her casual if not callous response to Seth's murder raised more questions about the truth of their relationship than she had answered in their forced jailhouse reconciliation.

Wig had been in regular rotation since his rumored engagement to Angel many years before. His addition to the evening would not only improve Paige's view across the booth but, owing to the fact that he was actually a model and didn't just play one on TV, he was more careful about his party habits due to their impact on his looks. Wig would have too much champagne, but he wouldn't actually get any stupider as the night went on. Paige would have someone he could talk to in the same language for the duration of the evening who, while he was not a master of said language, or even a native speaker, was not at all hard to look at.

Paige knew that Andy was bringing Wig for Paige's benefit and probably at Angel's request. It was almost as if Angel was thinking of Paige, considering his feelings—almost. It certainly wouldn't ruin Angel's fun when Wig inevitably went home with her that night.

Angel and Wig first met at a party at the World Music Awards in France. Wig was at the party as the date of a friend of hers. Angel dragged the unsuspecting clotheshorse up to her room. A house did not have to fall on Wig. He knew which fork to use for salad, how to hit his marks on the runway and that when someone famous, rich or important brought him back up to their hotel room, he was to take off his clothes and await further instructions.

Angel, of course, thought his enthusiastic nudity was a tribute to her irresistibility. Wig was just glad he'd been brought back to a girl's room for a change. He didn't feel strongly about it; it was just that night's mood.

When they emerged from her suite three days later, Angel and Wig announced their engagement to the world press. Bill E, Angel's husband at the time, was particularly upset about the news, though nothing ever came of it. Perhaps everyone concerned just forgot. Angel still delighted in the fact that, as an experienced runway model, "Wiggie" could get out of his clothes in record time and look pretty damn good doing it. All she had to do was get him up to her room, which was never very hard, and he knew just what to do.

"Green tea," the waiter said more than asked. He set the small raku teapot, unbidden, onto the table in front of Paige, along with a matched, handless cup warmed in anticipation of the delicate brew.

"Thank you," Paige said, enjoying the kind of service that Angel's celebrity accorded him in Los Angeles. He had not ordered the tea, but he would have and they knew it.

"And a kir royale," the waiter said, taking the perfectly chilled champagne flute off the tray and setting it in front of Angel.

"Goodie," she said, clapping. She took a girlish slurp and wiped her lip elegantly with the back of her hand. "Paige, you order. Lots of stuff."

"You and Andy won't eat anything," Paige said. He knew full well that food only spoiled whatever buzz the two of them were chasing, and that they'd be making fun of the entrée after only a couple of trips to the bathroom.

"Yeah, but Wiggie will eat. And I want him to keep his strength up. Order lots of pencil sharpeners," she said, her not-too-subtle code for aphrodisiacs. She toasted the air, downed about half the cocktail and signaled the waiter to bring another.

Angel was definitely the boy in that relationship, Paige thought. She was interested in Wig's looks and little else. In Wig's presence, Angel was always grabbing his ass or putting her arm around him because she knew, as did every old perv with a trophy wife, that Wig's attentions made her look better. Her lack of respect in his absence was breathtaking. She'd once convinced Wig to appear on an extremely demeaning reality television show for washed-up celebrity has-beens so she could make fun of him each week when she watched the show with a group of her friends.

Paige figured that, like any aging lothario, Angel reassured herself that if she was hot enough to snare someone who looked like Wig, well then she could still believe in the twentysomething version of herself that only still existed with a staple in its navel.

The two men arrived. "Hello, darling," Andy said furtively, looking around to see who was noticing him.

"Wiggie," Angel squealed, jumping up and down. Her bobbling breasts tested the skimpy out-of-season top she'd worn to call attention to them.

Andy looked annoyed at being ignored.

"*Engel*," Wig said earnestly. At nearly six and a half feet, he easily reached past Andy, taking both Angel's hands and gently kissing each one. "Are you okay?" It looked to Paige as though Wig actually had tears in his eyes.

"I'm fine," Angel said, looking past him for the waiter and her next drink.

"I'm so sorry to hear about Seth," Wig said, nodding seriously as he rubbed her hands against his face. "If there's anything I can do."

"No, no," Angel said. Taking her hands back, she gave them a bit of a shake. "This evening is about forgetting for a minute."

"Yes, how are you, m'dear?" Andy asked. He, too, took Angel's hand, obviously slipping something into it.

She clapped her hand to her lips. "*Greath*," she mouthed around the pill before tossing it back with the last of her champagne cocktail. The waiter replaced it with a fresh one.

"That should help you forget," Andy said.

She'd not even asked him what the pill was, Paige thought, as he sipped his green tea and felt invisible. Was that trust or reasoning born of too many brain cells lost to too many other mystery pills and kir royales?

"Vodka on the rocks," Andy sighed. He lowered himself into the chair opposite Angel's, divesting himself of scarf and leather jacket.

"Good to see you, Paige, *goedenavond*," Wig said. He clasped Paige's hand with a couple of the fingers of his enormous right hand. "What is it that you're drinking?"

"Green tea." Paige smiled at Wig's lack of killer instinct. He wondered what sort of cutthroat the supermodel turned into on his own turf in the dressing rooms in Paris and Milan. "*Goedenavond*. Good to see you too, Wig."

"I'll have a second cup and maybe you could please bring another pot?" Wig said to the waiter, picking up the rustic teapot by its twisted bamboo handle and testing to see how much remained. "Yes, another. You know, green tea is rich in antioxidants and clears your system of free radicals."

"Don't spoil it," Paige said playfully. "I was just enjoying a good pot of tea."

"It can help avoid *Al's Heimers*," Wig asserted. "And keep you from aging."

"That's my secret," Paige whispered. "I'm actually a hundred and three years old and I haven't seen *Al* since I was eighty."

Wig gave him a blank smile. Angel snorted champagne out of her nose. Still laughing, she leaped to her feet, trying unsuccessfully to avoid getting Cristal on her Gucci tube top.

"We'd better go get you cleaned up," Andy said. He pointed at his nose with all the subtly of coronary thrombosis as he helped her off to the bathroom.

"Angel, I thought that was you," came a familiar male voice from behind the obscene screen separating theirs from the next booth. "I'd recognize that snort anywhere."

"Oh, hi," Angel said, standing in front of the booth, offering an anemic little finger wiggle of a wave. "Good to see you."

"What's up this evening?" the familiar voice asked in a way that made it sound like he'd asked a much more personal question.

As the tone of Angel's conversation dropped below the kamikaze shouts of the sushi chefs, Paige leaned back to try to peer around the screen and see who was on the other side. The screen met the wall too closely to afford a glimpse. Paige decided to do the only socially correct thing that one could do at the hippest and loudest sushi restaurant in Hollywood. He stood on the banquette and looked over the top of the screen.

Angel was seated at the neighboring table, leaning to within an eyelash of the man sprawled across the bench. With his arms stretched out, draped across the padded leather seatback, he let Angel come to him like a patient fisherman with good bait.

Andy, sitting beside Angel, tried to look included as she examined the man's tonsils. She ignored the man's dinner companion, relating some tale or other in a chemically animated, whispery Marilyn voice. "Do all the rooms come with one of these?" she asked, concluding the story loudly enough to be heard.

The man threw his head back and laughed. His eyes met Paige's.

"Well, hiya, Paigeen," the man bellowed. "I didn't realize it was that kind of place, but what the hell." He punched a hole through the rice paper with his fist. "Put your dick through that and I'll blow you."

"Hello, William," Paige said, more amused than irritated. "This is why we can't go to nice places."

"This is a nice place?" William asked, guffawing. "And they let you in? Come to think of it, I guess they do serve shrimp here, eh, *maricón*?"

"The Spanish for shrimp is *camarón*, you idiot," Paige said, leaning on the top of the screen a little too hard and almost falling over.

"No wonder. That explains how I wound up with you instead of the tempura ebi," William said, howling at his own joke. "Oh, waiter, there's a fag in my soup."

"That's it, I'm calling GLAAD. You straight boys have to learn," Paige huffed theatrically.

Paige had met William Clifton during writer's meetings with Angel. He was her across-the-street neighbor, sometime overnight guest and the highest paid actor on the planet. It was a funny thing about her neighborhood and the little beach community around her. It was just people living kind of ordinary lives. Thanks to film and television, many of the locals were familiar to a sizeable percentage of the population of the planet, but they were, in fact, still just people. Paige and William had laughed about the idea of making a reality show that was just the security tapes from all the grocery stores, coffee shops, banks and drug stores in Malibu.

"Waiter, we've got a defective screen here—it has a hole in it. Can you take it away and push these tables together?" William went on. "You know Earl, don't you?" He said to Paige and his table. "Earl is my lawyer."

"Earl is my lawyer too," Angel said with a little laugh, smacking the back of William's hand. "I introduced you."

"I know Earl, too," Paige said in a NutraSweet tone. "He helped screw me out of two years' worth of income while begrudging me my pittance when I was stupid enough to fall for her book-writing scam." As the screen was taken away, Paige resumed his seat, now next to William, whom he actually quite liked.

"Now Paige, that's not fair," Earl said, surprisingly jovial considering Paige's in-one-breath excoriation. "I was just following orders. It was Grizelda's evil plan to screw you out of any profits on the books."

"Oh God, that old troglodyte," Paige moaned. He popped a couple of mushy edamame into his mouth. "What the hell ever happened to her?"

"We parted company before the first book," Angel said listlessly. Her pill was kicking in. "It was all starting to be about her. Everywhere we went there was an entourage and it was for her. I'm not that kind of person. I can just show up and sleep on the sofa."

"Yeah, right," Paige declared, tossing two of the steaming soybeans at her. "As long as they send a private jet to fly you there, pay your personal hair and makeup person to accompany you and paint a human face on that fiberglass husk and the sofa is in the parlor of your five-room suite at the Savoy on someone else's tab, yep, you're game to just rough it most anywhere."

There was more than a little laughter. Angel sputtered a bit but, to her credit, she joined in the laughter at her own expense. Paige thought it was her best—and possibly only positive—trait.

"I'm going to the bathroom to suck the rest of my drink out of this dress," she said, rising daintily. "Order me another one while I'm gone."

"A dress or a drink?' William asked.

"As long as *you're* paying," Angel said, wobbling down the aisle with Andy in tow, "suit yourself."

"Love to watch her walk away," William mused aloud.

"As long as she leaves." Paige shrugged as he turned back to Earl. "So, Earl, you said the book deal was Grizelda's idea?"

"Yeah," Earl said, joining in on the edamame.

"I always thought that the publishers came to Angel," Paige said. "That it was their idea and Angel just went along."

"No. Maybe that's what she told Angel, but it was Grizelda," Earl said, rolling his eyes. "It was her idea to brand Angel and set up all those friggin' deals for dolls and books and perfume and clothes and calendars and playing cards and dinnerware and you name it. Huge headache for me. Angel never showed up to do any of the work. That was an even bigger headache for Grizelda. Then the lawsuits started. Why haven't you sued her yet?"

"Can't afford it," Paige said.

"Hey, you're talking about the woman I'm going be having meaningless sex with later this evening, if one of us doesn't pass out first," William said.

"You are such a romantic." Paige clinked his teacup against William's glass.

Wig sat up like a thoroughbred hound on the scent. He regarded Paige warily.

Paige caught Wig looking.

Wig shot him a curious little smile.

"Yeah, I'm pretty irresistible," William agreed. "It's amazing how much twenty million a picture and points against the gross can up your fuckability quotient."

"Well, Grizelda sure dodged that bullet," Paige said, ignoring him and returning to his topic and Earl. As he spoke, he skinned another edamame. Wig caught Paige's hand, pulled it to his mouth and sucked the soybeans out of the pod. Confused and startled by the gesture, Paige smiled nervously and pushed the basket of edamame nearer to Wig.

"What do you mean?" Earl asked, not missing Wig's move but trying not to react.

Paige played it off, tossing the empty pod aside.

Wig stared at Paige intently.

"Well, she got out before all the lawsuits at least," Paige told Earl. He began demonstrating to Wig how to open the edamame pod, emptying it into his hand.

Wig pouted a moment and then began peeling.

"She didn't get out of anything," Earl said. "She was a partner in all of it. Her firing didn't really change her participation. She even maintained final edit on those books you wrote."

"Really?" Paige said. He choked slightly as Wig unexpectedly began feeding him. "Uh, thanks, Wig."

"I still don't see what this has to do with me," William said.

"Are you still here?" Paige asked. He turned his head to face William. Wig hit him in the side of the mouth with a handful of soybeans.

"Well, I didn't mean to interrupt you and the little Dutch boy," William said with a vaudeville eyebrow flash, poking Paige suggestively. "Looks like the dykes are safe tonight."

"What?" Paige asked, confused and flustered. He turned back to Wig just in time to get not only edamame but also a sizeable portion of Wig's index finger in his mouth.

"What did I miss?" Angel demanded, not-so-sweetly shoving into their newly enlarged booth beside William and snuggling up next to him. "What are they putting in your tea, Paige? Viagra root?"

"What is that supposed to mean?" Paige snapped, once he'd managed to withdraw Wig's suggestively long finger from his mouth. "It was an accident."

"Oh?" Angel said, slipping her hand into William's pocket. "What did you intend to put in your mouth?"

"Mmm," William moaned. He gave a start and a little shudder as Angel worked her hand deeper. "I finally see what this has to do with me."

"*Angel*," Paige said irritably, adding extra syllables.

He turned to Wig for support and got only an endearing smile.

Paige raised an eyebrow.

Wig's expression was not unclear to Paige and the prospect of spending the night with a supermodel not at all unpleasant. Somehow, the fight just went out of Paige. He wasn't sure what was going on exactly, but he could not for the life of him think of a reason to complain about it. Forgetting what he was going to say, he turned back to find an evil gleam in William's eye and an injured glare in Angel's that Paige was at a loss to understand, given the way the evening seemed to be unfolding.

"Well, my work is done here," Earl said, rushing to gather his things and get out of the situation before there was yet another murder. "I'm meeting Lefty at the bar and I see he's here. William, thanks for dinner. I'll get these contracts copied and messengered over to the studio in the morning. I'll send you copies once they've signed."

"Lefty's here?" Angel growled.

"Oh, yeah, that's so good," William said—regarding what, exactly, was unclear.

Earl chose to consider William's reply a conclusion to their business. "Great. Have a good night," he said, and fled the scene.

"Who's this Lefty?" Wig asked.

Angel nuzzled William's ear to show her irritation.

"Lefty's my manager," William moaned. "Easy, save some for later."

"He's also the only man who did to Angel what every man who knows her ends up wanting to do to her," Paige said, getting even.

Wig looked at Paige attentively.

Angel glared another baffling warning in his direction.

"What about me?" William said, giving Angel a squeeze.

"Oh, not that," Paige said, puttering his lips dismissively. "Everyone's done that."

"Hey," Angel said sharply.

"No, Lefty Flynn got even with Angel," Paige went on. "She tried to fuck him over and he took all her money."

"Bitch," Angel said, biting William's ear.

"Glass houses," Paige said.

Wig beamed at him.

Paige was uncertain what was going on with his astonishingly beautiful tablemate but he was determined to encourage it. If getting Big Wig in the mood meant tormenting Angel with the truth, Paige could not see a downside. "'Night, Earl," he called with a little laugh, even though the lawyer was out of earshot. "Give Lefty my best. I'll see you in court as soon as I can afford to sue." His laughter at his own wit was cut short when Wig almost choked him with a California roll. Clearly, whatever he was doing was working.

"Great," Andy said, returning from the bathroom and contemplating the erotic tableau at the table. Shaking his head, he scanned the bar hopefully. "Paris, darling!" he shouted, running from the dining room. Only Paige noticed and he wasn't sorry to see him go.

Two Years, 10 Months and a Couple of Weeks Earlier

Beginning on the Wrong Foot

Paige's first two meetings with Angel did little more than raise his starfucker stock and dinner party invitations; his eviction was still on the calendar.

"Honoria?" Paige said to his editor's voicemail. "I know you're getting these messages. It's heartless of you to ignore me. Clearly, I don't have the job or you'd have called me. But I had to pay for the lunch and take a cab home from my own kidnapping. I could really use the refund for things, like, you know, food. Please call me or call Grizelda and see if you can't help out getting me a little payback. Thanks."

He hung up with both hands and stared at the phone for a bit. It was time for a miracle and there wasn't even so much as a storm cloud on the horizon.

Failing divine intervention or even the courtesy of a returned phone call, Paige found himself with only one alternative. He gathered all the change from the sofa and the console in the car, walked to the neighborhood market, bought a quart of whole milk and a bag each of Oreos and Nutter Butters. Returning home, he put on his faux mink slippers and curled up on his bed in front of the television to watch what was left of the cable he'd gotten word was being turned off at any moment.

He woke up covered with cookie crumbs in the middle of *Madame X* after crying himself to sleep over *Imitation of Life* during a Lana Turner film festival on TCM. As he emerged from his sugar coma, Paige realized someone was alternately ringing his bell and pounding on the door.

He found the remote tangled in his bedclothes and turned off the TV set.

"Mr. Blanche? Are you all right?"

Fighting for consciousness, he staggered down the hall. Through his insulin-induced fog and the living room's casement windows, he found himself looking into the blue eyes and over the easy, sun-bleached good looks of the young beach bum who was earning his sex-wax money running errands. Clearly, Surfer Dude was knocking as much to rouse Paige from his stupor as to get him to the door. He succeeded on both counts.

"Great," Paige said, realizing too late the he had Oreo under his fingernails and milk spots on the T-shirt and pajamas bottoms he was wearing. He brushed at the light dusting of crumbs as the door swung open. Why was it that the cute delivery people only showed up when he looked like he was home waiting for news of his slip-and-fall settlement?

He took a deep breath. "Hi," Paige said. He offered Surfer Dude a winning smile. "What's up?"

"I've got a delivery for you," Surfer Dude said. He handed Paige a receipt book. "Sign, right here."

"What did I..." Paige began, trepidatious of possible eviction proceedings. He broke off as he saw the rolling cart, groaning under the weight of roses and la-de-da floral oases pricey enough to cover his rent for the rest of the year. "Oh, my."

"Yeah, you must have been pretty impressive at something to rate all that," Surfer Dude said with a wink and a careless toss of his shaggy locks in the direction of the head-of-state's-funeral's-worth of flowers.

"I guess," Paige answered, absently. He took the pad to sign for his delivery, his eye fixed on the awe-inspiring arrangement.

"And there's this," Surfer Dude said. He handed Paige a Louis Vuitton gift box with a bow almost as showy as the flowers. A rich creamy linen envelope with his name hand-printed on it peeked from beneath the thick ribbon.

Dear Paige:

Sorry I had to eat and run. That was so hot I can't wait to do it again and again!

How about breakfast at my place on Friday?

XXXO,

Zac

P.S. A little something for cab fare.

The box contained an LV wallet with ten hundred-dollar bills inside. He wasn't a fan of Vuitton, but the wallet's contents were more than enough to throw the wolves off the scent and possibly afford him some food beside self-pity Oreos.

"So, dude, what did you do?" Surfer Dude asked, trying to sneak a peek at the note.

"I could show you," Paige said, leaning seductively, he thought, on the doorjamb and smiling.

"Did you have something chocolate earlier?" Surfer Dude asked. He gestured at his teeth.

"Oh, right," Paige said, the mood and the smile gone. He tucked the wallet into the waistband of the pajama bottoms he remembered he was wearing. "Oreos. Could you put the flowers on the coffee table?"

He dashed in to rinse his mouth and returned in time to catch Surfer Dude sneaking a look at the card with the roses.

"Are these from…?"

"Oh no, it's a joke," Paige sighed. "They're actually from Angel Panderson."

"Well, I've got to shake your hand," the delivery guy said. "If you've got either of them sending you money and flowers, you're the man I want to be."

"Thanks," Paige said, grinning sheepishly at his unearned reputation. "Don't give me too much credit. The truth is—"

The phone rang just in time to kill it.

"Don't be modest," Surfer Dude said, backing toward the door with a little bow. "I'll just let you get that."

"Hang on, let me find my actual wallet," Paige sighed. He scanned the room for the phone and a tip source more in his budget than one of the Benjamins in the gift wallet. The cordless was never in the chargers on his desk or by his bed. "No worries," Surfer Dude said, holding up his own crisp hundred as he backed away. "Zac took care of me, too. I'm under strict orders not to take a thing from you. Well, any money, anyway." Surfer Dude shot him a suggestive grin before he turned to go.

"Thanks," Paige said, trying not to melt.

The phone kept ringing as Paige watched him go.

"You better get that," Surfer Dude called over his shoulder.

"Hello?" Paige said into the receiver he finally found on the kitchen counter.

"Paige?"

"Yes?"

"Did you get my flowers?"

It didn't make any difference that he was gay. She was irresistible. Her hoarse whispery voice in his ear, the gifts, the flowers, not to mention the boner-by-association the hot delivery guy now had for him—the seduction was on and it was working.

The Following Friday

He arrived at her beach house late that Friday morning feeling like a bit of a celebrity himself. The uniformed gate guard at the entrance to the private beachfront enclave gave Paige a knowing look when he uttered Angel's name.

Angel's pricey, fashionable and famous neighborhood, as is so often the case in Los Angeles, turned out to be completely underwhelming. Houses that ranged from modest to ridiculous were jammed in so closely to one another that it was not always possible to tell where one began and the next ended. In fact, the only thing that kept the place from looking like semi-detached condos on steroids was the fact that the architectural styles varied so jarringly. A New England saltbox looked as though it had a steel-and-glass wing and a stucco-and-tile-roofed garage.

Amid this strange and discordant architectural cacophony, Angel's house was, at best, inoffensive and on the modest end of the scale. Paige eventually managed to find a parking place, another less-than-fashionable aspect of the oh-so-chic compound. He rang the bell at Angel's front door, which opened literally onto the street. Had it opened outward, it would have scraped on the pavement.

"Paige?" the intercom by the door crackled. He could hear her voice from the window above as well.

"Zac?" he answered. "Is that you?"

She buzzed him in.

"Paige," Angel called to him as he made his way across a sort of courtyard front porch into the main door, which stood open.

What the house lacked on the outside it more than made up for on the inside. Standing in the doorway, Paige could see the tiny place was bursting with chintzy, overstuffed furniture and whitewashed and sandblasted tables and cabinets. Rusty accessories, mismatched crystal chandeliers and bushels of dead pink roses adorned every flat surface. It was a style of decorating called "shabby chic," but which Paige referred to as "they-saw-you-coming" school of interior design. It was like she lived in a very expensive yard sale.

Bounding down the stairs to meet him, she threw her arms around him as though they were old friends. In keeping with the L.A. hierarchy of fame being inversely expressed in fashion, her tangle of bleached blonde hair was stuffed haphazardly into a scrunchie on top of her head. She was clad in a beat-up, possibly recycled sweat suit that proclaimed itself "Juicy" in a banner emblazoned rather unappetizingly across her ass. "I'm so glad you could come. After those first two hell dates, I'd hardly expected you to still be speaking to me. Coffee?"

"No thanks," Paige said, following her the few feet into the kitchen/living/dining room.

"That's right—you're a tea drinker," she said, topping off her own huge mug from the coffee maker. "I could make a cup if you'd like."

"Thanks, yes, that would be great," Paige said. He took a stool at the island bar that was literally in the middle of the crowded room. He watched as she opened a series of kitchen cabinets, each one as randomly packed and cluttered as the rest of the house.

"I'm not sure how to start this," she chattered as she mounted the search for teabags. "I've been upstairs all morning going through boxes and boxes of notes, old letters, pictures. I realized I've been taking notes on my life for years—well, really all my life. Anyway, I'm not sure where to begin exactly, but maybe you can sort it out as we go along? What kind of tea do you like?"

Angel seemed not to be looking just for the tea. It was as though she was discovering what might be in each cabinet, like an archeologist exploring a strange and unfamiliar site. She found various boxes of chamomile, behind several of the mystery doors, but no proper tea.

"Well, there's nothing but herb tea, I'm afraid," she said, crinkling her nose endearingly as she leaned across the counter. Her face was very near his. Her cartoonishly large breasts strained the zipper that was already half-down the front of the flimsy sweatshirt. "What's your favorite? I'll have some here for next time. I thought we could meet here. I can cook you breakfast and tell you the story of my life. What? Every day? Every week?"

"Jasmine," he said, pulling one thread from her tangle of questions.

"What is?"

"That's my favorite tea," he said with a little laugh, realizing he'd answered the wrong question. As pedestrian as the surroundings and her appearance were, he was still more than a little starstruck. There was a kind of disconnect to it. He tried to resolve the very, very public person everyone on the planet had seen in a centerfold, on the big screen, all over TV, and having more sex than many popular porn stars, with the person who was standing on the other side of the kitchen counter drinking coffee from her three-dollar Starbucks mug.

"Oh, right," she said as she began ransacking the kitchen drawers in the same kind of unfamiliar way she'd looked through the cabinets. "There!" she crowed, triumphantly pulling a pen from one of the drawers and holding it up like Excalibur.

"What would you like?" she said, taking an envelope from a pile of mail and aiming the pen at it.

A quick glance at the huge double refrigerator revealed a souvenir shop's worth of random, kitschy refrigerator magnets, pinning up dozens of similar bits of recycled junk mail and other paper scraps, each scrawled with notes.

"For breakfast?"

"What? Oh, no," she laughed, realizing how it looked. "Hi, I'm Angel and I'll be your server this morning. No, what kind of tea?"

"Oh, right," he said, wondering about her short-term memory. "Jasmine or Jasmine pearls, but that's not bags."

"Okay, babe, I'm out."

Paige spun on his stool in the direction of the unexpected male voice behind him.

He found himself staring into the sleep-stained features of a man still wearing clothes he'd clearly put on for the first time at least a day ago.

"Okay, babe. See you," Angel said, looking up from trying to get the pen to write.

"I'll call you later on?" the man asked as he reached the foot of the stairs.

"Yeah, sure," Angel said. Discarding the dead pen, she crossed in the man's direction but stopped short. She turned abruptly away from him to rifle through the drawer of a frowsy looking sideboard.

The man seemed a bit lost. Paige felt as though he'd suddenly become invisible. Angel was simply oblivious.

"I'm Paige," he said, more to fill the uncomfortable silence than to introduce himself.

"Oh, I'm sorry, Paige," Angel said, scoring another pen. "This is Ron."

"*Ken*," the man said.

Angel began testing a cache of pens she'd discovered, throwing each dud over her shoulder as she went.

"Nice to meet you," Paige said, trying not to laugh. Clearly this was last night's trick and clearly Angel neither knew nor cared who he was or what he cared to be called. "How do you two know each other?" Paige asked, just to see the trick squirm.

"Just friends," Ron-Ken said, after a desperate look to Angel, who was not having much luck finding a working pen. "And you?"

"Oh, we're thinking about writing a novel together," Paige said coyly. "This is kind of our first writer's meeting."

"Well, I don't want to interrupt," Ron-Ken said, backing toward the door. "So, I'll see you around."

"Damn it!" Angel said. "You'd think we'd have one working pen around here."

"Well, that must be why you haven't written a novel before now," Paige suggested as he watched Ron-Ken hover near the door awaiting some form of goodbye from Angel.

"Yeah, that must be it." Angel laughed. "Do you have a pen?"

"Now you mention it, I do, actually," Paige said, handing her the one he had clipped to the cover of the composition book he'd brought for his notes.

Angel laughed as she took the pen. "Okay, one more time, what kind of tea?" As she looked around the counter for the used envelope, she discovered Ron-Ken loitering near the door. "Ron, you're still here."

"Um, Ken. Yeah."

Paige was actually beginning to feel sorry for the guy.

"Is there something you wanted?" she asked, as though he'd just stopped by instead of coming down from her bed.

"No, just saying goodbye," he said, with a pleading look that gave Paige pause.

Angel smiled sweetly and sidled over to him girlishly. All was forgiven, even getting his name wrong twice. She gave him a kiss and a cuddle and said something inaudible to him as she took his hand and led him the two steps outside the door. She gave him one perfectly-practiced-last-smile as she closed the door in his face.

Ron-Ken longingly watched her through the glass door as she walked away. Paige knew Ron-Ken was saving the memory. Oddly content, he slunk away. He would always be able to say that he slept with Angel Panderson. She would never mention it or possibly even remember it again.

Angel opened the refrigerator to reveal a daunting collection of takeout containers, expired milk and yogurt cartons and a highly questionable series of mismatched Tupperware. "Let's go out for lunch," Angel suggested.

"So, that was uncomfortable," Paige said as they piled into the front seat of her enormous white-on-white Malibu Barbie SUV.

"What? Oh, that." She waved the topic away dismissively as she backed the room-sized vehicle from her driveway. "Some guy I met last night. Not a keeper," she said, with a little laugh.

"Oh? Why not?" Paige asked. He was amazed at her candor and pleased with how quickly she seemed to be warming up to him.

"Well, he came on strong, but that's all he had." She shrugged. "All hat and no cattle. And he was sure no bull either."

"Hate that," Paige agreed.

"Don't you?" she went on, maneuvering the gas-guzzling tank easily into the traffic as she headed north on PCH. "I can tell you that even after spending the night together, he has no idea what I like to do in bed. Does that ever happen to you?"

"God, yes," he admitted. "Usually. This one guy finished in about a minute and a half, rolled off and asked, 'Did you get off?' Like, when was that supposed to have happened?"

Angel howled and blew the horn. She hit the button to lower the window and screamed out, "My G-spot is not between my shoulder blades!"

He couldn't help laughing. He couldn't help being taken in by her adolescent freedom, certainty and invincibility.

She darted in front of oncoming traffic in a rather daring left turn across the busy six-lane highway into the recessed driveway of Geoffrey's. The restaurant's name was pronounced *Joff-ree* by the locals despite the spelling, or perhaps because of it. It was the sort of place that would be chic even if it wasn't frequented by all the rich-and-famous residents of the California Riviera between Santa Monica and the Ventura County line. Hanging from a cliff above the Pacific Ocean with the grace of an Olympic diver, Geoffrey's served good food with gourmet views on the side.

The entry connects the highway above with a brick motor court by means of a brief horseshoe drive leading down the steep hillside. Paige drank it in as he stepped down from the running board. The blooming oleanders, lush palms, brick courtyard and effortless elegance of the place put him at ease as the valets helped them from the car.

"It's beautiful," Paige said, giving Angel a little one-armed squeeze as she walked up to stand beside him.

"You've never been?" She seemed surprised. "It's one of my favorites."

But their perfect moment changed in an instant.

It was like a summer thunderstorm. A flash of lights erupted out of the windows of the little herd of black SUVs poised on the horseshoe drive above them.

"Oh, my hair," Angel bleated. She darted quickly away, leaving Paige behind transfixed. He stood staring, still not entirely sure what was happening as attendants chased the paparazzi away.

As Angel's white behemoth pulled away, Paige turned back from the scene to follow her into the restaurant. The maître d' station was just off the courtyard along a winding, palm-shrouded walkway leading to the massive deck that served as most of the restaurant.

"Do you have a reservation?" the hostess asked.

"I doubt it," he admitted, as he turned to locate Angel. He was actually a bit surprised not to find her already there. No sign. "Did you see…" he trailed off, not wanting to sound like a stalker or a fan. "The woman who got out of that white Range Rover?" he started again. "Where did she go?"

"Oh, she left," the hostess answered cheerfully.

"I have got to stop having lunch with that woman," Paige sighed, still an unemployed writer, miles from home and his car.

20

By the end of the evening at C. Shore, Wig had fed Paige a lovely dinner of sushi, sashimi and house rolls. Paige hadn't a clue what was going on with Wig, but felt it would be rude to complain even when the big Viking fed him eel, which he despised. Annoyed at first, Angel was, eventually, too horned-out from the combination of whatever Andy had given her and making out with William to care what Paige and Wig were up to.

"Here," Wig said playfully, taking Paige's face in his hand. He dabbed at a bit of wasabi with one of the hot towels the waiter had brought at the end of the meal.

William, by virtue of being the richest person at the table, paid the check.

The car Angel had hired to bring them to the restaurant was summoned. The members of the Clifton/Panderson party tried to calm themselves enough to walk to the valet stand.

It was clear to Paige what was going on with Angel and William. He was less certain about Wig. Fearful of breaking whatever spell had been cast, he was afraid to say anything. Instead, he exchanged awkward, almost adolescent looks with the supermodel who'd more or less fed him dinner.

"I've got my car," William said softy to Angel. "What do you want to do now?"

Angel only laughed throatily in reply.

"Oh, that," William said. He put a finger on his chin in an absurd parody of shy. "Well, I guess we could. If you really want to."

"I've got a car and a driver," Angel said. "Are you out at the beach house?"

"Yeah, that would be best," William said.

"Perfect." Standing on tiptoe, she touched his lips with her finger. "They can take the car back to my house or wherever and I can ride back with you. It seems silly to take two cars when you're right across the street."

"Believe me," William said, running his hand down her back. "It won't seem silly once we get in the car."

Angel only laughed in reply.

"You two ready to go?" he asked Paige and Wig. He gave Paige a pat on the shoulder.

"Hmm? Oh, sure," Paige answered. The reminder of their imminent departure raised the unspoken question of accommodations for the night. He didn't want to presume, but he wanted to do whatever he could to encourage what seemed to be happening with Wig. "You ready?" he asked Wig as vaguely as was possible.

"I'll see if the limo's here yet," Angel said, dialing the driver's number on her mobile. "Paige, we're going to follow you two in William's car. You're welcome to my house tonight if you want it."

"That's great with me," Paige said, hoping for agreement or acknowledgement of some kind from Wig.

Wig only smiled obligingly. Effortlessly, he pulled out the table and offered Paige his hand. Paige was keenly aware that Wig had arrived with Andy, who had disappeared rather than accept fifth-wheel status. He decided that Wig could get in whatever car he wanted. His choice would be Paige's answer.

Slowly the little party made their way out to the valet trap. One of the more lucrative forms of Hollywood commerce other than sleeping with people for money, parts, power and status was the maître d'/paparazzi symbiosis. The formula goes like this: celebrity arrives at restaurant. Maître d' calls papz. Papz show up, grease maître d's palm. Papz take pictures of celebrity when they emerge and as they wait for their valet to bring them their car. Papz make fortune on pictures and video, more than enough to cover initial maître d' investment. Ergo, "valet trap."

The hired limo was idling where they'd left it. Wig stood with Angel and William, so Paige did, too. The digital lightning of the paparazzi's flashes was blinding. Paige had learned the trick was not to react. If you squint or wince, that's the picture they use to go with the breakup or rehab rumor. Their little impromptu party behaved as though they had randomly fallen into the trap together. Angel and William chatted politely and gave little indication that they'd all but conceived twins on the banquette inside. Cell phone photos from their fellow diners—also a local cottage industry—would later add that detail to the story.

Paige and Wig stood nearby, almost acknowledging that they might have eaten dinner with one or both of the other two.

As if to make their little deer-in-the-headlights moment more awkward, Earl and Lefty emerged from the restaurant to join them at the valet trap. Lefty had a tall, striking woman on his arm, dripping diamonds and money from her genetic-lottery-win frame. The three took up a place next to Angel and company to await their turn at the valet. Everyone tried to act as if they weren't acutely aware of the others.

"So," Lefty began, because he had the least to lose. "I hear you're a fan of mine."

He extended his hand to Paige. "I'm Lou Flynn," he said, taking Paige's hand when it wasn't offered. "Lefty. And yes, I took her for every cent she tried not to pay me."

Paige laughed weakly. He was torn between taking the high road or the scenic route. He didn't want to seem petty in front of Wig by scoring points at Angel's expense, though that strategy had seemed to work at the table. Lefty made the choice for him.

"Great work with the tea," he said, still pumping Paige's hand.

"Right?" Paige said, unable to resist acknowledging his triumph. "I can't see that video often enough."

"The hearts of a grateful nation." Lefty nodded. "Or at least every-fucking-body on YouTube."

"Really?" Paige asked blushingly. He never actually blushed but he tried to sound as if he was the sort of person who did. "I've been swamped and haven't had the chance."

"Angel! Sorry for your loss!" The paparazzi intermittently shouted in an effort to get her to look their way.

"Angel, did you kill him?" they asked in almost the same tones as they offered condolence.

Angel turned away slightly.

"Oh, right," Lefty said, shaking his head. "Tragic."

William put a supportive, almost brotherly arm around Angel.

"Easy, guys," Wig said to the zealous photographers.

Wig and Angel had been romantically linked in the past, so he was the man of record in their little tableau.

"Yes, dear," the woman with Lefty said to Angel. "It's customary to wait until after you're married to kill them."

"Hello, Lucrezia," Angel said.

Ah, Paige thought. This was Seth's ex-wife and evil stepmother to one-man protest movement Jay St. James.

"Lucrezia, should I offer you my sympathies?" Angel asked. "I mean, he was actually married to you."

"Heavens no, Angel," Lucrezia said. "We're actually celebrating. Since you jumped the gun, I still get his money. You just get the prison time."

"Sounds like that makes you a better suspect," Paige said to Lucrezia.

In response, she almost looked at him. "I'll wait inside, Lefty," Lucrezia said. "Let me know when the car gets here."

"Angel." It was Busby Barclay from *Star Reporter*. The maître d' was having a very profitable night. "It's Busby. Can we have a moment?"

"It's not a good time, Buzz," Angel said with an appropriately sad smile. You don't have to talk to the paparazzi, but if you don't talk to TV? Well, your career had to be going better then Angel's to snub syndicated entertainment television. Angel was too drunk and high to talk on camera but not so drunk that she didn't know it.

Paige held his breath.

"What do the police say?" Busby asked, undaunted.

"Nothing's certain," she said, breaking off as though she might cry.

William's cranberry Bentley Continental *deus ex machina* arrived.

Paige sighed, both tension and relief.

As William's car pulled up, the driver opened the back door of Angel's hired limo. Wig drew Paige protectively to his side, guiding him toward the open door. The paparazzi caught the scent. The pack's attention shifted. Was Wig out with a man? *Who*? Had they missed the story?

"Paige," Angel said, stepping away from William. She gave him a wink and the one-minute finger as she put an arm around Paige's shoulder and leaned close to his ear. "Sorry I got bitchy in there. Looks like there's plenty to go around. Forgiven?"

"Oh, Angel," Paige sighed into her ear. "I've got so many other things to hate you for. This one is hardly worth bothering about."

They laughed wickedly.

The gunshot shattered the window of the open limo door.

Lefty went down. Blood streaked his white shirt.

The next two shots shattered the rear window and blew off a corner of the valet stand. The limo driver dove for cover. Paige and Angel looked around, too startled to react or even understand what was happening for a moment.

The press went nuts. Torn between getting the shot and getting shot, their simultaneous retreat/attack instinct turned the scene into well-lit chaos.

Wig tackled Paige to get him out of the line of fire.

Angel ran behind William, the most expensive shield in Hollywood. The two dove into William's waiting car and within seconds squealed away.

Paige winced as several more random shots peppered the C. Shore entrance.

Oblivious, Andy emerged onto the sidewalk amidst the chaos, fresh from the bathroom with a couple of intimates. A stampede of parking patrons, paparazzi and staff poured past him screaming as they rushed back into the restaurant. Behind him, the giant lobby aquarium exploded, flooding the bar and the front of the restaurant with saltwater, shattered glass and brightly colored and very surprised tropical fish.

"Goddamn it," Andy demanded, scanning the scene. "Did they leave without me?"

21

The area outside C. Shore Sushi looked like the scene of a terrorist attack. The amount of destruction was startling. The few shots fired had missed their mark, but they had connected with a surprising amount of glass.

The glass in the rear passenger door and the windshield of the limo were shattered.

The plate glass doors and windows across the entrance to the restaurant had disintegrated into a snowscape of glittering cubes. The glass shimmered amidst a bed of kelp, seashells, tchotchkes, tropical fish and thousands of gallons of brackish water. The ruins of the enormous aquarium that disgorged across the lobby and onto the street added a shipwreck's worth of flotsam and jetsam to the crime scene.

Perhaps the most amazing part of the attack was the fact that only one person had been hit in the strafing the restaurant received.

Lefty Flynn, Angel's former manager and current enemy, had been winged. The bullet had grazed his arm. "A bullet wound on my left shoulder?" he joked with Paige and the EMS technician as he was taken away. "You can't pay for that kind of publicity."

In the end it would do more permanent damage to his expensive leather jacket than his arm.

Uniformed officers waved official traffic into the restaurant's small lot, jammed with emergency vehicles and the cars of trapped patrons. To minimize the chaos, police tried to expedite the interview process so that guests caught in the restaurant could leave as soon as medical personnel cleared them for release.

Paige watched as Lieutenant Roy Slade maneuvered his hulking, stealth-black, unmarked police SUV into the crowded lot. He hated that he would not get the chance to confer with Angel before they had to talk with their personal celebrity investigator. She still had not returned. Given her condition when she left, Paige considered the very real possibility that she didn't even remember the ambush and wouldn't think to come back at all.

He and Wig were swaddled in what looked to be aluminum foil. They sat on the rear deck of an ambulance like a couple of baked potatoes while they awaited their triage exams. The fact that he knew there was nothing wrong with him did not make Paige feel better. He feared it only made the incident look staged. Worse yet, the only person hit was someone with whom Angel had a longstanding feud. Slade had already busted them for their body-discovery melodrama in the hotel lobby. Paige knew the lieutenant couldn't prove it, but he was certain Roy knew, at the very least, they weren't telling the whole truth. Now, a sniper shooting in which neither was hit, but another enemy was?

Ever more suspicious.

Paige didn't wish Angel ill—well, not bodily harm; well, not permanent damage; well, not disabling; disfiguring was still under consideration. If only she had been nicked or gotten a flesh wound. Maybe she had. Maybe that's where she was. His spirits rose. Maybe she'd been shot. Maybe William had taken her to the emergency room. He sat up with a little shiver of anticipation.

Wig mistook his excitement. He put an arm around Paige's shoulder. "You are okay," he said gently, phonetically.

Paige caught the lieutenant's eye at just that moment. Was that an eyebrow flash? Was the lieutenant surprised? Intrigued? Jealous?

"If you could leave your keys in the ignition," one of the officers on lot duty called to the lieutenant. Roy tossed the officer the ring.

"Crime scene valet?" Slade shared a laugh with his beleaguered colleague loud enough for Paige to hear. "It *is* Los Angeles. I guess it was only a matter of time."

Paige watched as the lieutenant made his way toward them. As he got close enough for a good angle, Roy was blinded by the lights from the TV crews. Hidden by the glare, Paige stared at him.

The media formed a second perimeter surrounding the one police had established to cordon off the crime scene. The press was backed up by a growing crowd of lookie-loos, a traditional L.A. presence at all morbid events and awards ceremonies. The resulting mob, combined with efforts to secure and evacuate the adjacent strip mall where, it was supposed, the sniper had been positioned, virtually closed Third Street. Traffic snarled and imprisoned many at some of Beverly Hill's finest restaurants and screwed up dinner reservations for blocks.

Emerging from the bewildering blaze of camera light with the grace of a red carpet veteran, Roy caught Paige staring. They shared a tense smile as he made his way to where Paige was being examined by an EMS tech.

Paige looked away.

Wig tightened his protective grip.

"Paige?" Roy asked, with an urgency that surprised them both. "Are you okay?"

Startled by the tone and the question, Paige laughed. "Let's go with 'Yippy skip! I didn't get shot in the head,'" Paige said. "Dinner was great. I'd eat here again if they ever reopen."

"You sound pretty good," Roy said with the same off-putting tone of concern.

Paige could not decide if the lieutenant was actually worried about him or if this was another ploy to get him to drop his guard.

"Where's Angel? Was she with you?" Roy asked, resting his hand on Paige's shoulder.

"Oh, she probably got a room at L'Ermitage," Paige said. "She and William Clifton took off as soon as the shooting started."

"Hold still, please," the med-tech said, grasping Paige firmly. Her strong hands matched her muscular body.

"So you haven't heard from her?" Roy took a small Hermes pad from the inside pocket of his jacket and made a note.

"Not yet, no," Paige said warily.

The technician shined a flashlight in his eyes for some reason.

"Look up," the tech demanded sternly when Paige rolled his eyes in disgust.

"And you are...?" Roy asked Wig, pen poised to take it down.

"I'm sorry," Paige said, turning in the direction of Roy's voice, temporarily blinded by the tech's penlight. "Lieutenant Roy Slade, this is Ludwig Burgh, a... friend who was with us at dinner. Wig, this is Lieutenant Slade. He suspects me of being behind all this."

"How do you do?" Wig said, extending his free hand.

Paige could see his words had hit their mark, though the lieutenant never broke character as he greeted Wig.

The tech took Paige's head firmly in both hands. She turned him face forward as she continued to check for signs of concussion. "Follow the tip of my pen with your eyes," she instructed.

"Paige, we have to consider all possibilities," Roy said. Aside from the note and the handshake, he otherwise ignored Wig.

"Well, there was sniper fire and no one got hit." Paige cut his eyes sharply in Roy's direction, irritating the tech still trying to examine him.

"Lefty Flynn," Roy corrected, eyeing Paige.

"Yes, no one except Angel's mortal enemy," Paige conceded. "And only barely. Either they're the worst shots in the world, or I was just trying to make it look like I was a target to divert suspicion from me."

"You sound like a character on some cop show," Roy said. He almost chuckled.

"I'm a writer," Paige said, taking the bait. "We put the words in the mouths of all the characters in every TV precinct you've ever seen. You probably say stuff at work every day because you saw it on some cop show."

"'Just the facts, ma'am,'" Roy said in his best Joe Friday.

"I think it is most unkind of you," Wig said, encircling Paige's shoulders with his arm.

"I'm sorry. I don't mean to be glib," Roy began, clearly spotting the weak link. "No one is saying—"

"Paige makes light," Wig continued, with all the sincerity of a testimonial on a shampoo commercial. "The only reason that he was not shot was because I fell on him. The first shot hit the window in the door of the car we were getting into."

The tech sighed, disgusted. She tossed a couple of the implements she'd been using on Paige into a tackle box, slammed it shut and stalked off.

"All done?" Paige called after her in a saccharine tone.

"With *you*," she shouted over her shoulder.

"So, I'm okay then?" Paige persisted.

"If you were any better, I'd have to slap you," she said, turning to walk backward a step or two. Turning back, she made her way to her next charge.

"Worst luck," Paige said, taking it up with Roy again. "I'm not even hurt, so I must be guilty."

"There are no official suspects at this..." Roy began, trying to sound official enough to impress Wig and silence Paige.

"Paige?" The voice cut through the noisy scene. Television cameras and lights came to life again. Clouds of paparazzi fireflies erupted, revealing their positions in what had been the darkness surrounding them. "Paige!" Angel called out again, like Scarlett in search of Rhett in the fog. She held her position a moment to allow for a few good shots, then resumed her quest for him, though it was clear she'd seen him. The only thing missing was a swell of heartstring-tugging music.

"Over here," Paige groaned.

Angel and William made their way slowly, photogenically to the temporary med station where Paige still sat with Wig.

"You know what they're going to say on the news tomorrow, don't you?" Paige said to Roy in a confidential tone as she approached. "'Angel and William Seen Together at Hollywood Hotspot.'"

"Are you two okay?" Angel asked, embracing Paige and Wig in one huge hug. "What's so funny? I always feel like I just missed the joke."

"Why'd you come back? Did you forget your coat?" Paige asked.

"We came back as soon as we could; traffic is terrible and then we had to talk our way in." Angel sighed, hefting herself up to sit beside him. She clutched Paige's hand. "Hey, Roy."

"Angel." Roy nodded formally, but clearly getting a little charge out of being remembered and called by name. "Glad you're here. If you feel up to it, there are a few questions I'd like to get out of the way."

"Sure, whatever. Are you okay, Paige?"

Paige looked at her, surprised. She could be so selfish and self-absorbed. Sometimes it seemed she almost cared about him. She squeezed his hand and looked at him with what seemed genuine concern. Then a flash went off nearby and he remembered the cameras.

Two Years, 10 Months and One Week Before

Paige and Angel's first paparazzi photograph together had prompted Angel's abrupt departure, stranding Paige at Geoffrey's.

At the time, Paige vowed that he'd seen the last he ever would of Ms. Panderson and her evil minion Grizelda. He found it perversely amusing that they'd had their first and last photo-op together simultaneously. Not only would he have a story to dine out on, but there would be evidence to substantiate his claim should the photos ever turn up.

Far more pressing at that time were his concerns over getting back to work, getting a deal for his new manuscript and raising enough money to get that bankruptcy he'd been promising himself.

He needed an agent. A real one. What he had gotten was his first paparazzi shot.

Paige knew how to write. But to accomplish the million-to-one feat of getting a book into print, he knew he needed the help of a good agent. Truthfully, he had no idea what that looked like since he'd never really had one.

His first agents had done such a bad job negotiating the movie rights to his first novel that the studio had actually apologized to him. Paige's next agents pursued him until he signed on.

But once they had him, they kept insisting that he needed to go to writing school even though he was already a published author. Paige reckoned that he could manage to feel insecure about his work for free.

Then there was the woman from the name-brand Hollywood agency who'd made a big push to package Paige's work when his movie deal was hot. Later, whenever anyone called her office to inquire about his availability, she denied knowing who Paige was. The agent after that actually left the country, announcing she'd rather be a producer and make a movie in India to get the drop on a rumored SAG strike. The strike never materialized and neither did his agent. Paige's agent of record when Honoria first mentioned the mysterious celebrity book deal was Brittany. Brittany had come to him, drawn by her love of his work. She filled his ears with praise and promises until he signed with her. Like a bad lover, once she'd had him she was always too busy to return his phone calls, let alone keep her promises. As a courtesy, Paige called to let her know about the possible ghostwriting job when he first heard from Honoria.

Brittany's assistant Bicky told Paige that Brittany was on a conference call but would "return" as soon as she was done. That's how they said it in Hollywood. It was just too time-consuming to say that you'd return the call, so you said you'd "return." It was also important to "take meetings" and to "messenger" things over. Hollywood was a very efficient place, Paige mused, as he hung up the phone after Bicky unceremoniously disconnected him without so much as a cumbersome goodbye.

Several weeks later, Paige was at home working on his resume for a script coordinator's job on a children's game show a producer friend had told him about. His phone rang.

"Hello?" he said, only sort of paying attention. He was still reading the words dotting the screen of his laptop.

"Paige?" an unfamiliar woman's voice said tentatively.

"Yes," he admitted. As a rule he did not like to give out information to unidentified people over the phone, but he'd sent out several resumes and you never know.

There was a brief silence during which Paige reread a one-sentence job description of his stint as an office manager at USC. He tried to punch it up and make it sound more like production work.

"I'm returning?" the woman persisted when Paige didn't.

Interrupted by her assertion, he was reminded he was still on the phone. "What is this about?" Paige asked.

"I was thinking you'd tell me," the woman said, matching his tone.

"Well, I can tell you I haven't called anyone on the phone today," Paige said.

"No, well, I have a note from Bicky; it is from a couple of days back…"

"Brittany?" Paige asked. His tone would not have been much different had the call come from someone whose funeral he'd recently attended. "Well, how are you? Do you still live here in Los Angeles?"

"Well, yes, of course."

No sense of humor, Paige thought, shaking his head at the senseless waste of good material.

"I guess it has been a couple of days," Brittany said, taking up the challenge of his tone. "In fact, I haven't seen you in person in a while."

"Not so far this year," Paige agreed.

"Well, we should do something about that," she said in what Paige took to be a conciliatory tone. "I'm in West Hollywood on business for lunch. How about a coffee? Three-ish? Can it wait till then?"

"After three weeks…"

"Two."

Like that mattered. "What's a few more hours?"

In truth, Paige didn't know any more about the ghostwriting gig than he had when he'd originally called. He saw it instead as a chance for free pie.

"Great," she said. "Monkey Bar? Three? Gotta jet."

And the line went dead.

At 4:15, after two pots of genmaicha green, two budget-busting pieces of cherry pie and three I'm-on-the-way cell phone calls that did not even begin to come in until after 3:30, Brittany swept into the Monkey Bar like she was storming out.

"Paige, darling, I'm so sorry I'm late," she said, approaching a man at a nearby table with her arms outstretched. Tempting though it might have been to let the scene play out, Paige rose from his chair to greet her. She adjusted her course with a conviction that made him seem almost important to her.

She threw her arms around him, smacking the side of his head with a heavy canvas tote, the handles of which she had twisted around her wrist. Then she collapsed into a chair at the table he'd come to consider home.

"It's been crazy busy," she said as she always did before making excuses. Divesting herself of the bag and her purse, she let them fall to the floor on either side of her. "I'm so sorry you had to wait. Do you want anything?"

"No, I'm fine," Paige said, wishing he'd peed before she got there. The two pots of tea had completed their circuit, but he feared that if he got up from the table she wouldn't be there when he got back. "You?"

"I can't," she said, patting the back of his hand. "I've got another meeting I'm already late for, but I wanted to stop by and see you."

"Thanks," he said, irritated. Once again, they would not be talking about any of the career plans for him she'd spoken of so wistfully when she was courting him to sign.

"Anyway, let's get right to the point." She looked him in the eye.

"Okay, sure," Paige agreed, curious. He really only wanted her to call Honoria and he did have to pee.

"When we started working together we talked about all the plans I had for you," she said, taking over as though it was her meeting.

"Um, yeah." Paige nodded, startled by the tone and her choice of topic.

"And none of those things have come to pass," she went on as though he hadn't spoken. "I think that this isn't working, Paige. I think it's time we went our separate ways." As she concluded, she lifted the heavy canvas bag she'd smacked him with. Holding one handle, she upended the tote, emptying its contents onto the table.

Strewn across the tabletop was a complete collection of his writing samples. Screenplays, manuscripts, pilots and even published works, everything was there. All were in pristine condition, not a mark on them, not dog-eared or shopworn. In fact, it was as though they'd never been read at all.

"You're dumping me?" He scanned the table for something sharp.

"I'm not doing you any good, Paige," she said.

"Well, that's the truth," he agreed. You're not doing anything at all, he thought as he stared at her in disbelief. She'd collected her cut of the royalties and option checks all from work he'd brought to her. In return, she'd done absolutely nothing. And now that he needed her to actually earn that money, she was bailing.

"It's for the best." She looked at him earnestly, nodding as though it was the end of an affair rather than the sting of a con game.

"It can't get any worse," he sighed with a bitter smile as she rose to leave him.

"Good luck, Paige," she said, so genuinely he almost believed her. "You're a really great writer. I mean that. I hope you'll stay in touch when your career takes off."

As if.

"Thanks," Paige said with as little sarcasm as he could manage.

Then, she turned, left the restaurant and stuck him with the check.

The pie was good, he thought.

Out of options, he screwed up his courage and followed up on a manuscript he'd sent out.

The Morton Lynwood literary agency was one of those institutions whose client roster read like *People* magazine's "100 Most Fascinating." Paige had managed to scrape an acquaintance with the protégé of one of the founding partners through writer friends whose literary fortunes were less tenuous than his own. His colleague's success, he reasoned, was perhaps due in part to the fact that they were represented by agents who actually read and promoted their work. As unlikely at that seemed, it had always been a dream of Paige's.

"Paige Blanche for Morris Richardson," Paige said, trying for the same level of no-nonsense efficiency evinced by the British aristocrat who answered the agency's phone. Paige was transferred without further comment.

"This is Morris," a hearty and avuncular male voice announced. It was the sort of voice that always made Paige forget all of his own qualifications for being in the conversation in the first place.

"Oh, yeah, hi, this is Paige, um, Blanche—"

"Right, yeah, great. Thanks for the call. Listen, got the manuscript and obviously it's going to take a few days to carve out the time to give it a proper read."

"Obviously," Paige repeated like the congregation at vespers.

"Let's do this: I'll give you a call when I finish, but if you haven't heard from me by the end of next week, you call me again and give me a little hell, just in case. What do you say?"

"Next week sounds great," Paige agreed easily. "And thanks."

"You bet," Morris said, his voice already fading as, mission accomplished, speaking into the receiver at his end had lost its priority.

Paige set the phone aside, distracted. He began making tea and analyzing the conversation in which he'd actually only spoken fifteen words, two of them his name. Should he have said more?

Been more forceful? Asked for the sale? Talked about other projects? He was still lost in thought when the phone began ringing.

"Hello?" he answered. He cradled the receiver between his chin and shoulder as he poured steaming water into a teapot.

"Well, I don't know what you did, but you're the one," growled the husky female voice at the other end of the line.

"Honoria?" Paige said. "Where the hell have you been? I've been calling you for days. I've got no idea what's going on with the top secret Panderson project but—"

"What's going on is that you are the writer of record," Honoria said. "Get your agent to call me or I'll call, but she loves you. How soon can you get started?"

"She kidnapped me and left me stranded in Burbank. She came to lunch in disguise, started a fire and stuck me with the check. Then she got me out to Malibu under false pretenses and drove off and left me there. When did she decide that she loved me?" Paige demanded. "And more to the point, why in the hell would I want to work with her?"

"Because it's a job that comes with a publishing contract," Honoria said evenly. "Do you have something else lined up?"

"I'll have the agent call," Paige said quietly. He took her point even if it was straight through the heart.

"Great, I'll get in touch with her manager and get a meeting schedule set up," Honoria said. "And Paige, this should be a lot of fun, really."

"Thanks," Paige said, brightening a bit. It was not because his life was less bleak. It was not because he thought for a minute that it really would be a lot of fun. It was because of Honoria's efforts to make the rather demeaning project seem less hideous. A little kindness stood out sharply in such a harsh landscape.

He hung up the phone and sipped his tea. Technically he did not have an agent. He knew he could write Angel's book. What he didn't know was just what to do about setting up the writing deal with Angel. What's more, it was a deal that he didn't much want and knew absolutely that he really had to have.

He tried calling his attorney, but her reaction was less than encouraging.

"God no, you don't want me to do this," she said with a coarse blast of laughter. "Celebrity deals are a nightmare. It'll take forever if it works out at all. Especially with nutjobs like Angel Panderson. You'll spend any money you might make on the project on my legal fees. Trust me on this one. But call me after, babe. I'll take you to lunch. I can't wait to hear the horror stories."

So, despite the fact that it was decidedly uncool, Paige found himself calling Morton Lynnwood and Associates for the second time the same day.

"Morris Richardson," the agent said, answering the phone in a fashion identical to their earlier conversion.

"Morris. Paige Blanche, again. Something's come up here. I wanted to run it by you before I did anything else," Paige explained.

"Okay," Morris said. His voice showed no more interest or emotion than when he'd said his name.

"I've been offered a deal writing a book with Angel Panderson. I need someone to negotiate it," Paige said, more than a little sheepishly. He knew the agency represented literary giants, political gurus, spiritual leaders and opinion makers. Angel Panderson was a trendsetter in her own unique way but a little downmarket for Morton Lynwood, who had negotiated a book deal for the Dalai Lama. Still, what Angel lacked in gravitas she more than made up for in market share. "I know I don't have a deal at the agency yet, but I wanted to let you decide if you wanted to be a part of this. It's your choice. If you're not interested I totally understand."

"Angel Panderson," Morris repeated. He gave a long low whistle. "Well, that's interesting. Let me talk it over here and call you back, if that's okay?"

"Sure," Paige said. "But I need to move so let me know in the next couple of hours if you can."

Someone began hammering on his front door.

"I'll get right back to you," Morris assured him in a way that made Paige believe it might actually be the truth.

"Okay then, I'll wait to hear from you." Paige looked to check the wall calendar beside the refrigerator to reassure himself that whoever was still beating on his door was not the sheriffs come to evict him. "Thank you, Morris. I appreciate your consideration. It really would help out."

"No, it actually sounds like it has possibilities," Morris said. "I'll let you know."

Paige set the handset aside. Tentatively he peeked out the kitchen doorway. He craned his neck. If he stood in just the right spot he could see who was at the front door through the dining room windows. Alas, whoever it was stood too far to one side to be seen.

The pounding persisted.

It was clear to Paige that his forceful and persistent visitor was not going away. He sighed. The closer he got to the door, the more irritated he became with the incessant banging. He looked through the peephole. There was only an eye staring back at his. Paige's impatience got the better of him. He snatched the door open. "What the hell?"

The fist came laughably close to Paige's face. The forceful but misguided swing narrowly missed his chin. The momentum of the random roundhouse propelled his would-be assailant forward. As Paige stepped back to avoid the blow, his visitor literally fell past him, landing in a heap at Paige's feet.

A cloud of bourbon fumes filled the air.

"I'll kill you," the uninvited guest wailed at Paige's ankle. Despite his posture, he was still swinging wildly as he lay on Paige's entryway floor. Paige sidestepped to avoid the blows. Despite his guest's obvious intent, Paige was still too surprised to be upset.

"Uh-oh," the guest said suddenly going still. Then, as abruptly as his condition permitted, the invader struggled onto all fours and began crawling across the hardwood floor into Paige's living room. "Oh, God, oh, God," the attacker kept moaning as he neared a rather large schefflera near the front windows. He leaned over the edge of the plant's terra cotta pot and vomited.

"*Eeewww,*" Paige intoned, helpless.

He watched, more disgusted than concerned, as his guest's face slid down the side of the pot to fall in a mossy unconscious puddle on Paige's living room floor.

Tentatively, Paige made his way over to the body. He prodded it with his toe. No reaction. He prodded a little harder. Still nothing. He gave it a little kick. He got a little groan, but no more. Convinced of his safety, he turned the carcass over. To his great surprise, Paige found himself face to face with legendary rock-and-roll hooligan and mediocre musician Bill E Blaze, Angel's ex-husband.

Bill E was clutching a copy of the most recent issue of *Star* magazine. The vomit-spattered tabloid cover featured a photo of Paige and Angel, arm-in-arm in their first and, at that point, only photo together. Geoffrey's was visible in the background if you knew what you were looking for. Above the photo, the splashy headline read: "Angel & New Boytoy out on the Town." Below, black letters on a Day-Glo yellow comic book style explosion proclaimed, "Rumored Bill E Reconciliation Ancient History."

Paige could only laugh. Other than that, he was at a complete loss for what to do in the situation. He retrieved the cup of the tea he had been brewing as he considered his options.

Standing in the kitchen doorway, he peered through the dining room at the body lying by the window in his living room. Bill E was snoring, the sound of leaves caught in a pool filter. The videos of Angel's night in the VIP room had revealed to the world, among many things, that Bill E was exceptionally well-endowed. Paige had never seen the video but he'd heard the rumors. Briefly, he entertained the notion of having a little look to see what all the fuss was about.

The phone rang.

"Paige?" Morris inquired. It was as though he was telling Paige that's who he was, not asking.

"Morris," Paige answered.

"Is everything all right?" Morris asked. The quaver in Paige's voice was so odd that, despite their very brief telephone acquaintance, it was clear that something was amiss.

"Not really, no," Paige admitted. He was still not quite coming in for a landing as he circled the point.

"Anything I can do?"

"Maybe," Paige said, considering it. "Bill E Blaze is passed out on my living room floor. Thoughts?"

"Angel's ex-husband? *That* Bill E Blaze?"

"No, the other one."

"What happened?" Morris laughed a little. "I mean, we were just on the phone five minutes ago."

"He came by to beat me up, I think," Paige explained. "But he apparently fell into a vat of bourbon and drank his way out before he got here. So he only managed to knock himself down, throw up in my schefflera and pass out. I can't say for sure about the beating-up part. I don't think he came by for the nap or the planter, though."

"Did you call the police?"

"No, I was just wondering what I should do," Paige said. "The police, hunh?"

"He tried to attack you, didn't he?"

"He said he wanted to kill me, but he did a really bad job. If I call the police, it'll just give the *Star* more evidence of our feud over the affair that I'm having with Angel."

"The *Star*? That tabloid?"

"Yeah. My rival for Angel's affections brought a copy with him to my beatdown. I'm out on a hot date with Angel on the cover."

"Could be good for book sales," Morris suggested.

"Speaking of which…"

"I've talked to the partners and we're on board," Morris told him.

"Oh, Morris, that's great," Paige said. The body in the living room was forgotten. "Honoria said I should let her know something today."

"At Peters and Luge? I'll call her and get things started," Morris said. It always seemed to Paige that there were really only about twenty-five people in publishing because they always seemed to know each other.

"As for your guest, I'll see if Honoria can get me in touch with a manager or something through Angel's camp."

"Okay, cool. So, before you go, let me ask you," Paige said, reminded of his inert guest. "Do you think taking his pants off would be such a bad idea? Research for the book, you know."

22

"Listen, Paige." Wig spoke softly into Paige's ear. "William is going to give me a ride home. It's late and…" He shrugged his conclusion.

"Yeah, the shootout was a real mood killer," Paige said with a brittle laugh.

"But I'm in town for a while," Wig went on, with an awkward, ear-scrumming side-squeeze, his arm draped over Paige's shoulders. "Maybe I'll run into you again before I go. Or when you're in New York next?"

"That'd be great," Paige said. He got one last consolation hug from Wig, in honor of what was not to be.

"Okay then," Wig said, breaking off the embrace. "See you."

"Knock on the door when you get home," William said to Angel, lifting her down from the ambulance gurney where she'd been sitting. "Or surprise me. You know where I hide the key."

"And how you like to be surprised," she giggled.

He kissed her goodbye like it was World War II and he was leaving for a tour in the Pacific. Cover photos were duly captured.

Paige scowled as he watched the two men walk away.

Angel approached.

"He's meeting you later?" Paige asked forlornly.

"Yeah, he'll be out at the beach house." She leaned on the gurney next to him, facing in the opposite direction. "I'll see how I feel when I get home."

"A night with my first supermodel, ruined by an assassination attempt," Paige sighed. He watched William and Wig pulling away in William's Bentley. "I have the worst luck."

"I don't know. You might have gotten shot," Angel suggested.

"Yeah. I guess you have worse luck than me."

"Paige, really," she said, shaking her head. "If you were dead and I'd survived, then I'd be suspect number one. So, you see, my luck is much better than yours. I'm still meeting William later."

"Hag," Paige hissed. "This is all your fault."

"*My* fault?"

"You were the one who wanted to have sushi," Paige said, realizing the significance of what he was saying even as he spoke. "In fact, you set this whole thing up."

"Keep your voice down, Paige," she said under her breath. She crossed her eyes at him and offered up an *ixnay* look. "I'm sorry about Wig, but really he was my date and you went after him. There's no need to go making things worse."

"I did not go after him," Paige said, putting the end of his nose about two inches from the end of hers. "He came after me."

"Oh, I doubt that very much," she said, turning away grandly.

"Believe whatever makes you feel better, but he started in when you and Andy went to powder your noses on the inside."

Angel gasped. Maintaining her mannequin smile, she looked around to see if anyone from the police or, worse, the tabs was close enough to have heard.

"To be honest, I'm as surprised about it as you are. I was just talking with Earl and Wig started this thing with the edamame," Paige began. Then, remembering, he interrupted himself. "By the way, did you know that Grizelda had final cut on our books?"

"Grizelda?"

"Yeah, Earl said she had it in our contract with the publisher that she got the final edit," Paige said, annoyed, yet again, as he remembered it. "You didn't know?"

"First I've heard of it."

"Weird," Paige said, distracted for the moment. "Not that you wouldn't know what was in your contract. That I can easily believe. But, according to Earl, she exercised the option, too. Even after you two were no longer working together." Paige puzzled aloud, his voice trailing away. "I wonder how... *Honoria*," he cut himself off as he answered his own question.

"Who?"

"Our editor."

Angel gave him a blank look.

"Barbara?" he said, suggesting the name Angel had always used when referring to Honoria.

"Oh, Barbara, right," Angel nodded, as it came back to her. "What about her?"

"Well, first, her name is Honoria. And second, it was *her* double-dealing. She was running the manuscripts by Grizelda and then back to me. She claimed the edits were hers, or at the end maybe yours," Paige said in the same distant tone, reasoning it out aloud more than actually talking with Angel. "Some of her stranger edits totally make sense now. That snake."

"Barbara?"

Roy sidled up. "Where's Wig?"

"Oh God, not you too," Angel sighed, folding her arms. "Are we going to be able to go home at all tonight?"

"Sorry, I have other plans," Roy said, his eyes twinkling. "But you're free to go if you like."

"Can I borrow your car?" Angel asked, grinning flirtatiously. "Mine's ready for limo ER."

"Actually, your car service sent someone over," Roy said, pointing to a large black SUV idling just down the block.

"Oh, thank God," Paige sighed. He tossed his tin foil blanket onto the nearby gurney. "Why is it that they always put blankets on people? I mean, this is Southern California. It's never actually been cold here."

"People often get chills when they're in shock," Angel said, startling Paige into unaccustomed silence. "I already asked," she explained in answer to his incredulous look.

"So, you're okay?" Roy said, grasping Paige's shoulder and putting his arm around Angel's back. "You're both okay?"

"No one's dropped an anvil on my head," Paige said. "Yet."

"But it's still early," Angel said, taking Paige's arm and extricating them both from the lieutenant's grasp. "Let's go stand under a ledge closer to home."

"Sorry about all this," Roy said, walking with them toward the car as he helped to clear the way of barriers official and otherwise. "I'll try to catch up with both of you tomorrow morn—well, later today," he finished, with a quick check of his watch. He reached to open the car door. "Paige, maybe we could have that lunch."

Angel gave Paige a knowing look.

"That'd be great, Roy." Paige smiled. "But not sushi. I had that last night."

"You got it," Roy said, helping them both into the car. "I'll call you late in the morning so you get a chance to rest. You'll be out at Angel's?"

"Yeah, but I'll have the cell phone," he said, clutching his coat pocket to be sure and pulling out its shattered remains. "Yeah, I'll be at Angel's."

"I've got the number," Roy said with an easy smile as he held the door for them. "'Night, Angel."

"'Night, Roy," Angel chirped as he sealed the door in a final little burst of strength. She looked at Paige. "You have totally got to sleep with him."

The car pulled away instantly, as all oncoming traffic was still blocked off.

"I'll have you home in a few minutes, Miss Panderson," the driver called back to them to confirm that that was indeed, where they were going.

"He *liiiiiikes* you," Angel teased, ignoring the driver.

"Cut it out," Paige sighed, irritably. "You only want me to sleep with him so you don't wind up in the gas chamber."

"Do they still do that?" Angel said, putting her hand to her throat.

"God, I don't know, I hope not," Paige said with a shiver. "I think it's just something they say in noir movies."

"Seriously though," Angel said, checking her reflection in the window and fluffing her hair unconsciously. "I do think he's interested."

"I also think he suspects us of murder."

"After tonight?"

"He said as much."

"Really? How could he—"

"In the movies, having someone take a few shots at you and missing is the number one most-clichéd way to try to take suspicion off yourself."

"Well, I wish we'd thought of it sooner," she groused, as she rummaged through the car's obligatory built-in bar for something to drink.

"I'll tell you what I *did* think of doing..."

"You mean after you blow the lieutenant?" Angel asked. She pulled a split of Moët from the ice chest and set it aside for consideration.

"We need to talk to Grizelda," Paige went on.

"Well, you're on your own," she said, making flatulent noises with her lips. "She hates my guts."

"We should just show up at her office," Paige suggested. He leaned his head back on the deep leather seat. "If we act all nice, what's the worst she can do?"

"You've met Grizelda, right?" she asked. Giving up the search, she began peeling the foil off the little bottle of Moët.

"I'll call Honoria in the morning and see what I can find out," Paige said, not really paying any attention to Angel as he talked it through. "That starfucker will take my call if it comes from your number. They're three or four hours ahead there, I can never remember which."

"Four," Angel said confidently, untwisting the wire cage. "Unless it's Daylight Savings. Is it?"

He shrugged. "So, we can drop in on Grizelda after breakfast," he concluded. "And I'll still be able to make a late lunch with Roy."

The explosion was deafening. Paige threw himself to the floor. The driver almost lost control of the large automobile as the cork ricocheted around the interior compartment.

"I'm so sorry, guys," Angel managed to say through near-hysterical laugher. Champagne cascaded down her arm.

"Oh, *are* you?" Paige said nastily. Reaching into the ubiquitous burlwood-veneer ice chest, he pulled out another small champagne bottle. "I don't think you're nearly sorry enough." He gave the bottle a vigorous shake and began tearing the foil off the lid.

"No, Paige," Angel screamed, still laughing. "It was an accident! Paige, no!"

23

"See you for breakfast," Angel said in a stagey whisper. Still soggy with champagne, she kissed Paige on the cheek on the street in front of her beach house.

"Are you going to come in and clean up?"

"Yeah, *nobody* likes a champagne-soaked sexpot," Angel said with a laugh.

"Okay. Have fun," Paige said, still a bit dejected but trying to mean it.

"Paige, I'm sorry about Wig." She gave his hand a squeeze. "It would have been a perfect night if it had worked out for you, too."

"And without the shooting and all," Paige said. They laughed. He hugged her, squeezing a little trickle of champagne out of their drippy clothes.

"Yeah, total bummer," she said, bussing his cheek. "You remember the code, right?"

"Yeah, and the key?"

"Still under the rickshaw," she said over her shoulder. "See you for breakfast. Wear underwear. I may bring a guest."

Paige waved. He turned and walked the few steps inland.

William's place was an A-List, zillion-dollar oceanfront. Angel's house was on the more practical half-zillion, has-been side.

Paige put in the code—36-22-34. The buzzer sounded. The key code opened the courtyard door into the small garden space that buffered Angel's actual front door. He opened the door into the darkened courtyard. "Yeah, twenty-two. She wishes," he muttered. Rolling aside the small model rickshaw overflowing with wilted violets, revealed the key. "And thirty-four?" He laughed. How many years had it been since those much-vaunted measurements had actually been Angel's? Even though years of hard partying and harder drinking had left her body bloated and doughy, compared to its former glory, she doggedly maintained on her website and in press releases that she still wore clothes that fit the official description.

Sometimes, she actually did. In one incident Paige remembered from one of the stores on their book tour, an employee received minor injuries when a hook-and-eye blew under the extreme pressure of the bustier she'd insisted on wearing. The hook tore through the shirtsleeve and forearm of a young man who was helping to flap books for signing and lodged in the plaster wall beyond.

Paige smiled as he closed the front door behind him and tossed the key onto the small table at the foot of the nearby staircase. The glow of the outdoor security lights poured in through the glass doors across the back of the house. The pool rippled with reflected light, ethereal in the darkness beyond. Uncertain of the location of the light switches, Paige ran his hands over the walls. No sign, though he did dislodge a picture frame of some sort that fell and broke in the darkness.

"Who designed this place? Pee-wee Herman?" he growled. Feeling his way, he moved deeper into the house. Eventually, and a few broken and displaced items later, he found his way to the kitchen. He kept the refrigerator door open, standing in the brilliant pool that spilled out as he poured himself a glass of iced tea. He had made himself the pitcher of Lady Grey earlier and put it

24

Paige became aware of the shadow that fell over him.

He cried out as he fought for consciousness.

The events of the previous few days had him on edge, even in sleep.

"What the hell?" Angel, the source of the shadow, demanded.

"What?" Paige said, looking around to get his bearings. Why was Angel wielding that aluminum bat a baseball team had autographed for her under suspicious and, Paige had always thought, ill-explained circumstances? "Is everything okay?"

He was lying on one of a pair of white wicker divans on the deck outside the master suite of Angel's Malibu cottage. The two loveseats faced one another. Between them was a large, low, glass-topped wicker table, laden with a brunch feast. Toast, strawberries, waffles, whipped cream, fresh fruit, bread, chocolate—he smiled as he remembered the joyous trip to Gelson's Malibu.

"What is going on here?" Angel hissed.

"Brunch?" Paige said with a spokesmodel's gesture toward the spread.

Wig groaned and stirred, awakening as he became aware of the activity.

"I thought something happened to you," she said to Paige. Ill-concealed rage swept through her like summer fire through Topanga Canyon. "Hello, Wiggie."

"Hi, Angel," Wig said, standing and attempting to hug her. He was clad in only a pair of silk boxer shorts he'd left behind on one of his previous visits. "Would you like some breakfast?"

Angel shook herself free of his grasp. "I'm not hungry," she snarled.

"What's with the bat? Are you playing Xena, Warrior Princess?" Paige asked, nibbling on an enormous strawberry.

"What happened downstairs?" Still angry, she shook her finger in Paige's face. "There was broken glass all over the floor. The kitchen drawers were all pulled out. The cabinet doors were standing open. There was stuff everywhere."

"Oh honey, did we scare you?" Paige asked, rising and embracing her. "Were you coming to protect me? That is so sweet."

Angel stood board-stiff, fuming until he let her go.

"Where's Big Willie?" Paige asked, falling back onto the sofa beside Wig.

"Still in bed," she snapped. "What happened to my kitchen?"

"My bad," Wig admitted sheepishly. "I made brunch and you have the worst kitchen I've ever seen. Very confusing. Too much stuff jammed everywhere. One cabinet had underwear in it. I'll clean it up after we eat."

"It looked like someone had been attacked," she said too loudly. Plopping down on the loveseat facing theirs it was immediately obvious that the place had been set for William and her at the brunch.

"In a way I was," Paige said, giving Wig a playful shove.

"William talked me into coming back out last night after we left you two at the restaurant," Wig explained.

"Oh, he did, did he?"

"Paige was upset. You were going to be spending the night at William's. Paige would be here all alone. William knew the code here and where you kept the key. So I decided to surprise Paige after all."

"But his idea of a surprise was to sneak up on me in the dark and grab me," Paige added. "I'm amazed you didn't hear me screaming."

"Well, you *were* surprised," Wig said. "William didn't say anything? We agreed we'd all four meet for breakfast, since he's been staying at his Bel Air place. He doesn't have any food over there. We got enough for four."

"At least," Paige said.

"William's still asleep," Angel huffed, her face red with anger. "I didn't wake him."

"So, you didn't know," Paige said. His pleasant, morning-after fog burned away in a flash. She wasn't worried about him; she was just jealous. All her talk the night before had been just that.

"No. I didn't," she said.

"Well now, you do," Paige said biting each word off cleanly. "And so do I."

"Good."

"Great."

"What are you guys talking about?"

Two Years Earlier...

Beginning at Last

Once they began work on the book, Angel went out of her way to make up for the kidnapping, the fire, the dine-and-dash, the Malibu marooning and Bill E's drunken assault. She hired a private chef to cook breakfast for them so that they could focus on their work. The kitchen was stocked with Paige's favorite teas. There was always a steaming cup or a frosty glass in his hand. Their meetings were as much playdates as they were work. Paige was surprised less by Angel's hospitality than by how immediately she took him into her confidence. He found her candor strangely compelling. There seemed to be no guile or varnish at all. Her genuine openness and authenticity swept Paige off his feet. What made the seduction complete was that she took an interest in him and in his life.

Paige had lived in Hollywood long enough to know plenty of famous people. Most, he found, were only interested in you for as long as you could do something for them. He had learned that "let's have lunch" in L.A. would translate as "fuck off" pretty much anywhere else.

With Angel there had been no sense of L.A.'s indigenous disingenuousness.

Paige was tentative with her at first, but she was irresistible. Her openness was disarmingly refreshing in a city and a business run on, and often in, illusion. They talked easily about everything from their families to their childhoods to sex.

"My first time was so lame," she recalled. "It was like everyone was doing it. It just seemed like the thing to do. There was this guy who knew my best girlfriend's boyfriend. I don't even remember his name. Just that he had a great car." She gave Paige an innocent little smile and a shrug. "I mean, you want it to be special or memorable or you hope it will be but then..." She blew a raspberry and threw herself back on the matching, overstuffed, chintz-cushioned wicker sofa facing his. The crystal and silver remains of their brunch lay on the glass top of the distressed wicker coffee table between them on the deck of the beach house Paige had come to think of as a cozy consignment showroom. "What about you, Paige?"

"Me?"

"What about your first time?"

"What about it?" he said, suddenly shy of her.

"I tell you all this personal stuff about me." She grinned. Slipping off her sofa, she climbed onto his in a feline move that all-but-included purring. "Fair's fair. What was your first time? I just told you all about mine."

"The first time I had sex or the first time I fell in love?" he asked, setting aside the composition book he used to take notes. "The sex is so much less interesting, don't you think?"

"Hmmm, I guess it depends on who it's with," she said, and giggled. Leaning back against the arm on her end of the sofa, she put her feet on the cushion between them. "And the sex. I dated my first guy for a while, but I don't know if I really loved him. I'm not sure I was ever in love with anyone before Bill E. But you made me talk about me again." She poked him with her foot. "That's cheating. You tell. Your first time."

"He transferred into my high school at mid-term, ninth grade year," Paige said. He slipped off his shoes and put his feet up on the sofa, to defend himself at first. Then, at ease, he rested his feet next to Angel's and leaned against the opposing arm to face her. "He moved from Alaska. I think his father was in the army or something. I don't know that I understood about being gay, what it even meant or that I was or how it worked. But then I saw him in Miss Shoemaker's social studies class." Paige shrugged. "He was so beautiful. It was like all of a sudden I just knew."

"Well," Angel demanded, giving him a poke with her foot. "What happened?"

"Nothing," Paige said with a gust of breath. "I could never tell him. It wasn't possible to be gay when I was in the ninth grade. I hope it is for ninth graders now."

"I hate that," she said, a little pout on her face. "It's hard enough to be in ninth grade and madly in love and probably going to get rejected anyway, without being told that it's not even possible. I'm sorry, Paige."

"Thanks," he said, feeling a physical warmth.

"And," she said, leaning forward and tickling him mercilessly. "I'm not counting that as your first time."

"Okay, okay," he cried. "It was with a cousin who was visiting us while he was on leave from boot camp."

"Oh my God!" she shrieked. "That's so hot."

"It wasn't really. But it'll look great in the movie version."

"Better than mine," she said pensively, and then brightened. "We should make the novel say that she was date-raped. Like the guy took advantage of her. That'll be way better."

Together, Paige and Angel shaped her life into a story that would make for an interesting novel. They became friends along the way. Perhaps the most striking thing about getting to know Angel was the disparity between what he'd read about her in the headlines plastered over the magazine stands by the grocery store checkout and what actually seemed to be her life.

At the time, it was a source of outrage to him that she was constantly depicted as this out-of-control borderline menace to society. In reality, she seemed a bit of a homebody and even a little dull. More charming, still, was Angel's insistence on making a joke of herself before others could make a joke of her.

Her legendary breast implants, out-of-scale and oversized, had made her bustline an international joke. She'd capitalized on her punch line status, even naming her abortive attempt at a sitcom *Built*, the rice-paper-thin pun being that it took place in a real estate development office.

"My boobs succeeded," Angel said in one of their early interviews. "I just get to appear with them."

In an effort to provide Paige with greater insight, Angel introduced him to her famous friends and neighbors. Of course, there was William, but they were joined by lots of other celebrated locals. Like the famous comedian from down the block. "His sense of humor is not the only thing that's huge about him!" she giggled as they watched him walk home after he'd stopped by to join them for brunch. "He likes it wild."

"Really, like 'wild' how?" Paige asked, almost without thinking. Such questions had become as easy as their friendship.

"Like robber-and-housewife," she giggled. "Or secretary-puts-out-to-get-the-job, stuff like that."

Or there was the superstar actor, half of a recently dissolved Hollywood power couple. She met him at a party at the comedian's Beverly Hills home. Later, when they got together she got drunk and acted out scenes from her favorite movie, *Showgirls*. He never called her again.

At that same party, she'd also met the famous financier and up-and-coming media mogul Seth St. James. He'd already acquired the old Kensington Studios, so she sort of knew who he was and made nice. Seth's subsequent buying spree around town turned his operation into one of Hollywood's most high-profile media powerhouses. Still married, Seth bought a place at the beach just a few houses away from Angel's, so their visits could be chalked up to being simply neighborly.

To Paige's continuing delight and astonishment, Angel divulged all this and more to him, week in and week out. In addition to her unnerving openness, Angel was sometimes quite generous materially with Paige. She offered him little gifts and trinkets, but her generosity extended to where it meant the most to him.

When Paige first took the job, Grizelda had him swear to take the secret of his ghostwriting to the grave. With Angel's assurances that they were embarking on a prolific writing partnership, Grizelda and Morris easily convinced Paige to settle for a pittance up front, barely enough to cover his rent, his gas to Malibu and a better brand of ramen noodles. In exchange, he was to receive a healthy share of the profits that Grizelda confidently predicted would flow from Angel's extensive promotions of the book and the inevitable film exploitation of the project. He was even contractually promised the title of executive producer on the "inevitable" film. "Once vee get zis off zee ground, eet vil be a money machine," Grizelda assured him. "Beeg advances and a new book every zummer."

But Angel rendered the whole ghostwriting secret moot.

When she was appearing on the *Late Night Show* to promote her new fragrance Heaven's Scent, the host brought up her much-hyped book. "So, Angel, how's the writing coming?" the host asked. His eyebrows and incredulity rose at the idea of Angel reading a book, let alone writing one. "Do you write a little bit every day, or how's that work?"

"God no," Angel snorted. "I hired Paige Blanche to ghostwrite it for me."

"Well, Angel," the host pointed out, "If it's a ghostwriter you're not supposed to know who it is."

"Oh no, I've totally met him," she explained.

Not only did her revelation get big laughs on the show, it put an end to Grizelda's obsession with secrecy. It also served to dispel at least some of Bill E's suspicions. Much to Paige's relief, the "mysterious" threatening phone calls he was receiving stopped abruptly after the public confirmation. As the project progressed, Angel not only made it clear to anyone who asked that Paige was her "ghostwriter," but also insisted that his name, bio and photo would appear right alongside hers on the novel's cover. It was a shocking development for the publishers, who didn't want to dilute Angel's celebrity in marketing the book. As if to add to the indignity for the publishing house, Angel also insisted that she would bring Paige along on her book tour.

Paige failed to notice that Angel's acknowledgment that she had a ghostwriter also voided their agreement. Combined with her failure to pay him, in the end he was left with nothing but broken contracts.

The sting of the ending was worse for the promise of the beginning. The early weeks of their collaboration were among the happiest in Paige's recent memory, if not his life. Not only had he found a job that he genuinely loved, he'd found a wonderful new friend who just happened to be the most famous woman in the world.

25

Brunch was ruined.

Angel more or less threw Wig out of the house.

"The housekeeper will be here next week," she huffed. "She can clean up this mess then."

"This will be a much worse mess by then," Wig told her. "It will only take me a few minutes to clear up."

Angel raked all the food and dishes off of the granite counter of the kitchen island and onto the stone tiled floor in a shattered finale. "There. All cleaned up!" she shouted. "You can go now."

"Angel—" Wig began.

"Now!" she shrieked.

Angel and Paige's eyes locked in silent mortal combat.

"I will call you, Paige," Wig said. He kissed Paige on the cheek, then fled.

Paige stood still and silent, his stare unbroken.

"He doesn't have a ride back into the city," Paige said.

Angel only glared.

"Well, I guess the real mystery is why they murdered Seth and not you."

Satisfied with the gasp he got in response, Paige turned and stomped up the stairs.

"Be ready to go to Grizelda's office in thirty minutes or I'm stealing your car," Paige shouted over his shoulder at her.

It was a tense ride.

No one spoke.

The weather looked threatening. Dark clouds piled up over the ocean to their right as they sped down PCH.

Paige snatched Angel's bag. Fending off her wild swings at him, he located her phone, dumped the remaining contents of the bag on the floor of the car and kicked them around.

There were unpleasant noises, but still no one spoke.

He dialed.

It rang once.

"Angel, darling," Honoria announced into her phone.

Already annoyed with her, Paige was infuriated by the fact that she answered on the first ring, something she'd never once done for him when he'd called from his own phone.

"You viper," Paige began.

"Paige?" she said, confused and off-guard. "Is that you?"

"Yes," he said tersely. "You traitorous hag."

"Darling," she said, with a nervous laugh that sounded like a cage full of pigeons.

"Grizelda had final edit on my books? And you not only knew it but you fronted for her?"

"Paige, darling, you don't understand," Honoria said, as she scrambled for an explanation, which only served to further establish her guilt beyond question. "It was a legal thing."

"Is that what you're going to tell the police?" Paige asked.

"The police?" Honoria gasped.

"Yes, it's looking like your collusion in this little scam is going to figure into the murder investigation," Paige said calmly. "It's looking like it was something in the book that got Seth killed. So any funny business with the edit is bound to raise questions."

"Look, I didn't have anything to do with this plan. Grizelda came to me," Honoria rushed to shift the blame. "She said she was concerned about the legal implication of Angel naming names."

"It was a novel," Paige growled. "Fiction, you know?"

"But everyone knew who it was about," Honoria argued the corner into which she'd painted herself.

"Yeah? And what were they going to do? Take us to court and prove that the nasty things we said about them were true?"

"What is that supposed to mean?" Honoria said in a small voice. Her defense was folding up with her own logic.

"It means you didn't give a damn about who we named or didn't in the first book," Paige said. "So why would you think it was a problem in the second book?"

"When you put it like that..."

"Well, I do," Paige said. His tone had gone icy. "So the question remains, why did you secretly let her cut my book?"

"Well, some, I guess," Honoria admitted reluctantly. "But mostly she added stuff."

"Added stuff?"

"Yes." Her tone shifted as it became clear that Paige didn't know the whole story. "Grizelda's the one who came up with the original outline I gave you when we started. She's the one who decided who was going to be in the book in the first place. She even picked you. Your writing partner wasn't Angel—it was Grizelda. I'm sorry if you felt deceived, but that is the truth."

Paige hung up. He looked at Angel, who was driving and pouting.

He knew how obsessed Grizelda was with secrecy. Honoria's revelation reminded him of the *Mission Impossible*-style interview process he'd endured at her hands.

"If I don't wind up in prison, I'm writing a book about all this once I figure out what the fuck all this is."

"Prison is a great place to write a book," Angel snarled.

They rode on in silence.

She dialed the stereo up to deafening and continued to fume as Paige stared blindly out the window.

Angel took her anger out on the road. Making an abrupt and unnecessary turn, she smashed Paige's face into the passenger window. In retaliation, Paige began to look for ways to torture her.

"Maybe the four of us can go on a double date," Paige suggested, breaking the silence. "Wig and me, and you and Mr. Right Now."

She said nothing as she accelerated.

"After this is all over, maybe I should move to New York so Wig and I can be closer, don't you think?" Paige asked. "Thanks to you, there's nothing keeping me here except the authorities."

She turned up the stereo from "nerve damage" to "permanent hearing loss."

They fought over the button for a bit.

Eventually, when Angel refused to relent, Paige got bored and randomly hit settings and mode buttons, silencing the music. The move made it impossible for Angel to restore the music without pulling over and locating the manual. Paige used the silence as an opportunity to call Roy on her cell phone to confirm their late lunch.

"Lieutenant," he said, just as she managed to hit enough random buttons to get the music back. "Angel, it's the lieutenant—could you turn that down?"

"Paige? Is that you?" Roy guessed.

Angel turned up the sound.

"Hang on a second, would you?" Paige cooed into her phone.

He turned the volume down, pulled off the knob, opened his window, and made a show of tossing the knob onto the highway.

"There. I'm back," Paige said. "Sorry about that. The controls in these new cars are so confusing. I haven't of course been able to afford a new car, as my former business partner swindled me out of my money."

"I'm sorry to hear that," the lieutenant said, before he realized what Paige meant. "Oh, I see, yes."

Angel tried to get a grip on the knobless stem, but Paige smashed her fingers with his foot.

Angel swerved and nearly lost control of the car.

"So are you two going to be at Seth's funeral this afternoon?"

"Funeral?" Paige said, giving Angel a look. "So soon? I have to say, this certainly makes the family look as if they've got something to hide."

Angel began rolling down Paige's window from the master controls by her seat.

"It's more of a memorial than a funeral, I think," Roy said. "The availability for some of the principals is pretty tight, so the family decided to have an observance now."

Paige went to war with his window control, rolling it back up even as Angel rolled it down. She gave up long enough to for Paige to look away and then rolled down all the rest of the widows and opened the sun roof.

"Availability?" Paige asked incredulously. "They're casting Seth's funeral?"

Paige began tousling Angel's hair as she struggled to both drive and get away.

"No, of course not," Slade said. "But if they don't do it now, they'll have to wait until late next month to have everyone they want for the services back in Los Angeles. A lot of them are already in town for the ex-wife and Lefty's engagement party or still in town from Seth's, so they figured it was just easier for the family this way."

"They may have to have it in the rain," Paige said, eyeing the clouds.

"Oh, there's no graveside," Roy replied.

"You haven't even released the body yet," Paige said, getting it.

"Right. We haven't even had the inquest," Roy agreed. "Like I say, it's just a memorial."

"I love Los Angeles," Paige said flatly. "So his funeral is two days after his murder."

"That's the plan," Roy said, with a shrug in his voice.

"Have you worked out who inherits, yet?" Paige asked, trying to steer the conversation back to other suspects.

"The lawyer, Earl something, says that—"

"Earl?" Paige said before he thought. Earl Filou kept popping up everywhere. Were there no other lawyers in L.A.?

"Yeah, you know him? He says that there was supposed to be a new will, but that Seth never signed it, or if he did no one can find it, so the original will stands," Roy said. "You seem surprised."

"We hadn't heard that," Paige said. "And yeah, it is surprising since they were engaged and all. Still, even less motive for Angel and, by inference, me."

"Will you be there?" the lieutenant asked, pointedly not conceding the point. "It puts a crimp in our lunch plans, I'm afraid."

"Of course we'll be there, just as soon as we find out where *there* is," Paige said, trying to make the family look worse. "I mean, we haven't heard anything about it. But I'm sure Angel will want to take part. She is the one who's lost everything, after all." Paige reached over and patted Angel's cheek. She batted his hand away.

"Yes, she seemed very broken up last night at the sushi bar," Roy remarked.

"So thoughtful of you to say," Paige said in his most lugubrious funeral director voice. "She's been very emotional today."

Angel managed to slap Paige hard enough for the retort to be heard over the phone.

"Dammit!" Paige hissed.

"What was that? You okay?"

"Oh, just opened a can of Diet Coke and it went everywhere. So the service is when?"

"They were able to get the Hollywood Forever Columbarium, their first choice site, but they could only get it if they went at five this afternoon," Roy explained.

"So, first choice of location and the principals were all available?" Paige asked archly. "What a piece of luck that the murder took place when it did. Rain check on lunch, then?"

"Maybe we can meet up afterward?" Roy suggested.

"Sure. I'll call you when it's over," Paige offered.

"No need. I'll be there."

"You will?"

"Jay St. James asked me to be present."

"I see," Paige said, giving it all the tone he could manage. "Well then, I guess I'll see you there."

Paige hung up.

"Guess who's friends with your fiancé's son?" Paige said into the sulky silence. "You don't suppose the lieutenant and the Jay are special friends, do you? That would kind of make you Lieutenant Slade's stepmother-in-law. God, you're getting old. You'll feel right at home at Seth's funeral later. Maybe I should invite Wig?"

"Listen, Paige," Angel began, speaking at last.

Paige produced the radio knob he'd only pretended to throw out the window. With it, he ran the volume back up, and took the knob off again.

By the time they got to Grizelda's Santa Monica office, the clouds overhead were the least threatening signs of a storm to come. Angel was in a rage, but Paige's day was looking up.

One Year and Nine Months Earlier...

The Beginning of the End

After their first book together was complete, Angel had largely gone missing.

Paige figured that the *new* of their writing partnership had worn off. They were obligated to write a second book, but Angel just stopped showing up for their regular meetings. They still spoke on the phone to discuss details of the upcoming tour and promotion for their first book, but more and more often Angel "had a conflict" or "forgot the time" and had to cancel their writer's breakfasts.

They were only a few meetings into the second book when it began. Paige arrived at Angel's beach house only to find the place dark and empty. Angel and Grizelda had professionally gone their separate ways several months earlier under vague and mysterious circumstances that Angel coyly refused to clarify. So when Angel didn't answer the door that day, there was no one else for Paige or his agent to call.

"Oh my God," Angel gushed when he finally got her on the phone. "I lost all track of time by the time I realized my phone was dead and no one on the shoot had a charger. Do you forgive me?"

There were big apologies at first. Bushels of flowers and various consolation prizes arrived. But as Angel went missing more and more, there was less and less by way of explanation or apology. And then there was nothing, especially not Angel. Paige knew she was out-and-about. There were well-reported incidents and sightings enough to preclude alerting the authorities.

In many ways, it was a blessing to Paige. He loved seeing her and spending time together, but it wasn't as though he needed her help to write the books. In the end, all he needed was her approval of his final drafts. Other than that, she really just slowed him down.

What he did need from her was for her to do what she did best, attract attention and sell their novel. She was the most famous woman in the world, or at least she had been. Thanks to Angel, the pre-release buzz on their book was amazing. Meetings with major retailers—online and brick-and-mortar varieties alike—had brought assurances of support to make their novel a bestseller. So what if she stopped showing up for their weekly writer's brunch? It was all-systems-go for the part of their collaborations that was her undisputed specialty. All Angel and Paige had to do on the tour was get the word out to her fans and one-handed-readers everywhere and they were golden.

Best of all, Angel had insisted he join her on the book tour. Paige was looking forward to that and to the time they'd get to spend together traveling the country and the world. Meanwhile, he busied himself putting the finishing touches on volume two.

And so it was that Paige arrived with high hopes and a finished manuscript for their second novel at the private airport where they were scheduled to depart on the promotional tour for their first. The writing partnership had turned into a friendship, advance sales were in the stratosphere and the second book had practically written itself.

Paige was so optimistic that he spent most of his bankruptcy savings on new clothes for the tour.

Allowing himself to hope turned out to be the second worst mistake he'd ever made. The first, of course, was agreeing to write a book with Angel.

He could hardly blame himself for his optimism, though when the time came, he did.

Angel went on national television and spoke in glowing terms of their collaboration.

"It's the perfect partnership," she declared in one interview. "It's like I don't know where he ends and I begin. We've morphed into one person."

The tour literally took off in their private jet.

Paige's previous publisher had used his book tour more as an opportunity to swindle him than to promote sales of his book. He had been naïve enough to agree to spend his own money for travel. In return, the publisher humiliated him by not actually doing anything they'd promised to do to promote him or his work. Paige sat by himself in bookstores in cities across the country where no one had any idea he would be reading or signing because the publisher hadn't bothered to tell anyone he was coming. Paige entrusted them with his dreams. In return, they broke his heart, his bank account and every single promise they had made him. It destroyed Paige's relationship with Honoria—who was actually a remarkable editor—and came near to breaking his spirit.

Suffice it to say, the bar was pretty low for Paige's expectations as the date of their book tour approached.

Then the town car arrived to pick him up when it was scheduled.

The guard at the gate of the private airport addressed Paige by name and wished him a happy flight and good luck on the tour as he was driven onto the tarmac. They parked alongside the plane.

"Good afternoon, Mr. Blanche," the co-pilot greeted him as he held the car door.

The entire flight staff knew his name. The pilot took Paige's bag from the driver after introducing himself and the crew.

Evan, the flight attendant, brought Paige a steaming and perfectly prepared cup of Jasmine Pearls tea without his even having to ask. He nibbled on iced stone crab claws and leafed through *Vanity Fair* as the hair and makeup people loaded in and they all awaited Angel's arrival.

She was late, of course, but nothing could dampen Paige's spirits. His work was done. This was her area of expertise. He was just along for the amazing ride.

"I'm so sorry," Angel said, with a quick hug. An apology was fast becoming her most common form of greeting. "I was with Andy. We were doing a shoot for that new magazine *Elements*."

"We're ready to go when you are, Miss Panderson," the pilot said as the flight attendant sealed the door shut.

"That is the single best part of traveling by private plane," Angel declared, taking her seat. "We leave on my schedule! Is there champagne? I need to take some pills."

And their tour began.

Prior to their departure, Paige's only real experience of Angel had been as his fresh-scrubbed breakfast companion. She would arrive, hair wet, her make-up-free-face scrubbed and shiny for their weekly meetings, rested and ready to go. Other than his *telenovela*-outrageous interview process, he only really had Angel's word for who she was.

From the moment the G650 was airborne the scales began to fall from his eyes.

She swam across the country on a sea of champagne.

Because they'd arrived so late she had no chance to change or freshen up before their first event, a meet-and-greet with book store chain executives and influential retail types.

The good news was that the event was at their hotel. The bad news was that Angel was tipsy to the point of slurring her words, more than a little wobbly and wearing the costume and make up from her photo shoot prior to their flight. Though Angel had attempted to explain Andy's concept, as best as Paige could make out it was sort of the United Colors of Benetton meets Munchkin Land.

Clownish makeup and garish children's play clothes combined to make her look more like a journeyman with the Lollipop Guild than a newly published novelist.

The steps of their grand old hotel were thronged with uninvited guests thrusting handfuls of Angel's nude photos toward their subject for her signature. Beyond the amateur stalkers, the pros were on full alert. Paparazzi flashes lit the night like summer lightning. The hotel's valet opened the limo door and their little party tumbled out to be captured for posterity.

Angel managed to sign only a couple of photos before security whisked their party inside the hotel.

By the time Paige turned their luggage over to the concierge to be taken up to their rooms, Angel was being fawned over by every bookstore chain manager, marketing executive and middle-management executron who could justify a trip to Manhattan.

"I love what you're wearing," declared one breathless gabardine-swathed executive extending her hand as she arrived at the book-signing table.

"This old thing," Angel said, giving Paige a wink. "Why, I only wear this when I don't care how I look."

"It's so *recherché*," Honoria added.

"It's part of the new imperial collection," Paige said, winking back at Angel.

The tour quickly became one long inside joke between the two of them.

It wasn't for some time that Paige realized the joke was on him.

He was a newcomer to what he assumed was standard procedure in the world of celebrity promotions. Paige mistook Angel's drunken partying for working the tour. In fact, she missed many of the bookings and interviews that had been scheduled to promote their book. When she did show up she was frequently in no condition to talk about their novel or even, in some cases, to talk at all.

In one memorable radio interview, she refused to speak altogether, scrawling her illegible and incoherent answers on a yellow pad and holding them over her head like Norma Ray. In another notorious moment, after being up all night, Angel was so amped when they showed up for a morning talk show that she never let the host speak at all. In fact, she didn't even stop during the commercial break and returned during another guest's interview with the infamous declaration, "Oh, I forgot to tell you about my new book."

Everything she did occasioned comment and, presumably, sold books, but nothing on the tour got talked about more than the men.

It began that first night. Drunk, and clad in clothes only an emperor could love, Angel managed to seduce a couple of underfed young "dancers" who had been hired to perform at the event. Unaware, Paige arrived in Angel's room the following morning to discover that the pair were still in Angel's bed and wearing less than they had the night before at the launch party, which hadn't been much.

"Hello," Paige called.

"Hey, Paige," Angel called from somewhere amidst a battalion of upended champagne bottles, an armada of overturned furniture and a fleet of rolling wardrobe racks from the tour's stylist. Coming to the archway between the bedroom and the parlor, she posed against the doorframe in some of the clothes and what was left of the same makeup she'd had on when she'd boarded the plane the day before. "Take our picture."

Paige realized the young men were naked on the bed behind her. One of them playfully flipped Paige off. Undaunted and a bit encouraged by the antisocial behavior, Paige raised his camera phone and snapped the shot.

"Have you two met my ghostwriter?" Angel asked casually as she came into the parlor and took Paige's arm.

"We have now," Paige said, with a curt little wave. "Nice, um, tattoos."

"See anything else you like?" one of the pair asked, kicking off the rest of the covers.

From the unsubtle eyebrow wave he got along with the unobstructed view, it was clear to Paige that it was a genuine offer, though probably not a free one.

"Later, boys," Angel said. She waved to the two as she dragged Paige out the door of the suite. "Mama's got to go to work."

The first signing together was a completely new experience for Paige.

He'd been to book signings before—his own among them—but nothing could have prepared him for the experience that awaited them at their first and every subsequent book signing together.

As they emerged from the back of the limo, the only bit of pavement from the adjacent block of West 48th Street that was visible was the narrow pathway formed by the flimsy portable stanchions and the interlocked arms of the uniformed police officers who created an aisle from the car to the back doors of the bookstore. The rest of the block was obscured. The crowd literally covered every inch of the street and sidewalk between Fifth and Avenue of the Americas.

The noise was overwhelming. The crush of bodies surging toward them was frightening and thrilling. The police strained to hold their line.

Inside, the press and paparazzi began flashing as Angel and Paige were rushed into a small space to freshen up before their debut.

Makeup personnel gamely made a few magic passes on the ever-more-tragic, at-least-two-day-old makeup.

Someone from the bookstore said a few words and on cue, they emerged.

Paige stood staring at the phalanx upon phalanx of insatiable photographers.

"Okay, come on," Angel said. She put her arm firmly around his waist and led him out in front of the absurd legions of cameras. "Now, smile. Chin up. We'll start on the right and then slowly to the left. Now back." Angel taught him through the clenched teeth of her frozen smile that looked false and strange in person and perfect in the photos he later saw of the two of them on television, the internet and splashed about in papers and magazines.

Gently, she guided him through five waves of paparazzi, press photographers and video cameramen.

And then the fans came.

It was as amazing the last day of the tour as it was the first. Hundreds and often thousands stood in line, camped out the night before, drove all night. Some even traveled from city to city to follow the tour, just to spend a few seconds with Angel, get her autograph and maybe a picture.

It was just as Grizelda promised.

Books flew off the shelves. Their names ticked by on the belt of lights in Times Square and on the cable news tickers. Overnight, Paige became the bestselling author he'd dreamed of being.

The publisher hosted a dinner in their honor that first night at New York's famed L'Truque celebrating their triumphant launch. In a rare acknowledgement that Paige actually existed, let alone had written the book, or possibly it was just in deference to Angel's insistence, the publisher presented the co-authors each with a crystal angel engraved with their names, the title of the book and the publication date. It was a beautiful evening despite the fact that Angel brought the two young dancers from the night before.

"They are my physical therapists," Angel introduced them.

Paige and Angel grinned over another inside joke.

For their parts, Honoria and her bosses from Peters and Luge all gamely pretended that the strippers they themselves had hired for the previous night's event were Angel's medical consultants.

And when L'Truque insisted that the two wear loaner coats and ties, Angel insisted the young men discard their shirts and wear only the loaners.

As Paige remembered the dinner, it was probably the high point of the tour for him though he'd hardly noticed at the time.

Whatever Angel did was seen as creative or outrageous and always newsworthy.

Angel took to the stage one night when they had dinner at one of New York's finer strip clubs. She managed to get most of her clothes off before the tour publicist and the two freelance physical therapists managed to get her back to her seat. The video was viral on YouTube before they got back to the hotel.

Paige could only see the free spirit and missed the willful sabotage of the actual purpose of the tour.

Angel damaged promotional opportunities further when she arranged to meet guys at their books signings and appearances, ignoring fans while making time with the men who might or might not join the tour for a city or two.

In London, Angel took a fancy to one of the television presenters who interviewed them. She had him over to their hotel for the night. Next morning she canceled all their book promotions and interviews so she and the presenter could have breakfast in bed. To Paige's endless amusement, Angel then spent months trying to avoid the man.

"Why not see him?" Paige asked when she was trying to arrange her schedule to miss his visit to Los Angeles. "He's a babe."

"He is, but he was done before he started," she shrugged.

"A charmful little arm-full?"

"But a dreadful little bed-full," she laughed at yet another of their private jokes.

Despite the fact that Angel partied her way through the tour, hardly ever drew a sober breath, refused to do more than half of the promotions that had been arranged and, when she did turn up, revealed that she knew surprisingly little about her own book, the tour and their sales were a smash.

"I'm working on book five," she'd say, coming in from a night out with a band or a team of acrobats she'd picked up at some knockoff incarnation of *Cirque du Soleil*. It might have been just another inside joke but it was delightfully true.

All he and Angel had to do was make a success of the second book and not only would Paige finally get paid for his work, but they could secure a lucrative deal that would allow them to put out a new book every summer for years to come. They had only to build the fictional version of Angel into a sales juggernaut and he'd have been hard pressed to make up the stuff she was actually doing. There was even interest from competing publishers, which would help drive up future advances if any incentive was needed.

"It's all about that second book," Honoria said during a brief visit on their way back through New York at the end of their triumphant tour. "If you make this kind of magic happen again, you can write your own deal."

Paige smiled.

Not only was the next book already written, but the first book had only hinted at the fireworks he'd wisely saved for their second novel to assure an even bigger reception. Paige could not have known that the only surprises their second and final book would hold were for him alone.

26

Zeldom Films, Grizelda's production/management company, was located in a quirky old loft space on the Venice end of Santa Monica's Main Street.

Angel pushed Paige in first as she held the glass-and-wrought-iron wicket door that cut through the large wooden factory gate that took up much of the façade of the old repurposed industrial loft building. Inside, despite the cloudy weather, faux marble finished cement floors gleamed beneath the old wire glass skylights that had illuminated the shoe factory that once filled the space.

"Phanie," Paige said effusively to Grizelda's assistant/receptionist. They approached her fifties-modern, stainless-steel, green vinyl-topped desk.

"May I help you?" Phanie asked listlessly without looking up from her computer screen. She was perhaps just too lazy to be "Stephanie" with all those extra syllables. Her attitude and energy level elevated at once as she recognized them. She stumbled as she got to her feet. "Miss Panderson, Paige, how great you're here. I mean, what a surprise you're here. Grizelda's so swamped today, but I'm sure she'll want to see you. Can I send someone to Starbucks for you?" she concluded breathlessly, exhausted by all the effort. She began subtly herding them toward the conference room door.

"Low-fat mocha would be great," Angel said, her voice flat and irritable.

"A big cup of China Green for me, two bags," Paige said, with a genial nod. "And how've you been?"

"Totes dreamy," Phanie beamed. She slid the meeting room door open and ushered them inside with a grace Paige found surprising in one so indolent. "I'm sure you'll be more comfortable in here in case someone should come in or something. I'll let Grizelda know and I'll get someone on that Starbucks run, pronto."

"Thanks, Phanie, that's great," Paige said.

The door snapped shut behind her. Paige put his ear against it. He could hear only Phanie's footsteps echoing across the cement floor as she walked away.

Angel flounced into one of the leather and chrome swivel chairs nestled around the thick bottle-green glass tabletop. It had been sandblasted with the Zeldom logo and was balanced on what looked like oversized Oscar statuettes.

When Paige was sure the coast was clear, he abandoned his listening post. Angel sat with her head in her hands, leaning petulantly on the glass table. Grasping the back of her rolling chair with both hands, Paige gave it a firm yank. Angel's hands slipped from beneath her chin and she fell forward. A satisfying hollow *thonk* filled the room as her head struck the table.

"Ouch."

Paige spun her around. "Now you listen to me," he threatened, his face inches from hers. "You can be as angry at me as you like. I seem to remember you saying that you were sorry that things hadn't worked out with me and Wig—that it would have made the night perfect."

"Well, that was when I was sure you'd lost," she said fiercely.

"Oh, that's *nice*," he drawled. "Well, be that as it may, you seem to forget that we're here to try to get information out of

Grizelda about the book that's already gotten several people killed, almost including us. Now I've never seen any evidence of your acting abilities myself, but you've got a People's Choice Best Actress Award at home on the mantle that says that a sizable group of folks in trailer parks all over this great land of ours think you've got some talent, so," he said, grabbing her shoulders and shaking her for emphasis, "I need for you to suck it up and *act* happy to be here."

"But I don't feel like it," Angel said through gritted teeth. "Why should I?"

"To save your selfish hide," Paige said, folding his arms. He walked away and sat at the head of the table. "And, if you don't behave, I'm going to give up this crazy amateur sleuth nonsense and tell Roy everything I know when I see him later today. I'll wash my hands of this whole affair."

"You'd do that to me?" she gasped, her rage replaced by indignation.

"You better believe it, sister," Paige said, staring her down.

"Why?"

"Because if you don't help me find out who did kill Seth and the "head cases," it will confirm what I've had reason to suspect all along," Paige said. "*You* did it."

She only had time for one more gasp as the doors flew open. Grizelda swept into the room like floodwaters following a dam collapse.

"Angel, dah-link, you've come back to me," she bellowed as she bore down on them, dressed in what appeared to be a pin-stripe zoot suit.

"Zellie," Angel said. Transformed, she leaped to her feet and ran into the broad beefy embrace of the Teutonic Titaness.

"*Mon cher*, zo zorry to hear about Zeth."

"Zeth? Oh, right, Seth. Thank you."

The two of them made out like long-lost sorority sisters. They kissed, they embraced and they shrieked to one another in registers that only dogs and Sigmas could hear.

"*Unt* Paige," Grizelda bellowed. She bore down on him, dragging Angel in her wake. "My treasure, come to *mutti*."

"It's good to see you," Paige said, rising and bracing for the hit.

As she squeezed the life out of both of them, Paige exchanged a look and a thumbs up with Angel behind Grizelda's back. The pain helped them avoid cracking up and blowing their cover.

Mercifully, Phanie arrived with their Starbucks order. Grizelda freed them from her steely grasp. "To vat do I owe zee honor?" she asked, taking a seat at the table with them.

Angel and Paige each gave the other a go-ahead-look. "Well, to be honest we're hoping you can help us figure something out," Paige said after a *you-go-no-you-no-you* eye exchange with Angel.

"Yes?"

"We think something that we put in the books we wrote may have been what got Seth St. James killed," Paige said confidentially.

"No," Grizelda said, lowering her voice. She looked around melodramatically. "Vat?" she asked at last, satisfied that they were alone in the sealed room.

"We have no idea," Paige admitted.

"In fact, we think it may be something Paige made up," Angel added.

"How can I help?"

"Honoria tells me that you had a big hand in putting the book together," Paige said as tactfully as was possible.

"Tish-tosh," Grizelda laughed dismissively. "I put down zome notes from Angel and you did zee writing, Paige."

"Honoria gives you more credit than that," Paige said. "She said you worked very closely with the editing process."

"Fact-checking, no more," Grizelda said with a little wave.

Paige's smile broadened. Her nervous laugh gave her away as her composure slipped almost imperceptibly across her vast face. "You're too modest," he said, patting her hand. "I guess what we're trying to find out is if anyone pressured you about cutting a particular item? Or if Seth ever spoke to you about the book?"

"Vell, not really," Grizelda said. She rubbed her hands together thoughtfully.

"Anything that was cut out that you would have kept?"

"You know, now zat you mention it," Grizelda mused. She stared off at nothing, concentrating. "Zere vas von sing."

"Yes?" Angel prodded, showing real interest for the first time since her mocha arrived.

"It was that producer friend of Zeth's, Mitch Geller," Grizelda said, tentatively. "Zat *très riche* billiondaire."

"He was the one who helped Seth get the money together to buy the studio in the first place," Angel prompted.

"*Mais oui*," Grizelda agreed. "He actually loaned Zeth zee money."

"I didn't know that," Paige said. He wondered what that would mean now that Seth was dead. Was the investment lost? Or did Mitch own a shiny new media empire? It was the difference between motive and plausible deniability.

"Oh, *très* yes," Grizelda nodded emphatically.

"But what does he have to do with the book?" Paige leaned forward.

"It was just somesing zat he said to me at zee launch party," Grizelda said distantly. "I didn't sink anysing of it at zee time, but now, I am not zso sure."

"What was it?" Angel asked.

It was a good question. Impressed, Paige wondered if Angel actually wanted to know or she was just getting into her role. Either way, he was certain that she had no idea what to do with the information should Grizelda actually offer any.

"He said zat zee only reason he vould buy von of zee books vas to make sure he vasn't in it," Grizelda said.

"Is that all he said?" Paige asked. So far, it didn't sound very important. Mitch Geller was one of the richest, most powerful men in Hollywood. He was also one of the biggest closet cases on both coasts. Secretly financing the studio wasn't the only thing he'd have to hide.

"He offered me a hundred zousand dollars to read zee second book before it vas published," Grizelda said in such a way that Paige could almost hear the suspenseful music. "He said he'd dodged a bullet in zee first von and vanted to be sure zat his luck held in zee sequel."

"Maybe he was just kidding," Paige suggested, still not convinced.

"I sought zo, too," Grizelda said, nodding. "But zee next day a case vis a hundred zousand dollars inside vas delivered."

"What did you do?" Angel asked.

"I invested in real estate." Grizelda shrugged. "And messengered him over a copy."

27

"Mitch Geller," Angel mused aloud, once they were safely alone and back inside the car together. "Would he have killed Seth?"

"It seems unlikely," Paige said, closing the door and belting in. "But you don't get to be a billionaire by being nice to people."

Their argument momentarily forgotten, both were focused on what they'd learned from Grizelda and what it might mean. Angel turned the key and the car was filled with deafening music, a placeholder for where they'd left things on the way over. Paige located the radio knob in his pocket, restored it and turned the volume all the way down. The two were left laughing in the silence that followed.

"What now?" Angel asked when they regained their composure.

"Well, we could fight over Big Wig some more," Paige suggested.

"No, no, no." Angel cut him off. "Truce. I'm done with that. He's all yours. I deed him to you in the treaty."

"Signed," Paige agreed. It was a hollow victory, but he had bigger battles. "Okay then, we need lunch and I need funeral clothes."

"Oh, that's right," Angel moaned. "That bitch Lucrezia—can you believe that she'd plan my fiancé's funeral without even asking me to attend?"

"Right?" Paige concurred. "Especially since you've spent all that time mourning and planning and worrying about the arrangements. So brave in the face of tragedy."

"God, you're such a bitch," Angel snorted.

"If telling the truth makes me a bitch, I'm guilty as charged," Paige said. "Let's go by my house so I can pick up some funeral clothes and then maybe we can get some lunch somewhere on Sunset before the services."

"No shopping?" Angel whined as she pulled the great behemoth into traffic without so much as a glance of caution.

"Then there'll be pictures of us out shopping," Paige said by way of explanation.

Angel only shook her head.

"We'll be less likely to be convicted of a murder I didn't commit if there aren't pictures of us out living it up on Rodeo Drive the day of Seth's funeral," Paige said.

"Oh, yeah," she said picking up. "Still, I've got to wear something."

"I'm the only person on the planet who's ever heard you say that," Paige said. "Malibu is so far away. Is there anything in your luggage at the Argyle?"

"No," she lied.

"One, I don't believe you," Paige said. "Two, I guess we could go back to Malibu, eat at your house and then I could change on the way."

"Bleah," Angel responded. "Boo."

"Or we could go to Saks…"

"Gucci."

"Okay, but just one store…"

"And Ralph Lauren."

"You?"

"It's a funeral. I need serious clothes."

"Lipstick on a pig. But a quiet lunch—"

"The Ivy!"

They ended their shopping spree literally running from the paparazzi.

Word got out while they were hat shopping at Gucci. They had an entourage for the two-block stroll to Ralph Lauren. They sneaked out the back and still had to run like the rain had already started, shielding their faces with the Gucci hatbox with the wide-brimmed, black, felted velour fedora inside and the Lauren bag with her Black Label LBD that Paige had insisted was her shopping limit for the day. There was also a black Gucci consolation shirt for Paige, the price of his silence in their funeral day shopping argument.

Their pursuers shouted questions as they ran.

"Angel, do they know who killed Seth?"

"Are you a suspect, Angel?"

"What do the police say? Angel, is there any word on the investigation?"

"Who are you wearing?"

They dove into the conspicuous white Range Rover and raced the photographers to the Ivy, a few blocks away on Robertson.

Two lobster clubs and one *tarte tatin* later, they were all but conducting a full-on press conference under threatening skies from the steps above the valet trap in front of the restaurant.

"Don't you think it's too soon to be out celebrating, Angel?"

"Are you concerned that people will think you're guilty?"

"Do the police have any leads besides you?"

"Angel, is it true you found Seth's head in an ice bucket?"

"What do you say to the rumors that you killed Seth so you and Bill E could get back together?"

"Angel? Busby Barclay, *Star Reporter*. Do you have a minute for us?"

It was perfect timing. The cameras were rolling and the valet was rounding the corner with their car.

"Busby, you know I've got so much I want to say," Angel whispered into the camera, taking his microphone hand and drawing it near. "Losing Seth has been devastating." She paused. The light at Alden had changed and the car was stopped. Paige put a reassuring arm around her as she hid her tears in his shoulder and stalled for their exit cue.

"Take your time," Busby reassured her.

"I just want to say that all the harsh accusations aren't making this any easier," Angel said, turning back as traffic started moving. "We're here because we still have to eat. And I went shopping for a black dress to wear to Seth's funeral. You can think the worst of me if you want, but know that I'm mourning the loss of the most important person in my life. I would never have hurt Seth—he was irreplaceable to me." The conclusion of her sound bite was perfectly timed to coincide with the valet's arrival.

The car pulled up and they made a dash for it.

With a daring maneuver through the narrow residential streets south of Melrose, Angel managed to give the paparazzi the slip and put the fear of God in a group of children walking home from school. Still, just to be sure, they parked the car at the Argyle and sneaked down to Paige's. They crossed through Barrymore Park and made their way up the alley behind Paige's building. His kitchen door was still shattered. The plastic that had been carelessly taped over the scene of Angel's ham-handed B and E attempt was blowing in the breeze.

"Great," Paige sighed. "I'm so glad anyone can break into my apartment without risk of being seen. Thanks for not just knocking on the door, Angel."

He got the kettle off the stove. She dropped her shopping bags on the table and poked around absently.

"Like you'd have waked up," she accused, looking in the refrigerator.

"Oh, I'd have waked up," he said. "I just wouldn't have let you in."

"Really?" she asked, looking up from the empty icebox.

"Covered with blood and carrying a murder weapon?" Paige answered her hurt tone with bombast. "No, I think I'd have called 911."

"And that is why I broke in," she declared, closing the refrigerator decisively.

Paige answered with a sound of disgust as he continued to organize a pot of tea. The glug of the up-ended water bottle disgorging as he filled the kettle was the only sound for a few moments.

Angel pushed open the swinging door into the empty dining room. She leaned in and looked across the uninterrupted expanse of hardwood flooring that glowed in the afternoon sun. The piles and boxes of their unsold second novel and the dead schefflera were the room's only occupants. She leaned back and allowed the door to close.

"I think there may be a little coffee in the freezer, if you want," Paige said absently as he rinsed his mug with hot water and awaited the kettle.

"Tea is great," she said, looking around the room. "As long as it's black."

"Earl Grey," he offered. "No milk, maybe a sugar packet somewhere."

"Just tea," she said. "The living room is beautiful. No furniture yet?"

"No," Paige said. He stopped moving. "Not yet."

"Or food in the fridge?"

"I'm saving up for bankruptcy," he said tartly.

"Paige…"

"Not now," Paige said. "I can't start 'cause I don't know where I'd finish."

"Listen, Paige—"

"No. You don't get to feel better about this," Paige said.

They stared for a moment.

The kettle blew time.

Paige poured the water, took up the tray he'd laid with the pot and two cups and stalked off down the hall to his dressing room.

Angel followed silently. She perched on the edge of a built-in chest of drawers as Paige weighed his clothing options. He poured the tea and then began to dress himself for the funeral in silence.

He had just stepped before the mirror to tie the skinny black tie when they heard a loud creak.

They froze.

Angel's teacup was suspended midway between the dresser and her lips. She didn't move or breathe.

The broken glass from the back door crunched as it was trod upon by someone coming in from the kitchen door in the alley.

Paige leaned over and pulled the dressing room door shut. The key was still on the inside from their last visit. He turned the old-fashioned lock, pulled the cord and plunged the little windowless room into darkness.

"Paige," she whispered.

"*Shhh,*" he asserted in a clipped retort as his only response.

They could hear the sound of whoever it was rooting through the drawers in the kitchen. They combed noisily through the silverware and utensil drawers. The dishes clattered as they were removed from the cabinets; there were other random thuds and the sighs of the aging floorboards as the search progressed.

Angel's hand found Paige's. They clutched for want of anyone better.

"Phone?" he dared.

"Car," she sighed. "Yours?"

"Dead."

They went silent. The sound of sneakers squeaked toward their hiding place.

The linen cupboard door next to the dressing room groaned open. They heard the cottony rustle of sheet and towels as they fell to the floor.

The knob to the dressing room door turned and rattled. The searcher yanked on the handle and tried to force the old wooden door open. Paige and Angel fell into each other's arms. A pair of ostriches, he slammed his eyes shut. She hid her face in his shoulder.

The door held.

The searcher swore and took it out on the bedroom. Glass broke. Things were overturned. The bathroom was more of the same as their increasingly frustrated guest raked the contents of the medicine cabinet shelves onto the unforgiving ceramic tile floor.

There was a pause. Without warning, the assault on the dressing room door resumed. They had to bite back the urge to scream. Clearly, the apartment's third occupant believed he was alone. He had little or no concern for noise.

It was only a matter of waiting for the door to give. The assault was unrelenting and clearly would end only with the door open or in splinters.

Paige tried to fight off Angel's terrified embrace enough to arm himself, but she was too powerful to escape and his options were too few. They each took a wooden hanger in hand for what good it would do them when the confrontation came.

"Paige?"

A familiar voice rang out in the distance, from the front of the apartment.

The attack on the dressing room door stopped abruptly.

"Paige is that you?"

The housebreaker remained still.

There was the sound of someone struggling with the key in the front door.

Paige and Angel were treated to the blessed sounds of retreating footfall as whoever it was fled down the hall and out the back door.

They remained frozen, afraid to breathe. At last Paige heard the difficult lock on the front door give way. "Paige?" the new guest called. "Are you here? Oh my God! Paige? Are you all right?"

"Armie?" Paige risked a timid bleat. "Is that you?"

"Paige? Paige!"

"In here," Paige called softly, still unable to let Angel go.

"Paige?" Armie shouted, grabbing the dressing room doorknob and taking up the struggle where the intruder had left off. "Oh my God, are you in there? I'll go get a key."

"No, don't go," Paige said. The thought of being left alone finally inspired him to action. He freed himself from Angel's insistent grasp and unlocked the door from inside. The two more or less fell, panting, into Armie's arms.

"Well, I'll be," Armie said, starstruck even under the circumstance.

"Armie, this is Angel," Paige said, with an eyeroll but not the least bit sorry to see the incorrigible old starfucker. "Angel, this is my landlord, Armie."

"Such an honor to meet you." Armie trailed off, tongue-tied.

"That's what I thought at first, too," Paige said. He switched the dressing room light back on and took one last look in the mirror. "But suffice it to say that Angel broke the window in the kitchen door and will be happy to pay for the repairs."

"Such a memory for slights and grudges, that one," she said, chucking Armie on the shoulder. "Still, the window's on me. As for the rest of this place…"

"Oh my God, my house," Paige wailed, emerging to get a first look.

"What happened?" Armie asked following as Paige surveyed the damage.

"Son of a bitch," Paige said softly. "I have no idea. We came by to change for the funeral…"

"Funeral?"

"And somebody broke in and did this," Paige said, throwing his arms out expansively. "Looking for something?"

"My dress!" Angel moaned. She dashed to the kitchen, only to find that the shopping bag and hatbox had been upended and flattened on the dusty hardwood floor. "I'll kill them."

"But I'm the grudge-keeper?" Paige said. "Here, I've got a roll of masking tape. We should have you in shape in no time. Armie, can we borrow your steamer?"

"I'll go get it," Armie said, nodding.

"And my new hat," Angel roared, holding up the crushed remains.

"As it happens," Armie said, "I think I can help you with that, too."

With Armie's star-crush-driven assistance, Paige and Angel were soon well turned out in their funereal finery, though the apartment was still totaled. He had always been a good friend to Paige, but when Armie broke out his prized Tallulah Bankhead, black-veiled, picture-frame hat from the Newport, Rhode Island production of *The Little Foxes*, well, Paige knew it was true love. He stood in the doorframe and watched as Armie carefully pinned the ludicrously massive chapeau on the pile of Angel's bleached blonde hair the two had contrived while Paige pointed at his watch.

"What are they going to do, start without me?" Angel sniffed when Paige called time.

"Yes." Paige nodded. "They most certainly will."

"Mmmm," Angel cooed as Armie draped the veils just so.

"What do you think?" Armie asked Paige as he fussed.

"She looks like she's got a turkey platter on her head," Paige snorted.

"You look divine, my dear," Armie assured her, offering Paige a dismissive cluck.

Taking Angel by the arm, Paige propelled her out of the dressing room. He reached back and grabbed an umbrella just in case, though the clouds so far had done no more than menace.

"I like him," Angel said of Armie as they made their way up the impossible Barrymore Park steps to Sunset.

"Well, I'm sure he'll gladly have your children," Paige gasped, out of breath from the exhausting recent turns in his life, let alone the past few hours and the dauntingly steep steps.

The camera flashes and inappropriately provocative questions began almost as they stepped onto the sidewalk of Sunset, headed to the Argyle where the journalists and paparazzi had laid their ambush.

"Angel, will you be speaking at the services?"

"Are you crashing the funeral or were you invited?"

Paige was pleased that he'd called ahead and asked the Argyle's valet to bring the car around.

"Will you inherit Seth's fortune now that he's gone?"

"Angel, do the police have any new leads?"

"Angel, did you kill Seth?"

That one turned her head. They got the shot just as she was stepping up onto the running board of the Range Rover. With a haughty head toss, she launched herself aboard the gigantic white SUV. The exquisite Ralph Lauren LBD, Angel's hair up and her face framed by the amazing hat—all of it contrasted against the white on white interior and threw the stunned expression on her face into stark relief with Paige's shocked face over her shoulder as he climbed in on the passenger side. He knew it would be the shot of the day and then some. It was the kind of celebrity snap that could earn a photographer a month's expenses. As they careened away into traffic, yards of Tallulah Bankhead's black veil trailed them, caught in the door that Angel had slammed in her haste to escape.

28

Hollywood Forever Cemetery is to death what the Chinese Theatre is to movie premieres. The storied final resting place of some of the industry's brightest stars and the site of about two-thirds of all the graveside scenes ever filmed, the cemetery is as famous and recognizable as Hollywood's iconic hillside real estate-promotion sign. The man who put up the sign and "founded" Hollywood was buried at Hollywood Forever along with Rudolph Valentino, Fay Wray and several of the Ramones. Paramount Studios was actually built on former cemetery property. Only a wall separates Hollywood's departed from those artists still thriving only a few feet away.

Angel didn't even try to outrun the paparazzi posse.

"You know they know," she said ignoring the shouts at every stoplight on the short drive between the Argyle and the graveyard.

"I know," Paige said, trying to remember to keep eyes front. "There's no point in trying to escape. It's like we're driving into a trap."

"Totally," she agreed. They rode in silence for a few blocks. "So who the hell was in your house?"

"I'm still trying to figure out what they were looking for," Paige said, fighting to keep his funeral face on as they rode to the services in the rolling fish tank surrounded by cameras. "I don't mind telling you that was the second most terrifying thing that's ever happened to me."

"Oh, right, meeting me was worse," Angel said, forgetting and rolling her eyes and then trying to play it off as fighting back tears as the paparazzi snapped.

"No, you ruined my life and there were a few tense moments—still are—but you're not even close to being terrifying," Paige assured her.

"Um, thanks?"

"Stupefying might be a better word," Paige said, trying not to get caught laughing.

"Okay, that's enough," Angel ordered. "Stay in character. No fair playing crack-up."

"Point taken," Paige said, and nodded. "Still…"

"I mean it."

They rode in silence the rest of the way. Playing the paparazzi game was her turf, and Paige ceded to her seniority. Neither of them could afford to look anything less than shocked and grief-stricken until the police had someone else in custody.

Soon enough, the gates of the famous cemetery were in sight. The blue-tiled dome of the Hollywood Forever Cathedral rose majestically above Hollywood Discount Mufflers and Elite Car Stereo, both of which were in the strip center that bordered the graveyard on the Santa Monica Boulevard side. A liveried attendant waved them past the cemetery museum and gift shop and into the valet line.

To their relief, in addition to the paparazzi, the police had been tipped off and were enforcing a well-defined boundary between the press and the mourners. The weather had held, even letting some late afternoon sun peek through. Valets shagged cars in the shade of the cathedral's terra cotta tile-roofed-covered entry drive. The press was relegated to the adjacent mausoleum parking lot. Mourners who wished to interact with the media could easily do so by walking a few feet. For those who preferred not to speak with reporters, the entrance was far enough away from the press line that it was possible for the bereaved to avoid hearing them, though it was not possible to avoid being photographed attending. No one got everything they wanted, but it was a workable solution and, for the most part, the press respected the boundary.

As Paige and Angel waited for their turn at the front of the valet line, they had a moment to revel in the red-carpet-level celebrities making their way inside to pay their last respects to a man they hardly knew.

"Look at these vultures," Angel said, nodding sadly to a network primetime staple who touched her heart to acknowledge Angel as she passed. "They didn't know Seth. Hell, *she* doesn't even like me." Angel smiled sadly and touched her heart in tribute and reply to the multiple Emmy-Award-winner.

"Glass SUVs, darling," Paige said.

"Well, what are we doing here?" Angel asked, hiding her face with a handkerchief that Armie had loaned her along with a black beaded clutch.

"I don't know about you, but I'm here to meet the other suspects," Paige said. "I didn't know Seth either and he was certainly not at the top of my Christmas list after what he did to my last book. Look at that, would you?"

"What?"

"Look who the lieutenant has his arm around," Paige said, gesturing with a nod.

"Jay St. James," she intoned. "Do you think?"

"His arm's around his hip, not his shoulder," Paige said, brow arched. "That's all I'm saying."

"If Jay's a suspect, does that mean the lieutenant—?"

"Cheese it, here comes the valet." Paige cut her off. "So, you be upset and I'll comfort you."

"Oh, I wanted to be brave," Angel whined as the valet drew nearer.

"It'll just come off as cold," Paige said with a somber shake of his head. "You don't have to throw yourself on the coffin—I mean, hell, there won't even be one. But a good swoon wouldn't hurt."

"Got it," she said as the valet opened her door.

Realizing that it was Angel, the reporters overran the line, and they were surrounded by the time Paige met up with Angel at the front of the car.

"Angel, this way! Angel!" they shouted, practically in one voice.

"Angel, who killed him? Was it you?"

Angel turned to the reporter, chin trembling. Her lips moved as she began to comment, and then she crumpled. Paige caught her and helped her up as the photographers and video cameras closed in.

Suddenly the crowd parted.

"Get back or I'll have you all ejected from the property," Lucrezia St. James boomed in a tone that sent the reporters and the faint-of-heart scattering. She was the sort of imposing woman who could strike fear into the souls of the most hardened Hollywood jades. Her supermodel height, glossy dark hair and thoroughbred bone structure made her Seth's physical equal. But it was the titanium self-assurance that gave Lucrezia the force of authority. Built out of money and privilege, she was a woman who had never once been troubled by doubt.

"Angel, darling, it's okay," she said in a deep, reassuring voice.

Together Paige and Lucrezia helped Angel to the curb.

"Leave it to you to turn this into a circus," Lucrezia muttered, dabbing photogenically at Angel's crocodile tears the moment they were out of earshot.

"I didn't plan this horror show," Angel said, grabbing Lucrezia's hands and hanging on as she swooned for effect. "What's your rush, Lucy? Something to hide?"

Paige was impressed. Angel was just the sort of white trash to be completely uncowed by Lucrezia's patrician authority.

"Don't call me Lucy," the great woman commanded with soft menace. Getting an arm behind Angel's back, she more or less dragged Paige and Angel inside. "There's a film shooting here for the next two weeks and this is where Seth wanted to be buried. You'd know that if you were anything more than window dressing."

"What?" Paige asked, wondering at her implication.

"Between his engagement party two days ago and mine the day after tomorrow, everyone who we would want to attend is already in town," Lucrezia said, releasing Angel.

"Paige was right," Angel said, grabbing at Lucrezia. "This *is* about casting and location?"

Lucrezia did not slow her pace.

"Sounds like you're just the ringmaster at this circus," Angel yelled. "You're not even a featured attraction, let alone a star."

Everything went silent. Lucrezia froze, though she did not turn back. The press was on the move. There was an explosion of flashes and questions as police and event security struggled to hold the media at bay.

Paige could see the steel in Lucrezia's spine stiffen. As deliberately as she'd done everything in her whole life, she resumed her stately departure.

"Bitch," Jay St. James hissed at Angel as the lieutenant dragged him past.

Roy nodded nervously at the two of them as he struggled to get Jay into the sanctuary. Paige gave the lieutenant a you're-not-fooling-me look that got a sheepish smile in reply.

Jay and Angel's eyes locked. With the lieutenant to navigate his path, Jay never turned away. He maintained his icy glare for as long as he could see her.

Angel blew Jay a kiss as he disappeared inside.

"Welcome to *Meet the Suspects*," Angel said, extending her elbow. "Shall we?"

"Have you done this before?" Paige whispered as she propelled them inside.

With the confidence of a victory march, Angel strode to the front of the chapel.

Lucrezia had taken up her position on the front pew on the groom side of the sanctuary. She was joined there by Lefty, Jay, Lieutenant Slade and what Paige could only suppose were various other members of her family and household. Whoever they were, they looked like pillars of money got up in funeral weeds. The rest of the domed room was filled with just the sort of be-spoke-masters-of-the-universe one might expect to people the rarified world that had been the natural habitat of Seth St. James in life. Sprinkled among these were the boldface celebrities and wannabes, peers only in that both were trying to scrap a reputed acquaintance with a man in no position to dispute their claims.

Paige knew this was a regular occurrence in the industry following a notable death. People, downright strangers who could not place so much as a photograph in evidence to support their claims, told elaborate tales of intimacy and loss to anyone with a camera and a willingness to listen.

The three-time Emmy-winning actress and a number of Seth's fellow cosmic commanders had taken up the other front pew, bride's side.

Angel simply walked to the front and took up a position.

She stared.

The room, already hushed with the affectation of reverence, real or not, fell deadly quiet. The Emmy-winning actress was turned in her seat, speaking to someone in the pew immediately behind her and was the last to realize and fall silent. She turned and found herself caught in Angel's affronted glare.

In a moment worthy of Mack Sennett, the party on Angel's row rose and moved house left, *en masse*, to make the aisle seats available to her. Lucrezia misread the moment and made an exasperated noise, which led everyone to glare at Lucrezia. They blamed her for the slight to Angel, who was, after all, the dead man's fiancée, whatever you thought of the sincerity of their relationship. Angel had become the grieving widow by default.

It was actually Lucrezia's fault. She had intentionally only asked that the front row be reserved on the one side for herself and made no provisions for Angel whatever. She had inadvertently cast herself as the villain and made it apparent that her only interest was in fulfilling the social obligation of hosting the memorial. She was clearly an ex-wife and one who would not be mourning the departure of a husband who had left her a long while before.

"You're winning the funeral," Paige whispered to Angel.

"Stick around," she said.

The Emmy winner, re-seated to Paige's left, reached across him and took Angel's hand reassuringly before giving Lucrezia the stink-eye so everyone could see how close she was to Seth, a man she'd never once met.

And so the bizarre service began.

Earl, the ubiquitous entertainment/family lawyer, officiated. "Friends," he began. "We were all friends of Seth's and so today at least, we are all friends here; friends who have come together to remember and to say goodbye to a man who left us too soon and too tragically. I've been asked, um, well, if it's okay with everyone..." He stumbled and gave Angel a pleading look. "We, or rather, I thought it would be best to do this informally. Those who wish to speak may do so."

Angel shot him a sad but studied smile and a quick nod.

For a moment, the lawyer looked a little too happy to be the officiant at a funeral. Adopting a more solemn tone, he made some short remarks about how he'd only recently become a part of Seth's world and how sad he was that they wouldn't be working together as they'd planned.

"I'm just glad to have had the chance to get to know this remarkable man," he concluded. "Now, if anyone else would like to say a few…"

Angel made as if to stand. Paige grabbed her hand, fearful of what she might say. In the hesitation, Jay leapt to his feet and raced to the little lectern that served as a mic stand.

After shouldering Earl out of the way, Jay shot Angel a withering glare of victory. In return, Angel nodded to him gently, as though giving him permission to be next. Visibly shaken by even the appearance that Angel would be in such a position, Jay was so tongue-tied with rage that he could barely speak.

"My father was a man that few people got to know well," he began, haltingly. "He was a man of many interests and many accomplishments, which meant he was a man with very little free time. He was more generous with the fruits of his success and I have been blessed with a life of great privilege thanks to my father, but sadly not with as much of my father as I would have liked. And now, though his generosity continues even as he has moved on, he took his greatest gift with him when he was taken too soon by this tragedy."

Jay glared at Angel.

He managed to stumble through, expressing regret that he might not have made it clear to his father how much he meant to him and how grateful he was, but Jay never recovered. Instead, he sounded angry, resentful and neglected by an absent father who had ignored him most of his life which, Paige figured, was probably closer to the truth. "My daddy was taken away from me and it's not fair," he said, dissolving and sobbing into the microphone. After a minute or two of his amplified tears, Roy rose and helped Jay back to his seat. He continued to cry on the lieutenant's shoulder as Roy kept him wrapped in a protective arm.

Lucrezia declined to speak, which only made her look more like what everyone already knew perfectly good and well she was. Seth was her ex-husband; still it was she who had invited everyone to the uncomfortably premature memorial.

Lefty was there only as a show of support for Lucrezia and because, presumably, there would be food at some point, so he said nothing. Some of Seth's business associates and a few distant family members spoke. But quickly it became clear that, other than being shocked by the tragedy and sorry for the loss, no one had much to say.

Paige scanned the room during the long, uncomfortable silences when no one had yet taken the unspoken invitation to speak. A pianist filled the uncomfortable moments with movie themes.

"Mitch Geller isn't here," Paige said to Angel under his breath as he turned back.

Angel was clearly focused elsewhere. She had only made a move as if to speak at the outset. With Lucrezia's refusal, it seemed that perhaps Angel too would hold her peace.

"Well, if there's no one else," Earl began.

Angel stood.

There wasn't even breathing.

Paige sat motionless. He could not comfortably reach her to stop her. All he could do was hold his breath in anticipation of her impromptu eulogy.

Angel took a breath and then, gathering her strength, she walked to the mic.

Earl helped her onto the little raised area where she took up her place next to an absurd amount of flowers and a giant photo blow-up of her fiancé that had clearly been taken many years before or heavily retouched or possibly both.

"Thank you all for being here," she said softly.

Paige could almost hear Lucrezia's teeth grinding. He wondered if she would do a rebuttal after Angel sat down. He almost laughed when he imagined Angel rising to speak a second time after Lucrezia's rebuttal and the two speaking in rounds until their respective camps dragged them away or, better yet, it came to blows. He gave a little bleat of laughter that he played off as a sob and only just managed to keep from losing it altogether. Angel gave him a look but waited for him to settle.

"It means a lot to me that so many people showed up on such short notice to pay respects to a man who changed my life," Angel said. "I bet he changed your life too. I bet that's why you're here. I bet you wonder, as I do, what we're going to do next. I bet you wonder how we're going to go on without Seth to make everything possible. I'll tell you, I was a little surprised to see the sun came up the next day without Seth here to make it happen."

There was a little soft laugher and some sobs.

"That's who my Seth was. That's how important he was to me. I bet he was that important to you, too. I bet you were as surprised as me to see that the world kept turning without Seth there to set it spinning. I bet you're as mad as I am that someone would take someone like our Seth away from us. I bet you want know who would kill our Seth, our own saint. And you want to know what else I bet?" she said leaning into the microphone and going for it. "I bet his murderer is here in this room right now. And whoever you are, you better hope the police catch you before I do."

She said some other stuff too, but after Lucrezia overturned the mic stand and tore the wires loose, there was just a lot of shouting and the deafening sound of amplified feedback. There was that and the unforgettable spectacle of Angel beating Lucrezia with a huge bouquet of Casablanca lilies as she chased her out of the Hollywood Forever Cathedral and into the waiting arms of the press.

Sometimes Paige didn't hate spending the afternoon with Angel.

29

"Can you believe that?" Angel demanded, exhilarated. She smacked the steering wheel for emphasis. Still swanked-out in their Hollywood funeral attire, they were speeding west on Pico under ominously dark skies. Angel had given the paparazzi the slip with a clever maneuver in the Beverly Center parking garage when they gave chase after the press storm that concluded Seth's crappy memorial. The catfight at the end between Angel and Lucrezia was actually the best, nay, the only good part. The two ladies had literally rolled around on the carpeted front walk, pulling one another's hair and liberally using both the "C" and the "B" word. Jay and Lucky pulled Lucrezia free while Paige made a halfhearted attempt to extricate Angel from a battle in which Lucrezia was getting a beating he felt she richly deserved.

"This isn't over, bitch," Angel screamed, shaking her finger at Lucrezia.

"Actually, he's still dead, so it *is* over," Lucrezia replied smoothing her dust-and lint-covered black Chanel suit. "And I won."

Perhaps Paige had not held on to Angel as tightly as he might have. Perhaps he pushed her in Lucrezia's direction. Who could say?

Whatever the cause, Angel landed a good solid punch under the taller woman's jaw and sent her sprawling into the water feature in the serenity garden. As the other side struggled to extract the soaked, indignant and squawking woman from a tangle of water lilies, Paige and Angel beat a hasty retreat. With the help of a starstruck valet, they retrieved the car and sped away before further reprisals could be exacted.

Paige wondered why the paparazzi needed to chase them after that. Unless they knocked over a bank on the way home, there was no topping *that* exit.

"Once we figure out who killed Seth, we're going to have a proper funeral," Angel declared. "And that B-I-T-C-you-next-Tuesday can sit in the back, if she's not in jail."

Gone was even a trace of the animosity she'd shown toward Paige on the ride into town that had begun their day.

"Yeah, but first we're going to have to figure out who the murderer is ourselves," Paige said, thinking over the thankfully growing list of suspects. "Doesn't look like we're going to be able to count on Lieutenant Spokesmodel."

"Right?" she said. "I *said* you should have gotten in there. Now he's working for their side."

"Or at least sleeping with the enemy," Paige added.

"I guess your lunch together is off."

"Well, it explains why he was so well-informed on the memorial service," Paige said with a little who-cares-anyway head toss. "Did you notice Mitch Geller wasn't there?"

"No, really?" she said. "Does that make him look guiltier?"

"Or did he just flee the country on his private jet?"

"Or yacht."

"To his private island," Paige concluded.

"That and paying off Grizelda to keep his name out of the book makes him look like a prime suspect," she said. "I hope it's Lucrezia. I never liked her."

"But what in the book could Mitch have thought was about him? Why the big deal?"

"You implied that he was a big fag," Angel pointed out.

"He *is* a big fag," Paige said with a shrug. "And everyone knows it. And besides, they are fictional characters. It's a novel."

"You said that he was an evil monster who destroys his enemies. That he made most of his money selling out the record labels he started at the top of music trends—and that he left the buyers and the artists who made him rich to twist in the wind when the trends went bust."

"I thought you hadn't read the book."

"I haven't, but that's what I told you, right?"

"Yeah and I put it in the book, though it sounds like a lot of sour grapes to me," Paige said with a dismissive sniff.

"But it got changed, right? It wasn't in the second book?"

"I can't remember anymore," Paige said. "I'll have to look at my notes. Or worse yet, read the book. It got so crazy on the second book with changes from you and Honoria and Seth and, it turns out, Grizelda. I'm not sure what's in there and what's not anymore."

"Well, if it's not?" She let the question hang in the air.

"Then we may have our first real lead," Paige said with a whistley little exhale.

"Where are your notes?" Angel asked. She gave a genial smile to the paparazzi camped outside the gates of her Malibu compound. They raised their cameras halfheartedly. Nothing could top the show at the funeral. The guard raised the gate and waved them through. Angel waved back and made her way the last few blocks.

"The notes are at my apartment," he said, checking the car's clock.

"Well, I'm going to have a really long hot bath and a nap," she said, snatching the emergency brake as she brought the huge gas guzzler to an abrupt halt in front of her house. "It smells like we're finally going to get the storm we've been promised all day and the sound of rain on the roof makes me sleep like a baby. We can go in for dinner later when the photogs get bored or washed away, then stop by your place for your notes."

"Why not?" Paige grinned. "Dinner went so well last night."

"What are the odds of that happening again?" She shrugged.

"I can look over the second book while I'm here and see if I can find anything incriminating," Paige agreed, a little reluctantly. "If the rain doesn't put me to sleep, doing that certainly will."

"Or you could just have a nap, too," Angel said evasively as she punched in the code. He followed her through to the door. "We can worry about the book and the notes after dinner."

A nap didn't sound half bad.

He stopped.

"You don't even have a copy of the book, do you?" he demanded.

"Maybe somewhere," she said evasively as she rolled the rickshaw aside. "It seems vain to keep mementos of yourself."

"You don't have it!" he shouted.

She tried the door, rattling the handle, then returned to the rickshaw.

"Where is it?"

"You know perfectly good and well whether or not you own a copy of the book we wrote together!" Paige huffed.

"No, where is the key?" she said, exasperated as she tried the door again.

"Don't you have one?" Paige asked.

"Yeah I do," she said mockingly. "I keep it right here, remember?"

"No, I mean, don't you have one in your purse?" Paige asked more irritably.

"In my purse?" Angel said reproachfully. "Of course not. Why would I keep one in my purse? I have hundreds of purses. Should I have a key for each of them? I borrowed this one from Armie; should he have one?"

"The reason I asked is because the one that used to be under the rickshaw is inside on the hall table."

"Paige!" she wailed.

"I'm sorry," he said abjectly. "But I was scared when I got home last night. We'd just been shot at. I thought I was alone in the house. Then today, I just figured it was a spare key."

"Why would I need a spare when I have one right there, under the rickshaw?" She smacked him on the shoulder with her purse. "What are we going to do?"

"Maybe the glass doors in the back are open?"

"God, come on," she said, disgusted. He followed her and her giant black hat down the narrow alleyway carved between hers and the house next door. The outrageously expensive homes were surprisingly close together. There was a fence between Angel's and the house next door with three feet of space on either side of that. The neighboring residence belonged to an Australian woman who'd suddenly become household-word-famous singing pop music in the '80s. Then, just as suddenly, she'd vanished from view and public consciousness. Occasionally during lulls in their writers meetings out back by the pool or on Angel's deck upstairs, Paige had heard her still-beautiful voice as she sang her old tunes around the house, just like anyone else might and yet—in that the songs were her million-sellers—not quite like anyone else.

That afternoon, the only sound was the crunch of white marble gravel under their feet as they made their way through the claustrophobic passage into the sumptuous but compact backyard.

Angel marched across the patio, grasped the handles on the double doors and pulled fruitlessly. "Dammit!" She yanked on the doors a few more times in frustration. "Now what are we going to do?"

"We could break the glass."

"You can't," she said in a nasty singsong tone. "They're double-insulated and unbreakable."

"Do you have bulletproof glass in your windows?" Paige asked. His tone was both mocking and accusatory with just a dash of impressed.

"Yes," she said defensively. "I'm very famous. You just never know."

"Well, lately anyway," Paige said. He spotted some rusty metal boxes and gardening implements by her tiny swimming pool. "What's that?"

"I was having some work done on the sprinkler system. I guess they left their stuff or they're not done," she answered, following as he made his way to the tools.

"Just what we need," Paige said, producing a hacksaw triumphantly from one of the bins.

"Wait a minute," Angel said, following him back to the patio doors. "What are you going to do?"

"This is the kind of saw they use to cut metal pipe," Paige explained as he took the tool apart. "I'm going to take off this blade, thread it between the two doors, saw through the bolt, and presto, we're in."

"Paige, do you have any idea what you're doing?"

"None whatsoever." He managed to slip the blade through the space between the two doors and forced it down to rest on the bolt.

"That's what I figured," she said, rooting around in her purse for her phone. "I'm calling a locksmith."

"No, this should work." He started sawing.

"Honestly," she sighed, surfing for the number. "All this amateur detective stuff has gone to your head."

"O ye of little faith," he said, sawing vigorously.

"Are those sparks?"

"Don't worry."

There was a blinding flash.

The last thing they both felt were the sensations of heat and of flying as they catapulted through the air on waves of liquid flame.

Witnesses would later say there was a huge noise, but Paige and Angel never heard it.

The house disintegrated into matchsticks and was replaced by a fireball twice its size.

30

It turned out that Angel's bulletproof glass doors worked in both directions.

Paige and Angel had been flattened like bugs on a windshield as they flew across her backyard. The doors blew off the back of the house, propelling them into the relative safety of the swimming pool. The force of the rest of the explosion and its deadly household shrapnel passed above their heads.

By the time they resurfaced, what was left of the house was on fire. Most everything that would and could have killed them was scattered over a six-block radius. The fireball that was formerly Angel's house passed over their heads as they watched from beneath the ripples. When they first breached the surface of the pool, flaming rubble continued to fall from overhead. They struggled through the debris in the water.

Paige dragged Angel under the diving board. They remained there, heads above water only far enough to breathe, until things settled. There were a few small explosions following the first mother blast. The enormous bricked-in gas grill was propelled from its resting place at the side of the patio, leaving a huge hole through the hedge and fence at the back of the property in its trajectory, and splashing down in the marsh beyond.

Once things calmed to the relative quiet of a mere four-alarm fire, the two climbed out of the pool. They tried unsuccessfully to make their way to the street. The blaze was too hot and the path to the street too narrow. Several minor explosions thwarted them further and sent them running for cover behind the burned-out hulk of the armoire that had formerly housed one of her enormous televisions. They gave up the idea of waiting the fire out and decided on escape via the grill-shaped hole in the hedge at the back of the property.

Clinging to the back fences of the residences of the Malibu Colony, they worked their way along the narrow swampy embankment of the tidal estuary that ran behind all of the houses on the leeward side of the street. At the bank's end, they reached the gate in the chain link fence where Angel's road ended and the beach began. As they turned to make their way back, Paige's blood froze in his veins. Roy was seated calmly on the hood of his car, watching the fire a safe distance beyond the house.

"Look," Angel said, a little too loudly, their ears still ringing from the noise of the explosion. "It's Lieutenant Sl—"

"*Shhh*!" Paige dragged her past the fenced-off dead end of the little street and onto the darkening beach.

"What's the matter?" Angel demanded.

"Think about it," Paige snarled under his breath. He was trying to whisper, but he was as hearing-impaired as Angel and was really only shouting more quietly. Their voices were covered by the roar of the nearby Pacific that neither could yet hear. "Who was it who knew where we'd be this afternoon? Or when we'd be back? Or where we were last night?"

"Santa Claus?" Angel suggested, palms turned heavenward. Her clothes were in shreds. Leaves and chips of house paint tangled in her singed hair.

"Roy!" Paige said. "Now there he is, watching the house burn like a horny arsonist. How did he even get past the house to be down at this end of the street? Or why would he?"

"Oh, you'll say anything to get out of going out on a fix-up date," she said, rolling her eyes as she picked tiny pieces of her kitchen counter off of her tattered blouse.

The sounds of approaching sirens interrupted them.

"We've got to get out of here," Paige said, looking around to see who was on the beach. The few people still there were either staring in the direction of the fire or heading towards it.

"Where the hell are we going to go?" she breathed.

Paige could tell she was annoyed, but not unconvinced that he was right about the lieutenant and frightened enough not to want to take chances.

"We need to go somewhere that no one will ever think to look for us," he said.

A sly smile split her sooty face as she looked down the beach.

"I know just the place," Angel said. "Follow me."

31

Their ears were ringing but the sound of thunder made them both flinch.

"So, do you believe me now?" Angel asked as they slogged through the soft sand in the rapidly deepening darkness.

"Believe what?" Paige replied, irritably. He was wet, scorched, bruised and covered in abrasions from their little adventure.

"Do you believe that I'm innocent?" Angel persisted, running to keep up with him as they made their way down the beach.

"Great, make this all about you," Paige growled.

"I'm just saying that I'd hardly have blown up myself and my house as a cover story," she said, matching his tone.

"I'll start a collection for your stained glass window, okay?"

"Will you ever just forgive me?" she said, shoving him so hard that he tripped and fell over in the sand.

He tried to get up, but she pushed him down again, sobbing.

"This is so completely the problem with you," he said. He threw a handful of sand in her face so that he could escape her and get to his feet. "You squeezed all that you needed out of me. Then you tossed me aside like a used toothpaste tube. Now you want me to give you absolution?"

"All I want is for you to let me off the hook!" she screamed into his face, pounding on his chest.

He managed to catch her wrists and hold her in check. They were the same height and pretty evenly matched, so it was a standoff. They stood panting, glaring at one another, straining to hold their positions in the shifting sand.

Another thunderclap wrinkled the air above their heads. Dark clouds boiled up out of the ocean. Paige hardly noticed the makings of the spectacular sunset banding the horizon.

"You know, maybe if you weren't such a complete waste of skin, and actually made a positive contribution to the lives of anyone other than yourself, you wouldn't need me to exonerate you," he said quietly. "Maybe if you'd treated me decently in the first place you wouldn't need to be let off the hook."

The first heavy drops of rain fell hesitantly from the sunset-infused clouds. It spat against them, cold, hard and shocking.

Angel broke the stalemate, wrenching her arms away.

The deluge began.

They ran down the beach.

They chose their destination for its randomness and beach access.

The downpour came in what Paige called Los Angeles torrents—not like rain at all but simply water pouring, uninterrupted, from the sky. Instead of getting hit with individual drops, it's more like getting blasted with a hose.

The rain made the beach tough going, but it allowed them to travel unseen. The last people they'd come near on the beach were the fleeing refugees from a children's birthday party who were far more concerned with scrambling for cover than star sightings as the storm clouds rolled in and the lightning and thunder began.

Los Angeles dissolves in the rain. Because rainfall is so rare, the city has no coping skills for it. Despite its natural state of drought, L.A. doesn't even have a means of catching rainwater. Escalators are uncovered and outdoors. Interior furniture is commonly used and stored outside, unprotected. The city simply ceases. Events go unattended or are simply cancelled altogether. The freeways and roadways turn into carnage because no one has the least notion how to drive in the rain. The prevailing wisdom seems to be to drive as fast as possible to get home sooner.

In the rain, Angel and Paige, despite their rather frightful appearance, were able to make their way down a public beach in one of the most populous areas of the world completely unobserved. The enforced silence between them was welcome as both still smarted from the brutal honesty of their exchange.

"This is it!" she cried out, trying and failing to raise her voice above the thundering rain. She raced to catch up with Paige. He resisted when she grabbed his arm. Silently he followed her toward the steep and forbidding rock face that bordered the disappearing strip of sand under foot. The rocky wall they were pressed against offered minimal shelter from the tempest. Angel led him along, feeling her way.

Then, as abruptly as *open sesame*, they came to a cleft in the rock wall that led them onto a staircase carved into the stone. Their cover diminished as they ascended. Nearing the top of the bluff, they were again pounded by the relentless cascade. Ocean winds, whipped into frenzied gusts by the cliffs and the storm, made the driving torrent into lashes, slowing their progress still more and threatening to toss them over the edge.

A single light flickered in the distance. They edged toward the pale beacon. As they neared the source, it revealed itself. A blue glow filled the ground-floor windows of an otherwise dark and lifeless house. The imposing structure was large enough to look like a continuation of the rock face they had just scaled.

As they drew nearer, it became clear that the lighted windows were actually a series of glass doors. The doors wrapped around one side of a patio that had at one time been covered by an awning. All that remained was the rusted steel frame that had once supported the canopy. The rain beat on the naked glass.

Angel and Paige approached and tried the door handles. Locked. They pressed their faces against the glass to see if there was anyone inside to hear them.

Inside, a glowing television screen flashed a news report with pictures of a huge house fire. It gave way to a blue screen for a second or two and then was replaced by the sepia glow of a low quality, under-lit video. The blurry footage revealed an over decorated VIP room in a bar, long ago and far away. It took a moment for Paige to realize what he was seeing. The video that had made Angel and Bill E so very famous had replaced the televised news of the fire at Angel's house.

A still-youthful Angel flickered into view. "Be quiet, we don't want to wake him up," she said with a giggle to the lead singer from Bill E's former band. The camera zoomed in on a young, sated Bill E, who was passed out naked on a nearby sofa.

The infamous video had first appeared on the internet and went on to become one of the bestselling adult videos of all time. It later came out on DVD and became a bestseller yet again. It was the beginning of a storied and eventually clichéd Hollywood tradition.

Celebrities of a certain stripe—typically those whose only claim to fame is youth and looks, rather than any actual talent—release their "private" sex tapes in desperate and obvious attempts to grab their own piece of immortality and unearned fame. The prevailing wisdom is that if two such self-absorbed, meritless, no-talent has-beens as Bill E and Angel could command such media attention with the technological equivalent of boastful words written in a public bathroom stall, then anyone with large genitals and a few minor film credits or a well-known family name could do the same.

The sickening spectacle has led to more than a few of Hollywood's more visible and unwarranted careers as each new amateur porn star takes their brief turn in the spotlight.

Angel's recorded moans and cries could be heard over the storm as they echoed through the beachfront mansion. The place was, Paige realized, surprisingly empty. He had heard it was for sale. The furniture, the toys, the gadgets, the mementos, even the awards that had once stuffed the overproduced manse, had all been sold off. All that remained were a lube-stained sofa, a ridiculously large flat screen TV, a disc player, Angel and Bill E's DVD and the memories of former grandeur.

Angel and Paige began pounding for admittance like a pair of Flintstones.

32

They laughed, despite the horror of their afternoon.

Bill E, shirt unbuttoned, fly open, his torso bathed in the glow of the television, the room's only light source, looked up from what he was doing to see the laughing faces of his dead wife and her dead former best friend smushed against the windows of his den backlit by storm and lightning.

The two outside, peering in half drowned, looked every bit as though they had been thrown from an exploding house. Bill E, medusa-haired and face frozen in a rictus of horror and disbelief, looked more like he had his finger in a socket rather than where his hand had oh-so-obviously been. It was hard to say who looked worse or more surprised. Bill E was torn between terror and abject humiliation. Human pride being what it is, he only managed a strangled scream as he dove behind the sofa to zip up. Safely tucked away, he fumbled for the remote to silence the rutting noises and turn off the images emanating from the screen, which reverted to news coverage.

Angel and Paige kept pounding the glass until Bill E ran to the doors. He paused just as he got there. Unable to decide what to do, he stared into Angel's knowing eyes, uncertain. She and Paige stopped pounding. He stood.

"Open the door, you idiot," she shouted, loud enough to be heard inside over the rain and the television. Her tone and volume cleared up any remaining doubts that Bill E might have harbored about the corporeal nature of the visitation. He turned the latch. The doors gave way to the pressure of the two people on the other side. Angel and Paige tumbled into the room, wet and disheveled.

"What were you up to in here?" Angel demanded with a coarse laugh.

"I was just watching some TV," he answered, a little boy with his hand caught in the X-rated cookie jar.

"Well, it really is as big as they say," Paige remarked, as though Bill E was not in the room. He shut the doors and surveyed the unoccupied space that surrounded them. "Congratulations, dude. Could we get a couple of clean towels?"

"Yeah, sure," Bill E said, still too stunned and embarrassed to fully comprehend the moment. "Angel, what are you doing here?"

"We needed somewhere safe to hide out," she said with a shrug. "I thought, *Now where's the last place on earth anyone would look for me*? And here we are."

"Oh my God," Paige said. He stood, dripping, near the television watching the news report that had replaced Bill E's DVD fantasy. "Angel, look; we're dead." Paige pointed.

"If you're just joining us," the anchor announced. "Actress Angela Panderson and bestselling author Paige Blanche are missing and believed dead following a massive explosion at Panderson's beachfront home on Malibu's Pacific Coast Highway. LAPD special homicide detective Lieutenant Roy Slade says that foul play is suspected. Authorities have begun the process of sifting through the wreckage of Panderson's home but now suspect that the two lost their lives and that their bodies were vaporized in the extreme heat of the explosion…"

Grabbing the DVR remote, Paige rewound the live footage as far as it would go. It stopped just at the beginning of the breaking news coverage.

"Good evening, I'm Curt Reed, and this is L.A. Live at Five Evening News," the anchor began. "We have stormwatch coverage coming up. But first, an explosion, seen here in home video taken at a children's birthday party being held on a nearby beach, destroyed the Malibu home of actress Angela Panderson. Panderson and her bestselling writing partner, Paige Blanche, are missing." The screen filled with a frame of the video taken of the two of them outside the Argyle, frozen just before Angel threw Paige's tea in her own face. "The two are seen here in recent video during an altercation outside a Sunset Boulevard hotel just hours before the body of Panderson's fiancé, the movie studio mogul Seth St. James, was found in their suite at that hotel."

"Ah, happier times," Paige said.

"Here, live from the scene with L.A. Special Crime Unit homicide detective Lieutenant Roy Slade, is our own Erica Laurelson. Erica, what can you tell us so far?"

"Erica Laurelson, live from Malibu," began an extremely blond correspondent, trying to look very serious. "Here with me on the scene of this tragic explosion is Lieutenant Roy Slade, liaison for the Los Angeles Police special crimes division."

Behind them Paige could see the still flaming wreckage of what had been Angel's house. Firemen were battling the blaze. Unlike many live scene reports, there was no one in the background other than emergency personnel. Not even the children of the high-profile residents of the high-end hood made impromptu media appearances without stylists and PR handlers.

"So far, it's unclear just what caused the explosion, Curt," Erica went on, clutching the earpiece to her ear so she could hear over the goings-on of the very busy disaster scene around her. "Lieutenant Slade is here to fill us in. First, lieutenant, any indications that anyone was in the house at the time of the explosion?"

"Erica, at this point we aren't certain if anyone was inside the house when the explosion occurred," Roy said. He cheated his answer to the camera, IDing his interviewer and rephrasing her question as he replied. Paige was sure he'd learned the technique in an on-camera interview class. That way, his answers would be easier to use later as wholly self-contained sound bites. "What LAPD and the Los Angeles Sheriff's departments have discovered in our joint investigation of this case is that it is believed Ms. Panderson and Paige, um, Mr. Blanche, had just returned to the residence. The gate guard waved them through only minutes before the incident and Ms. Panderson's car was still in the drive near the door at the time of the explosion."

The camera panned back to show the flaming wreck of Angel's SUV, burning itself out on the few square feet of concrete between the asphalt and the charred frame of what had been her garage door.

"So, you are still not certain that they were inside?" Erica prompted. The camera continued to follow firefighters' efforts to knock down the flames enough to protect the very nearby houses, though the two on either side had clearly been scorched in the conflagration.

"Well, it's too early to say for sure whether or not Mr. Blanche or Ms. Panderson were in the house at the time of the explosion, but LAPD and the Los Angeles Sheriff's department can confirm that there has been no word from either at this point and efforts to contact them have, so far, gone unanswered. On the other hand, there is no sign anyone was inside the house so, at this point, there is no way to be sure either way."

"Lieutenant Slade, this is Curt Reed," the anchor said, breaking in, as planned, with a question from the desk.

Roy clutched his earpiece in response. "Hi, Curt."

"Lieutenant, are there any leads so far in this case? Who might have done this?"

"Well, as you know, Curt, LAPD and the Los Angeles Sheriff's department are currently conducting a joint investigation into the recent suspicious deaths of Ms. Panderson's fiancé Seth St. James as well as several of Mr. St. James' business associates. In addition, there was an apparent attempt on the lives of Ms. Panderson and Mr. Blanche last night at a restaurant in Beverly Hills, which we are also looking into with the full cooperation of Beverly Hills Police. These events, along with today's possible tragedy, seem likely to be related, though it's too early in the investigation to say for sure. LAPD and L.A. Sheriff's officials are pouring all available resources into halting this apparent rampage."

"So, lieutenant," Curt said, prefacing an unprecedented second question. "If there was an attempt on Angel's life last night, why no extra security precautions today?"

The look on Roy's face made it clear this was the question he'd come to answer.

"As you can see, Curt, the existing high-security setting of the location itself includes a limited, guarded entrance to the area, regular armed security patrols and Ms. Panderson's own elaborate security system. These factors, along with the heightened awareness and stepped-up presence in the area, were as much as could possibly have been done short of assigning Ms. Panderson a personal police escort. Even that would not have prevented the explosion."

"But what about police presence on the scene?" Curt persisted.

"I was here at the time of the explosion," Roy said. "My presence did not stop or mitigate the blast. The question now concerns who could have gotten through the security perimeter. When we know the answer to that, we'll have our suspect."

"Thanks, Erica, and thank you, Lieutenant Slade, LAPD," Curt said, taking the shot back to the studio. Roy and Erica were relegated to a large monitor near the anchor desk.

"Thanks, Curt," Roy said with a winning and practiced smile.

A clap of thunder, one of the rarest of L.A. events, took Roy and Erica by surprise. Both turned to raise their arms defensively against further explosions from the bombed-out ruin behind them.

"And there's live proof from Malibu that there's much-needed rain in our forecast," Curt said, grinning. "More stormwatch coverage ahead. But first, what *you* need to know about breast augmentation. Is bigger *really* better?"

Paige muted the coverage.

"We are dead," Angel said taking the remote and fast-forwarding to real time.

"And it looks like it's going to rain," Paige said, squeezing water out of what was left of his suit jacket.

"Cool," Bill E intoned with an appropriate whistle.

"That's terrible," Angel said.

"No, it's wonderful," Paige said. "If they think we're dead, not only will they stop looking for us, they'll stop trying to kill us."

"Well, there's that." Angel sank onto the sofa to watch as the station began a little retrospective of her work, featuring clips of her wearing next to nothing on various crappy television shows over the years.

"Do you have a car, Bill E?" Paige asked.

"Of course I have a car," he snorted.

"Well, there's not a lot else here," Paige said. "I just thought maybe."

"We got a discount on the lease if we paid up front," Bill E sighed. "It may be my new address if I don't catch a break soon."

"Yeah, well, I may be in the market for a roommate, so I'll keep you posted," Paige said, not in the mood to be one-upped. "Meanwhile, a towel and something dry to wear would be nice."

"Sure, yeah, this way," Bill E said. "Angel, some of your old stuff is up here."

"Like that'll still fit," Paige mumbled under his breath to Bill E. They laughed, co-conspirators.

"Hey," Angel called after them. "I heard that. I'm the same size I was when I first got to Hollywood."

"Honey the only thing that's still thirty-six, twenty-two, thirty-four is your security code," Bill E muttered. He and Paige laughed among themselves again, the camaraderie of the fallen. Bill E led him up the stairs through the vast and absurdly empty house, which swallowed and echoed Angel's graphic reply.

33

A half hour later, clad in Bill E's old jeans and a couple of his sweaters, Paige and Angel were in Bill E's Mercedes hurtling through the pouring rain toward Paige's apartment. Paige, after much heated argument, was behind the wheel. He'd finally won out when he admitted that it was the car of his dreams and he just wanted to drive it. Bill E had graciously offered them the keys and stepped aside, electing to return to a quiet rainy evening at home with Jack Daniels.

"As if," Paige said as soon as the window was up and they were on their way. "Mr. Daniels will not be the only Jack on Bill E's dance card this evening."

"Well, that may not work out quite like he hopes," Angel said, pulling the DVD from underneath the oversized sweater she was wearing.

"What's that?"

"It was in the DVD player," she cackled. He gallantly hit the button to lower her window and she hurled it into the night. "To be honest, it's nothing he hasn't already seen."

They parked on the street between Paige's apartment and the Argyle. It felt eerie and strange. The intruder from their earlier visit was invested with more menace by subsequent developments.

The wet streets and the rain only heightened the sensation of sustained, dread-tinged déjà vu. Paige turned off the engine. Both sat motionless in the car, staring at the darkened apartment.

"Well, he won't come back to kill us a second time," Paige said aloud what they were both thinking.

A quick look around, and they made a dash for it, slipping in through the back door from the alley.

"Great, Armie still hasn't done anything about this door," Paige groused.

"So you'd rather be locked out?"

"Worked out pretty good for us last time," he said, feeling for the light switch.

The lights revealed that Armie had made a fine start at straightening up the place from the ransacking. Things weren't back to rights by any means, but most everything was off the floor and piled in heaps to be sorted and put away.

"Aww, Armie has a crush on you," Paige said. "But he's going to kill you when he finds out you lost his hat."

"Oh, that's right," she said, grasping her head involuntarily. "In all the, you know, I forgot I even had it on."

"He'll remember," Paige said.

"Where are your notes?" Angel sank into one of the battered old kitchen chairs.

"Hang on a sec," Paige said, putting together things for a pot of tea. "I figure we're going to be up for a while. You want gravy?"

Angel smiled. The old joke name Paige had given her too-strong coffee reminded her of easier, less-murderous times. "Gravy? Yeah, that'd be nice." She explored the little room where Paige had written her bestselling book. A strange expression spread over her face.

"Here we go," Paige said, putting down their mugs after a bit. Kneeling, he opened the cabinets under a corner cupboard that was filled with books and dishes. "Oh good, they're still here," he crowed, relieved that they wouldn't have to shift through the detritus to find them. "Our burglar had no interest in these, I guess."

"Maybe he just didn't know what they were," Angel suggested. "I sure don't."

"Maybe." Paige pulled out several large stacks of typed pages, bound with enormous rubber bands and illuminated with blue and red pencil marks. He spread the various versions of his manuscript of their last book out on the table.

"What is this?" Angel asked, taking an unladylike slurp off her mug. "Perfect coffee."

"Thanks," Paige said, trying to get the manuscripts straight. "This is the first, the second, and the third drafts of our second novel, before you lost your mind and wrote that draft in crayon."

"I told you about that," Angel said.

"Yeah and I've been pretty clear on the subject too, I think," Paige said, unconvinced and unswayed by the Seth-made-me-do-it-in-exchange-for-a-multimillion-dollar-contract-but-I-didn't-mention-it-until-it-was-convenient explanation. "More tea?"

"I'm on coffee, remember?"

"And the tea was on you, as I recall," Paige said with a mean little smile. "You wanna see the video before we get started? I never get tired of it."

She answered with a look.

"Okay, we'll just dive right in then," he said laughing, pleased with himself. "Now, what we have to do is find the references to the Mitch Geller character, Griff Miller, in this version. Then we compare them to how it was changed in this version before the hundred thousand dollars he paid Grizelda. Then figure out what, if anything, was changed here, after the payment."

"I'm confused. We think it wasn't something you accidentally came up with that got Seth killed?"

"Not sure," Paige said. He began to leaf through the original and scan the pages for references to the character Griff. "The burglar wasn't even interested. But if it was Mitch, it's the only motive we can use to catch him."

"So, you think Mitch killed Seth?"

"Well, he probably *had* someone do it."

"And framed us?"

"Well, I know *I* didn't do it."

"Nice," she snarled sweetly. "Why would Mitch plant the extra manuscript in the hotel suite?"

"I can't figure that one out," Paige nodded. "I guess that was to frame us somehow for blackmailing Seth instead of him? But it doesn't make sense to me. Okay, here's the first reference. On or around page thirty-two, we're talking about how little it is."

Angel snickered as she began flipping through the second draft. Paige flipped through the third draft to find out what if any post-payoff changes had been made.

"'She called him Sweet Gherkin because it reminded her of the diminutive treat,'" Angel read aloud laughing. "That's funny."

"Yeah, too bad it never got published," Paige said with a bitter little laugh. "Oops, no, that's the same in all three pre-massacre versions."

He took up the original and began leafing through again. "Okay, page seventy-six talks about the music business. 'He was so cheap that he preferred hustlers because he knew how much they would cost him up front.'"

Three pots of tea and innumerable mugs of gravy later and they'd been through every page of all three drafts.

"It's insider trading," Paige said with an air of finality. "It has to be. It's in the last version, the one Seth read before you started editing with the machete and blasting caps. We said that Mitch made his first billion by taking stock options in lieu of money when he sold one of his record labels to a big media conglomerate, which he knew was about to be bought by an overseas conglomerate."

"You made that up?"

"Sort of," Paige shrugged. "At least I think so. There aren't any notes from you or Seth or Grizelda or whomever other than the ones to take out the description of how he made his money in the music business selling short and screwing over so many people."

"Is it in the final version?"

"He's not even in the final version," Paige shrugged. "Nothing is."

"How many times do I have to say I'm sorry?"

"You can stop," he said, rinsing the cups and plates as she handed them to him. "'Sorry' will never give me back the last three years of my life or make you feel better about yours."

She stared at him silently as he finished washing up.

"Okay," he said, drying his hands. "You want to pick out some clothes that fit before we go pay a visit to the eighty-third-richest man in the world?"

34

Mitch Geller's home is a local legend.

Towering above the Pacific Coast Highway, the elaborate Alhambresque palace demands both attention and privacy. Poised on the bluff just north of Bill E's home, Geller's estate has a commanding view of both the ocean from the top of the seaside cliffs and the storied Pacific Coast Highway that drops off sharply to sea level just beyond. As a result, his Xanadu can be seen for miles in the massive basin below as well as by anyone driving along a heavily traveled public road that leads into one of the most populous cities in the world.

The estate's entrance on the highway is a huge forbidding walled façade complete with turrets, guardhouses and even a portcullis. It resembles a medieval fortress more than the entrance to a private residence.

The drive leading up to the gate and the property itself is lined with dozens of gigantic, ancient sago palms, each imported from its original location to the lavish private compound. When the massive trees arrived, PCH traffic was stopped in both directions, backing up cars for miles. The air overhead filled with the obligatory helicopters reporting the event. Such is the nature of privacy in Los Angeles.

In the lavish private setting, Geller held Gatsbyesque parties peopled entirely by beautiful young men and the old lechers who admire them. Yet Mitch was not out to the world. He very publicly dated some of the most famous women on the planet while maintaining a string of boys more to feed his ego than to share his life or his wealth.

Formidably bordered on two sides by dizzying cliffs and on the fourth by another equally secure estate, Geller's domain is impenetrable by frontal assault.

The fact that Paige and Angel were enjoying being dead complicated their unscheduled arrival. Paige was not interested in surrendering their cover by showing up at the front gates of the Geller estate and posing for the security guards and their video cameras.

"Don't worry about it," Angel said. "I know how to get us in."

"Yes, I remember your amazing break-in at my house," Paige said, unconvinced. They sat in Bill E's car parked on the side of PCH opposite Geller's. The windshield wipers squeaked a steady rhythm. Angel was once again behind the wheel.

"I've been to a zillion parties here," she said.

"I thought he just had boy parties."

"Darling, I'm the official fag hag to the rich and famous," Angel said. Accelerating abruptly, she cut back onto the busy roadway, sliced across two crowded lanes and made a U-turn across two more, all without so much as slowing down, signaling or looking over her shoulder. The thrill-ride maneuver left traffic in an uproar and rendered Paige speechless with terror.

"You see," Angel went on, authoritatively. "All the security is in the show window, out on the street. He's such a closet case that there's not much in the house because he wants to keep his privacy. They count on the front wall line of defense. Once you're past that line, the walls are there more to keep secrets in than to keep people out.

"The cliffs are the biggest part of his security system. If we were going to rob the place we'd be out of luck," Angel went on, talking like a cat burglar. Paige stared in silent disbelief. "But the cliffs are our advantage. Aside from being on his regular guest list, I'm also his former neighbor. I happen to know that he was having an affair with a twinkie-boy-movie-star who he moved into one of the other houses further south along the cliff. They cut a path along the rock face to connect the two houses so they could each appear to be at home and still hook up."

"Really?" Paige said. His desire for dish exceeded his fear of Angel's death-defying driving. "Who?"

"His house is right next door to Bill E," Angel hinted broadly. She pulled up to the gate of Bill E's and punched in the code.

"No kidding?"

"How do you think he keeps getting cast, with no talent?"

"I don't know—how'd you do it?"

"Shut up."

35

The rain had subsided by the time they were scaling the wall onto the neighboring estate. They used a ladder on their side. Paige was surprised to find that Bill E still owned a ladder. His huge house's only other furnishings were the sticky old sofa and a mattress on the floor in the master suite, which Paige had seen when they were changing.

"It belongs to the gardener," Bill E admitted when Paige pressed him on it.

"You still have a gardener?" he asked.

"Just to get the place ready to sell," Bill E replied sadly.

Paige was a little touched. In a way, he could identify with Bill E's fate. He, too, had been used up by Angel and then left discarded, destitute and a bit worse for wear. Still, Bill E had an estate to lose. Paige was still hoping for home ownership and dreaming wistfully of health insurance.

Using the ladder, their climb up the wall was a cinch. Dropping to the ground on the other side was a bit more challenging.

Angel handled it by doing a fancy drop-and-roll maneuver that she'd learned from a stunt coordinator during her painfully brief action-adventure movie career. In addition to losing millions and helping to make her the laughing stock of an industry that already found her pretty amusing, the movie also landed her in the hospital—twice. It wasn't too surprising then that her drop-and-roll maneuver got mud on the black cotton mock turtle she'd borrowed from Paige and got *her* a whack on the head from a rock in a nearby flowerbed border.

Paige was dubious of Angel's technique. He straddled the top of the wall and watched as she clutched her muddy head and jumped up and down.

"Oh shit, oh shit, oh shit," she swore.

Once he got bored with the show, he hoisted the ladder over the wall from the top, then climbed down on the other side. More graceful perhaps, but very hard on his back because he was seated on the wall at the time and the ladder weighed quite a bit.

Both methods were particularly hard on the neighbor's landscaping. They tucked the ladder out of sight, crushing still more shrubbery.

"This way," Angel said in a TV whisper.

"*Shhh*," he hissed.

She led Paige to a break in the hedge where she thought the pathway began. In fact, it was just a break in the hedge. Confidently she marched right over the edge of the cliff. For a moment she hung, Wile E. Coyote-style, just at the brink, frantically windmilling her arms to maintain her balance and cheat death. Paige caught her hand and dragged her back from the sheer cliff face, sparing her from the rocks far below.

"You saved my life," Angel said in a hoarse whisper.

"Damn it," Paige said, smacking himself in the forehead with the butt of his hand. "Well, it actually made my back feel better, so it wasn't a total loss."

Angel just hit him.

Together they located the start to the secret path, which—what do you reckon—was concealed in the hedge, being secret and all. It was dark and slow going. They'd brought a tiny Maglite that they'd stolen from Bill E's glove compartment. In spite of the danger and dark, they were reluctant to use it except in places where the footing was completely obscured, for fear of alerting whatever unknown security awaited at the Geller estate end of the path.

To calm themselves along the perilous walk, they talked nervously.

"What exactly are we trying to accomplish here?" Angel asked tentatively. She clutched the side of the cliff and inched along.

"Well, I guess to gain his confidence," Paige reasoned. Inching along behind Angel, his hand frequently touched hers as much for reassurance as by accident. "We need to find out somehow that he was guilty of insider trading. And to determine if he'd kill Seth or have him killed because Seth knew about it and maybe told us."

"Is that all?" Angel scoffed. "And just how do you propose we do that?"

"I have no idea."

"Should we just go in and ask him?" Angel said in disgust. For a moment she forgot her precarious surroundings and frightened herself when she realized.

"In the movies they'd play good cop/bad cop and sweat it out of him."

"How does that work?" she asked as though it was a serious consideration.

"Well, one of us would pretend to be tough and violent and scary," Paige explained, his voice thick with sarcasm. "The other would be kind and reasonable and win Mitch's trust by trying to protect him from the scary one. Since neither of us has yet reached the height of five-eight and we're about as cuddly as a couple of cacti, I'm doubting that's going to be our best approach."

"Then what do you suggest, Sherlock?"

"The best thing would be to find some document that says he did it," Paige sighed. He longed to scratch his nose but was too afraid to let go of the rock face long enough. "I think our only real option is to bluff."

"How do we do that?"

"We act like we already have the proof and maybe try to extort money from him," Paige speculated. "That way if he agrees to pay it's the same as admitting guilt."

"But isn't that why we think he killed Seth in the first place?" Angel asked after a moment's calculation. She stopped and turned back to face him. In the darkness he collided with her, terrifying them both.

"Yeah, that's the downside," Paige agreed when he was able to get his breath.

She turned back and they resumed their slow progress along the ledge.

"What's the upside?" Angel asked.

"He probably didn't do the killing himself?" Paige suggested, as hopefully as possible under the circumstances.

"I hate that plan," she said flatly.

"It's not perfect."

"Not perfect?" she squawked. "We're trying to get the murderer to kill us to prove that he's the murderer."

"There's that."

"Well, I don't know about you but I'm sick of him trying to kill me."

"How is this any different?"

"You're right," Angel said without conviction. "That little closet-case bastard has been trying to kill me for days."

Paige took her silence as assent to his plan.

36

It started to piss rain again. Cold and soggy, they finally emerged from the hedge on the lawn below the blue glass-tiled infinity pool.

Angel gave a gasp of recognition.

"I've got it," she said aloud. "I know how to get in."

"*Shhh*," Paige ordered irritably.

She nodded empathically. With tiptoe hand gestures and pointing, she indicated that Paige should follow her lead. He rolled his eyes, nodded, then crept with her to the edge of the pool. Angel gave him the one-minute finger. He waited, looking around nervously, while she popped her head quickly up to pool level to check.

The pool was dark and surprisingly still, given the constant flow of water over the infinity ledge just above them. Raindrops pocked the smooth surface.

She ducked back down to Paige and gave him the thumbs up. Then, to his astonishment, she began to remove her clothes.

Confused, Paige gave her a little shove to get her attention and then turned both palms up in silent bewilderment. Angel responded by pulling the tail of his black Gucci dress shirt out of the waistband of his black DKNY jeans to indicate that he should do likewise. She returned to stripping down. Paige again gave her a push, nearly knocking her over as she was on one leg struggling out of his black Calvins. In response, she slapped him and began angrily trying to yank the clothes off of him.

Paige was outmatched. Angel had a great deal of expertise in this particular area. When he was defending his shirt buttons, she was on the zipper. If he was on zipper patrol, she was unbuttoning the shirt. Paige eventually surrendered, giving her the timeout sign and holding up his hands in defeat. He preferred to limit his humiliation to simply getting naked to break into a mansion to which he'd coveted an invitation all his adult life. It seemed excessive to add to his shame by being pantsed by a girl.

Angel took their clothes and stuffed them under two nearby chaise lounges, where they would be accessible for a quick getaway. Then, in the chill of the night air, she led the way up and into the infinity pool. Tugging Paige's hand, she began to swim in the darkness toward the house. Stopping abruptly and treading water with her feet, she turned to face him, took a deep breath, and held her nose, indicating he should do likewise.

With a dubious shake of his head, he complied. Before he'd had time to roll his eyes in disgust, she dragged him under, pulling him along below the surface. Then rising, she swam him, as he spluttered, nearly drowned, to the edge.

When Paige managed to clear his nose and eyes of water, he realized that they were inside the house in a room that looked like a luxury spa. Angel was standing over him pulling on a fluffy white terrycloth robe. She extended a hand to hoist him out of the water; the other held a towel of luxurious and opulent properties.

In a moment, he was dry and wrapped in a robe of his own, gathered from a heap of similar lavish white terry robes piled on a teak cart that looked as though it had been custom-built just for the robes. It had been.

He checked his hair in a nearby mirror and gave her the thumbs up.

Angel smiled and led the way. She had spent many lovely evenings in that house, wandering amidst tangled bodies and negotiating webs of deceit and intrigue. Angel proceeded there with confidence.

37

Paige followed her up a couple of stairs from the pool's spa room and into a larger wicker-filled glass-walled room that faced the pool. She paused, ran her hand along a shelf stacked with more of the opulent towels and effortlessly flicked a concealed switch. A panel slid aside, revealing a circular stone stairway.

Silently, and without question or protest, Paige followed Angel to the top of the stairs, where she slid aside a similar panel. The two stepped into a brightly lit apartment that made the rest of the house look tatty. Gilt furniture, marble columns, Renaissance tapestries and imported Italian ceiling frescos were reflected in acres of gleaming inlaid wood flooring sprinkled with handmade silk oriental rugs. Despite a massive, intricately carved rosewood bed, the room resembled a museum more than a bedroom.

Flickering light spilled in through an alcove on the far side of the room. The amplified sounds of a movie interrupted the plush silence of the magnificent chamber.

A peek through the alcove revealed a spectacular private movie theatre. Three descending raked rows of luscious velvet sofas and chaises faced an immense screen, where a twenty-foot-tall Norma Shearer had cornered a magnificent black-and-white Joan Crawford in the ladies' room and was valiantly defending her marriage. A lone figure sat rapt before the towering image, lost in every word.

"*The Women*?" Angel's shrill voice shattered the silence. Her sudden outburst frightened Paige as much as it did the reclining figure of Mitch Geller. "And people are supposed to think you're not gay?"

"Angel?" Mitch said. He clutched his chest where his pearls would be. "I heard you were dead." Touching a glass panel on a nearby table, he muted the movie's sound; Joan and Norma continued their dust-up in silence.

"I got over it," she said, closing the distance between them.

"What are you doing here?" Mitch asked. He was not so much upset as unsure what to make of the sudden arrival of someone not unfamiliar but certainly unexpected.

"Sit down," she said. She pushed him back onto the sofa. "I'll be asking the questions, fruit fly."

"Angel I don't think there's any need for—" Paige began.

"This little head case thought he'd killed us this afternoon, and you don't think there's any need?" Angel shrieked.

"You think I tried to kill you?" Mitch asked, clearly confused.

Angel backhanded him with such force that he almost fell off the sofa. "I told you I'd ask the questions," Angel said in a singsong voice, leaning down near his face.

Blood tricked from the corner of Mitch's mouth. He sat up. His back was pressed hard against the arm of the sofa, as far away from Angel as he could.

"What is it you want to know?" he asked, wiping at his mouth.

"That sounded like a question!" Angel bellowed. She grasped an open bottle of wine from a nearby table where it sat with a glass and some cheese and crackers laid out to be Mitch's movie popcorn. The bottle shattered against the low brass railing that separated one level from the next. Advancing on Mitch, she gripped the bottle's neck threateningly in her hand. She menaced him with the jagged remains.

"Okay, Angel, take it easy," Paige said, afraid to get too near her. He figured she'd been more upset by their narrow escape that afternoon than he'd realized. Maybe it was post-traumatic stress or PMS or something. He knew if he didn't get her to snap out of it they'd have another murder to deal with and this time they'd actually be guilty.

"I'm sorry, I'm sorry," Mitch said, cowering into the sofa. He held up a silk tasseled pillow to ward off her attack.

"Okay, look," Paige said. He took a tentative step between them. "Mitch, we just want to know about Grizelda and the hundred thousand dollars."

"What about it?" Mitch whimpered.

"That's a question, Tinker Bell!" Angel shouted.

"Give me a minute, okay?" Paige pleaded. He avoided looking into her crazy eyes as he tried to steer her hand with the broken bottle away. His breath caught in his throat.

"That's more time than I had this afternoon when my entire house and everything I owned was blown sky-high and I was set on fire and tossed through the air like a flaming baton!"

"Okay, so Mitch," Paige said, giving him a desperate look. "Why did you give Grizelda a hundred thousand dollars?"

"Because she asked me for it," he said with a little shrug. He hid his face in a pillow and began to cry.

"She asked you for it?" Angel asked rhetorically. She lowered the bottle slightly as she considered.

"Yes," Mitch nodded, peering over the top of the pillow. "I paid her to take out the stuff about the record business. But then the book said that I'd made my money through insider trading. I didn't know how she'd found it out but that's how I got the money to finance the new studios with Seth. I'm so sorry about Seth, Angel, so very sorry."

"*Then-why-did-you*-kill-*hiiiiim?*" she howled, lunging at him and ripping into the pillow he reflexively held up in his defense. Down flew through the air like December flurries at

Mammoth. Mitch stared at her, blinking through disbelief, terror and feathers.

"You think I killed Seth?" he asked. The fluff began to stick to his tears. "I loved Seth; he was my—best friend."

"Oh my God, were you sleeping with my fiancé?"

"Yes," Mitch nodded. "But you weren't."

"True," Angel admitted.

"So why would I kill him?"

"Because he was threatening to expose you to for your insider trading?" Paige suggested.

"He'd have lost the studio if I lost my money," Mitch shrugged. "That's why he wrote the will the way he did."

"What will?" Angel asked, completely thrown.

"He was going to give it to you after the engagement party," Mitch said with a sigh. "After you'd both signed the prenup. He'd already signed it and he wanted to make a gift of it. I guess he never got the chance."

"So she's an heiress?" Paige asked, hopeful of being paid at last.

"More or less," Mitch said. "It's in a trust, but it's hers for life."

"*Whose* life?" Angel asked, menace creeping back into her voice.

"Yours," Mitch said, trying to lean farther away from the jagged bottle still in her hand. "I'm your trust administrator since, technically, it's my money he bought the studio with."

"So who inherits if Angel dies?" Paige asked, trying to keep up.

"The trust reverts to Lucrezia, the last wife," Mitch said with a shrug. "Then Jay, his son from the first marriage."

"But you remain as administrator."

Mitch nodded.

"Then why did he change the manuscript?" Paige asked, sitting on the sofa beside him.

"To protect me," Mitch managed. He began to sob again.

"So Grizelda came to you?" Angel asked, squinting.

"Yes," Mitch quaked. "She figured it out. She hit Seth up for money, too. And several other people that I know of. I think that's the main reason she put together the book deal in the first place. All those other branding ideas she'd set up for you with the perfume and the clothes and what-all were turkeys, 'cause you were such a drunken deadbeat and all she got was sued. Sorry, but you know it's true."

Angel shrugged. She did.

"She hit on the book thing to raise some cash. I got the idea she was going to run out on you and leave you holding the bag for all the lawsuits. I mean, they were your own fault, but still. Seth was trying to protect me and to help you at the same time. She must have killed…"

Mitch broke down, doubling over in tears.

"Oh, you poor man," Angel said. Rushing forward to embrace him, she nicked his neck with the forgotten bottle still in her hand. He cried out.

"Oh God, I'm so sorry," Angel said. She began weeping herself. She tossed the broken bottle away. It smashed against the ebony wall paneling.

"First aid, anyone? I'll see what's in the bathroom," Paige said.

By the time they got the bleeding and the crying stopped, everyone was best friends again and it was clear that Grizelda was the murderer. The only question remaining was how to prove it.

Mason, an adorable twenty-something butler Mitch dispatched to fetch their clothes, returned them without so much as a raised eyebrow or the appearance of interest in how they had become separated from their clothes in the first place.

Over tea, drinks and *hors d'oeuvre*, Mitch offered to help any way he could. He began by dispatching his car to drive them back to Bill E's. He even promised to see that the ladder was returned to the right side of the fence; the other house actually belonged to him anyway.

"Paige, you are now officially on the guest list," Mitch said, with a warm and genuine hug. "I can't imagine how we've missed inviting you before now. Angel, my darling," he said, kissing both her cheeks. "Always a pleasure to see you, circumstances notwithstanding. Grief does terrible things to people."

"Thank you, Mitch," she said, stepping into the back of the car. "Thank you for understanding. I'm so sorry about your neck."

Mitch waved it away, touching the bandage with his other hand. "It's a part I was going to have removed anyway. Be careful, you two," he called in from the door. "Don't get killed a second time."

"Mum's the word, now," Paige cautioned him from deep inside the sumptuous interior of the black Phantom limo.

Mitch made as if locking his lips and tossed away the key. He waved goodbye as the butler held the door for him.

Paige sighed as they pulled out of the gate.

"Well, that went great," Angel said, invigorated by their progress and the late supper.

"Angel," Paige said, taking her hand. "I had no idea you were so upset about this afternoon. I should not have asked you to go tonight."

"Oh, I was up to it," she said with a manly shrug. "Not crazy about the whole attempted murder thing, don't get me wrong, but still, happy to be alive."

"Angel," Paige said sincerely. "You were out of control in there."

"Oh, that." She laughed. "Don't be silly. I was just playing bad cop."

"Bad cop?"

"Yeah. Your other plan sucked."

38

By the time they got back from Mitch's to retrieve the Mercedes, Bill E was passed out. He lay on the tawdry sofa where they'd left him. His pants were around his ankles. More traditional porn played on the DVD player.

Rather than disturb him, they simply took the keys out of his easy-access pocket.

"He's a real show-er," Paige said as Angel fished for the key.

"Yeah," she said, rising. "The problem is what it's attached to. Okay, let's roll, Danno." She gave the keys a smart little toss and caught them again.

"It creeps me out how much you're getting off on this," Paige said.

She didn't deny it.

He followed her out the front door.

"I was a smokin' bad cop," she said with an air of pride.

"Yeah," he said, walking past her. "You have a real talent for abusing men."

"You have no idea," she said as she slammed the door. "Bitch."

★

39

It was very early morning by the time they got to Grizelda's offices. Angel and Paige left Bill E's big, bad Mercedes at the curb across the street from Zeldom. They tried the doors. It was too late and too early to worry about being observed or seeming suspicious. They could afford to be fearless with no risk of being caught or blowing their whole tragic-death cover story.

The doors at Zeldom were locked, of course.

Heedless, they began, none too subtly, to look around for another way in. A chain link fence crested with razor wire secured the alleys on either side of the old loft-style building. Even so, doors and ground floor windows were barred and wired for alarms in the street-gangsy-Venice-adjacent-hood. Angel tried climbing up on the bars. Hanging on and doing a little dance, she attempted to use her body weight and gravity to pull them loose but to no avail.

"That's a good look for you," Paige commented. He tried breaking the glass with a stone and hit Angel with the ricochet instead.

"It was an accident," he insisted.

She "accidentally" stomped on his foot as hard as she could.

Their incompetent break-in attempt was well suited to the early hour in the frowsy neighborhood of the vast but sleepy, provincial city.

"Any ideas, bad cop?"

"Kiss me," she said, grabbing him.

"What the hell are you—?"

The liplock cut him short. He struggled to get away until he saw the police cruiser rolling by. Reluctantly, he submitted to her all-too-realistic smooch until the instant he was sure the patrol car had rolled out of sight around the next corner.

He shoved her away. "Sheesh, do you not even know what acting means?" He wiped his mouth with the back of his hand.

"Shut up, bitch," she said.

"There's no need—"

She grabbed him again and began groping him savagely.

A van pulled past them and parked at the curb nearby.

"Go mama," one of the van's uniformed occupants called. His similarly clad crew joined him. Angel and Paige's performance earned appreciative howls and wolf whistles from the little group as they stepped out of the van and pimp-walked their way to the doors of Grizelda's little fortress.

Despite Paige's struggles, Angel stepped up her attentions. In the guise of passionate abandon, she managed to turn so they could both watch what was happening at Grizelda's door and make out at the same time.

The leader of the crew produced a huge ring of keys from the pocket of his baggy trousers. They jingled as the doors swung open. Angel and Paige continued to paw each other for a bit until they were reasonably sure that the coast was clear. Once he was certain, Paige pushed her away again, spitting and sputtering.

"Doesn't that do anything for you?" she asked, straightening herself up.

"Sorry, no," he said. Turning, Paige crossed over to the van to get a closer look "'Kalifornia Klean-up Krew'? Can you believe that these guys call themselves the KKK?" he asked, reading aloud from the side of the van. "Do they not even teach history anymore?"

"It's open," Angel whispered. She held the glass door slightly ajar and motioned violently for Paige to hurry up. He dashed across the sidewalk to join her.

Just in time, they ducked behind Phanie's huge steel desk to avoid being caught by a Krew member crossing the lobby to the front door.

"Now what?" Paige whispered, as soon as the Krew guy was gone. The two were squeezed into the foot well of the enormous desk. Despite its monumental size, it was still far from a comfortable fit.

"How the hell should I know?" Angel said. She hit her head on the desktop trying to give him a look.

"*Shhh.*"

The Kleaner returned from outside, pushing a rolling cart loaded with supplies. He wheeled it deeper into the recesses of the offices. The cart's wheels squeaked across the shiny faux finished cement floor, subsiding into the distance.

"I guess we'll have to wait them out," Paige murmured.

Suddenly the place was filled with deafening music.

"Well, at least we won't have to whisper," he said.

"Totally, but there's no room to dance." Angel tried to move to the rhythm in the impossibly small space but only managed to hit her head again.

"Get off me," Paige ordered, as he struggled to escape her crushing gyrations. "Maybe we can move into another area." He ventured a peek and surveyed their options. "There are some cabinets in the conference room that we could maybe fit inside."

Angel sniffed the air. She pushed him out of the way and stood up.

"What are you doing? Be careful!" Paige said. He grabbed at her hand, trying to restrain her.

She sniffed again, taking a few steps from behind the desk.

"Do you smell that?" she asked. A grin spread across her face.

"Smoke," he said, alarmed. "A fire?"

"Calm down," she said, taking his hand. "It's a very controlled burn." She laughed as she walked toward the sound of the music.

"Angel, what the hell are you doing?" Paige hissed after her. With a plaintive groan, he gave up and followed.

"Just come with me," she said. Their path led to an open area filled with the desks of assistants and support staff. The Krew sat in a little half circle comprised of various rolling chairs. Their "KKK"-emblazoned uniform smocks were draped over the backs of their chairs. Feet up, they were passing a joint.

Angel walked to the player from which the deafening music was issuing. She switched it off.

"What the hell is going on in here?" she demanded.

Paige took his cue, folded his arms and scowled.

Sparks flew and chairs were overturned. The Krew members leaped to their feet, too late to conceal what they were so obviously up to.

"We, um, we work here," one of the terrified young men in the group managed.

"Oh, so you get paid for this?" Angel demanded, marching over and picking up the still smoldering roach. She waved it in his face.

"Hey, you're Angel, aren't you?" one of the young women staffers asked. She pointed at a framed poster of Angel and her failed signature cologne, Heaven's Scent, on the wall nearby. "I thought you were dead."

"I got better," Angel declared, wading into the little group. "Which is more than I can say for you if you don't get your ganja-smoking asses out of here by the time I count to ten."

"But what about—"

"One."

"Are we supposed to—?"

"Two."

"Okay, we're going," the crew leader assured her. They started to gather up their things.

"Three," Angel said, grabbing the phone and dialing.

Mops and buckets hit the floor as the kids ran for the exit.

Angel and Paige stood silent, trembling with fear and exhilaration. They listened for the sounds of keys in the lock and the van squealing away from the curb. Then they began to breathe.

"Four."

"Okay, this bad-cop thing is really starting to freak me out," Paige said.

Angel grinned and took a hit off the still-smoldering spliff.

"Put that out," he chided.

Angel answered with a huge drag.

"Until later," he sighed.

She knocked the fire off onto the cement floor on the edge of one of the steel desks and stomped it out. Grinning, she tucked the dead roach behind her ear.

"Classy. That's what I like about you," Paige said. "Which way's her office?"

"This way, remember?" Angel groaned. "You need to lighten up. No wonder you don't have a boyfriend."

"You're giving out relationship advice now?" Paige asked. "What's next on your career list? Acting lessons or financial planning?"

She flipped him the bird over her shoulder.

40

Angel swung open the corrugated-steel warehouse double doors that led to Grizelda's inner sanctum and switched on the light.

They stood for a moment stunned by what they saw.

Grizelda's office was a world where everything had equal value or perhaps just none at all. Childish refrigerator-ready-art from her children, now long grown, hung next to high-art photography, centerfold nudes, signed movie posters and awards, framed, not framed, taped, nailed, mounted and thumb-tacked to the walls. The rest of the office was organized along the same lines. Sample magazines of clients' work were on the coffee table with back issues of *Entertainment Weekly* and out-of-date IKEA catalogs.

"What exactly are we looking for?" Angel asked.

"I'll resist the urge to say matches and lighter fluid," Paige answered.

Both had been in the office before but the edge never came off the shock. The idea of conducting business in the room seemed impossible if not just plain ill-advised.

"What we want is to show how she was blackmailing Mitch, right?"

"Yeah," Paige said, taking a seat at the desk. He started to go through the drawers. "Notes on our book would be great."

A large bottom drawer on the desk yielded file folders on hanging racks. Paige flipped through, not expecting much.

"*Fallen Angel*," he said aloud, startled at the find.

"What's that?" Angel asked. She looked up from the pile of handwritten notes, deal memos, magazine clippings, bills and store coupons she was leafing through.

"It's a copy of the manuscript you found in Seth's hotel room the night of the murder," Paige said, mystified. "This just doesn't make any sense at all."

"Unlike everything else up to this point?" Angel cackled as she vaulted herself onto the desk and took a seat.

"Point to you, Double-D," Paige conceded. He dropped the manuscript back into the folder and continued his search. "And here are her notes on the book." He squinted at the pages. "In an unlocked drawer, in a file labeled 'Angel Book Notes.' That just seems impossible."

"That the file is labeled?"

"Stranger still," Paige nodded. He swept some of the debris from the desk to make room for the notes. It was instantly apparent to Paige that this was how Grizelda herself began work each day. The detritus he'd swept away was undetectable amidst the semicircular debris field where it landed. "The whole thing seems perfectly planned and then here are the incriminating notes in an unlocked drawer, in a file labeled 'smoking gun.'"

"Well, we're dead and who else is looking?" Angel pointed out.

"True that, Sergeant Bad Cop," Paige conceded. "Still, it's like there are two levels of organization. The murders are carefully set up to frame us. Then there's this blackmail scheme. Frankly, the fact that you and I were able to crack it is more an indictment of the scheme than a testament to our superior detective skills."

"You better watch how you talk to Sergeant Bad Cop," Angel said, smacking the back of his head.

"Okay, that's enough." Paige swatted away her hand as he began to pore over the notes.

"Do you have a light?" Angel asked. She reached past him to try to get into a drawer on the far side of the desk, the roach lodged between her lips.

"Not now," Paige groaned. "Can't you just wait?"

"It'll give me something to do while you read."

He pushed her. She tried to shove his rolling desk chair away from the desk so she could continue her search for matches.

In a fit of defiant, childish rage, Paige dragged his sneakered feet and held onto the desk. They were, as always, pretty evenly matched. The struggle persisted for a few moments. The two grunted and strained against each other. Their tenacity in the petty brawl was fueled by disputes that far exceeded the position of Grizelda's desk chair. The stalemate held until Angel leaned down and stuck her tongue into Paige's ear.

He shrieked and grabbed for the side of his head.

The sudden shift left Angel pushing Paige's chair, unopposed, with all her strength.

Paige's rolling chair rocketed across the room. It crashed into a mirrored glass cabinet filled with keepsakes, framed photos, awards, magic markers, used coffee cups and trail mix.

The casualties were many.

"I think she's going to notice that," Paige said. He moved in slow motion as he attempted to stand and shake the broken glass off his face and clothes without cutting himself.

"Oh, look," Angel said. She retrieved one of the framed photos that had fallen to the floor in the collision, its glass cracked. "It's me with Grizelda and Bill E at the Opernball. And here's one of me at the Venice film festival." Temporarily distracted from her quest for fire by her own image, Angel began to sift through the debris for other pictures of herself.

Freed from her invasion, Paige returned to his own search of the desk.

"Hey, score one for Sergeant Bad Cop. Look at this. It was behind that picture of me in Venice."

"What?" Paige asked, not looking up.

"You know—*hidden*?" she pressed. "Under the picture. Under the glass."

"Is it the picture of the creepy family that came with the frame?"

Frustrated by his inattention, she unfolded the piece of paper she'd found under the picture and held it up to see what was written on it.

"Mitch Geller, selling short," she read aloud. "Seth St. James securities fraud. Steven Spielberg—"

"What are you —?" Paige began, looking up. "What's that?"

He reached for the scrap of paper and she pulled it away.

"It's a clue that *I* found," she said, taunting him with it.

"Let me see that," Paige said, rolling after her.

"What do you think?" she asked. "It's a clue, right?"

"I think you've earned this," he said, holding up a book of souvenir matches from Caesar's Palace that he'd discovered in his search of the desk.

She reached for them and he pulled the matches away.

"Trade?"

She handed him the paper, holding on until he surrendered the matches.

Angel took a seat on the edge of the coffee table next to a pile of Eva Gabor wig boxes.

Paige began comparing the list to the notes. In short order he found and matched each of the names on the list with the changes to the manuscript. Equally as important, he noted the instances when there had been no changes.

By the time he was done, Angel was baked.

"You know," she said, abruptly and apropos of nothing.

"Know what?" Paige asked, looking up after a moment or two.

"What?"

"I'm asking you."

"Asking me what?"

"Yes, what?"

"What do you mean 'yes what'?"

"I mean I'm asking you what?"

"What?"

"How can you say *what* when you know what *what* is?"

"What?"

"You're stoned."

Angel began to laugh. Then her laughter faded away. "What's so funny?" she asked.

"Don't start that again," he said. He emptied out a couple of folders inconspicuously onto the floor and loaded them with the pages of the book, the notes and the list. "Come on—we've got to get out of here."

"What about this mess?"

"This is how her office always looks."

"Not the broken glass and stuff," Angel said in a girlishly accusative tone.

"Hang on," he said. "I have an idea." He set the folders on the desk. Angel leafed through an old fashion magazine as she lay on Grizelda's filthy sofa.

Paige quickly returned at a gallop, wheeling the abandoned Krew Kart. The cart smashed into what was left of the cabinet at full speed.

For her part, Angel had clearly forgotten that Paige had left the room or, for that matter, that he was still in the building. His sudden return, and the unexpected impact, caused her to sit up on the sofa and scream.

"Pipe down, tough guy," Paige said. He scribbled a note on a neon-colored Post-it and stuck it onto that wreckage.

"You scared the hell out of me," she complained. She stretched as she arose from the couch and crossed to where he was gathering up the folders once again. "What does that say?"

"*Lo siento*, Senora Grizelda," Paige answered absently.

"I mean, what does it mean?"

"'Sorry about that, Miss Grizelda,'" he translated. Tucking the folders under his arm, he headed for the door. "Let's go. And I am *so* driving."

"We'll see," she said. She tucked the keys into the front of her pants and followed. "Where are we going, anyways?"

"I think we have to try to get in touch with Roy," Paige said, heading through the empty building toward the front doors.

"I thought we didn't trust him," Angel said, sobering.

"I still kind of don't, although I'm not sure how he could be connected to Grizelda," Paige said, thinking out loud as much as explaining. He walked past Phanie's desk and across the lobby. "The thing is, we have to trace these payments from the people on this list to Grizelda. I don't have any idea how to do that, do you?"

"Duh, but why don't we just go to the police?" Angel said, laughing as she said it.

"Right?" Paige said. He laughed with her as he leaned against the front door. "Or we could just hand-deliver typed confessions. Roy still thinks we're dead. So let's say I set up a meeting from a phone booth or something and disguise my voice. I'll tell him we've got anonymous information about Grizelda blackmailing a whole bunch of Hollywood A-List types. Then, maybe, if he checks it out, he'll find out who killed us?"

"Do they still have phone booths?"

"I have no idea," Paige admitted. "They put cell phones in specially marked boxes of Cap'n Crunch now. Maybe we should call from here."

"That's a great idea," Angel agreed enthusiastically. "That way the caller ID will show this place and make it look like the call is coming from someone on the inside."

"*Fur sher*," Paige said in his best Valley speak. He held up his hand for a high five.

"Oh, that's so last millennium," Angel said, wincing at the gesture.

Disgusted, Paige smacked her with his still extended hand, then stalked over to Phanie's desk.

"Hey, buzzkill," Angel said, indignantly. "That's not funny."

"Welcome to the twenty-first century," he said, taking a seat behind Phanie's desk. Paige picked up the receiver and tucked it between his shoulder and his chin. He rooted through his pockets in search of the card with Roy's number.

"I'm dying," Angel said. "I wonder if there's anything to eat in here?"

"There's a bar or something in the conference room," he said in an effort to get her to go away so he could think.

"Right," she said drifting away.

He found the card and began dialing.

"Oh yeah, there's practically a whole kitchen in here," Angel shouted back to him. "You want anything?"

41

"Hello?"

"Is this, like, Lieutenant Slade?" Paige asked. He spoke in his best Valley-Girlese into an empty paper cup that he held next to the receiver of the phone at Grizelda's reception desk.

"It is," Roy answered, sounding half-awake.

"Okay, so like this is totally anonymous, 'cause you know, like I could get so fired." Paige's absurd voice was muffled by the cup even as it was magnified by the cement floor, brick walls and glass-skylit ceiling of the cavernous room.

"What can I do for you?" Roy asked, somewhat less fuzzily.

"Well, so, like, I have the 4-1-1 on some of old Grizelda's totally shady dealings."

"What kind of dealings exactly?" Roy asked.

It seemed to Paige that the Lieutenant was pretty quick on the uptake. "Dude, like blackmail and stuff."

"Blackmail? Who?"

"Totally. So, here's the dealio. I've got a list of who was getting punked but I only know that one person on the list paid up to the tune of a hundred-K. So, like, it would be way excellent, if you could, like, connect the dots on who paid Grizzly Grizelda, 'cause, like, it looks like she did the deed."

"The deed?"

"Murder, dude."

"Grizelda?"

"Looks like."

"Can you prove it?"

"As if. Isn't that, like, your job?"

"Okay, so how do I get this list?"

Angel's screams cut their conversation short.

"Not another one!" she shrieked running through the reception area. "It's happening again."

"Is everyone okay there?" Roy asked. "Is that Angel? *Paige?*"

Paige hung up as soon as he heard his name.

"What the fuck, Angel?" Paige demanded. "I was on the phone with the lieutenant. You totally could have blown our—"

"I don't care," she called, running for the front door. "We have to get out of here."

"What the hell is going on?" Paige said.

He stood up. One of the phone lines began ringing. "LAPD" was all it said on the caller ID.

"Great," he said under his breath, regretting his brilliant plan even before he had the chance to put it in place.

"I'm leaving now," Angel said from the door. Her hand rested on the crash bar.

There was banging on the door. Instinctively she screamed and retreated.

Paige's scalp felt like his hair was on fire.

"What the hell is going on with you?"

Angel was running back across the lobby toward him.

"This is the police," a voice shouted through the door. "Is everyone okay? Please open up."

"How did they know we were here?" she said grabbing Paige's hand.

"He alerted them the minute he got the call," Paige said, realizing what a fool he'd been.

"Who did?" she said. "Come on, we've got to get out of here."

"Do we?"

"Yes."

"Why?"

"Open this door!" the police called. "This is your last warning!"

"There's another head in the refrigerator in the conference room," she squeaked, pulling on his arm.

"*What*? Whose?"

"Grizelda."

42

Clad in purloined KKK Kleaners smocks, fade sunglasses and Eva Gabor wigs, Paige and Angel watched the police from a safe distance. Peering over an ornamental hedge in the unlighted parking lot of a nearby bank branch, they could observe the comings and goings at Zeldom.

They had managed to escape the police through Grizelda's secret exit. The door, concealed behind an armoire hinged to the wall in the lounge, opened onto the alley behind Zeldom. Angel knew of the private entrance and had used it to conceal her arrivals and departures in happier, less eluding-a-killer-or-arrest days. It worked equally well to escape the police as it had the last time the paparazzi cared whether or not she was alive.

The alley connected with cross streets at either end of the block. There was no idling stretch limo like those that once awaited Angel there. Instead, they crept to the end of the alley and circled back to get a better view.

"So I guess Grizelda isn't the murderer?" Angel said as they watched a Grizelda-shaped-black-zippered-body-bag emerge, strapped to a gurney and wheeled to the coroner's van.

"No," Paige said, wishing for a cup of tea. "Grizelda was just a blackmailer. Looks like it's us."

"Us?"

"Thought you'd be pleased," he snorted. "Congrats. You're back at the center of attention."

"Don't be silly, Paige," she said, patting his hand. "We're dead. It can't possibly be us."

"Even after that phone call?"

"He didn't see us."

"And our fingerprints absolutely everywhere?"

"We were there earlier today, before the explosion."

"And our guest appearance at the KKK rally?"

"Oh, yeah," Angel said. "Could be trouble. They seem like the sort of young people who'd go straight to the police with information on a murder committed in a building they had the only keys to."

"And Bill E's car?"

"It's parked on the wrong side of the street," she said, smiling.

"Street cleaning." He smiled. "It'll be gone before they think to look for it. You're a better criminal than a bad cop."

"Missed my calling," she said, folding her arms. "Just one teensy-weensy problem."

"Us?"

"Where the fuck do we go?"

"Batcave," he said, looking around.

"Batcave?"

"We just need a Batmobile."

They watched the lieutenant emerge. He spoke with several of the other officers.

The sky was starting to lighten. It was going to be one of those *après*-rain, blazingly clear Los Angeles days. Paige knew they'd have to move soon. They needed the dark for cover. He didn't know what to make of the lieutenant. The news report he'd seen at Bill E's made it clear Roy didn't think he had any reason to hide the fact that he was outside Angel's at the time of the explosion. Still, up until that moment, the lieutenant was the only person who knew where they'd be and where they wouldn't be.

"Why would he kill Grizelda?"

"Grizelda the blackmailer? Grizelda the swindler?" Angel mugged. "I can't imagine."

"Exactly," Paige said. "What could she have had on the lieutenant?"

"The lieutenant?" Angel asked, screwing up her face. "Are you still beating that horse?"

He heard the sound before he saw it. A smile melted gently across his face like butter on fresh pancakes. The lights came into view as the tow truck rounded the corner. Flashing lights, beeping back-up noises, the clank of chains and the whine of hydraulic motors; the police never even looked up. Just the noises of the city waking up. The driver began the rodeo-cowboy-swift lasso of Bill E's errant chariot.

"Let's get out of here," Paige said, turning back toward the street they'd come from. "Bruce Wayne awaits."

"Bruce Wayne?"

"Billionaire playboy?"

"Oh," she said nodding. "That's really clever. Cause he's got skin in the game now."

"I just don't know how we get out there," he said, as they made their way toward the Pacific.

"I got this one," she said. "Butch it up and follow the fag hag."

43

"The Seahorse?" Paige asked, a tone of contempt in his voice. "That's your plan?"

"I know, princess," Angel said with a nasty little laugh. "Not really your sort of place I'm sure, but trust the hag on this one."

He was tired, his cheap wig itched and his feet hurt too much to argue.

They had walked from Zeldom in Santa Monica to Venice Beach's most notorious hustler bar.

"It's closed," Paige pointed out.

"This way," Angel said, leading them past the front entrance on Rose and around the corner onto Speedway, a winding pathway of a street that was little more than an alley. From there, they turned up a grimy and anonymous access way. As casually as making her way up her own front walk, Angel stepped over a pair of half-naked sleeping bodies, passed out mid-blowjob and snoring lustily.

When Paige hesitated, afraid to speak and afraid to go on, she turned back, gave him a wink and extended her hand. He took it, strangely warmed by her manner. Stepping gingerly over the unconscious copulaters, he followed her to a door so filthy he could not tell what color it had once been.

She tapped a strange rhythm on the door, then wiped her knuckles on her KKK smock.

After a short wait, a little panel in the door slid open.

"Yeah?"

"Is that any way to talk to a lady?"

There was a pause.

Angel lowered her shades enough to peer over the top of the blackout lenses.

The *tsk-tsk* of a clicking tongue was, at first, her only reply.

"Girl," their inquisitor said at last. "That is one sad wig."

The comment was followed by the sequential unlocking of a ludicrous number of chains and deadbolts. The door swung wide.

"You better come in here before someone sees you," said an enormous man in full drag as he made a grand and sweeping gesture.

"Whose reputation are you worried about?" Angel asked, following their hostess.

"It must be theirs," Paige said, bringing up the rear and pulling the door behind them. "Not sure how a bad wig in Blowjob Alley is inconsistent with your reputation."

The laugh was as big as the drag queen.

"I'm Queen B," she said at last, extending her hand.

"What's the B stand for?" Paige asked, taking her hand.

"Bob."

She began relocking the half-dozen locks on the alley door.

"Nice," Paige said with sincere admiration. "I'm Paige, Paige Blanche."

"I know who you are," Queen giggled huskily. "Even if I hadn't known before, and I did, but even if I hadn't I would have known you after your little tea escapade at the Argyle. You should have been a drag queen, *chéri*. No one knows how to throw a drink in someone's face like a drag queen. You've got mad skills."

"I'm standing right here!" Angel pointed out.

"You hadn't been so famous for a long time," Queen B said, tapping Angel familiarly on the tit. "You ought to have people throw tea in your face more often. Come on, the both of you, and let's see what we can do about that hair."

They followed Queen B into the bar area which, despite the Seahorse being closed, was as busy as happy hour. Hustlers were finalizing deals and developing new ones with plentiful clients. The music and lighting were subdued. No hint of the day breaking outside intruded on the scene. Those few who took note of them eyed Angel and Paige suspiciously.

"Come on," Queen B said. "There's commerce going on up in here. I's about to get out of these work clothes. Come to my office and you can tell me what the hell you're doing here at this hour. Especially since you died yesterday."

They followed her across the little stage at one side of the room. Colored lights played across them as they passed through the Mylar strips that comprised the curtain at the back of the runway.

"God knows you wouldn't be here unless you wanted something," she sighed as she disappeared through the glittering shreds.

44

Queen B's office was part dressing room, part office and mostly residence.

"Sit down, won't you?" She took up a place facing the mirror. "Can I offer you anything?"

"A cup of tea would be lovely," Paige said, in the vain hope his request might yield something other than laughter. He was wrong.

"I daresay," Queen B said, wiping away tears of mirth and a deal of mascara. "Tea? Where'd you find this one, LB?"

"LB?" Paige asked.

"It's nothing," Angel said.

"A lot of old queens used to use bags of rice as boobs," Queen B said, catching Paige's eye in the mirror. "The showy ones used a whole pound."

"LB." Paige nodded. "I like it."

"Great," Angel said, rolling her eyes.

"Only I'd say she looks more like ten pounds in a five-pound bra," Paige said to B's reflection.

"I see why you keep him around," Queen B remarked to Angel.

"I'd be happy to leave him with you," Angel replied, stacking arms.

"You'd think someone who calls so much attention to herself would be a better sport about getting it," Queen B said to the Paige in her mirror.

"Oh, Queenie," Angel said. "I'm not a drag queen, I just play one on TV."

"That's the way, girl," Queen B said with a proud nod. "Say it before they say it about you. It might as well be *your* laugh." She swept her eyes over both of them. "So what the hell do you want, showing up at my place at this hour with the police looking everywhere for you? And it had better be good. I don't need your trouble in here."

"Can you call Mitch for us?" Angel said in her little girl voice.

"Mitch who?" Queen B asked, brows arched higher than the ones she'd painted on.

"That's the one," Angel said. "We need for him to send Mason out to pick us up in one of his Stealth-UVs. We need to hide out at his place till the heat's off."

"Till the heat's off?" Paige said. "What is this, a gangster film all of a sudden?"

"He's a keeper," Queen B confirmed.

"Feel free," Angel said, cutting her eyes in his direction. "And yes, I think this is starting to be just like a gangster picture. We're up to three heads now. What would you call it?"

"Three heads?" Queen B asked, turning to look over her shoulder. "I hope that's a figure of speech."

"I wish," Angel said. "But no, it's actual heads. And I found all of them."

"*Mmmm*, LB," Queen B said, turning back to her mirror. "I like my head right where it is. We need to get you two out of here."

"The sooner the better," Angel said. "I woke up with my fiancé dead on top of me with his head bashed in. And that turned out to be the least horrifying thing that's happened in the last three days."

"St. J. was a nice man," Queen said.

"You knew him?" Paige asked.

"He was in here now and again with 'Mitch Who,'" Queen said, giving Paige a meaningful look in the glass. "Mind you, I didn't know him as well as I know the son."

"Really?" Paige said, leaning forward.

"Oh, yeah! Jay Bird?" Queen B said, as she began smearing her face with Noxzema. "He was in here all the time. Did a lot of business here until he met that new man of his. They'd come by, late mostly, just for ambiance. Hire a little trick to take home and slap around. Paid good, though. That new man of his was a big believer in you-broke-it-you-bought-it. Nothing serious, but serious enough for a little paid leave."

"Jay St. James?" Paige asked.

"The boyfriend mostly, I think," Queen B said with a vigorous nod. "Jay came in with a shiner or two. He's good with concealer, but you can't fool an expert."

"Poor Jay," Paige said reflexively.

"Who was the boyfriend?" Angel asked.

"Don't know," Queen said. "Rich, I guess. Dressed nice. His own money. It was nice to see Jay Bird with someone who didn't have a hand in his pocket."

"Just a fist in his eye," Paige said, shaking his head.

"Yeah," Queen B said. "So, did you two come here to talk?"

"Aren't you enjoying our company, Queenie?" Paige teased.

"You don't know me long enough to call me that," Queenie chided.

"So you're saying you want us to stay longer?" Paige asked.

"Okay, hand me my damned phone," she ordered, beckoning with a wave of her glittering talons.

45

Angel and Paige followed Mason down the alley behind the Seahorse. The tricked-out black Escalade stretch with the black windows idled at the curb on Speedway. The sun was just barely up. Their sunglasses looked only a little less ridiculous than they had when the two arrived. The sleeping blowjob couple was gone.

Paige and Angel moved swiftly without talking.

Mason held the door as they dove into the back.

"Well," Mitch said. "This is heating up. It's all over the news that Grizelda's dead." He pointed to a video screen in the console. A tightly dressed young woman was pantomiming the weather as the local morning news update played with the volume muted.

"Thanks for getting us out of here, Mitch," Angel said, patting his knee as she took the seat beside him. "I don't know what's going on."

"This shoots down the whole Grizelda theory," Mitch said.

Paige took the seat facing them as they pulled away.

"It wasn't us," Paige said. "We just—Angel just found the body—the head—in the conference room fridge. I don't know where they found the body."

"It couldn't have been you who killed Seth," Mitch said. "Grizelda was the proof that you didn't do it."

"Thanks for believing," Angel said. "I'm so confused. I'm starting to wonder if we *are* guilty."

"Speak for yourself, LB," Paige said, looking out the window uneasily. "Have they officially found the body? Did they say?"

"They're not even admitting to the head," Mitch said, scrolling on his tablet. "They are saying they think it's connected to Seth's murder."

"Anything about us?" Paige asked. "Are we still dead?"

"No mention either way," Mitch said. "I have heard that there's going to be a press conference later this morning. It's really gone national. Six deaths so far—if you count you two."

"Which I don't," Paige said. "But, yeah, it really is turning into a crime spree. I just can't figure out what the crime is."

"You mean other than the four dead bodies?" Angel said, leaning her head on Mitch's shoulder.

"I mean if it's not the blackmail," Paige said. "What's going on? I brought you this, by the way." Paige handed Mitch a folder.

"What's this?" Mitch asked.

"Hostess gift," Paige shrugged. "It's everything Grizelda had on you, I hope."

"You're very kind," Mitch said, regarding the blue folder. "It's hard to believe all this is about blackmail."

"Right? That plot doesn't really make sense," Paige agreed. "Yet."

"I'm too tired to think," Angel moaned. "I can't even remember the last time I slept. How many days have we been up?"

Paige actually had to pause to consider his answer. "It was at the beach, the night after sushi," Paige said wistfully, after a moment. "And that house isn't even there anymore."

"We'll get you two something to eat and you can get some sleep," Mitch said, stroking Angel's hair.

"I appreciate you doing this," Paige said.

"He meant a lot to me," Mitch answered. Tears were in his eyes suddenly. "And then the whole insider trading thing."

"Well, she's dead and I'm not telling," Paige said and smiled.

The exterior of Zeldom appeared on the video screen.

"Turn it up," Paige said pointing.

"...where police discovered the body in a posh Westside talent agency," the anchor continued. "The victim, born Grizelda Louise Lamar in Buffalo, New York, in May nineteen..."

"Buffalo?" Paige declared. "I knew that accent was a fake."

"Hmm," Mitch said, smiling a little. "Sometimes it was German, sometimes Hungarian, sometimes French."

"Always ridiculous," Paige concluded.

"...Lamar was a celebrity manager, guiding the careers of many noteworthy celebrities, including Angel Panderson, presumed dead following a suspicious explosion at her Malibu home seen here in amateur video shot from the beach nearby," the anchor narrated. "Police declined to confirm whether or not the Lamar death was related to the growing string of deaths that seem to stem from the recent murder of media titan Seth St. James."

There were tears in Mitch's eyes again.

"This is an active crime scene," Lieutenant Slade told the reporter outside Zeldom. He was attractively disheveled. "We're going to focus on the investigation here, but there is a press conference scheduled for later this morning to discuss the St. James case and other recent developments. So we can talk about this at that time."

"We will have the news conference live in its entirety, here on..."

Mitch ran the sound down again.

"Good news, Angel," Paige said. "We're still dead."

Angel began to snore.

46

"...This is Erica Laurelson coming to you live from the Santa Monica police station," the somewhat-fatigued-but-determined reporter said. She had a death grip on the microphone and wore the same outfit she'd had on at the scene of the fire at Angel's in Malibu the day before. It was clear she was not about to let go of this story. "The LAPD, Santa Monica PD and the Los Angeles County Sheriff's West Hollywood and Malibu divisions have called a press conference to address grisly developments overnight in the growing so-called St. James Spree killings."

The camera focused on a well-lit rostrum, bristling with microphones and emblazoned with the Santa Monica city seal. It was centered on a raised platform flanked by a UN's worth of state, local and national flags. The wall behind the panoply was fashioned from the same blond wood as the lonely lectern.

"The crime spree began with the murder of billionaire media mogul Seth St. James sometime following or during an engagement party for him and his fiancée, former television star Angela Panderson," Erica droned on, filling time until someone official took the stage. "Until this morning's grisly discovery, Panderson and her writing partner and close friend Paige Blanche were believed to have been the latest victims in this bizarre series of as-yet-unsolved crimes, their lives claimed in a devastating explosion that flattened Panderson's multi-million dollar Malibu home. Oh, I see LAPD Lieutenant Roy Slade is moving to the podium. Slade is the spokesman for this multi-department, multi-jurisdictional investigation. He is accompanied by representatives from the many municipalities and jurisdictions that have been touched by this crime wave."

"Good morning," the lieutenant said into the microphone.

"He's been to hair and makeup since his guest appearance at Grizelda's," Paige said. He was still a little touchy about the whole Jay St. James double-play.

"*Shhh*," Angel hissed, eating breakfast for the second time that morning.

"Yeah. I'd hate to miss out on what we already—"

"*Shhh*!"

"I'm Lieutenant Roy Slade with the Los Angeles Police Department." Roy's voice was a little too loud and there was a scramble to adjust the volume as he continued.

"I have a brief update on some late breaking developments," Roy went on. "And then I will turn the microphone over for further statements and questions."

Blinding camera flashes lit up the brass arrayed on stage. Reporters leaned in with their own mics and devices to try to capture their own versions of the proceedings.

"After an anonymous phone tip alerted authorities early this morning, Santa Monica police and LAPD were called to the scene of what appears to be another related murder in this on-going investigation," Roy read. "The victim was Grizelda Lamar. She was found dead, believed murdered, at her place of business. No further details are available to report at this time, but based on specific evidence found at the scene, all departments believe that Ms. Lamar's death is related to what seems to be a series of murders that began with the death of Seth St. James, three days ago."

"Refrigerators full of heads," Angel huffed, smearing strawberry preserves on a heavily buttered English muffin.

"*Shhh*," Paige shushed her.

"We can report at this time that two people presumed dead in yesterday's Malibu explosion, Angela Panderson and Paige Blanche, are no longer believed to have died in that blast and are wanted for questioning."

The questions and disturbance at the press conference went up a few dozen decibels after that.

"Son of a bitch," Paige said, joining the chorus.

"And finally," Roy said, riding over the racket. "If I may, just before your questions? Finally, we can report that the body of Los Angeles attorney, and attorney to Mr. St. James, Earl Filou, was found at the scene of the Malibu explosion. We are unable to say whether or not Mr. Filou died in the blast but we have positively identified his body. Thank you, that's all from me. I will now turn the proceeding over to…"

The set went mute.

"Holy fuck," Angel said, putting down the remote.

Paige stared at the screen. A spoonful of crème brûlée hung in midair between his mouth and the Wedgwood bowl in which it had been served to him.

He was now a wanted fugitive and suspected serial killer. They had stayed up to watch the press conference and get something to eat, but a morning nap seemed unlikely, given their new circumstances.

"Earl?" Paige said, still unable to process it. "What does Earl have to do with all of this?"

"We're like Robert Downey Jr. and Juliette Lewis from *Natural Born Killers*," Angel said.

"No, we are actually not spree killers," Paige corrected, tossing his spoon into the bowl with his half-eaten dessert. "And I think that was Woody Harrelson, who is nothing like me."

"So you're saying I'm like Juliette Lewis?" she asked, considering.

"I have too much respect for Juliette to say anything of the kind," he retorted. "Besides, I think it's way more like *The 39*

Steps. He's just trying to help and he gets accused of murder or spying or… I can't remember, exactly."

"*The 39 Steps*? What the hell is that?"

"It's Hitchcock, you cretin," Paige snapped. "It's a classic. Don't you know anything about movies at all?"

"I know I've been in more movies than you!"

"One," he said, holding up a finger. "*One* more movie than me."

"You both just need some sleep," Mitch said, putting an understanding hand on both their shoulders. "It's *Thelma and Louise*—it's much more like *Thelma and Louise*."

"Totally," Paige said, bopping himself in the forehead with the heel of his hand.

"You're right," Angel said. "I'm totally Louise."

"You are such a Thelma," Paige hooted.

"No way."

"Way," Paige insisted. "Lookit, she gets drunk and gets into trouble while Louise is just trying to help. She sleeps with Brad Pitt and loses the money. She gets crazy and robs that liquor store? Louise is practically an innocent bystander. Like me."

"I am way more of a Susan Sarandon than you will ever—"

The phone intercom interrupted.

"Mr. Geller?"

"Yes," Mitch said, picking up. "Uh-huh. Kind of early. What do they want? No, a warrant won't be necessary. I'll meet them in the drawing room."

He hung up.

Angel and Paige stared at him.

"The police are here for you," Mitch said.

"How the hell?" Angel said.

"What are we going to do?"

"Well," Mitch said. "Fortunately we have a safe room and plenty of doughnuts."

47

The prospect of gaining access to the Geller estate was a coup not to be missed.

Brass from both the LAPD and the county sheriff showed up for no other reason than to say that they had been inside the legendary home of the legendary billionaire. The expeditionary force was composed of the best, brightest and most opportunistic among the lower ranks. But as the morning progressed, the upper echelon officers who had populated the dais at the press conference adjourned to the Geller mansion.

Mitch played the gracious host, welcoming the authorities into his home and thanking them for their service. He offered them coffee, doughnuts and the run of the vast estate. Once Roy and company had exhausted themselves and their options, Mitch sat down with the lieutenant and two of his superiors to discuss the case and answer questions.

Though Mitch's lawyer had arrived by the time of the interview, Mitch spoke easily and candidly with Roy and his associates while his lawyer listened in for the record.

"They did come by last night," Mitch said. "I was watching a movie and they joined me for a bit."

"Did they say why they'd come?" Roy asked, refusing the plate of cookies that Mitch passed his way.

"Well, obviously they were both very rattled after two attempts on their lives," Mitch explained. "We mostly talked about how upset they were. Particularly Angel. She'd lost everything in the explosion."

"But why here?" Roy persisted.

"They wanted to know about Seth's business dealings," Mitch said easily. "I was financing his expansion into the industry. I think they were just looking for a motive for whoever was after them."

"Did they say why they didn't go to the police?"

"No," Mitch replied with a shrug. "My guess? They were afraid. There had been two attempts on their lives and people around them are dropping like flies. They said they felt safer being dead. I guess they were using you as their alibi, if that makes sense. Now that you've made it clear on national television that they are still alive, I'm sure they'll go into hiding."

Roy smiled in response to Mitch's thinly veiled accusation; his associates not so much.

"And you haven't heard from them since?" Roy asked.

"I'm not sure why you think they would contact me again," Mitch said. He had not quite answered the question, so he hadn't quite lied to the police. "Why do you think they did it?"

"We're working on a number of theories," Roy said, rising. "If you have nothing else for us, Mr. Geller?"

"Please call me Mitch," Mitch said. "I don't have anything else to add."

"Thank you, Mitch," Roy said, taking the hand Mitch offered. "If you wouldn't mind, could my colleagues and I just have a private minute?"

"Please," Mitch said with an expansive gesture. "Make yourselves at home," he added to the Safety Officers Convention assembled in his living room. "Cook is putting together a couple of trays of sandwiches. Shall I have them bring you some lunch?"

"That's very kind of you, but—" Roy said. The nods and murmurs of assent from his bosses brought him up short.

"Not at all," Mitch said. "Again, thank you for your service."

He left, closing the doors behind him.

"So, where are we?" asked Captain Ferrell. He was Roy's boss from LAPD. No pushover, he clearly had faith in Roy.

"We know from Bill E that they survived the explosion," Roy said.

"Bill E? That son of a bitch," Angel said, smacking the monitor. The large HD screen was one of more than a dozen mounted on the wall in Mitch's panic suite. Other than an absence of windows, there was little to suggest panic in the self-contained, fully equipped, well-stocked and sizeable apartment. They could have survived a lot more than a visit from the police. In fact, they could have lived there for years. And with the help of an extensive system of hidden cameras throughout the property, they could keep track of goings-on anywhere on the estate.

"*Shhh*," Paige urged. "This is it." It was the moment he'd been waiting for all morning. He'd monitored every step that Roy and his law enforcement associates had taken while they poked around the huge mansion and grounds.

"The question remains—was the blast an attempt on their lives or an attempt to fake their deaths?" Roy was saying, reviewing files on his tablet. "The presence of Earl's body in Angel's house seems to suggest that they were planning an escape and tying up loose ends. But it could just as easily be an attempt to frame them for the murders."

"But they survived," Commander Moore, the L.A. Sheriff Bureau Chief, pointed out. "That seems improbable given the size of the explosion."

"Tell me about it," Angel said.

"Have we got a cause yet?" Ferrell asked, helping himself to more cookies.

"Nothing conclusive," Roy sighed. "They're leaning toward gas leak. They haven't turned up any evidence of explosives or even accelerants. Either way, my problem is motive."

"Any theories?" Moore persisted.

"With the exception of Grizelda, everyone murdered so far worked for St. James," Roy said. "His murder seems key. On the one hand, there's money and inheritance, which doesn't really involve Blanche and Panderson, at least not that we can turn up. We're still looking into how Panderson might benefit from St. James' death."

"Have I missed anything?" Mitch asked, joining Paige and Angel in the panic room with a tray of sandwiches. "Is there coffee?"

"I think you're just in time for the big reveal," Paige answered, not looking away. "And no, we couldn't figure out how to work the machine. There is tea."

"On the other hand?" Moore prompted from the living room monitor.

"There's growing evidence of some sort of blackmail," Roy said. "We're not sure exactly how it works, but it seems to have had something to do with Blanche and Panderson's books. We're piecing it together from what we found at Zeldom, but Grizelda seems to have been the central figure in the scheme to use their books to blackmail the subjects of their little peek-a-boo tell-all. And there was another book that Blanche was cagey about writing, found at the second scene."

"I gave him that book," Paige complained to the screen. "He's trying to make us look bad."

"And we found more evidence tying the books directly to the blackmail at the Zeldom crime scene," Roy went on.

"Because I called you and told you about it!" Paige shouted.

Roy and the others paused as their lunch was delivered.

"I told you, you should have slept with him," Angel said.

"What?" Mitch called from the panic room's kitchen. "Is something going on with you and the lieutenant? I thought I got a vibe from him." He rejoined them, setting down a tray with coffee.

"Paige was playing hard to get, but Jay St. James put out and now Lieutenant Blue-Eyes is batting for their side," Angel said.

She began to load cream and fake sweetener into one of the cups. "How did you make coffee so fast?"

"It was already made," Mitch said. "I had the room set up earlier. Why so reluctant, Paige? He's a babe."

"Well, to be fair, he blew up Angel's house and killed us both before I had the chance to go out with him," Paige replied.

"What?"

"I wasn't sure," Paige said, shaking his head. "But now the way he's skewing the investigation against us? Leaving out my cooperation?"

"Well, you did disguise your voice," Angel said. She shot him an accusing look.

"He totally knew who it was," Paige said. "Especially once you started screaming about finding another head. And I think he was with Jay St. James all along—before the investigation *or* the murder. You saw them together at the funeral. And why else would Jay show up at the WeHo Sheriff's station with your pre-nup? And at just the moment we were leaving in front of all that press."

"That's right." Angel nodded. "It was pretty convenient."

"Unless someone texted him and told him we were coming out," Paige said, triumphant. "And the only person who knew besides us was..."

"The driver?" Angel guessed.

"Besides him," Paige said pointing at the monitor.

"Roy?" she tried again.

Lunch served, Roy resumed his explanation of the case to his two superiors. Paige grew angrier as he listened.

"And now he's totally setting us up for this," Paige snarled.

"He totally did send the po-po as soon as you called him on Grizelda's phone," Angel said. "Huge mistake."

"It was your idea," Paige grumbled. "Still think I should sleep with him?"

"There's always conjugal visits," she suggested.

"At least I'll be in a separate prison from you," he said, glaring at the screen. He stuffed half a smoked salmon finger sandwich into his mouth.

"So, Mitch," Angel began. "Are these cameras everywhere throughout the house?"

"Guilty secret," Mitch sang out.

"You must have some steamy tapes," Angel said.

"All I'll say is that it's a good thing for a lot of people that I don't need the money!"

Paige turned up the volume to drown them out.

"So," Roy concluded. "It looks to me like Angel and Paige are rolling up their blackmail network. They killed Seth after he discovered what they were up to. We figure his business manager tipped him off, and that's why they took him out—and the assistant. Grizelda's financials make it clear that Earl was in on the blackmail scheme, probably supplying confidential client information. They're both gone. And the shooting and the explosion were both smokescreens."

"Are there any other possibilities?" Ferrell asked.

"The only other theory points to the ex-wife," Roy said, and shrugged.

"Whose?" Moore asked.

"St. James'," Roy explained. "There's a rumor that there was a new will that favored Angel, but it's gone missing. So the existing St. James will is still in force unless someone can produce a later version."

"And if Panderson and Blanche are guilty, it's a moot point," Moore added.

"And the ex-wife is still the beneficiary," Ferrell concluded.

"Exactly," Roy agreed.

"Pretty powerful," Moore suggested. "We're talking what, billions?"

"With an s," Roy said. "The problem is there's nothing linking the ex-wife to any of this or any of the other people killed. She's completely oblivious to the investigation. She and her fiancé,

Lefty Flynn, were even possible targets. Her fiancé was the only person shot in the incident at C. Shore Sushi."

"And the fiancé was Angel's former manager?" Ferrell pointed out. "There was no love lost between the two of them."

"That's true," Roy agreed with his superior. "Further motive for the shooting."

"Shooting is too good for that weasel," Angel said, throwing a doughnut at the screen.

"*Shhh*," Paige insisted.

"The ex-wife and ex-manager's engagement party is tomorrow night," Roy said.

"Will we have security there?" Ferrell asked between bites.

"We do, they do and I'll be there," Roy volunteered. "Her son is a good friend, so I was already planning to attend."

"The lieutenant is Jay's abusive boyfriend," Angel said, realizing. "The one Queen B told us about."

"Oh my God," Mitch said. "They're going to kill Lucrezia."

"But not Lefty?" Angel asked with a tone of disappointment.

"Maybe," Mitch said. "But with you out of the way and Seth's will missing, Lucrezia is the only thing standing between Jay and Seth's fortune."

"I thought it was in a trust you control?" Paige asked.

"That's in the second will," Mitch explained. "The one that's missing. In the original there's a trust for Lucrezia until her death and then Jay gets it all outright."

"We should warn her," Angel said without conviction.

"Security going forward?" Moore asked Roy.

"They are actually leaving the country following the party," Roy answered. "They're having a little civil ceremony and then taking an extended honeymoon."

"They're going to kill her at the party tomorrow," Paige said. "It's their last chance."

"Oh, well, too bad we weren't invited," Angel said with an air of finality. "Is there more tuna?"

"Maybe we don't need an invitation," Paige said, rising from his chair.

"Oh no, you totally need an invite," Angel said, shaking her head. "I've tried to crash her parties before. That place is tighter than virgin ass."

"How vivid," Paige said. "I actually meant that we might be able to head off her murder if we can prove what Jay and the lieutenant are up to."

"Yeah, 'cause our track record with that has been going great," Angel said, loading yet another plate.

"Isn't that like your third or fourth meal so far today?" Paige asked.

"Well actually, suck my dick," Angel said, throwing a little egg salad sandwich triangle at him.

He caught it and took a bite. "*Mmmm* Are there more of these?"

The police luncheon was wrapping up and Paige binged on little sandwiches as he watched the group making their good-byes. Angel busied herself trying to guess the celebrity names in Mitch's private video collection, mining her memory of old guest lists and gossip for candidates.

"Okay," Roy said to Ferrell, his immediate superior and the last to depart. "I'll be here until the warrant is fully executed."

"Keep me posted," Ferrell said, softy enough not to be over-heard by the others.

Roy nodded in acknowledgement of the unspoken meaning.

"And there'll be a conference call for you and the other chiefs this evening and in the morning," Roy concluded.

"I know," Ferrell said, with a quick look over his shoulder. "But don't stand on ceremony."

"Got it." Roy smiled in acknowledgement.

Ferrell gave him a wink and left him.

Paige watched as Roy, left alone, began to organize himself. He stacked papers, he sorted files. A junior officer stopped by with questions. Roy handled his request with dispatch and was soon on his own again.

Paige couldn't help but feel a little regret. Had he dodged a bullet or been too slow out of the gate? Maybe the lieutenant *was* that slick. Maybe he'd fooled Paige and Angel. Or maybe Jay had just been quicker on the uptake. Roy wasn't hard to look at, but after seeing what a snake he'd turned out to be, was Paige better off for having waited? Or had Roy been in it from the start? It looked more and more as if he had been. Did he get himself assigned to steer the investigation away from the two of them?

As Paige was beginning to daydream, the lieutenant's cell phone rang.

Paige watched, riveted, as Roy took the phone out, checked the number and started to answer. Hesitating, he rose and crossed to the door and opened it. He leaned into the hallway to make sure there was no one about. Then he closed the door, locked it and quickly answered the call.

"Hi," he said softy. "Sorry, it's been crazy this morning."

Paige turned up the volume and leaned in.

"Yeah, I know. Me too. How about tonight? Well, just tell them we're going to the shooting range. It worked because it's true. Or it has been. Okay. That sounds great, yeah. Yeah." The lieutenant laughed in a way that Paige wouldn't have minded making him laugh. "About eight? Okay. I might be a few minutes late. I'll call if I'll be much longer. Mangia? Meet you there."

Roy hung up the phone and smiled like he had a secret.

Paige smiled because he was sure he knew what the secret was.

"Mitch, we need your help," Paige said.

No response. Angel was holding forth, relating a sexual war story Paige had heard before.

He tossed a sandwich at her and scored a direct hit.

48

Mangia turned out to be a dive-chic, hole-in-the wall Italian restaurant near the business end of Marina del Rey. This was good news on several fronts. First, there would be no paparazzi anywhere near the marina. Second, and most important, since Angel and Paige had absolutely no clue what they were doing, it would be easy to catch up with the lieutenant and tail him from there.

On the downside, Paige and Angel would have to figure out where the marina was and, worse yet, go there.

"We should wear disguises," Angel suggested.

"Like fake mustaches?" Paige suggested. "Too bad you don't have a couple of days to let yours grow in."

Angel punched him in the shoulder hard enough to bruise.

Paige let her take charge of the cloaks in their cloak and dagger plot.

He regretted it.

Clad in Hawaiian prints, extra padding and wigs, they looked as if they had disguised themselves as tourists from a '50s comedy film. In order to be able to make a quick getaway and so they wouldn't actually have to find the place, they arranged for Mason, Mitch's driver/butler/resident hottie, to drop them near the restaurant in Mitch's least-conspicuous Lincoln Town Car.

On the way, Paige took advantage of the car's Wi-Fi and a tablet he'd borrowed from Mitch to research what was happening with the investigation. Once again, Busby Barclay proved to be both invaluable and a fair-weather fan. His blog at AvengingAngel.org had taken a decided turn toward their prosecution.

www.BusbyBarclay.com/
AngelPanderson'sHollywoodCrimeSpreeUpdate

<u>In the latest bizarre twist in the St. James murder spree, we can exclusively Star Report</u> that the latest victim, Hollywood Manager/Producer Grizelda Lamar, does not exist. Despite appearances, Grizelda Lamar (<u>seen here at the Hollywood premiere of Angel's Box Office Bomb "Ember Poison, PI"</u>) is actually a wanted criminal under various aliases. The alleged talent manager is wanted in numerous states on charges of extortion, blackmail, embezzlement, and fraud. Lamar, AKA Zelda Louise Lamar, AKA Belinda Louise Hershel of Buffalo, New York, has apparently been using her production and management company as a front for her extortion business. Sources inside the LAPD have revealed exclusively to <u>StarReporter</u> that Lamar's blackmail schemes figure prominently in their investigation of the St. James and subsequent murders. (<u>Mugshot from Lamar's arrest in NYC after the jump</u>)

Those closely involved in the case tell me that the fugitive Angel Panderson and her alleged writing partner were using their books as a means to blackmail prominent Hollywood figures. The two have been missing since the death of Lamar and the discovery of the body of Lamar and Panderson's well-known Hollywood attorney, Earl Filou. Anyone who spots Ms. Panderson or her companion is advised to notify police. They are considered very dangerous and you should use caution when approaching.

Next Story: <u>The secret Hollywood doughnut diet the stars use to melt away ugly belly fat</u>

Previous Story: <u>The smoothie cancer cure, find out how you can cure cancer with a blender</u>

"No exclusive for *him*," Paige concluded after reading the column aloud.

"Why would I kill Earl?" Angel asked. Her question seemed more absurd than usual, considering she was dressed like a background extra from *It's A Mad, Mad, Mad, Mad World*.

"I know why *I* would," Paige said, setting the tablet aside. "But I'd have killed you first. The whole blackmail angle to this doesn't make sense."

"Unless we did it," Angel said.

"Right," Paige nodded. "And we didn't. So the blackmail is just an elaborate frame that happens to be real. At least the 'AKA Grizelda' part."

"It would just be easier to confess," Angel said, and sighed.

"Yeah," Paige agreed, a bit dejected. "Maybe they're just trying to wear us down."

"It's working."

They found Mangia at the end of one of the Venice canals at just the point where they do not join the lagoon at Marina Del Rey. Their flagging moods worsened right away when their plan to watch inconspicuously from across the street was foiled by their discovery that across the street was actually the Ballona Creek channel. It was a lovely place to watch the yachts from the marina sail out to sea, but a tough spot to blend in, unless you were a seabird.

"Wait for us around the corner, Mason," Paige instructed as they climbed out onto the street. "Be ready. We'll call when the target is on the move."

"The target?" Angel said.

Mason only nodded, ever noncommittal.

"Whatever," Paige said. "We can't say their names."

"Makes sense," Angel said. "We'll attract much less attention dressed as Fred and Ethel Mertz and talking like assassins in a spy movie."

"'Cause that was exactly my plan," Paige said. "For the record, you picked these disguises. Let's just go get a table in the back and we can watch them from there."

"That was *my* plan," Angel said.

"We are not here for dinner," Paige asserted, already tired of the argument.

"We have to order something so we blend in," Angel said reasonably.

"What is with you and the eating?" Paige asked, holding the restaurant's plate-glass door. "Maybe an *hors d'oeuvre*."

"I'm stressed," Angel said, pushing past.

"And sober," Paige said under his breath, following.

The restaurant was an Italian restaurant of the dimly lit, plastic-checkered-tablecloths and candles-in-Chianti-bottles variety. Dusty plastic fish and lobsters wound with seashells into matted fishing nets with blown glass floaters hung on the fake, dark-wood paneled walls. A sooty brick pizza oven was visible beyond the promotional menu board, soft drink clock and beer-company-Tiffany-shaded light fixtures.

They were early. There was no sign of the lieutenant or anyone else they recognized. Since Paige wasn't certain who Roy was meeting, he knew they had to keep their guard up. This was made more difficult by the fact that there was hardly anyone else in the place. While Paige considered their options, Angel took charge of developing their cover.

"Hey, *calzone*," Angel shouted, in the worst low-end, Long Island accent since *Jersey Shore* went off the air. "Could we get some service over here?"

"*Ixnay*," Paige muttered under his breath, giving Angel the elbow.

"Sit anywhere you want," the big-haired young woman at the counter replied, without looking up from her cellphone.

"Nice tawk," Angel went on, attracting the attention of pretty much everyone except the waitress. "You kiss ya motha wit dat mout? *Fogeddaboutit*."

"If you don't shut up I'm going to stab you to death with a plastic fork," Paige said as he dragged her to the farthest booth at the back. It was the perfect spot from which to observe the restaurant. They were situated near the bathrooms and a rear exit should they need to make a timely departure. "Wait here," he instructed, shoving her onto the semi-circular, red vinyl banquette.

Paige hurried down the short hallway and into the men's room. He took a minute or two to wash his hands and to make his trip look convincing. Opening the door slowly, he saw that no one was looking. Angel and the waitress were conferring so he took his chance. The back door swung open into an alley. At one end he could make out the whitecaps of breaking waves between the houses on the beach. At the other was Channel Walk, a paved pathway along the jetty that wound inland along the channel to the tony Marina Del Rey developments and the boat slips of the marina.

"Can I help you?" A large man, a cook or kitchen worker in a stained white apron, fixed Paige with a hostile stare. He had a cigarette hanging from his lips and a bandana tied on his head in that confident-hip-beach-bum way that some men could pull off.

"Oops, sorry," Paige said. He resisted the urge to ask how the man got the bright blue handkerchief to stay on his head while managing to avoid looking like *Tante* Jemima or a complete hipster douchebag. "Wrong way."

The chef stubbed out his smoke and followed as Paige retreated back into the restaurant.

"Yeah, it's real confusing," the man said, giving Paige the eye as they walked down the not-the-least-bit-confusing short hallway into the restaurant. "This is the restaurant."

"Yeah, thanks," Paige said, not looking up as he slid into the booth beside Angel.

"I got yous a nice beer, J-Pop," Angel said, too loudly.

"I don't drink," Paige said under his breath.

"It's part of the cover," Angel insisted, speaking through clenched jaws but still clearly audible from the front entrance.

"I'm still allergic, even undercover," Paige growled. "And keep it down."

"Can we get some iced tea over here?" Angel said, appropriating the beer.

"Yeah sure," the waitress said listlessly as she deposited a large bottle of Chianti on the table, along with some bread and a basket of mozzarella sticks. "I thought you wanted wine?"

"I like my beer with a wine chasa," Angel said, laughing like they might not hear her in the back row. "The tea's for J-Pop, here. He's a totaler."

"A what?" Paige asked.

"A teetotaler, you know?"

The waitress walked off while they were talking, clearly not interested or possibly not even aware that they were talking.

"Will you keep it *down*?"

"I'm trying to give my character depth," Angel said. "You might try to do a bit more with J-Pop."

"Angel, the idea of undercover is that you try to be nondescript, not memorable," Paige said. "It's not an acting gig. We're not trying to get good reviews. We're trying *not* to get noticed."

"I don't think that's true," Angel said, knitting her brow. She downed the glass of draught and let off a huge belch as she slammed the mug back on the table.

"Choice, J-Cow," Paige said, waving his hand daintily in front of his face.

"My name is Shotzie," Angel whispered loudly.

"I like J-Cow better."

"Well, I hate it," Angel said taking a swipe at him and missing.

"So, J-Cow it is."

"Your tea," the waitress said slamming the misshapen, red, plastic tumbler onto the table in front of him. "You need sweetener?" she asked, as she set up a round metal stand on the table.

"I'm good. Maybe lemon?" he asked. "What's that?"

"It's for the pizza," the waitress said, stalking off. "Your antipasto will be up in a minute," she called back to them. "I'll bring it with your salads."

"What did you order?" Paige demanded.

"This and that," Angel said. She tossed back a glass of the thick red wine and poured another. "I just wanted to look like regular people at a pizza place."

"But you hate solid food," Paige groaned. "What's up with the binge eating? Why can't you just be—"

The bell on the doorframe jingled.

Paige broke off and sank down in the booth. He raised his menu to conceal most of his face, peering over the top in a manner only slightly less obvious than everything Angel had done since their arrival.

"Look who's here," Paige said in a whisper. "I knew it."

"Who?" Angel demanded.

"Your stepson." Paige grinned.

"I do not have—"

"Shut up," Paige said sharply.

"That's no way to talk to the lady," said Bandana Guy. He paused by their table, arms loaded with loaves of cheap, unsliced white bread.

"Oh no, I didn't mean it like that," Paige said with a nervous laugh. "I meant it like 'get out of here' or 'you don't mean it,' *that* kind of 'shut up.'"

"Words can hurt," Angel asserted grandly in her terrible accent.

"I've got my eye on you," Bandana Guy said, glaring at Paige before departing.

"Way to be inconspicuous," Angel teased.

"The lieutenant is meeting Jay," Paige said ignoring her. "I knew it."

"Maybe Jay just stopped by for a slice," Angel said, holding up her menu and peering over the top of it.

Paige only raised an eyebrow at her in reply.

"Yeah, even I don't believe that," Angel said. "They're fucking, I *told* you."

"Probably," Paige agreed. "But I think it was going on before. They're too familiar. I think the lieutenant is totally in on it. We need to keep an eye on—"

The bells jingled again.

The lieutenant walked in. He leaned down and exchanged a quick hug with Jay.

"Bingo," Paige said, menu firmly in place. "Here we go."

"Lieutenant, hey," Bandana Guy called warmly. "We've got your usual coming up."

"Bodhi!" Roy acknowledged the chef, then took his seat across from Jay at a table by the front window.

"I wish we were closer," Paige said from behind his menu. "I can't hear a word from here."

"Do you still need those?" the waitress asked, setting a basket of fried calamari and clams on the table, along with an enormous antipasto platter.

"I'm sorry?" Paige asked, confused.

"The menus, you still need them?"

"Oh, yeah, I think I'll hang on to mine," Paige said. "I just want to see what all you have."

"Well, she ordered most of it," the waitress said. "You could just wait and be surprised. Suit yourself."

"Why did you order all this food?" Paige asked.

"We're at a restaurant," she snapped. "You wandered off. I was trying to blend."

"Everything okay over there?" Bodhi called.

Everyone including Roy looked their way.

Paige gave the chef a thumbs-up and raised his menu higher.

Bodhi handed the waitress a pizza box and a takeout bag and did the *I've-got-my-eye-on-you* thing with his index and middle fingers, pointing at his eyes and then at Paige.

To Paige's horror, the waitress delivered the takeout order to the lieutenant and Jay, who rose as she approached.

"Oh my God, they ordered to go," Paige whispered violently. "We've got to pay and get out of here."

"Don't look at me," Angel said, stuffing rolls and calamari into her otherwise empty wicker pocketbook. "I don't have any money."

"You don't have any…" Paige trailed off in a rage. "You were in charge."

"Of money?" Angel said, looking up. "I usually pay with the black card, but it has my name on it so I left it at Mitch's. We're undercover, right? I don't have a Shotzie Amex."

"Well, I don't have anything," Paige said, beginning to panic. "And I didn't order all this food."

The lieutenant handed the waitress some cash and then waved off the change. They chatted easily as they walked to the front door.

"Come on," Paige said, seeing their chance. "I've got an idea."

Quickly he headed down the adjacent hallway and to the exit.

"Dine-and-dash?" Angel giggled following. "Paige Blanche! You'll be drummed out of the Princess Brigade."

"Just come on!"

They hit the fire exit door at a run and took off down the alley.

Pausing for a minute, Paige tried to find a gap between the buildings to get them back out onto the street in front of the restaurant.

"There they are," Paige pointed, spotting the lieutenant and Jay, arm-in-arm, strolling down Channel Walk toward the marina.

He took off at run. Angel did her best to keep up.

"Slow down!" she called after him. "It's hard to run in these shoes in the dark."

"Yet you picked them for a stakeout," Paige said, maintaining his pace.

He stopped short and crouched in the shadows of a stand of trees on a triangle of parkway beside a lookout near the water, just where Channel Walk turned toward the marina.

Angel almost fell as she came to an abrupt halt behind him.

"Be careful," he snapped.

"Sorry, it's just that—"

"Shut up."

"Is that the 'get out of here' or the 'you don't mean it' kind of shut up?"

"It's the 'shut up' kind of shut up, now *shut up* shuttin' up," he snarled.

"You want a roll?" she asked, snapping open her pocket book and helping herself. "You're getting really grouchy. Maybe something to eat?"

Paige abandoned her and moved to catch up with the lieutenant and Jay.

Angel followed, quieter, with her mouth full of purloined rolls and antipasto.

They kept to the shadows and in the shrubbery along the curving path and were somehow able to follow unnoticed, despite their complete incompetence at doing anything unnoticed, ever. The lapping water, growing darkness and marina noise covered their clumsy efforts. Also, the fact that Jay and Roy were far more interested in each other than in their surroundings probably contributed to Paige and Angel's unlikely success.

As they came around the corner, the channel opened up into the marina.

Jay and the lieutenant strode out onto one of the floating docks that ran alongside the many boat slips. Paige and Angel took cover next to a manicured boxwood hedgerow near a fountain on a little plaza. The splashing waters emanating from a leaping pod of verdigris dolphins helped to further conceal them and allowed them to speak normally.

"Does Jay have a boat?" Paige asked as he watched to see where their unsuspecting subjects were headed.

"I don't know."

"What about Seth?"

"More than one," she said with a tone that implied that the answer was obvious. "But none here that I know of."

"I guess it could be the lieutenant's," he considered.

"As if," Angel snorted.

"Yeah, probably too pricey for public servant pay."

"Oh, yeah," she agreed. "I hadn't thought of that."

He resisted the urge to ask her what she *had* thought of.

"We'll see where they go," Paige said. "Once they're inside, we can sneak out onto the pier and try to eavesdrop."

As he spoke, the two men climbed aboard an impressive but not insanely extravagant mahogany sailing yacht.

Angel whistled. "Nice one."

"It's got to be Jay's," Paige said, emerging from the shadows as the lieutenant and Jay disappeared below deck. "We'll just give them a minute to get settled in. Then we'll follow them out there and see if we can hear—"

There was blinding pain as Paige fell heavily onto the brick walk.

Once he began breathing normally, his vision cleared and he found himself pinned, on his back, looking up into the face of Bodhi, the greasy bandana-coiffed chef from Mangia.

"I knew you were nothing but trouble," Bodhi declared, and slammed Paige into the bricks a couple of times to make it clear just how certain he was.

"Wait, wait," Paige gasped. "I can explain. It's not what you think."

"I get it," Bodhi said. "You figure you can follow a couple of our best customers home and roll them, just because they're gay? Well, I got news for you—one of them is a police lieutenant and you'd have been plenty sorry if you'd succeeded."

"No, that's not it at all," Paige said.

"I was half-a-mind to let you get a rude little shock," Bodhi went on, explaining and pounding. "But nobody runs out on a check on my watch. *Nobody.*"

"We'll pay," Paige gasped. "Angel, call Mason, for fuck's sake, and get some money for these nice people. You ordered all that food."

"Don't talk to the lady like that," Bodhi said, slamming Paige again for emphasis. "I told you. And picking on people just for being gay? You oughta be ashamed."

"I'm gay," Paige shouted. "And so far, I'm the only one getting bashed around here."

That had some effect on Bodhi, who stopped pounding Paige into the brickwork long enough to take a closer look. He seemed unconvinced.

"*You?*" Bodhi said. "You don't look, I mean, you don't seem like, I mean…" He trailed off, unable to think of a way to say it without sounding like what he was accusing Paige of being.

"I know I don't look gay," Paige said, trying to capitalize on and extend his respite from pavement pounding. "I'm in disguise. This is my best friend Shotzie. She came along for moral support. Roy and I have been together for years and I was pretty sure he was sneaking around seeing someone, but I couldn't figure it out until I overheard him making a plan to come to Mangia. It's a lovely restaurant, by the way. Shotzie, angel, call our friend Mason and get him to come bring some money."

Paige went heedlessly on, afraid to take a breath for fear Bodhi would resume his rhetorical pounding. He could see that Angel was digging through the calamari in her purse for the phone. "Sure enough, in they came. Jay is a good friend of mine. I knew his father from the bank where I work—so sad."

"Right?" Bodhi agreed.

"Such a loss," Paige rushed on. "Anyway, they came in, and we realized we hadn't put money in our disguises and so we ran off to confront them. I'm so embarrassed."

"Well, I don't know," Bodhi said. "Roy and Jay have been coming in for a while."

"Did Jay come in on his own before?" Paige asked.

"Sure. It's his boat," Bodhi said. He shrugged. "He lives out here a lot of the time. They're loaded so he's got a lot of places, I guess."

"Right, but Roy only started coming in with him recently?" Paige persisted.

"Mmm, not that recently," Bodhi said, pausing to think. "What do you think, Teresa?" He turned to the big-haired Mangia waitress, who was drumming her fingers on Angel's shoulder, half-heartedly holding her back.

"Little over a year," she said. "Little more, little less."

"I guess that's about right," Bodhi agreed.

"You see?" Paige said. "Roy and I met in college, so it's been a long time and I guess he just lost interest. Jay is so much younger and loaded. How can I compete?"

Paige's eyes filled with tears, acting his ass off, even though it wasn't his audience who was captive.

"Oh, you poor man," Bodhi said.

And just like that, even though he was still sitting on him, Bodhi embraced Paige and rocked him in his big, garlicky arms.

Mason arrived. Ever the soul of discretion, he gave Teresa and Bodhi the price of dinner and a crisp hundred apiece for their trouble.

Bodhi promised to keep Paige's secret—for the time being—to give him a chance to try to work things out with Roy.

"I really have been too lost in my work," Paige confessed to Bodhi. They were back in the restaurant. Teresa was packing up all the food Angel had ordered. "I can't put all the blame on him."

"You're a good guy, Mickey," Bodhi said, giving him a punch in the shoulder a little too heartily. "If things were different—a whole lot different—you're the kind of guy I'd want, if I was gay."

"Thanks, Bodhi," Paige said. He was as touched as it was possible to be under such completely fictitious circumstances. "That means a lot."

In a cloud of hugs and tears and with promises to see each other soon and in happier times, they parted. Angel and Paige piled into the back of the Lincoln with a shocking amount of Italian takeout. Their operation complete, if not completely successful, they headed north along the coast.

"Oh, my God," Paige groaned. "If we weren't already dead I'd go to the emergency room. Mason, is there a doctor we can trust?"

"Mr. Geller has several on retainer," Mason answered, nonplussed. "I'll phone ahead."

"God, I'm starving," Angel said, tipping open a pizza box. "Want some calamari?" she asked, offering Paige her purse.

49

"Well, this proves it—there really is a first time for everything," Paige sighed. "You're right, Angel. I just never thought I'd say it."

"It's the perfect solution," Angel said. "We can be anywhere at the party. And not only will no one recognize us, but they will actively aggressively ignore us."

"I said you're right," Paige admitted. "I just don't have to be happy about it."

And so, hidden in the back of a catering truck and dressed as mimes, the two made their way to Lucrezia St. James' engagement party. If they were going to find the murderer and clear their names, they were convinced they had to catch him in the act as he made an attempt on Lucrezia. Paige reasoned that the party was the killer's best opportunity.

Their first hurdle was police security. LAPD was taking the lead in locking down the over-the-top affair.

Mitch had used his influence with the caterer to get the two of them in as his "surprise" for Lucrezia. But they still faced actual police inspection just to gain access to the gated Holmby Hills compound. The Beaux Arts/Hollywood Regency, 30,000-square-foot confection had been built in the 1930s by oil-rich locals trying for the same sort of instant pedigree and heritage that had been the inspiration for Paige's own architecturally fanciful neighborhood. In the end, both turned out to be more backlot than substance.

Like the Hacienda, Chateau and Tudor Castle apartment buildings of West Hollywood, the granite façades of Holmby Hills offer a veneer of respectability to residents far from certain of their legacy. The neighborhood itself is for those to whom Bel Air and Beverly Hills seem a little trendy and downmarket. Self-conscious insecurity manifests itself into the formidable walls and gates and isolation designed as much to protect locals from what other people think of them as from any physical threats they might face.

The history of Lucrezia St. James' home stretched back almost eighty years, a candidate for the historic register by L.A. standards. Beyond the gilded fretwork of the Beaux Arts iron gates and the cadres of Prada-clad private security was a very visible perimeter of Tinseltown's finest. Clearly, Paige and Angel were not the only ones who counted Lucrezia's head as the next candidate for the fridge. The only debate seemed to be over who was racking up the grisly head count. The authorities thought—or had been led to believe—that Angel and Paige were collecting scalps. Paige was of the mind it was Seth's son Jay, with the inside help of Lieutenant Slade, who was taking such a toll on local necks.

The officer guarding the six feet between the street and the gate opened the rear doors of the van. "Step out of the vehicle, please," he ordered.

Paige got a little thrill of terror as he met the uniformed patrolman's gaze with only a layer of clown white to protect him. He moved to climb over some of the hired stemware toward the policeman.

Angel grabbed Paige's white gloved hand with her own and pulled him back. Pushing herself to the front of the line, she batted her eyes at the officer with a silent but exaggerated bit of flirtation, smiling coyly.

Getting the idea, Paige grabbed her hand and snatched her out of the way. He extended his hand to the officer in greeting.

Angel in turn snatched Paige back. They managed one more round.

"Okay, enough with the clowning around," the officer bellowed.

Angel and Paige collapsed, convulsed in fits of silent laugher. They kept that up for a bit longer than was funny.

"Let's see some ID," demanded the officer, who hadn't found any of it funny.

Paige leaped to his feet and began extracting an endless piece of paper from his pocket, covered with meaningless scribbles.

"No ID, no entry," the officer snapped, trying to cut the routine short.

Angel again stepped to the front. She pulled a wad of fake bills from her bra and surreptitiously handed them to the policeman. Expressionless, he looked at the money and then back to her.

Angel sighed, opened her tiny black purse, and tossed a handful of confetti into the officer's face.

"That's it, I see some ID or you two are out of here," the officer said, brushing confetti off his uniform. "Any more antics and I'm taking you both in."

"Officer!" It was Lance, a caterer cohort of Mitch. He pushed past the gate to meet them. "The mimes are a gift from Mitch Geller. He wanted to surprise Mrs. St. James. My apology for not clearing it with you."

Mitch's name had a magic effect, even in a city as jaded as Los Angeles. Combined with the caterer's vouchsafe on their behalf, the tumblers dropped. The officer, relieved to be done with them, waved the van through. House security did likewise, holding up their hands in surrender and waving the little party onto the estate.

"Follow the drive to the left and park in back," the security guy muttered. He spoke into his headset as they passed. Paige and Angel did a little pantomime of hanging on to a speeding van, although they could have walked faster than the van was traveling. Their mime was terrible, to say the least, but it had its desired effect. Security actually turned away, averting their gaze, though it was hard to tell. Between the five-hundred-dollar Persol sunglasses, cordless headsets and the custom designer suits, the security staff might just as well have worn diamond tiaras, Paige thought as he held onto his beret.

Once the van was parked, he and Angel silently disembarked and set off to find the murderers, clear their names and warn Lucrezia. On the plus side, their disguises worked perfectly. People fled when they saw them coming.

"God, mimes? Really?"

"What? Is there an eighties theme?"

"How much to leave us alone for the whole party?"

"Mommy! Make them stay away!"

Everyone hates a mime.

It was as though they had the house to themselves.

The downside was the fact that they couldn't ask anyone where Lucrezia was or anything else. They couldn't even talk to each other. Silently, they strolled through the public rooms of the mansion, doing their dreadful rendition of the finding-their-way-in-a-blackout routine. Feeling their way along the walls, around corners and past guests, Angel actually got slapped by a woman she accidentally groped.

Reviled and ignored, they easily sneaked behind the velvet ropes and upstairs, which had been closed to party guests. There were dozens of bedrooms and sitting rooms. Paige and Angel made quick work as they were able to abandon the mime conceit. They found no sign of Lucrezia or anyone else upstairs at all. The only resistance they met was a single locked door on the backside of the house. Paige put his ear to the door, heard nothing but the pulse of the air conditioner and dismissed it as a storage room.

They took a bathroom break in the master suite, the last of the rooms they explored upstairs. Angel went first, doing a desperate and slightly appalling pantomime to indicate. Paige rolled his eyes as he bowed and gestured her in.

The suite was larger than his apartment, with a large sitting area, huge bedroom, two dressing rooms and two matching private bathrooms, one decidedly decorated for him and the other for her. Paige would have been happy with either, but someone had to keep watch.

After what seemed an eternity, Angel emerged, miming something that he could not decode. He closed the door in her face as she gesticulated wildly.

She was still at it when he reemerged.

"Angel, for Christ's sake," he said, catching her hands and trying to hold them still. "We are not mimes and we are alone—you can just tell me."

"Oh, right," she giggled. "I was in character."

"Another first," he said.

She took a half-hearted swing at him.

"So what is it?" he asked.

"Come see!" She dashed to one of the huge French windows that lined the walls. "It's her—I think. By the pool. See?" She pointed through the window, unable to stop miming.

Paige wasn't certain from that distance, but he was pretty sure the woman in the fifty yards of ivory silk and lace, draped over the gilded Quatorze fainting sofa on what was more or less a stage, was likely the guest of honor. Either that, or some dame on her own float was stealing Lucrezia's thunder.

"Yep, I think so," he mused. "Now, how the hell do we get to her to warn her?"

Before Angel could offer a stupid answer to his rhetorical question, they were interrupted.

"I'll start at this end—you check the master suite," said a stern voice in the hallway. "There was definitely someone at one of the upstairs windows and there's not supposed to be anyone up here."

50

"Angel," Paige whispered loudly. They clung to the trellis beside the ornamental iron balustrade just outside of the second floor French windows. "For future reference, just because someone is ignoring you doesn't mean you are invisible."

"Oh great, make it my fault," she whispered loudly, putting her hand on her hip and almost toppling from the ledge.

"Try not to attract any more attention to yourself!"

"Are they gone yet?"

"I don't hear anything. But it's a big room and it's too soon to risk looking."

They clung silently to the trellis.

Angel managed to terrify Paige by turning herself around to face the party below.

"Be careful," he ordered.

"Too late," she said. "Oh, look! Fireworks. I love fireworks. It'll be dark soon. I hope we're still here."

"Fireworks?" Paige said, struggling to see over his shoulder. "In this tinderbox?"

"There's a golf course just down the hill from here."

"So what?"

"They do fireworks over golf courses here. There's less fire risk," she explained.

"I'm not sure if that's true."

"Maybe not, but I can see a golf course just down the hill from here."

"That's it!"

"I told you," she said.

"No, I meant, that's how we'll get her to ourselves."

"What is?"

"Do you think we can climb down these trellises—is that the plural of trellis?"

"Is *what*?"

"Trellisi? Trelliste?"

"Did you forget to take your meds?"

Paige took a tentative step down the latticework. "I think we can—"

He plummeted into the rosebushes below. Lying on his back on his bed of thorns, he watched as Angel began to climb down the trellis on her side of the window, backwards.

"Are you okay?" Angel asked, trying—unsuccessfully—not to laugh.

"That's nice," he groaned. He wasn't badly hurt, but he wasn't in any hurry to get up. "The thorns are the worst part."

"What?"

"Nothing."

"*Ow*, there are thorns. Why didn't you—*ow*—warn me?"

It made him feel better.

From this vantage point on his back, Paige saw a dormered window swing open in the roofline on the floor above the master suite.

"Get down," he ordered. "Hurry."

"*Oww, ow, ow*," Angel bleated as she ducked into the rose bushes. "Now what?"

"*Shhh.*"

There was activity on the third story sill. Paige prepared to be discovered by security or worse. But, although the window remained open, nothing else happened.

"Okay," he said. "I think we're good. Let's get out of here."

"It's like you're at a different party," she groused. "*Ow, ow, ow.*"

"We need to get to the fireworks. Follow me."

"It's not dark enough yet," Angel said, struggling out of the bushes. Paige was almost to the entrance to the garden promenade by the time she caught up with him.

A long, winding pathway led through a terraced garden down to the pool at a leisurely slope. A little *Arc de Triomphe* served as entrance to the path. Actually, the arc wasn't that little, Paige observed; it was only slightly smaller than the original.

Paige and Angel tried doing a smell-the-flowers routine to edge through the partiers along the path, but it proved too slow for Paige's purposes. To speed things up, he tried to get Angel to engage in a little hide-and-seek chase through the crowd, but he could not speak and he could not make himself clear. Angel continued her oblivious exploration of the garden. He tugged on her arm but to no avail. After a few other more subtle tactics failed, he adopted a new strategy.

As she bent over the little iron railing along the edge of the path, sniffing marigolds, he delivered a swift kick to the obvious region. She almost lost her balance, nearly tumbling over and falling to the next level of the terrace. Once she recovered her footing, they exchanged a heated look.

She glared.

He shrugged.

After that, all he had to do was run. He made it into a game, hiding behind and running circles around the guests they encountered on the path. Really, the only difficulty he had was staying ahead of her.

In short order they were at the pool level and barreling toward Lucrezia.

Paige scouted the crowd for Roy or Jay but didn't spot them. He found no immediate threat but plenty of the haute-fashion-police-security-detail around Lucrezia. Two guards stood immediately behind her—presumably to keep watch for Angel and Paige. There didn't appear to be any uniformed police to spoil the motif, though Paige couldn't be sure of undercover guest police.

Behind their hostess, at the far side of the pool, was an ivy-covered, Hollywood Regency pool house. The two wings were divided by an open area sheltered under a high, gentle archway that was, at that moment, serving as Lucrezia's proscenium. Beyond the pool house were the fireworks they had seen from the trellises.

The guards and the guests ignored Paige and Angel, but Lucrezia did not. Spotting the two mimes over the heads of her guests, she shot them a withering glare. She looked away and motioned to one of the security guards. Paige led their little game of chase around the hedge at the end of the pool and quickly behind the pool house.

As Paige paused at the corner of the cabana to check on coastal clarity, Angel collided with him and the two tumbled into a heap at the feet of one lone security guard in the fireworks area.

"What the hell are you two doing back here?" the guard demanded.

After a brief skirmish they managed to get back on their feet—though Angel did get in a couple of good kicks in the process—and blithely danced away from the guard, who followed them.

As he continued their game of chase, Paige was able to scope out the arrangement. The fireworks were set up on a series of racks that ran five deep all across the back of the pool house. All the racks were connected to cables that led to a laptop sitting on a gate-legged catering table in the grass at the far side of the cabana.

"You are not supposed to be back here," the guard admonished.

Paige signaled to Angel with a little tilt of his head that she should distract the guard.

Of course, Angel just mirrored his head toss and then kicked him again.

Paige slapped her, which actually got a laugh out of the guard. It was the first laugh they'd gotten from anyone at the party.

As Angel's eyes filled with fury, Paige ran straight for the guard. Angel pursued and Paige made the hapless staffer into their maypole.

"Cut it out!" the guard shouted. "Get away from me! You're not even supposed to be back here. Knock it off!"

Paige grabbed Angel's hand and shoved it into the guard's crotch.

"Whoa, ho, ho!" the guard cried out.

Angel and Paige's eyes connected. They shared a smile. At last, she understood.

As Paige backed away, Angel began to do a lot more than mime the guard a lap dance.

Once it was clear to the guard just what her baggy, striped mime sweater was concealing, she had his attention.

Paige made his way as swiftly as he could to the fireworks control table.

The program was pretty straightforward. There were a series of routines with onscreen buttons and timers and a master execute clickable button that it seemed to Paige would start the whole routine. Someone had clearly spent hours carefully setting each routine to successively longer and longer times so that it would be possible to click on the master button on the monitor and start a timed release, chain reaction.

Angel pulled the guard's zipper down and got his full attention as the two began to struggle with his pants. Paige had lost that same game with her only a couple of days before and knew he could proceed at his leisure. He carefully reset all the fireworks for the same time delay and then clicked the master execute. As near as he could figure, he and Angel had about a minute and a half before all the fireworks would begin to go off at the same time.

Job done, he took off at a run past Angel and the guard and around the corner. Once out of range, he waited for her to catch up. It took her a surprisingly long time.

"Where were you?" he demanded when she finally came strolling around the end of the pool house.

"Making a date for later," she said.

"Are you serious? We're trying to prevent a murder. It's literally life-and-death, and you're working out a booty call?"

"Of course not," she said, giving him a look. "Though I'll tell you, you didn't cop the feel I copped. Pretty impressive. But no, if I'd just run off, he'd have followed."

"Oh," Paige admitted. "That's actually pretty smart."

"I'm pretty good with men," she added. "I just suck at picking them. Once I've got 'em though—putty."

"Come on," he said, moving toward the hedge that shielded them from view and the pool. "We've got less than a minute."

They peered through the hedge and waited for their cue.

"Well, who says there's never a policeman around when you need one?" Paige growled as the lieutenant strolled into sight.

51

The countdown had already begun. There was no time to figure out how to stop it.

"Okay," Paige said. "Here's the deal. When the fireworks start, run straight for the lieutenant and knock him into the pool. I'll get to Lucrezia. With any luck we can warn her before Roy has the chance to kill her."

"You know, I don't really like her that much," Angel said.

"For the millionth time," Paige said, teeth gritted. "We need her on our side and we don't really have time to—"

That was pretty much all they got to say on the matter. The simultaneous detonation of hundreds of thousands of dollars' worth of fireworks was deafening. Everyone froze, then took flight from what seemed like a terrorist attack. It was perhaps the only conditions under which two charging mimes might possibly be a little less conspicuous.

Paige bolted toward Lucrezia.

"What the fuck?" Lucrezia demanded. She seemed almost as angry about the uninvited mime bearing down on her as the series of explosions threatening her pool house.

The bullet hit her just as Paige did. The two went down, and Paige felt the razor-sting of a second bullet graze his backside as he rolled the two of them off the back of the stage for cover.

The last thing Paige saw before they went over the edge was the lieutenant, gun drawn, stepping out of Angel's way as she charged him. She rocketed out over the water. Paige heard the splash just as he and Lucrezia thudded into the grass.

"I've been shot," Lucrezia howled. She sounded more indignant than troubled about it.

"I know," Paige said. "I couldn't get to you in time. Your stepson Jay and Lieutenant Roy Slade of the LAPD are trying to kill you to get their hands on Seth's money."

"*What?*"

"They're lovers," Paige shouted over the last of the fireworks. "They've been killing off everyone between them and the money and you're next."

Everything went quiet.

The explosions stopped as suddenly as they had begun. There were some distant screams as the party guests continued to flee up the long bridle path.

"*Paige!*" Roy called out. "I know you're back there!"

"He's got a gun," Angel called from the edge of the pool.

"Great work," Paige called back to her. "Thanks."

"He tricked me," Angel yelled.

"By taking a step to the right?"

"I didn't see it coming!"

"Okay, Paige," Roy shouted. "Come out where I can see you."

"You stay here," Paige whispered to Lucrezia. "Okay," he called out. "I'm unarmed."

Slowly, hands in the air, Paige raised himself above the lip of the little stage.

Roy crouched, gun aimed right at him.

"Don't shoot," Paige said, so that it might at least be clear to witnesses that the lieutenant was the cause of Paige's imminent death. "I'm unarmed. And you didn't manage to kill Lucrezia, so there's no point in killing—"

"*Look out*," Angel screamed.

The lieutenant fired twice.

Paige dove for cover.

"Okay, Paige," the lieutenant called. "It's safe to come out now."

"Safe for *what*? Safe for you to try to shoot me again?"

"No, Paige," Roy said, trotting across the stage. He looked down at Paige, gun at his side. "Are you okay, Mrs. St. James?"

"Are you serious with that question?" she demanded, clutching her bleeding arm. "Among other things, you shot me."

"It wasn't me who shot you," Roy began.

"Dude, you *shot* me!" a strangely familiar voice cried out from behind them. "That really fucking hurt!"'

"Stay down, then," Roy said, sharply, moving past Paige and Lucrezia.

Paige wheeled to see Bill E, dressed as one of the high-fashion security guards. His Persols were missing, his headset was askew and there was a hole in his Prada suit, but it was Bill E.

Writhing on the ground beside him was another man, similarly clad. It took Paige a moment before he realized.

"Wig?" he said. "Is that you?"

52

"Stay back, Paige," Roy said. He kicked away a couple of guns near where Bill E and Wig lay. "Hands on top of your heads. Both of you."

"You shot me, dude!" Bill E wailed.

"*Do it*," Roy commanded.

Slowly and painfully, Wig and Bill E moved their hands to their heads.

"What the fuck is going on?" Paige asked.

"Bill E just tried to kill Lucrezia," Roy said, cuffing the still-whining rocker. "I think it was Wig who shot you."

"Wig?" Paige said. "*You* shot me?"

"I wasn't aiming at you," Wig said apologetically.

"Well, that makes it all better, doesn't it?" Paige said.

"Is somebody going to help me out of this pool?" Angel shouted.

"You're the only one who isn't shot," Paige said. "Just this fucking once, could it not be all about you?"

"Lucrezia? Darling, are you okay?" Lefty called as he bolted down the terraced path. "I'm coming."

"Lefty," Lucrezia called. "I'm here. I'm wounded but I don't think it's serious. This man—Paige, right?—Paige saved me."

"Oh, I hardly recognized—Paige, I remember, we met. I thought you were the murder..." Lefty trailed off. "You know this isn't a costume party, right?"

Paige smiled. What, exactly, is the socially correct response when thanking the chief suspect in a murder investigation for saving your fiancée?

"Good to see you again," Paige said. "Despite what the lieutenant may have told you, I'm actually not a crazed serial killer."

"Well, I hardly..." Lefty said, cradling Lucrezia as he wrapped her arm in a tablecloth.

"Sorry, Paige, Angel," Roy said as he cuffed Wig, who was more compliant than Bill E. "The evidence was there."

"Don't feel bad," Paige said. "I thought it was you and Jay."

"*What* was me?" Jay St. James asked, arriving on the scene. He was in the company of a sizeable number of high-fashion security guards and a growing number of police and sheriff's personnel. "Lucrezia? Are you all right?"

"Why do people keep asking me that?" Lucrezia wailed. "There was a shooting at my engagement party and *I* was the one who got shot!"

"So, no?" Jay queried. "Is there anything I can get you?"

"An ambulance would be lovely," Lucrezia sighed.

"One is on the way, ma'am," Roy assured her as several uniformed officers took charge of Bill E and Wig. He tossed Paige a pile of cloth napkins. "Here, put some pressure on that."

"What about us?" Bill E groaned.

"What *about* you?" Angel asked.

"We're injured."

"Want to try for DOA?"

"Roy, good to see you, especially under the circumstances," Jay said as he stepped forward and took Roy's hand. The two men embraced.

"How do you two know each other?" Paige asked, archly.

"Shooting range," Roy volunteered. "At first, at least. We realized we had other things in common. The usual."

"Shooting buddies—*sure.*" Paige gave him a knowing smirk.

Jay and Roy helped Lefty get Lucrezia on her feet and onto a chaise in the nearby cabana.

"Why me?" Roy asked, looking over her shoulder at Paige.

"What?" Paige asked, confused by the question.

"Why did you think it was me?"

"Oh, well, you always knew where we were when things happened," Paige said. "And then we saw you outside Angel's after the explosion."

"I was there to meet you," Roy said, shaking his head.

"You were just sitting there watching it burn."

"Hello, not a fireman," Roy said.

"And then you just failed to mention that I gave you the book and the blackmail evidence," Paige said, realizing his admission too late.

"I *knew* it!" Roy said. "I thought I recognized the smell of fish at Mitch's and I don't mean the tuna sandwiches. That impromptu policeman's luncheon was a little too gracious. I figured Mitch was setting us up. That's why I left you out."

"Oh, you *meant* to do that," Paige said, knowingly.

"What other motive would I have?" Roy asked.

"We thought it had something to do with the new will," Paige said, shaking it off.

"No, that wasn't valid," Jay said, leaving his stepmother to Lefty and joining them. "Dad and Angel never signed the prenup."

"So, let me get this straight," Angel said. She was still in the pool, standing at the near end, elbows resting on the marbleized coping. "*Bill E* and *Wig* are the murderers?"

"Right?" Paige said. He turned to face her and rolled over onto his hip. "*Ow, ow, ow!*" He struggled to his feet in an effort to ease the pain.

"What?" Angel asked.

"I got shot," Paige said, and leaned on a chair for support. "Why did you shoot me, Wig?"

"I was trying to shoot *her*," Wig replied.

"Lucrezia?"

"No," Wig said with a shake of his head. "She seems lovely. And that was Bill E's job."

"*Me?*" Angel said, realizing. "Why were you trying to shoot *me?*"

"'Cause I lost," Bill E said.

"What?"

"We flipped a coin and I lost," Bill E said with a little coughing laugh.

Angel erupted out the water like Esther Williams. She strode across to where Bill E was lying. Standing over him, she paused, dripping, her mime makeup mostly washed away.

They regarded each other a moment.

She kicked him in the gut.

"Jeez, babe," Bill E groaned.

"You really shouldn't kick the suspects, ma'am," one of the nearby uniformed officers cautioned.

"What? You mean like this?" she asked, kicking him again.

"Pretty much, yeah, ma'am," the officer said, stepping between them.

"You were trying to kill *us?*" Paige asked. "Her, I understand, but me?"

"Hey," Angel said, kicking Bill E again. Ready for her, he caught her foot between both of his and nearly knocked her over. The officer caught her before she fell.

"We were just trying to frame you for the murder at first, Paige," Bill E said. He tried to roll away a bit to defend against further attacks from Angel, who was already back on her feet and dancing around, looking for an opening. "I stole that crystal angel thing from you to make you look suspicious. It had your name on it." Then he grinned. "But that tea in the face thing was poetry, man."

"Wasn't that great?" Paige agreed.

"Paige! Whose side are you on?" Angel demanded.

"Do I have to decide right away?" Paige asked.

"You kind of did our work for us," Bill E said. "I was surprised I could still find your place again. I was pretty toasted the last time I was there. Sorry about puking in that plant."

"Why Seth?" Paige asked, ignoring the apology.

"Poor fucker. He just got in the way." Bill E shrugged it off. "He was going to have a meeting with that Grizelda chick and caught us in the suite. And then his business manager and his assistant caught us with the body. The only thing that saved Grizelda was that she didn't have a key to the room. Accidents happen."

"*Accidents happen*!" Angel screamed, circling the wary patrolman as she tried to get in another kick. "That man was the key to my comeback and now I've got nothing in the pipeline or even on the distant horizon!"

"Touching, hunh?" Paige said to Roy and Jay.

"Babe, I wanted to kill you. Do you think I care if I screwed up your career?" Bill E asked with a simple shrug. "Plus, I'm still your beneficiary."

"And why were the heads in the fridge?" Roy asked.

"Yeah, out-of-hand, right?" Bill E managed a grin. "Well, we got the idea to try to frame Angel and Paige for doing in old Seth but after they walked in on us we had to lose the extra bodies. Only they wouldn't fit in the trunk that we were trying to get them out in. With a little alteration we got almost all of them to fit and we got most of them out. We were coming back for the other one but Angel showed up so drunk she literally took the fall and we just never got around to it."

"And the second head?" Paige asked.

"By then we were trying to throw suspicion on you two for the whole mess and what else were we going to do with it?" Bill E said. "We were looking for the letter opener and the glass thing we'd planted so we figured you must have them. Angel called to tell me she was okay and so I knew you were there."

"How did you get in?" Angel asked.

"Maid scam," Bill E said. "From the old days on tour."

"You screwed *another* hotel maid?" Angel sounded disgusted. She tried half-heartedly for another kick but the officer intercepted her.

"So, why Grizelda?" Paige asked.

"The crazy bitch was trying to blackmail us," Bill E began. "Somehow she found out what was really going on."

"Lieutenant," Lefty said, his voice rising. "I feel like I'm in the final scene of a fucking Charlie Chan film. My fiancée has been shot; must we endure this?"

"I'm sorry, sir," Roy said, placing a reassuring hand on Lefty's shoulder. He was reluctant to do more as he was getting the answers he needed in front of witnesses and without arresting anyone. "But this *is* an active murder investigation."

"Honestly," Lucrezia huffed. "Who do I have to shoot around here to get an ambulance—or a cocktail, at the very least?"

A member of the haute-security detail moved toward the bar to oblige their charge.

"And Earl?" Roy went on.

"He was in it with Grizelda," Bill E said. He shook his head. "What she knew, he knew."

"Wig, what do *you* have to do with all this?" Paige asked.

"He wanted to kill her as much than I did," Bill E said with a breathy little laugh. "Maybe more." He looked Paige in the eye. "Don't *you* want to kill her?"

"Only when I'm awake," Paige said. "No, that's not true. Sometimes I dream about killing her, too."

"Then you know," Wig said, raising his shoulders to his ears. "To know Angel and let her into your life is to want to kill her."

"I'm actually still here," Angel said. She stomped on Bill E's foot.

"It's why I blew up your house," Wig said, squirming around so he could address her. "You put me out without even a ride back into town or a second thought. The place was open. I walked in, dumped the body, turned on the gas and locked the door."

"So it was *you* who knew we were at C. Shore," Paige said, realizing. "Why did you spend the night with me?"

"I'm sorry for that, Paige," Wig said, sucking air through his teeth. "My bad. You seem like a good guy. But I really only did it to hurt Angel. To let her know how little she meant to me."

"I see." Paige nodded. He paced nearer to where Wig lay. "Looks like you missed your mark twice and got me instead."

"It was not my intention, either time," Wig said. "I owe you more than an apology."

EMS personnel were making their way across the pool area to the scene.

"Well, it was a night I will certainly never forget," Paige said. "What with the sniper and your surprise visit. And now I'll have this scar from where you shot me to remind me of it all. So I guess I owe you a debt, too." Leaning in, he gave Wig a mighty kick.

Wig doubled up. Paige stumbled backward, his ballet-slippered mime foot mightily stubbed on the bony model. Tripping on an overturned side table, he fell into Angel's soggy arms.

She looked down into his face and pursed her lips.

Paige waved a finger in her face. "If you say I told you so…"

"I was going to say thank you," she said with a smirk. She pulled his arm over her shoulder and helped him into a nearby chair. "I know I didn't give you any reason to help me. Thanks, anyway."

He sat down hard and was quickly and painfully reminded of exactly where Wig had shot him. He shrieked and leaped to his feet. His injured foot gave way and he fell against Angel. The two hardly resisted as they tumbled into the pool, laughing.

53

"That's really all we found," Paige said almost apologetically as he handed over the last of the evidence that he and Angel had taken from the scene of Seth's murder and stored in the Argyle Hotel safe.

The lieutenant stared at him silently for a moment, recovering.

The Argyle lobby was largely empty of guests. A few paparazzi lingered outside the glass doors in hopes of yet another shot.

"That's it, is it?" Roy asked tensely.

"Yeah, just the stuff that they planted to incriminate us," Paige said. "Well, that and the manuscript that I already gave you. That's the real reason I put the pages in those binder sleeves. Though I am pretty anal, to be fair to Angel—and don't tell her I said that."

"It'll be our secret," the lieutenant said. "You know, Paige, in some circles, like law enforcement for instance, removing evidence from a crime scene is considered a crime."

"But we used it to help solve the murder for you," Paige said. "*With* you," he corrected genially.

"And only five people died, while five more were shot," Roy said, as patiently as he could manage. "Including you. Next time, how about you leave crime to the professionals?"

"*Next time?*"

Angel emerged from the hotel office. Flashes lit up the lobby as the glass was suddenly plastered with photographers. Hotel staff held the doors closed.

"I'm going to take the longest shower in history," Angel announced grandly.

"And then I'm going to break your record," Paige said. "No. Bubble bath with a book, that's it. I'm staying under till I prune."

"I got us a suite together," Angel said. She gave Paige a questioning look. "I can't stand to be alone. And I can't go home."

"Thanks, but I just want to sleep in my own bed," Paige said.

"About that," Roy said. His face betrayed just the tiniest bit of satisfaction.

"What about that?"

"You can't," Roy said. "Crime scene."

"Being innocent is really hard work," Paige said.

"Come on," Angel said, taking Paige's arm. "It won't be so bad. You can have the master bedroom. It's got that giant tub. Perfect for bubble baths."

Paige sighed. He really was too tired to argue and there was some appeal to the fact that his bath, bubbles and bed were only an elevator ride away. "Can I at least go home for a few things?"

"Sorry," Roy said. He shot Paige a lame smile. "We only learned about *this* crime scene a couple of hours ago. It's going to take a while to process."

"Miss Panderson?" Manager Bob had emerged from his office.

"Bob, you darling man," Angel cooed. "Can I get a pair of white silk men's pajamas sent up to our suite? Make it two pair. Extra short?"

Paige huffed but he was too tired and more than a little charmed by her gesture to really complain.

"I'll leave you both to it," Roy said as he moved toward the lobby doors. He paused. "Off the record? Thanks for your help."

"Get *us*," Paige cackled. "Solving crimes." They headed for the elevators, arm-in-arm.

"Miss Panderson?" Bob called again.

"Yes, Bob?"

"I'll get those pajamas up to you as soon as we can get our hands on a couple of pair," he said.

"Barneys is open till eight," she called over her shoulder.

"Miss Panderson...?"

"Bob, I told you Mr. Geller would be taking care of everything."

Paige was impressed. "Really? That's so sweet."

"You saved him about a billion in legal fees," Angel replied under her breath.

"Yes, ma'am," Bob persisted. "I understand. And there's this."

He held up a beautiful inlaid box, tied up with yards of lush pink satin ribbon.

"What the hell?" Angel said. "Bob...?"

"Oh, no, ma'am," Bob demurred, blushing. "Not that I wouldn't. But this is from—well, it's from Mr. St. James."

"Seth?" Angel's tears had found their moment.

"Yes, ma'am," Bob said, thrusting the box toward her.

She made no move to take it.

"It's a gift for you," Bob explained. "He had it stored in the safe. He said that he wanted to surprise you after the party."

Angel made a small strangling sound that Paige had never heard before. He reached out and gently took the package from Bob.

"Thank you," Paige said. "It's very kind of you to hold on to this. Come on, Angel. There's a steam shower and a case of Cristal with your name on it."

Bob nodded. He gave Paige the thumbs up signal to let him know that he understood the unspoken room service order for enough champagne to drown a bison.

"That's a girl," Paige said, walking her onto the elevator. "Here we go."

The paparazzi grabbed a couple of last shots as the doors closed. The two ascended in silence as Paige faced the prospect of comforting the most insensitive person he'd ever known.

54

"So I'm not as bad as you thought, right?" Angel said, flossing her wet hair with a huge hotel towel.

"Have some more Cristal," Paige encouraged. He was bundled up in a hotel bathrobe and sipping jasmine tea. He had deferred his bubble bath and taken some time to get Angel calmed down. He had never seen her emotional, other than when she was angry. In the end, he settled for getting her drunk.

"No, really." She flounced onto the parlor sofa. "Most of what you blamed me for was Grizelda's doing. And Seth's, I guess." She stared at the box on the coffee table.

"Angel, let's just be glad that, tonight at least, no one is trying to kill us." Paige burrowed deeper into the pillows on the chaise he'd arranged to allow him to sit without aggravating his bullet wound. "Top up that champagne and let's put a pin in the question of whether or not we want to kill each other."

She complied.

Angel stared at the box from Seth. It rested unopened on the coffee table in front of the sofa where she sat. "Maybe it's jewelry," she said. "I could sell it and pay the taxes on the house that burned to the ground."

"I'm sure there's insurance for that," Paige pointed out. "The house, not the taxes. Tax insurance? Wouldn't that be a great scam?"

"The insurance is already spent," Angel said. "So much debt."

"I don't think insurance works that way," Paige said. "Maybe you can sell the house after they rebuild it?"

"Seth was my plan," Angel said. "And now he's just gone. We've been so caught up in being Cagney and Sherlock that I haven't really had time to think about what I've lost."

There were tears again. Just enough to fill her eyes, but enough to threaten more.

"It's scary to put your faith in someone," Paige said, as tactfully as he could manage. "But it's not as hard as having that faith destroyed when they... leave."

She looked at him.

"That's what I did to you, isn't it?"

"Not tonight," Paige said. He felt his own tears at the ready.

He raised his gilt-edged Royal Doulton teacup. "A toast to Seth," Paige said. "The author of our feast."

"To Seth." She lifted her champagne flute, tossed back its contents and poured another.

He sipped his tea in silence.

"I'm going to open it," she announced. She knelt in the space between the sofa and the coffee table. One tug and the bow collapsed. The ribbon fell away to reveal a glossy wooden box with a sliding lid, which she gently pushed open.

Inside was a rolled sheaf of paper, tied with the same pink ribbon.

She tugged at the bow and unrolled the pages.

Her eyes traced each line, slowly at first and then more and more swiftly.

She pushed back, rose, and sat on the sofa, still reading.

"What is it?" Paige asked.

Angel shrieked, rifled through to the last page, shrieked again, leapt to her feet and began jumping around the room.

"*What?*" Paige asked again.

She pulled him up from the chaise and kissed him on the lips.

"Angel, what the hell?"

"It's the will," Angel shouted joyously. "The one Mitch told us about. And it's *signed*. I'm rich."

She tossed Paige the will and raced back to the coffee table. Taking up the half-empty bottle of champagne, she put her thumb over the top and gave it a good shake. Squealing with delight, she proceeded to spray the room and the both of them with Cristal.

"Jesus, Angel," he said, ducking for cover. "Signed? Really?"

"I'm rich, I'm rich, I'm rich," Angel sang as she danced around toasting and showering in her newfound wealth.

Paige ducked behind the chaise, protection against further downpours, and read.

"I'm going to get a Bentley. I'll get *you* a Bentley. We'll go to Paris and buy our clothes right off the runway. I'll sell the old house and move to the ocean side of the colony! Maybe I'll give you the old house—well, a new one where it used to be—and I'll buy three on the other side of the street just to tear them down and build one great big giant one! Or maybe—"

"Hang on, Spenderella," Paige said, rising from behind his barrier chaise. "Don't sign the check quite yet."

She froze, staring at him.

He couldn't tell whether her look was terror or fury so he kept the chaise between them.

"Turns out the will is only valid if you and Seth have signed the prenup," Paige said. He held up the document, folded to the correct page, and pointed at the clause.

She rushed him.

He flinched but held his ground.

She snatched the will out of his hands.

Spinning, she read.

"No, no, no, no, *noooooooo*!" she yelled, tossing the will aside. "That lying, cheating, closet-case son-of-a-bitch!" she screamed. She threw herself on the sofa, wailing and beating the pillows in a childish tantrum.

"There's the selfish cow I know and love—but not in that way," Paige said. Gingerly resuming his seat on the chaise, he poured himself a fresh cup of tea. He took a sip and watched her for a moment. Her tantrum showed no sign of flagging. "Sorry, old girl. Jay was right."

He slurped at his cup and watched, amused. Is this what I look like, he wondered?

"Wait a minute," he said. He set the tea aside as he stood. "Wait *just* a minute."

He stared into the middle distance, paralyzed by his realization.

"*Wait just a minute*!" he shouted with such vehemence that Angel paused, mid-bitch-fit.

"What?" she asked.

"Jay was right."

55

"The murder is solved but the mystery continues," Busby Barclay voiced over shots of the red carpet coverage of Wig and Bill E's perp walk. "Media titan—and Angel Panderson's fiancé—was murdered by two of Angel's high-profile jealous exes. Rock god Bill E Blaze and supermodel runway king Ludwig Bergh have been charged in the scandalous murder that is all anyone in Hollywood can talk about. But there's a new mystery."

Paige watched the live coverage from the safety of Mitch's panic suite. He and Angel had been sequestered there ever since their third escape from the Argyle on the night following Lucrezia's engagement party. Both had dived into the back of Mitch's Phantom still in their bathrobes, after sneaking down the stairs to the street behind the hotel and in front of Paige's apartment. They kept the hotel room as their decoy but remained in hiding at Mitch's beach house.

The perp walk and promotional footage of Wig and Bill E dissolved into coverage of a paparazzi riot outside Mitch Geller's gates. "And now—who inherits Seth's billions?"

As Busby continued, the TV flashed shots of Jay and Lieutenant Slade arriving outside the Mitch Geller estate. A limo disgorging Lucrezia and Lefty was mobbed.

"*Star Reporter* has learned that St. James' controversial *second* will was discovered after his death, signed and wrapped as an engagement gift for Angel," Busby went on, live in front of the same gates. "Speculation is high that Angel may be Hollywood's newest billionaire." Found footage of Angel with Paige played as Busby's narration continued. "Rumor has it that she and writing partner Paige Blanche have been hiding out at the home of fellow Hollywood high-roller Mitch Geller, where the will is scheduled to be read to the rich and famous beneficiaries later today. Meanwhile, I have it on good authority that Angel and Paige are hard at work on their next project, a movie version of their recent ordeal, entitled *Ordeal*.

"I'll have more on the will—and the movie version of the entire scandal—exclusively tomorrow on *Star Reporter* with Busby Barclay," Busby said as he pitched breathlessly back to the studio. "Coming up: fashion missteps of the stars and how you can avoid them by shopping at Burlington Coat Factory, with *Star Reporter* fashion consultant Bree."

Paige muted the sound. He had taken control of their story by leaking most of the details to Busby. They'd fled the hotel and taken refuge at Mitch's in the wee hours that first night after the engagement party shootout. Once all was in readiness, he revealed their hideout and used news of the second will as bait to summon Seth's family—and the media—to Mitch Geller's gates.

"Let's go, Angel," he called. "It's showtime."

56

"I've always wanted to see the inside of this house," Lucrezia said in lieu of a greeting. She and Lefty were dressed more appropriately for the red carpet than the reading of a will.

"Lucrezia, Lefty, welcome," Mitch said, as graciously as he was able. "I'm only sorry that it couldn't be under happier circumstances."

"I'm not actually all that upset," Lucrezia replied. She pointedly ignored the hand Mitch offered her. "But then, I wasn't as close to Seth as you were, Mitch. If I'm cut out of the will, then we can talk about being upset."

Mitch recoiled.

"Everyone else is already here," Paige interrupted before Mitch could explode.

"We're ready to begin," Lieutenant Slade called from across the pointed, cathedral-arched colonnade that formed the central hallway in Mitch's Malibu palace.

Mitch gestured for his two late guests to precede them. Lucrezia nodded grandly and strode toward the lieutenant. The little party made their way down the immense hallway. Paige stifled a laugh as Mitch made threatening hand gestures behind Lucrezia's back.

The two men had become quite close over the previous few days. Mitch had been very generous when Angel and Paige had invited themselves over for an extended stay.

"We have proof that all of the killers are not yet in custody," Paige had explained. "We need your help to flush them out—and we need a safe place to stay while we do it."

"Why not just go to the lieutenant?" Mitch had asked.

"We think he's in on it," Angel said before Paige could stop her.

"Really?" Mitch said, intrigued and a bit excited. "*Again*?"

"We can't say any more at this time, but we have a plan to expose the scheme *and* the killers," Paige said.

Mitch was in.

"Why would Mitch help us with this?" Angel had asked on the ride out to the seaside fortress in Mitch's Phantom, with trusty Mason, as ever, at the wheel. They got the drop on the paparazzi by sneaking out of the hotel the same way they'd broken in the night of Seth's murder.

"Mitch cared about Seth," Paige said. "And I think he's grateful for our help with his little blackmail issue. But I think it's mostly because it sounds exciting to him."

"Exciting? He's one of the richest people in the world."

"Yeah, well, I'm sure it's great to be a billionaire," Paige mused. "But there's still only so much you can do in the world even when you can do everything. Billionaire boredom is probably a greater threat to humankind than anyone has paused to consider. In any case, I'm glad he's on our side—and mum's the word. The less he knows the more intrigued he'll be."

And so, in the intervening few days, with Mitch's help and considerable resources, they put their plan in motion. The conclusion of their efforts was the announcement that they had found Seth's signed last will—something which, initially, had startled even Mitch. Then they invited those they said were named in the will to Mitch's estate for a reading—and the game was afoot.

By the time the day arrived, they were more than a little terrified.

"What if it doesn't work?" Angel asked Paige over breakfast in the panic suite where they'd been living.

Paige shrugged. "Then Bill E and Wig are the whole story. They really did kill most of those people. Maybe all of them."

"Who didn't they kill?" Angel asked, frightened enough to care.

"Maybe Earl," Paige suggested. "Maybe Grizelda. What's interesting is who they *didn't* try to kill."

"You have been at this too long, Hercules," Angel snorted. "You sound like an Agatha Christie character."

"I think you mean *Hercule*," he grinned. "But I'll take Hercules over Miss Marple, thank you."

She paused and examined his face from several angles. "Not yet," she pronounced.

"Bitch."

They did their best to keep their spirits light, but the old fear was back.

While they were nervous about the will reading and what they hoped it would reveal, it was nothing compared to their apprehension that there was still someone out there who wanted them dead.

57

Paige closed the library doors behind the last of their little group.

Lefty and Lucrezia greeted Jay warmly. Paige learned from the lieutenant that Jay had moved back home with his stepmother following the incident at her engagement party. Nevertheless, Jay had arrived with the lieutenant, with whom he sat. Along with Mitch and Angel—and the lawyer Paige had hired to fill in for Earl—they were the extent of their little group.

"This is so dramatic," Lucrezia said. She sighed.

"We're just trying to respect Seth's final wishes," Paige told everyone. He took a seat beside Angel. "You are the people mentioned in this most recent will. So it's just family. No need for drama."

"It's a pretty dramatic family," Lefty said in a snide tone and with a pointed look at Angel. "*You're* not mentioned in the will, are you, Paige?"

"No, Lefty." Paige nodded. "And neither are you. I'm guessing we're both just here to support those who are. I know I am."

"Sure," Lefty said. "Very noble and all that."

"All right, everyone," the lawyer said, taking a seat at the desk in front of them. "Let's get started, shall we?"

His voice echoed through the vast mahogany-paneled library. The immense space made their little party seem more intimate. Twin carved mahogany spiral staircases twirled up to the second level of books lining the walls and filling two stories of mahogany bookcases. Comfortable leather wingbacks and Chesterfield sofas were clustered around numerous fireplaces throughout the room.

Lefty and Lucrezia perched on one of the sofas. The rest of the party sat on the padded leather-backed chairs that surrounded several ornately carved mahogany library tables stationed at intervals down the center of the room. Each chair was stamped with a gold crest and Mitch's monogram at the back. Thick oriental carpets that covered much of the polished inlaid wood floor tamped down some of the echo, but the vaulted stone ceiling reflected and magnified the slightest sound.

"It feels like being in church in here," Angel said, shifting in her seat.

"Something to confess?" Lucrezia asked.

"*Hmmm,*" Angel said, considering. "I confess that even though you're older and have been living off of him longer, you're not any different or better than me. And you can stop acting like it. He's dead. If you feel like acting, try acting like you give a shit."

Jay snickered.

Everyone else hid smiles as Lucrezia made indignant, bird-like noises.

"Due to the untimely demise of Seth's attorney, Earl Filou, Angel has asked me to summarize Seth's last will for you today," the lawyer said. "It is a long and complicated document detailing the disposition of what I'm sure you are aware is a vast fortune accumulated during a remarkable life. There are copies for each of you of the signed documents as well as official certification of his signature and statements from the will's notary and witnesses also signed, notarized and witnessed.

"The bequests and provisions break down into several main parts in sum as follows.

"Smaller bequests to staff, more distant relations and intimates, who will be notified separately, amount to thirty-two million dollars."

There was no perceptible reaction from any of the principals, Paige noted, as he reeled at the sum of the "small" bequests.

"Charitable endowments to various existing organizations and establishing particular charitable trusts in the amount of one point two billion dollars," the lawyer went on.

Angel squirmed a bit and there were signs that the others were at least listening, even as the amount exceeded Paige's ability to imagine.

"For Lucrezia St. James, there is a trust of fifty million established to support you for the remainder of your life."

"What?" Lucrezia said.

Everyone seemed to wake up at this.

"And the Holmby Hills estate is your home for as long as you care to remain. A separate trust is established to care for the estate. At the time of your death, Lucrezia, the money from the trust along with the Holmby Hills house reverts to Jay St. James."

"I don't..." Mitch began, but cut himself short.

"The balance of the estate is left to Angela Panderson, the testator's intended wife at the time that the will was written and signed."

That got everyone's attention.

Even Lefty was outraged.

"I don't know how, but this will is a fraud," Mitch insisted. "There were trusts for Angel and Jay."

"I don't know what you're trying to pull," Jay said to Angel. "But it's not going to work." He rose from the sofa.

"Jay, we should leave this to the lawyers and the police," Lefty said, putting a hand on Jay's arm.

Jay jerked his arm away, advancing on Angel.

"The original will stipulated that you and Seth had to have signed the prenup before it took effect," Jay continued. "Dad knew what a slut you were. He knew you'd cheat, which would invalidate the prenup, which would invalidate the will. It was all a smokescreen anyway to leave the money to his true love—Mitch Geller."

Paige stood and placed himself between Angel and the much taller Jay St. James.

"Yeah." Paige nodded. "That's what you said at Lucrezia's engagement shootout. My question is—how do you know?"

"What?" Jay demanded hotly. His focus was on Angel. Paige's sudden interference surprised him.

"How do you know what was in Seth's will?" Paige repeated.

Jay looked to Lucrezia and Lefty.

Then, in the move that Paige had anticipated, Jay turned to Roy.

"I don't see why I have to answer these kinds of questions," Jay said to Roy, pleading. "I think the question is who falsified this will?"

"Oh, *I* did," Paige said before Roy could speak. "The original is here in a safe. And this isn't a lawyer. I couldn't get one to do it—something about ethics, of all things. This is my landlord, Armie. Take a bow, Armie."

Armie rose, blushing, bowed and nodded, acknowledging his audience graciously.

Angel alone applauded.

"No," Paige went on. "I just wanted to see who knew what was in the original will because *that* is the person who planned and carried out this whole elaborate string of murders. And it looks like it's you."

Paige pointed at Jay.

"The murderers are in jail," Jay said, backing away.

"Oh, I'm sure that Bill E and Wig are where they belong," Paige said, moving toward Jay. "Especially if they get boiled in oil on a more-or-less regular basis after what they put me through. But they don't have a motive for *all* of this. Or the smarts to plan a road trip to Vegas, for that matter. Their *only* possible motive is that they were both broke. And they aren't mentioned in any of

Seth's wills. My guess is that someone was going to pay them off once he inherited."

"But that wasn't me," Jay insisted. "I don't inherit."

"No," Paige agreed. "That's the tricky bit. You see, it's all about the order that the crimes took place. First, Seth had to die before he could sign the prenup, or the will that I'm guessing Earl told you about. Or was it Seth's business manager or his assistant who told you? They were all in on it, right? That's why they all had to die?"

"That's a lie," Jay said, retreating and bumping into Roy as Paige advanced.

"Is it?" Paige asked. "Then how did you know? And why is Earl dead? Or for that matter, Seth's business manager and his assistant? Why would anyone kill them? Bill E and Wig don't have a motive between them. They didn't really even have an opportunity."

"It had to be Bill E and Wig," Jay said, tapping Paige on the chest with his index finger. "They blew up Angel's house to dispose of the body. They killed the business manager because he got in the way. You heard them—we all did. They were trying to frame you, Paige."

"Wig and Bill E blew up the house because you couldn't find the will," Paige went on. "Was it you who searched my apartment? Did you even know we were behind that locked door?

"I don't know what you're—" The look of surprise on Jay's face answered Paige's question.

"Grizelda was blackmailing Seth with whatever she'd found out. But when Bill E and Wig killed her golden goose, the stupid cow tried to go on blackmailing *you*, didn't she? So you killed her, or you had Tweedledee and/or Tweedledumbass do it. And they killed the business manager and his assistant because they were at the scene of the first murder to witness the signing of the prenup they had put together, and you couldn't let that happen. Yet somehow you had the prenup in your possession to deliver to the sheriff to try to incriminate us."

"You can't prove any of this," Jay asserted, putting one of the leather library chairs between the two of them.

"So, with Seth dead before the prenup could be signed, the second will missing if not destroyed or at the very least invalid because you killed Seth before he could sign it, the only person standing between you and billions is Lucrezia."

"That's not true, Lucrezia!" Jay said, wheeling to face her. "We've had our differences but I would never—"

"That was what kept eating at me," Paige went on. "We didn't crash Lucrezia's party just to warn her that Bill E and Wig were trying to kill her. We showed up because we knew that with her dead, you would inherit. Everyone had to die in the order they died, so you could inherit Seth's fortune. You're still in danger, Lucrezia."

Lucrezia shifted warily.

"In the valid will, Seth's money is only yours in trust till you die, Lucrezia," Paige explained. "Then…"

"It's Jay's," Lucrezia said, her voice level and lifeless.

"No," Jay said. "No, I would never."

"It wasn't Wig who shot me, though I think he *was* aiming at Angel when he fired," Paige said, patting his still-tender backside. "It wasn't even Bill E who shot Lucrezia, though I'm sure he tried. I'm not even sure either of them knows how to shoot a gun. All the other murders were bludgeonings—crude and brutal. You're the shooter, Jay. The shooting at C. Shore was probably your first attempt. Lieutenant, you've fired guns at a shooting range with Jay. Does he have the skills to shoot Lucrezia, by the pool, if he's aiming from the attic floor of Lucrezia's house? Does he have the ability to shoot us from the strip mall across the street from C. Shore Sushi?"

"I'm not certain," Roy said, his face white. Clearly rattled, he exchanged a desperate and confused look with Jay.

"On the day of the engagement party, the door to the third-floor staircase was locked. It was the only locked door on the second floor of the Holmby Hills house that day. I checked,"

Paige said. "And I saw the attic window open while I was, um, reconnoitering during a strategic readjustment."

"Was that before or after you fell off the house?" Angel murmured, though her voice echoed.

"I say 'strategic readjustment.' You say 'two-story fall,'" Paige said, throwing up his hand. "Potato, *pomme de terre*. The point is, one shot—Lucrezia's—was through-and-through. The other—mine—only grazed me. So, from our wounds and in all the confusion the direction of the bullets was misleading. Bill E and Wig were shooting at us and their bullets were where you expected to find them, lieutenant. But you didn't look for the other bullets and you didn't find them because they were fired from the opposite direction."

As they'd planned, Angel handed Paige a folder of photographs, which Paige passed on to the lieutenant.

"These are photos of what the ballistic experts that Mitch hired for us found, along with their data from the attic where Jay did the shooting," Paige explained. "We left everything in place because we aren't the police. It's yours to solve, but here's a hint: it's Jay."

"*It isn't!*" Jay shouted, charging Paige, getting close enough to tap the smaller man threateningly on the chest. "And you can't prove it."

"Then tell us how you knew that the will was invalid because they hadn't signed the prenup?" Paige asked him calmly.

"I don't have to tell you anything," Jay blustered.

"Why not tell us?" Roy asked.

"Looks like my work is done here," Paige said. "Roy, before you take over, can I ask a favor?"

"I suppose," Roy said with a trace of hesitation in his voice.

"If you would have your men remove Jay first, there's one more point I'd like to make," Paige asked. As Roy jogged to the hallway to summon assistance, Paige turned to Lucrezia and Lefty. "If you'll indulge me?"

"You have saved my life twice now," Lucrezia said. "It would be gauche of me to deny you anything, I think."

To Paige's amazement, she actually smiled at him. Lefty shrugged his deferral to her wishes.

Soon, Roy's deputies were escorting a stunned and protesting Jay out of the library.

"Well, then," Paige said. "It was lovely to see you, Jay. Close the doors behind you." Several more deputies stationed themselves nearby.

"What is this all about?" Roy asked, his patience clearly wearing thin.

"There's one more little point, Lieutenant Slade."

Roy gazed at him in anticipation.

"I said, 'There's one more little point, Lieutenant Slade,' " Paige said more loudly, his voice echoing through the hall.

"Yes, Paige," Roy said, irritably. "I heard you the first time."

"I *said*, 'There's one more little point...'"

The library doors burst open.

"Keep your wig on," Queen B bellowed regally. She rolled into the room like a battleship on the water.

"Hi, Queenie," Paige said. "Have I known you long enough to call you that?"

"You have," Queen B said with an imperial nod. "But don't think you can get all familiar."

"Never would," Paige said, bowing. "So, do you see him?"

"Mm-hmm," Queen B said. "That's him. That's the man."

58

"Are you sure that's him?" Paige asked.

"That's him," Queen B persisted, nodding like a monarch at a knighting. "I told you he was a snappy dresser."

"Yep, you did," Paige said. "I've got to learn to be a better listener."

"Who is this woman?" Lefty demanded.

Angel, Queen B and Paige had a good laugh. Mitch looked uncomfortable.

"What's going on?" Roy asked.

"I've gotta tell you, I'm not entirely sure anymore," Paige said, still laughing a bit. "I hate to be the one to break it to you, Lucrezia, but your fiancé is having an affair with your stepson."

"That is outrageous!" Lefty said, rising and storming toward the door.

"On the plus side, Lucrezia," Paige said. "It looks like I've saved your life a third time."

"Don't leave, Lefty," Roy ordered. His men stepped in front of the library doors.

Lefty stopped in his tracks. He wheeled on their diminishing little party.

"I will not stand here and be accused of such a disgusting and reprehensible act," he threatened.

"Lucrezia, where were you going on your honeymoon?" Paige asked.

"A cruise," she said, dejected. "The Mediterranean on a private yacht."

"I take it you're not a strong swimmer?" Paige asked.

"That is just..." Lefty spluttered. "Lucrezia..."

"The good news is, you do get all Seth's money," Paige said, shooting her a tight little smile.

"Great," Angel muttered.

"This is insupportable," Lefty said. "That I would—with that little worm? Why, the thought repels me. I would never lower myself to touch that doughy, inert great hulking nothing. Without his father's money, no one would ever have noticed Jay at all."

"*You* did," Jay shouted.

Lefty, turned, turned again, looking.

"Up here," Jay said.

Everyone looked to see Jay standing on the upper balcony at the back of the library.

"What's the play here?" Roy asked under his breath.

"Full disclosure," Paige said. "I was going to prove that you were Jay's lover and accomplice. There's private security everywhere to take you into custody."

"*Me?*"

"You were dating the murderer!"

"I'm not sure I'd call it dating, exactly."

"Shooting buddies? Really?"

"Well, maybe not just shooting buddies," Roy admitted.

"So, are you going to let me take the rap for the whole thing, Lefty?" Jay demanded, near tears. He stood in handcuffs, flanked by uniformed policemen.

"Shut up, you stupid..." Lefty trailed off. "We're not saying anything else until we've seen our lawyers. Don't tell them anything, darling. I'll get you out of this. I'll take care of you. I promise," he called up to Jay as the officers closed on him. "I love you, baby."

"I love you, too, Daddy."

"Ugh," Paige said.

"And you were a shit manager, too," Angel called after Lefty as the officers escorted him away.

"The *manager*, of course," Paige said, realizing at last.

"Is that everything now?" Roy asked, looking at Paige.

"God, I hope so," Paige answered.

"You really should have taken me into your confidence."

"I wish we could have, but we had to think you were in on it," Paige said.

"Still?"

"It was just weird you being 'shooting buddies' with Jay," Paige said. "Too convenient. I should have seen it for the misdirect that it was, but it just made such a good story. Oh my God. I just realized. Jay shot *Lefty* at C. Shore. He did it intentionally to make Lefty appear innocent. It *is* love. Great device. And he hooked up with you to be on the inside of the investigation. I bet it'll turn out that you were requested personally. Ask Commander Ferrell. The whole story is clear when you see all the pieces."

"This is not a story, Paige," Roy said. "This is murder."

"If you're a hammer, everything looks like a nail," Paige said. "If you're a writer..." He left it at that.

"Well, it just shows I was right all along," Angel declared, rising from her leather chair.

"Right about what?" Paige asked.

"You totally should have slept with him," Angel said.

59

It took Paige a moment to realize that the kettle was boiling.

He typed one more sentence, then rose to pour the water for more tea.

The television droned on in the background. The updated strains of "Hooray for Hollywood" filled the busy little kitchen as *Star Reporter* came on.

The glass in the back door had been replaced. The finger-printer's dust had mostly been vacuumed away, but little else had changed in Paige's apartment. He'd been too busy with the screenplay. The new collaboration with Angel was pretty much like the old one. Paige did most of the writing and Angel took most of the credit.

He didn't mind. They owned equal shares of the project. It was, after all, *their* story to tell. The rumors were true; they were calling it *Ordeal* and he had started the rumors to get the buzz going. It was based on their story-writes-itself experiences around Seth's murder and their well-publicized roles in helping to solve the crime in order to clear their names.

With any luck at all, Paige thought, there might soon be real furniture in his living room. Or maybe even a whole new living room somewhere else.

He had left much of the crime scene tape where the police had hung it, mostly because he hadn't had time to think about anything but the screenplay. He only ever left the office kitchen to pee and occasionally to sleep. The shabby little room felt cheerful and safe after the events of just a few weeks ago.

The lieutenant kept them posted on developments, but the investigation had quickly turned into a finger-pointing rush of confessions. Bill E, Wig, Jay and Lefty had, in true Hollywood tradition, struggled to outmaneuver one another for the best deal. With the flood of admissions and accusations, Roy and his contacts at the district attorney's office did not think there would even be a trial.

Paige and Angel had both said they were willing to testify, but it was looking like it was all over but the ripped-from-the-headlines movie version. Getting the script ready was pretty much all Paige had been doing ever since the crime-scene people had let him return home and Armie had gotten the door fixed with shiny new bars over the glass.

Lucrezia went on her honeymoon alone, but before she left she had arranged for flowers to be delivered to Paige's apartment every day—for life. The place was bursting, and Paige had struck up a speaking acquaintance with the hunky surfer-dude delivery guy. Between their flirtation and regular calls from Mitch to find out if he needed anything, floral deliveries and takeout had been about all the recent the human contact he'd had.

Paige and Angel had not resolved everything, but they had agreed to a new working partnership. They had plans to try to work through their past disputes after the screenplay was written and off to market.

Paige was about as happy as he had time to be. The world seemed to have changed around him, despite the fact that everything was pretty much the same as before. The kitchen/office was no longer a depressing dungeon. The empty living room and dining room had been filled suddenly with hope and possibilities. And the pain of Angel's betrayal seemed, if not healed, at least on the mend.

Tea in hand and lost in the scene he was still writing in his head, Paige returned to his laptop on the kitchen table. He began to peck at the keys.

It was hearing Angel's name on the television that caught his attention first.

"And there's exciting movie news from everyone's favorite amateur detective, Angel Panderson," the *Star Reporter* hostess *du jour* said into the camera with the same level of excitement that she would use to announce world peace or a zombie apocalypse. "Here with the inside story is *Star Reporter*'s Star Reporter, Busby Barclay."

"Hi, Bunny," Busby said, live from some poolside at some resort somewhere. "Busby here, with who'd-have-guessed-it-super-sleuth Angel Panderson and her soon-to-be costar, box office superstar Tyler Hunt."

Paige's head snapped up.

Screenplay forgotten, his attention was fully engaged.

Tyler Hunt's face filled the little screen.

"Hi, Buzz," Tyler said, in an easy, familiar way offering up a toilet-bowl-white smile. Tyler's poolside attire was more blinding still. His improbable physique was actually better than his poseable action figure version.

"Busby," Angel squealed, bussing him on the cheek.

"So, what's this news I hear?" Busby asked.

"You mean about our super-secret special appearance in Times Square, next Monday at eight A.M. Eastern time?" Angel said.

"It has something to do with a certain food crisis in this country," Tyler said.

"Well, I'm sure we'll all tune in to find out about that," Busby said, without showing the slightest interest in any food crisis. "But there's some *other* news I'm starving for that we can serve up right now."

"Well, yes," Tyler said. "Angel and I just signed a deal with Mammoth Studios to bring Angel's recent headline-making personal tragedy and triumph to the big screen."

"Really?" Busby played along.

"Yeah, that's right," Angel said. "After a long vacation, I'm finally ready to return to the big screen. I guess I was just waiting for the right story."

"So you're going to play yourself in the movie?" Busby asked.

"Totally, Buzz." Angel nodded enthusiastically. "It's a chance to work through the personal tragedy of my fiancé's murder and my personal, real-life struggle for justice."

"And Tyler, what about your role?"

"I'll be playing the real-life police officer who worked tirelessly with Angel to solve this heinous crime and fight corruption in Hollywood," Tyler explained.

"Is there a title yet?"

"It's called *Ordeal*," Angel stated.

"Ooh, I like it," Busby cooed.

"We'll be in production soon," Tyler added. "And in theaters hopefully next summer."

"Meanwhile," Angel said, grabbing the microphone from Busby. "Don't miss our special appearance in Times Square this—"

Paige turned off the set.

"And so it begins again," Paige said. His voice echoed in the empty house.

He picked up the phone and began dialing.

"Yes, hi, Mitch," he said into the receiver. "Can I borrow your jet? I need to get to New York and I need your help with a little project. Do you have any pull at the networks?"

60

His flight back from New York was awful but Paige laughed all the way.

The airport traffic was hideous and Paige couldn't stop smiling.

They'd even lost a piece of his luggage and he could not have cared less.

Paige was in one of those just-got-laid-got-the-dream-job-I-think-it's-love-bulletproof kind of moods where nothing can bring you down.

West Hollywood had never looked better, despite road construction and tourist drivers. "Walking on Sunshine" came on the radio and he turned it up and sang along. The song ended as he pulled into his pokey, dusty, cobwebby parking slot. Paige glowed at the perfect timing. The front door seemed more stubborn than usual and Paige found it charming.

Still singing under his breath, once he finally got inside he ditched what was left of his luggage and headed for the kitchen. He switched on his miserable excuse for a television and checked the DVR.

"Banzai!" he cried when he saw the contents of the now-playing menu. First, he saved the show forever and fast-forwarded to the perfect moment. And then he let it play.

As he started to make tea, the recording of that past Monday's edition of the morning show *Sunrise* came on, already in progress.

"Well, here's something you don't see every day," Atlanta, the heavily made-up newsreader on the network morning show, gushed as they cut to live video of Angel, clad only in strategically glued-on lettuce leaves, waving from a Jacuzzi-sized glass salad bowl, where she perched on a bed of what appeared to be chopped Romaine. "It's the biggest salad bowl I've ever seen, there in Times Square. But this salad is dressed with none other than TV favorite Angel Panderson."

Paige opened a bag of gourmet caramel corn he'd been saving for a special occasion. He stuffed a handful into his mouth as he angled the set so he could sit at the kitchen table.

"Panderson is no stranger to good causes," *Sunrise*'s dashing co-host, Bric, cut in. "And today, for Angel, giving her all means all of her clothes apparently. All in order to call attention to her vegan diet."

The camera circled the titillating shot as the hosts continued to voice-over the pictures from their studio several blocks away.

"That's right, Bric," Atlanta followed up. "She's wearing nothing today but lettuce as she appears here on a bed of greens in this giant salad bowl made especially for this event by Panderson's friend, the visual and performance artist Plastique, who is live in studio with us this morning."

Bric and Plastique appeared in a box in the corner of the live shot of Angel in her salad bowl. The artist's suit was white with enormous Wonder Bread polka dots, but his most striking feature were the hot dogs he had wound into his hair like sponge-curlers.

The whistle on the kettle blew. Paige moved to pour the water over the tealeaves without ever taking his eyes off the screen.

"Welcome to *Sunrise*, Plastique," Bric began. "Tell us a little bit about this morning's installation."

"Thanks, Bric," Plastique said in his flat, oddly foreign accent—odd because he was from Queens. "As part of our commitment to animal rights and healthy eating, we are staging today's protest installation, which I call *Awe Naturale*. Angel is wearing only organic, locally sourced non-GMO butter lettuce as a statement about the crisis we as Americans face at the dinner table each day—"

"Wait— is it? Yes, it is," Atlanta interrupted. "It's surprise guest, Paige Blanche, Angel's writing partner and recent partner-in-crime."

"Crime-*solving*, that is," Bric cut in.

Remote in hand, Paige put his feet up on the kitchen table and grabbed another handful of caramel corn from the bag as he watched himself enter the shot with Angel.

"Right you are," Atlanta agreed. "And it looks like he's climbing fully clothed into the salad bowl with her."

"She seems to be throwing lettuce at him," Bric went on narrating, confused but no less enthusiastic. "Tell us what's going on, Plastique."

"I'm not entirely sure…" Plastique's voice trailed off.

The little box in the screen's corner with Bric and the artist disappeared.

"Let's go live to the scene with our man in the clouds, weather guy extraordinaire Bart Storm," Atlanta said, jumping to the weather recap, typically the show's most-watched minute. "Take it away, Bart. It seems Angel has some company."

"You bitch!" Paige screamed, diving at Angel as she struggled to escape him amidst the piles of lettuce surrounding them. The more they struggled, the deeper they sank into the lettuce. "While I'm slaving away on the script that you tricked me into writing, you sell the project out from under me?"

"Paige, I'm sure we can get them to hire you to write it," Angel said, shielding her face from a barrage of lettuce.

"You are a liar, a cheat and a pig," Paige shouted, pulling a huge plastic bottle of barbecue sauce from under his coat. "And you know what real Americans do to pigs?"

"Uh-oh," Bric commented from the safety of the studio. "Is that barbecue sauce?"

Paige began to douse her liberally with the red goopy marinade as Angel scrambled to get away.

The weatherman looked on helplessly as volunteers attempted to climb into the giant salad bowl to break up the brawl.

"Looks like a repeat of their teacup incident that went viral a couple of months back," Atlanta remarked, visibly excited about the potential for a little viral-video help with their sagging ratings.

"Maybe we should check out the local weather report," Bart suggested gamely.

"Don't you dare," Bric insisted, clearly a little disappointed that he wasn't included in the live shot that would be heard around the world.

"Okay, then—" Bart began his weather script as best he could. "It's a beautiful day for a salad—or a barbeque—here in Times Square." Behind him through the glass bowl, Angel and Paige sank farther into the bed of lettuce as they smeared each other with barbeque sauce.

The paparazzi broke through the line and began to intrude into the live shot.

"Looks like there's a new Hollywood feud on the horizon, as high pressure and spicy goodness roll in from the west," Bart reported, doing his best to ad-lib through the ruined remote. "*Sunrise* wants to help you choose the right dressing, whether it's salad days or barbecue temps in your part of the world. Here's a look at your local weather."

Paige froze the action just as his Monday-morning self pinned Angel against the side of the bowl, both of them behind the weather stats facing the camera as he poured the bottle of sauce over her head. He sipped his tea and had a little more caramel corn.

A satisfied smile spread across his face.

With a contented sigh, he rewound the clip and started again.

Acknowledgements

The road to the *Write Murder* has been as rocky, perverse and circuitous as any mystery story I might have imagined.

And so, though there are many to thank for their help in getting this novel written and published, I would be remiss if I did not begin by thanking those who helped me, quite literally, to survive the process.

Of course, Anne and Christopher Rice, to whom the book is dedicated, for their collegial and familial friendship, invaluable advice and professional example. I just couldn't do this without you.

My darling Sophia Stuart, who gently pressed the tools I needed into my hands and then patiently, taught me how to use them.

Efrem Seeger for his unwavering good sense and complete dis-interest in my extemporaneous, dramatic histrionics. And honorable mention to his sister Mindy Seeger for telling me the truth whether I wanted to hear it or not.

As always, my love and gratitude to my family of origin—Ron, Genie, Sarah, Dan, David, Angelica and Marcos—who keep me grounded by reminding me what is important and whose unconditional, standing offer of safe haven, should the world cave in around me, gives me the courage to risk failing at my dreams, which is after all, the only way to attain them.

Miriam Divas for taking such good care of me so good naturedly for all these years.

Patricia Nell Warren for inspiring me to write books in the first place.

Cynthia Gilliam for showing me that I could be anyone I wanted to be.

Patricia Cornwell, who took the time to share her wisdom and invaluable advice on how to write a successful murder mystery. Here's hoping it took.

Dame Agatha Christie and Carolyn Keene, AKA Mildred Wirt Benson, for inspiring my love of murder mysteries.

Richard Morris for convincing me to write this book, even if that's all he did.

Gregg Hurwitz and Marc Glick, whose faith and encouragement came just when I needed them most.

And the staff and crew of *The Dinner Party Show*: Brandon Griffith, Brett Churnin, Benjamin Scuglia, Cathy Dipierro, Christine Bocchiaro, Bobby Lea, Miriam Divas, Billy McIntyre, Sergio Rocha, Jasun Mark and Jack Mikesell.

For the skill, expertise and sheer labor that it takes to get a book put together and out into the word my special thanks to:

Amy and Rob Siders, Corey Hodgson, Kasi Alexander, Benjamin Scuglia, David Groff, Asha Hossain, Kim Guidroz and, of course, Christopher and his "Passion Posse."

Last and most certainly least, she-who-shall-not-be-named, to whom I can only say:

"You're so vain, you probably think this book is about you."

Eric Shaw Quinn's debut novel, *Say Uncle*, the comic tale of an eccentric gay man who receives custody of his nephew, took ten years to find a publisher and was immediately optioned for film upon its release. As Quinn Brockton, he wrote two original novels (*Never Tear Us Apart* and *Always Have, Always Will*) based on characters from the hit Showtime series *Queer as Folk*. His time as the "ghostwriter" for a certain celebrity landed him a spread in the National Enquirer and earned him the title of Amazon's #1 chick lit author for 2004. *The Prince's Psalm*, his historical romance based on the Old Testament Books of Samuel, will be published in June 2016 by Itineris, a new imprint of Dreamspinner press. He is also the co-host and executive producer of the popular podcast, The Dinner Party Show with Christopher Rice & Eric Shaw Quinn. — www.TheDinnerPartyShow.com

Write Murder is the first in his all new mystery series.